Having Ca
distraction

Lauren could t
had a strong ef
wanted to back
on him, and another part of her – the part that hadn't had a lover in too long, the part that remembered what an incredible lover Carson was – wanted to pull him against her and kiss him.

She desperately wanted to reach out and touch the light stubble along his jaw. She couldn't help imagining what it would feel like against her face, her breasts, her belly...

The aching between her legs was getting to be too much, and she shifted in her seat.

"You have had a vision about yourself, haven't you?" Carson said.

Lauren smiled. "What I'm having a vision of right now is you and me on that bed, naked. Think you can accommodate me?"

"Are you trying to bewitch me to distract me?"

"Call me wicked," she said. "I won't deny it."

TAKEN

BY
TORI CARRINGTON

&

CALL ME WICKED

BY
JAMIE SOBRATO

First published in Great Britain 2008
by Harlequin Mills & Boon Limited,
Eton House, 18-24 Paradise Road, Richmond, Surrey TW9 1SR

ISBN: 978 0 263 86723 7

14-0908

Harlequin Mills & Boon policy is to use papers that are natural, renewable and recyclable products and made from wood grown in sustainable forests. The logging and manufacturing processes conform to the legal environmental regulations of the country of origin.

Printed and bound in Spain
by Litografia Rosés S.A., Barcelona

TAKEN

BY
TORI CARRINGTON

Dear Reader,

"Well-behaved women rarely make history." This Laurel Thatcher Ulrich quote is one of many that grace our office walls. Women who push the boundaries of accepted behaviour are a popular theme for us, so when it was proposed that, along with Leslie Kelly and Julie Elizabeth Leto, we consider adding members to THE BAD GIRLS CLUB, we immediately signed on.

In *Taken*, Seline Sanborn is a sexy con artist. And self-made millionaire playboy Ryder Blackwell is the handsome mark. When Seline breaches his company's inner circle by posing as a successful account executive, Ryder falls for her hard. A one-night stand quickly turns into full obsession. But what happens when he wakes up to find the angel in his bed gone…along with an interesting chunk of his company's capital? Is he capable of redefining everything he believes about life and love and the law in order to be the one man skilled enough to earn Seline's trust and steal something worth far more than money – her heart?

We hope you enjoy every twist and turn in Seline and Ryder's unconventional journey towards happily-ever-after. We'd love to hear what you think. Contact us at PO Box 12271, Toledo, OH 43612, USA (we'll respond with a signed bookplate, newsletter and bookmark), or visit us on the web at www.toricarrington.net.

Here's wishing you love, romance and *hot* reading.

Lori & Tony Karayianni
aka *Tori Carrington*

TORI CARRINGTON

Romantic Times BOOKreviews Career Achievement Award-winning husband-and-wife duo Lori and Tony Karayianni are the power behind the pen name Tori Carrington. Their over thirty-five novels include titles for Mills & Boon® Blaze® and Special Edition lines. They call Toledo, Ohio, home base, but travel to Tony's home town of Athens, Greece, whenever they can. For more information on the couple, their books and where they plan to appear next with a fresh batch of Tony's Famous Baklava in hand, visit www.toricarrington.net.

We dedicate this book to fellow lifetime
Bad Girls Club members Leslie Kelly, Julie Leto
and our shared editor Brenda Chin. And to bad
girls everywhere: keep knocking down those
walls and breaking through those glass ceilings.

1

IT WAS a temptation she couldn't resist.

Heat slid over her skin, igniting every nerve ending, making her hyper-aware of each breath she drew in. Tension. Anticipation. Longing. All combined in her muscles, clamored for release. Demanded she unleash the more primal part of herself kept under wraps for far too long.

It was July, it was hot and Seline Sanborn sat alone in her leased glossy-black Audi TT roadster convertible with the top down, her Dior shades parked on her nose, tendrils of blond hair stuck to her chin and lips. Yearning, pure and strong, shuddered through her. How long it had been since she'd allowed herself the indulgence of taking off her mask? One month? No, it was closer to two. Two months since she'd taken on the identity of conservative Carol Lambert, senior account executive moved to New York City from Seattle, Washington. Eight weeks in which she'd gained the confidence of the higher-ups at Blackwell & Blackwell Industries. Sixty days since she'd traded a lifestyle with few boundaries for long twelve-hour days, and nights spent reviewing carefully laid out plans rather than enjoying romantic sunsets with a special someone.

Then again, it had been time immeasurable since she'd spent a romantic anything with anyone.

Which probably explained why she'd decided to take the sporty rental car to her uptown lunch meeting rather than a taxi. And why she'd let the top—and her hair—down afterward.

Of course, the success of the meeting had also contributed to her desire to cut loose. If all corporate endeavors could be as powerfully engaging, she'd seriously consider hanging up her hat and going legit. The problem was that there was much more paperwork and tedium involved in the life of a corporate exec than big-ticket deals like the one she'd just brokered on behalf of Blackwell & Blackwell.

Or rather, just brokered on behalf of herself using a shell company she'd anonymously staffed through a temporary employment agency. A company that would cease to exist by this time tomorrow, guaranteeing her rush would survive at least as long...and the security the funds from she'd make off with even longer.

Which was why she much preferred the title of con artist. Forget that the job was the only one she knew. What other position would give her quick access to the type of money she needed? Not even Carol Lambert's nice salary could cover an overhead that went beyond the expensive leased cars and designer duds she needed for her cons. Well beyond.

Of course, the impulsiveness of her current actions went against one of her top rules, developed out of necessity: do not, under any circumstances, let your guard down until the con is over. And seeing as only a day and a half—thirty-six short hours—remained in her current job...well, her uncharacteristic recklessness was spotlighted all the more.

"It's a car ride, that's all," she said quietly. "What harm can come out of a car ride?" She pressed the power button for the high-end CD player. The guitar riffs of "Radar Love" by Golden Earring instantly drowned out the cautionary voice that whispered in her ear, along with the sound of the purring engine now idling at a stoplight.

Until the rumble of another equally impressive engine turned her attention to her left.

She smiled with deliberate pleasure.

It didn't take a car lover to appreciate the sleek lines of the XK Jaguar. But seeing as she knew the 12-cylinder engine that growled beneath the attractive hood inside and out, her interest quotient notched upward.

Too bad all she could make out through the heavily tinted windows was her own reflection. Which looked damned good, if you asked her.

She tilted her head and made a play at nudging her sunglasses halfway down her nose to get a better look at the driver even though she couldn't see him.

The response was a revving of the potent engine.

Seline righted her glasses and looked forward.

Having been raised in New York, despite the fact that she could no longer live there unless she was on the job, she knew times were few and far between when traffic opened in front of you. And this appeared to be one of those rare occasions when the big city and her many denizens offered up a precious gift of space and opportunity. She had every intention of greedily taking advantage of both.

She put the car into first gear, easing up on the clutch even as she floored the gas pedal. The car's back end immediately jerked as the back tires spun against hot asphalt. The Jag's engine revved louder in answer.

She watched the opposing traffic light. A moment after it turned red, and a split second before hers turned green, Seline released the brake and the Audi shot forward in a cloud of white smoke and burning rubber. She was no fool. She knew the Jag could do cartwheels around her car…if the driver was equal to her and if she played fair.

But she wasn't known for fair. For survival's sake, she'd learned to take full advantage of any opportunity to get ahead. In this case, literally.

She switched gears into third, then quickly into fourth, watching as the speedometer needle leapt upward.

The Jag easily caught up, staying even with her. Ahead, a taxi seemed to be at a dead stop in the middle of the road. She veered right even as the Jag swerved left, within moments the two of them running side by side again.

Seline shivered at the feel of her hair whipping around her face, the sound of the engine and electric guitar filling her ears, and the sights and smells of midtown Manhattan around her.

Damn, but this felt good. And it had been a long time since she'd felt good. Much longer than two months.

She and the Jag ran like that for another four blocks before the other driver blew his horn. She shot him a look, having noticed two lights back the white-and-blue NYPD cruiser parked at the next intersection. What she didn't know was if the other driver would have the guts to continue the street race or if he would drop back.

To her surprise, he kept up with her, even upping the ante as he blew past her.

The stopped squad car immediately turned right and gave chase after the Jag.

Seline thrust the gear into Neutral and made a squealing right-hand turn, then another, until neither the Jaguar nor the cops were any longer visible.

Yes.

Seline relished the rush even as she turned the music down, slowed to the speed limit, then headed back to the offices of Blackwell & Blackwell where she would have to play Little Miss Manners for the next four hours before knocking off work…with nothing but a saucy little smile to remind her of her brief excursion.

"THANK YOU, officer."

Ryder Blackwell accepted the speeding ticket from the unsmiling NYPD officer then leaned back in his dormant Jaguar and watched the patrol car drive away.

He'd purposely raced by the hot babe in the Audi, hoping to place her squarely in the patrol's crosshairs rather than him.

Then she'd turned off and rather than following her, the police officer had targeted him instead.

He grinned and shook his head, thinking of the provocative blonde in the black car—the personification of every teenage boy's dream. And, apparently, a grown man's, as well.

"Can I take that for you, Mr. Blackwell?"

He'd only been a block up from the Blackwell & Blackwell building when he'd been pulled over, so the red-haired, freckled-face valet who usually parked his car had sprinted over to meet him.

Ryder got out of the XK and tossed him his keys. "Sure, O'Malley. But why don't you take her through the car wash before parking her back in the garage."

"Yes, sir, Mr. Blackwell."

Ryder chuckled quietly as he retrieved his briefcase from the back of the Jag. He knew the nineteen-year-old valet would take the car for a spin first. But that's what hot July days were meant for. If you couldn't have a little fun in a kick-ass car on a day like this, what was the point? He would have loved the opportunity when he was O'Malley's age.

He straightened his tie and was crossing the parking-garage driveway when he was nearly hit by the woman he'd never expected to see again. Ryder squinted at her. At least he thought it was her. Gone were the trendy sunglasses. Up were the Audi's top and her wild blond hair. And if he didn't know better, he'd think she'd exchanged scarlet lipstick for neutral beige.

"I'm sorry, Mr. Blackwell," she said, looking everything like yet nothing like the woman who'd tempted him into a ticket. "I didn't see you."

"So, is that going to be the story?" he asked with a grin.

She looked confused.

He nodded toward where O'Malley was taking off his black hat and getting into the Jag. The tires squealed as he pulled away from the curb.

When she looked back at him, he saw a definite shimmer of challenge in her green eyes.

"I'm sure I don't know what you're talking about, Mr. Blackwell."

A car pulled up behind her and the driver lay on the horn. Ryder stepped aside to let both into the parking garage, shaking his head as he went.

Carol...Carol...he repeated her name in his mind. Lambert. That's right. Her name was Carol Lambert. Coleman had hired her a couple months back.

It wasn't all that surprising that he'd had trouble remembering her name. Although she'd been present in meetings, she usually sat back from the table in a way that guaranteed he barely noticed her, rarely contributing anything, although he understood from Coleman that she was doing a hell of a job since signing on.

He stepped inside the lobby and went straight to the elevator dedicated to his top-floor offices.

Perhaps he'd have to invite the wild Ms. Lambert into his office to see how hot her personal engine ran.

DAMN, damn, damn. She *so* hadn't made that mistake. Had she?

Seline sat at her desk behind a door she never closed but had closed now, hoping against hope that what had happened earlier would stay outside the office. But even though three hours had passed, and she was just a short time away from knocking off for the day, she knew that

Ryder Blackwell wasn't the forgetting kind. And judging by the hot suggestive look he'd given her, he wasn't the timid kind, either.

Of course, she already knew that. Ryder Blackwell, the sixth in a line of wealthy Blackwells—although she understood that Ryder's grandfather had squandered a great deal of the family's fortune…a fortune that the grandson had spent a great deal of time earning back and then some—was not only touted as one of the city's most eligible bachelors, he was also a notorious ladies' man, never seen with the same woman at two consecutive events.

"It's said that men love the thrill of the chase," he'd said in an interview with *GQ*. "But I think women are equally intrigued by a challenge."

It wasn't all that difficult to see why he rated high with both the ladies and the NY press. Money aside—and that was a big aside—he was the epitome of tall, dark and handsome, with just the right amount of devil in his smooth grin and one deep cheek dimple. His attractiveness had been exactly the reason why she'd steered a wide berth around him. And if she couldn't avoid contact, rather than looking up to meet his gaze, she tucked her chin into her chest and murmured responses that he had to ask her to repeat.

Then she'd gone and challenged him to a street race in the middle of Manhattan.

The telephone at her elbow rang. Seline froze and then she forced herself to answer.

"Yes, Rita?"

"Ms. Lambert, Mr. Blackwell says he'd like to see you before you leave for the day."

"Here?"

"No. He'd like you to go up to his office. Just ring his assistant when you're ready so she can signal the elevator."

Seline sighed. "Thanks, Rita."

Signal the elevator.

Oh, she'd known the layout of the building like the back of her hand before she'd ever set foot in it. Architectural plans were easy enough to access. But she'd never had reason to venture into Ryder Blackwell's professional domain. And she didn't want a reason to now. Not with such a short time remaining before a punch of a button would transfer a significant amount from Blackwell & Blackwell's business accounts into a series of dummy front accounts and eventually make its way, untraceably, into her own.

She could pretend she hadn't got the message. Blame the miscommunication on Rita. After all, who she was—or rather wasn't—and why she was really here would become painfully obvious soon enough.

She swiveled restlessly in her chair. This was exactly the reason she'd established a strict set of rules to work by. And today the breaking of one of them had snowballed into the breaking of Golden Rule Number 1: Stay under the radar of the higher-ups.

And in this con they didn't come any higher than Ryder Blackwell.

She clicked through the documents on her computer, then made a couple of notes. There was no way in hell she was going up to that office.

Seline remembered his sexy grin and her panties grew tighter. A reaction that had nothing to do with July sunshine and fast cars, and everything to do with sex and a great candidate to have some with.

2

"UH OH. I know that look."

Ryder turned his leather chair from the clear view he had of the Empire State Building from the forty-fifth floor of the building his company owned. He considered his second-in-command and longtime best friend, John Coleman. "What look?"

Coleman sat back in the righthand guest chair and gave him a wry expression of his own. "That one that says you're about to do something dangerous. Or stupid. Or both."

Ryder grinned, not so much at his friend, but at himself. "I don't know whether I should take offense or be amused."

"Oh, God. You *are* about to do something stupid and dangerous, aren't you?"

"When have I ever done something stupidly dangerous?"

"Oh, how about that impromptu trip to Alaska

two months ago to drop from a helicopter and snowboard down some virgin mountain when we had a meeting to close the deal with Trump? Or the month before that when you disappeared so you could hike up the side of the Montserrat volcano before it was due to erupt?"

"You call that dangerous?"

"I definitely call that dangerous."

Ryder leaned forward in his chair. "That's because risk to you is whether or not to wear the pink tie your new wife gave you for Valentine's Day."

"Yes, well, someone's got to keep their wits about them around here."

Ryder's mind wandered to the clock. Four-thirty.

"So what are you considering now?"

"What?"

"Isn't there a hurricane due to hit Florida's east coast? Are you having your surfboard waxed?"

"Nothing quite so unimaginative."

"But you *are* considering something."

Ryder picked up his pen and tapped it on his desk. "Maybe."

It all depended on one very inscrutable Carol Lambert.

Granted, he'd been privileged to enjoy the

company of a lot of women in his life. And he knew that outer wrappings often were deceiving. There was the raunchy pop star he'd gone out with who had pretended to be an exhibitionist sex kitten in public, but the minute he got her home she'd folded in on herself then passed out from the stress of having to put on such an act all night. He recalled having waited around until morning in that case, convinced the sex—when he got it—would be worth it. But it hadn't been. One-on-one she'd been shy and hesitant, the exact opposite of the image she portrayed for everyone else.

Then there was the icy socialite he'd briefly—very briefly—considered marriage material. She headed the right charities, boasted the right pedigrees and was the perfect hostess of myriad social events. But behind closed doors she was a borderline nymphomaniac. She had nearly shredded his back with her nails and broken his eardrums with her loud and X-rated demands of what she wanted him to do to her for what had to be a record-breaking ten hours straight.

It had been the one and only time that Ryder had been more preoccupied with whether he'd survive what his sex partner might do to him than with the sex itself.

Then there was Carol Lambert.

He leaned back in his chair, ignoring his friend.

There was something about Carol. Something different. The first thing being that the hot lady who'd challenged him to race didn't seem to fit her name, forget the person she turned into the minute she entered the front doors of Blackwell & Blackwell. He'd even consulted her employment records to try to solve the mystery, but nothing from her file had helped him to reconcile the two women with whom he was acquainted. *Acquainted* being the operative word.

And something he hoped to upgrade to *having intimate knowledge* of when she came to his office that afternoon.

"Should I call legal and make sure your insurance policies are up to date?" Coleman asked.

"What insurance policies?"

Coleman stared at him.

Ryder chuckled and got to his feet. "Go home to that pretty wife of yours, John, and stop being such a worrywart. You sound like a nagging mother." He smacked his hand against his friend's back on their way toward the door.

"Promise me you won't do anything I wouldn't do."

Ryder raised a brow.

John sighed. "Okay, then. Promise you'll be careful."

"I'm always careful."

"Why doesn't that make me feel any better?"

The minute John was on his way down the hall to his own office, Ryder's secretary approached.

"There were three calls for you while you were occupied." She said, offered up the message slips.

"Hold on to them, Mrs. Newman. I've got a meeting to make."

"Meeting?" she asked his departing back. "I have no meeting on your agenda."

Ryder grinned at her as he turned inside the elevator then pressed the button for the floor he wanted. "It just came up."

IT TOOK a bit of doing, but Seline managed to push everything up by twelve hours. Which meant that the minute she stepped out of her office, the con would be done and she would be free to shuck Carol Lambert's conservative suits and identity for good.

It also meant that her personal accounts would be that much fatter, while Blackwell & Blackwell's accounts would be that much slimmer.

And, ultimately, it meant that she could duck out before anyone would miss her. Specifically, Ryder Blackwell.

Of course, it went without saying that she also wouldn't have an excuse to see whether or not Ryder growled in bed as satisfyingly as the engine of his car did on the road.

But that was part of the price she paid in her line of work. It came with the territory. Even if the rules she lived by didn't already make involvement with anyone personally connected to any company she targeted off limits, it just made plain business sense to keep her attention focused on the job rather than indulging sexual fantasies that would only endanger her and the con. No matter how delicious the temptation.

And Ryder Blackwell was the epitome of delicious and temptation.

She'd been around long enough to understand that if she were lucky there would be only a handful of men she would connect with in a way that transcended your run-of-the-mill attraction. And she'd felt that connection strongly with Ryder upon realizing who he was when he'd blocked her access to the garage. Within a nanosecond, his gaze had communicated an understanding, an awareness, to her that sometimes years with another person couldn't accomplish. An "I see you" gaze that left her feeling…no, *knowing* that he had seen her. Not the details. Not what her favorite color was or what she was up to. But, rather, more fundamental elements. Almost as if the past, present and future had melted together to become immaterial in light of their meeting, their connection.

Oh, well. While it was certainly the first time she'd had such an experience with a mark, she had the feeling it likely wouldn't be the last. And, probably sooner than she currently believed, she'd forget all about his electric-blue eyes and dimpled cheek and the surge of her blood every time she'd thought about him that afternoon, and use the money she'd stolen from him to further more important plans.

She stuffed the last of the items that could be connected to her inside the cavernous depths of her Louis Vuitton bag and wiped her prints from the drawer she'd closed.

"Going somewhere?"

Seline froze at the sound of Ryder's voice. Somewhere in the back of her mind she gave herself a pat on the back for not having jumped. Even if his sudden presence was definitely of the jump variety.

Not that she hadn't half expected him to show up at her office, despite his request through official channels to see her in his. Mostly because of that connection she'd shared with him. She'd instantly sensed that—not unlike herself—he was someone used to getting what he wanted. And he wanted her.

Her. The woman in the car who'd challenged him to a race. Not Carol Lambert. Although she had to remind herself that he didn't know there was difference. A vast and damaging difference.

It had been that knowing that had prompted her to finish up her business and get out of here posthaste.

Unfortunately, she'd been two minutes too late.

Seline turned her chair to face him in the doorway, giving him her best Carol Lambert tucked-chin smile. "Hello, Mr. Blackwell. I was just getting ready to come up to see you."

"Why do I get the impression you were getting ready to leave instead?"

She tried to act surprised, but she made the mistake of meeting his stimulating gaze. And the challenge there left her incapable of ignoring the desire to rise to it.

So he thought he could handle her, did he?

Thought he knew who she was and by extension thought himself up to the task of tussling with her without consequence?

She found herself smiling.

She had two weaknesses. One was for a good, clean, risky con; the other was proving to a powerful bachelor like Ryder Blackwell how powerless he truly was when it came to a woman like her.

And while she should pass on this one, she found she didn't want to.

All cons came with their risks. And so far this one had run like clockwork. Boringly like clockwork. Maybe a tryst with Ryder was just what was needed to spice it up a little bit.

"Was there something you needed to discuss with me?" she asked, getting up from her desk and coming to stand in front of him.

She watched him watch her approach. His black pupils dilated slightly as his gaze dropped first to her baggy blouse as if searching for the lacy bra underneath, then to her legs, which she knew were killer even in the low-heeled, unappealing shoes she wore.

Seline leaned forward, brushing her breasts against his chest. She had to give him credit for standing still, not giving away with a blink or an intake of breath that her actions surprised him. She picked up a file on the side table behind him, then broke contact as she put it into her bag.

"There are several things I'd like to discuss with you, Ms. Lambert."

She put her bag on the table then reached for her suit jacket hanging on the back of the door. He took it from her and she easily turned so he could help her into it. If his movements were a little more languid than the occasion called for, if his fingers lingered a little too long at the collar, against the burning skin of her neck, she wasn't going to let him see her reaction. Even though she sensed that he knew. Just as she knew that he wanted to touch her in far more intimate ways.

"I only have a few minutes," she said, turning back to face him. "I have a meeting to get to."

His gaze swept up from her neck over her chin to her lips. "Cancel it."

She smiled in a way designed to transmit that he'd just tipped his hand. "Surely whatever is on your mind can wait until morning?"

Until she was long gone and he would begin the process of discovering exactly what she'd been doing while she'd been there. And that it had nothing to do with sex and everything to do with money.

"Actually, it can't. Have dinner with me."

She picked up her bag and edged the handle up to rest over her shoulder. "Dinner? Sounds personal. Doesn't that violate the company's no-fraternization rule?"

The right side of his mouth budged upward, revealing the single dimple that made her tongue tingle with the desire to taste it. "I'll put it on my agenda to change that rule first thing in the morning. One of the benefits of being the boss."

Seline couldn't resist leaning closer to him. The new proximity filled her senses with a scent of lime that made her mouth water further. She dropped her voice to a provocative whisper. "Yes, but that still leaves the rule in effect for tonight. And seeing as I'm a new employee, I wouldn't want to do anything to endanger my position. You know, like having sex with the boss."

"Who said anything about sex?"

She tilted her head so that she was looking into his eyes. "You did. And do. Every time you look at me."

"Astute woman."

"Shameless man."

His chuckle sent a shiver skidding over her hypersensitive nerve endings. It had been a long, long time since mere conversation with a man had made her wet. But if the dampness between her thighs was anything to go by, Ryder had accomplished exactly that.

"Look, Mr. Blackwell—"

"Ryder."

"No matter what guarantees you make, the truth is that sleeping with the boss is never a good idea. Chances are you'll come in tomorrow morning having regretted our…intimacy." She watched as he swallowed thickly. "And then where would I be? Aside from sharing the title of one-night stand with no doubt countless other women in the company?"

"I don't sleep with employees."

"But isn't that what you're proposing now?"

His grin widened. "No. I'm offering dinner."

Seline shivered again and clamped her thighs tightly together, reveling in the luscious sensations rolling through her. "Nothing more?"

"Let's just say that the rest…well, I'll be offering. It's up to you whether or not you take me up on it."

She blinked slowly then smiled. "Your car or mine?"

3

RED-HOT. Reckless. Dangerous.

Ryder couldn't be sure where the danger part came in. All he knew was that the instant they entered the elevator in his Upper East Side building, Carol Lambert stopped playing coy and began playing hard. Not hard to get, but hardball—letting him know exactly what she was after. Which happened to be the same thing he was after. But despite his time with the nympho socialite, he wasn't accustomed to this unabashed display of carnal desire. Or his own feral response to it.

Carol shoved him against the mirrored back wall of the elevator, kissing him hungrily even as she pushed his suit jacket over his shoulders. One of her legs edged between his, her upper thigh pressing boldly against his erection.

Ryder rolled her so she was the one against the wall, pulling open her blouse to reveal the sexy garments underneath. The black lace should have surprised him, but it didn't. Rather he experienced a sense of relief that the woman he'd raced on the street was evident in the racy underwear. No pretend sex kitten here. She was one hundred percent the real thing.

He grasped her right breast, pressing the circle of her areole more tightly against the lacy cup, then fastened his mouth over the fabric and the flesh beneath, drawing both deeply inside even as he worked his own leg between hers, raising his upper thigh until it met with her crotch. Bracing himself, he lifted her until she slid up the mirror. Her knee-length skirt bunched around her lush hips, revealing that she wore no stockings and that the black thong she had on was all lace.

He groaned, holding her against the wall with one hand even as he lowered to his knees, at eye level with the decadent undergarment. Dipping a finger inside the edge, he tugged the lace aside until her gloriously bare swell of flesh was exposed to his hungry gaze.

His vast experience with women left little doubt as to her arousal. Her labia were swollen, making her sex appear like a fresh fruit just waiting to be plucked. He blew lightly and watched as the skin reacted, contracting so that the pink bit of delicate flesh between her folds peeked out, tempting his tongue.

And it was his tongue he offered.

Carol moaned even as the elevator climbed up the thirty floors. He ran the length of his tongue against the slit, then flicked it over and around her clit, pulling the bud deep into his mouth. Her hands left his hair as she braced herself against the wall. Ryder took in her provocative, half-lidded expression even as he drank deeply of her.

The scent of feminine musk, the sound of her shallow, ragging breathing, filled his senses, increasing his desire for this woman who tasted like fresh peaches and cream but was as naughty as the day was long.

He grasped her right leg and positioned it over his left shoulder, then followed suit with her left leg over his right shoulder. She quickly joined her ankles behind his neck, balancing herself against the mirror even as he dove in for another taste of her.

He was aware of her impending release and moved to delay it, moving his attention from the bud to the blooming entrance just below. So slick. So tight. He lapped her slowly, purposefully. As soon as he heard her breathing even out a bit, he traveled back up to the fleshy button and fastened his lips around it again, sucking deeply.

She came apart instantly, her legs tightening, her cry echoing against the elevator walls at the same time an electronic ding sounded.

Ryder thought she might panic at the thought that someone might see them. Instead she rode out the wave of her orgasm then collapsed against the wall, making quite the provocative image with her wild hair, her skirt bunched around her waist, her legs still crossed around his neck as he looked up at her.

She smiled at him languidly. "My, Mr. Blackwell, you do appear to have your skills."

He chuckled as he freed her legs. She found her footing and he rose to stand next to her.

The elevator doors slid open to reveal his warmly lit, empty penthouse. During the drive home—they'd taken their separate cars—he'd called his butler Jonathon, asking for discretion. A silver ice bucket holding a bottle of champagne, a tray of chocolate-tipped strawberries and a bowl of cream and the soft strains of old Motown melodies were the only evidence that Jonathan was anywhere in residence.

"After you," Ryder said.

For just one night Seline wanted to forget the past...forget the future. She wanted to live in this one moment, and this one moment alone.

She'd need all the help she could get. Because both the past and the future were difficult to ignore for even one night.

She looked around. She'd always appreciated a man with good taste. And Ryder obviously had it in spades.

Languidly strolling into the penthouse, hyper-aware of every nerve ending in her body, the chafing of her nipples against her bra, the throbbing of her womanhood, she took in the mammoth living and dining area, colorfully yet sparsely decorated. Probably it had been put together by an interior decorator. She snatched a strawberry from a tray and bit down on the succulent fruit even as she moved to consider a small framed Manet over an antique, ivory-inlaid banquet. A very good decorator who had taken Ryder into consideration during the planning process.

And likely Ryder had taken the decorator right on the huge ottoman that served as a coffee table between two long sofas.

She shivered.

It had been so long since she'd indulged herself with casual sex. So long that she felt her emotions exaggerating the not-unfamiliar sensations. Her elevator orgasm just as the compartment had stopped moving had rocked her to the marrow. Even now, she was uber-aware of every move Ryder made even though her back was to him.

A crystal flute was placed in front of her. She put it down on the buffet then scooted to sit on the surface, spreading her legs wantonly.

"Nice place."

Usually when she made a comment like that, the person in question took a look around as if seeing through her eyes. Not Ryder. He trapped her gaze with his and didn't blink, secure in the knowledge that it *was* a nice place. And that it had nothing at all to do with the reason she was there.

"Thank you."

He put his flute down on the other side of her, his gaze dropping to where her blouse bowed open, then lower still to her bared thighs.

"Are you hungry?" he murmured.

"Mmm." She caught the waist of his slacks and yanked him forward, his suit jacket long since discarded by the door.

Then she set about showing him exactly what she was hungry for.

Many women she knew sorely underestimated the importance of a good kiss. And oh, did, Ryder

Blackwell know how to kiss. His lips were firm yet malleable, his mouth damp but not too wet. And he didn't go for her tonsils as other men she'd known over the years had made the mistake of doing. Instead he lingered with his lips on hers, his mouth not quite open, not quite closed, his tongue dipping out briefly before he finished the kiss.

Seline grew aware of her shortness of breath. That and he hadn't touched her beyond their kiss since they'd entered the penthouse.

She scooted forward on the buffet, her softness instantly meeting his pants-covered hardness. She briefly bit on her bottom lip, an ache the size of Manhattan gaping within her. An ache that only he could satisfy.

His hands squeezed her legs near her knees then slid up. Her instinct was to throw her head back and allow him to do what he would.

Which was why she instead caught his hands, slid down from the table, then led him toward the wide, open staircase to their right. Swaying her hips suggestively, she climbed three or four steps, aware of the view he was being afforded from the back. She felt a hand on her ass and she paused, allowing the hot branding to ripple through her. Then he was pulling her toward him, forcing her to lie against the carpeted steps as he fitted himself between her thighs.

Seline groaned, welcoming his weight as she pulled at his tie and shirt, then abandoned both for the fastener to his slacks. He hungrily kissed her as she tugged his zipper down, working her hand inside his boxers until the scalding length of him filled her palm.

While their clothed fondling had left her with little doubt as to his size, it had masked how very impressive he was. She idly measured his length, finding him going well beyond the stretch of her fingers and palm together. She encircled the turgid flesh, finding that she could barely touch thumb to fingertips.

Mmm…

Seline's mouth watered with the desire to taste the silken flesh. She trailed her hand down the thick shaft, feeling his heartbeat at the root, her own heart beating hard against her chest in awareness of his reaction to her touch.

He reached for his back pocket and took out a condom while she worked his slacks down his hips, then he rid himself of the constricting material. Next was her skirt, his shirt, her blouse, his briefs, until finally they lay against the steps completely nude, the glass wall on the other side of the stairs reflecting the golden globe of the sun beginning to set off to the west. Seline helped him sheath his erection then arched her back in preparation for his entry.

Instead, he grasped her chin in his right hand, holding her still as he deeply kissed her.

Seline blinked open her eyes. Her chest contracted to the point of pain and she lost her breath.

She immediately labeled the sensation. She'd felt it only one other time. And back then it had been much more about intimacy than sex.

And she wanted strictly sex.

She switched her attention from his face to his shoulder, biting lightly as she wriggled free of his grasp and turned, climbing a couple of more steps then arching her back, presenting him with a carnal view she knew no man could resist.

She knew a moment of disappointment when he followed where she led, grasping her hips as he positioned himself from behind. But that emotion was banished to the winds as he fit the head of his penis against her opening then thrust into her to the hilt.

All coherent thought left her, and sheer sensation quickly filled the void, pressing outward until she was afraid she wouldn't be able to contain it.

So good…

He rocked against her, his sac swaying against her swollen womanhood, then withdrew, his right hand circling her hip to find the bit of flesh and give it a pinch. Seline threw back her head and moaned as he thrust again, and again, causing her bare breasts to sway, her sensitive nipples repeatedly grazing the carpeted step beneath them. His strokes grew from controlled to more frenzied as Seline bore back against him, longing for an even deeper penetration. She reached down between her legs, gently grasping his balls and coaxing him to slow his movements. Whenever he thrust, she rubbed the globes against her slick flesh, shivering at the sensation, then released so he could withdraw.

All too quickly she could no longer concentrate on the move and dropped her hand. The instant she did, he increased the frequency and urgency of his thrusts.

Flesh slapped against flesh, moans competed against groans…

Then finally she was toppling over the other side of the virtual staircase out over a vista she hadn't seen in a very long time, everything shaded in red.

SELINE lay back against the Egyptian cotton sheets. She was naked, she was spent and she was having a hard time concentrating on anything other than the delicious throbbing in her various body parts. Patches of stubble burn marred her inner thighs, her breasts and her chin. She had rug burn on her knees and elbows from the stairs. Her nipples protested when she tried to drape the top sheet over them, so she left them bare as she listened to the sound of the shower in the other room.

The purple-hued world outside the tall, floor-to-ceiling windows told her dawn would soon break. And that it was way past time to hightail it out of here. It wouldn't be too long before Coleman got to the office and discovered what she had done. While she'd built in certain mechanisms to delay the discovery, she knew Coleman was no fool and that he was also the type of dependable guy who would check account activity every morning.

She glanced toward the clock on the nightstand, finding a pillow covering it. Seline dragged it off and the clock fell with it. She picked it up from the floor.

Five forty-five. Damn.

She could count the times she'd had such great sex on two fingers. With Joey Caprioti when she was nineteen and just coming to know her own sexuality. And now.

She smiled stupidly. Yes, Ryder Blackwell was

definitely no slouch in bed. She'd known men who were roaring lions in the boardroom but lazy cats in the bedroom. Not Ryder. He was as ambitious between the sheets as he was outside them. Sheets being optional.

In fact, they hadn't hit the bed until sometime after 3:00 a.m. And only then because they'd risked serious injury in the kitchen when he'd hoisted her onto the counter and knocked over a stand of butcher knives.

The shower shut off.

Seline bounced up from the bed, collected her clothes, then headed at a run for the door.

No matter how good, no sex was worth the risk of a long prison sentence.

4

WHEN RYDER had emerged from his shower to find Carol gone, he'd been amused. He'd hoped the sound of the water would wake her and entice her to slip under the multi-jet spray with him.

Instead she'd left.

When she hadn't shown up to work by ten, he suspected she'd gone back to her place and fallen asleep. He thought maybe she'd be in later.

Then around eleven, John Coleman had requested an emergency meeting.

By 4:00 p.m. Ryder was furiously aware of everything one Carol Lambert had done. Only it hadn't been Carol Lambert but the sexy woman he'd slept with last night. Because Carol Lambert was a thirty-eight-year-old brunette who still lived in Washington State and hadn't transferred to New York and his company, but rather was taking extended time off to have her first child.

"How much are we looking at?" he asked Coleman.

"Three quarters of a mil."

Ryder sat back in his chair as if hit in the chest with a punching bag.

"This woman was good. She brokered a deal between Blackwell and a sham company that as of this morning no longer exists."

"Get the money back."

"Easier said than done. The instant the money hit the sham company's account it was then automatically transferred out to various other accounts, and I'm guessing even more accounts from there. The minute the money left our bank it essentially became untraceable." Coleman shook his head as he considered the printouts he held. "This woman was a pro. She knew exactly what she was doing." He looked up. "Johnstone says this was a set-up from the get go. She borrowed the Lambert woman's résumé, burrowed deep into the company, then meticulously set us up."

Ryder rubbed his face, as much to wake himself up from the nightmare he was in the middle of as to rid himself of the erotic images that kept sliding through his mind from last night.

Coleman didn't know he'd spent the night

sleeping with the enemy. Sleeping—hah! They hadn't slept at all. He'd had Carol, the con artist, every which way it was possible to have a woman. Hell, he'd had more sex with her in one night than he'd had in the entire year.

And he'd been stupid enough to believe he'd be getting more of it.

And still wanted it despite what she'd done.

"Johnstone's got nearly every detective firm in Manhattan working the case now."

"So he's confident she'll be caught."

Coleman grimaced. "Look, Ry, I've never been one to mislead you. The truth is, given the professional nature of the crime, with every moment that passes the trail gets colder."

"You mean there's a chance we won't catch up with her?"

"More than a chance. A probability."

Coleman's cell phone rang, and he answered. A minute later, he rang off.

"The apartment she rented came furnished and was in Carol Lambert's name. And it was wiped clean. Not a print anywhere. But they think they got a couple of hair samples."

"Security cameras?"

"The staff is going over Blackwell's videos now. But routine dictates that they erase tapes after a twenty-four-hour period so all we'll have is the footage from yesterday."

Ryder looked at his watch. The woman had left his place just before six. Nine hours ago. Which meant she could be pretty much anywhere in the world by now. Probably collecting the cash she'd stolen from his company.

"I want to see the footage as soon as it comes in."

"I don't expect to get much," Coleman said. "She always walked as if staring at something on her shoe. I thought it was because she was self-conscious, but now we know the real reason."

Ryder also knew the real reason she'd originally rebuffed his advances yesterday after finding out he'd been the one she'd raced with. No doubt number one in the con artist's handbook was "Fly under the radar."

"Ryder?"

He blinked at Coleman.

"Are you okay?"

No. He was far from okay. Because he was all too aware that if he hadn't taken the woman back to his place last night, he wouldn't be obsessed with the situation right now. He'd have left everything in Coleman's capable hands and gone on with his day full of meetings overseeing expansion plans, financial realignments and mergers. While the amount of money wasn't anything to sneeze at by any means, it wasn't enough to warrant the type of attention he was giving to it. The company lost that amount in a day if truck drivers went on strike in the Midwest.

Despite all that, he'd cancelled everything, mentally incapable of doing anything but concentrating on this one thing. This was personal.

"I want to talk to Johnstone," he said, naming the head of security.

"I can do that. Don't you have a meeting regarding Stanton?"

Ryder got up from his chair and put his suit jacket on. "I cancelled it."

"But we're in the final stages of closing the deal. Everything's set to go into motion the instant the takeover papers are signed. Do you think that's a good idea?"

No, it was a decidedly bad idea. The not-altogether-friendly leveraged buyout of his second-largest competitor would give him a marketing edge in the nation's distribution system, one of the many areas in which Blackwell & Blackwell owned businesses. But Ryder couldn't help himself. He was going to find this woman who'd impersonated Carol Lambert, the woman in the rented Audi, and he was going to find her now.

BY THE END of the week, Ryder had been forced to accept that his finding her wasn't going to be easily checked off his agenda.

It was a Sunday and along with Blackwell & Blackwell's own security team, he was paying three detective firms double their going rate to find her.

Only it was beginning to look like no amount of money was going to be able to uncover the true identity of the woman who'd screwed him... twice.

Coleman told him that perhaps it was time to admit defeat and move on. Besides, the company could write the loss off. There was the Stanton deal in limbo and very possibly in danger of unraveling altogether. But Ryder couldn't seem to think of anything else.

"Are you all right, son?"

Ryder looked at his father, walking next to him along the Coney Island boardwalk. The place where he'd grown up, but now only visited when he saw his father every other Sunday.

"That's the third time you've asked me," Ryder said, shoving his hands into the pockets of his Lauren khakis.

Growing up, he'd heard countless times how much he and his father looked alike. Some of the family's relatives had even taken to calling him Junior, though his father's name was Alan. But time had erased those physical similarities. And while Ryder only lived across the river in Manhattan, it might as well have been across the Atlantic as far as their lifestyles went. His father would take the train into town every now and again for coffee and to go to a museum exhibit or an off-off-Broadway show, but otherwise their lives were separate. And had been since Ryder's mother had died of breast cancer fifteen years ago.

Of course, it didn't help that their differences extended to their own personal ideologies.

Being born a Blackwell, his father had once told him, was no different than being born under any other name, despite the historical and cultural significance it once held in New York. Ryder would always remember that conversation, held when he'd come home soaked on a rainy Tuesday in April. He was nine and he'd just learned that his ancestors had been instrumental in the building of Manhattan and that even his grandfather, his father's father, had enjoyed great wealth, until the mid 1950s when the family had been bankrupted.

His father? His take was that it had probably happened for a good reason. While Alan Blackwell had been educated at Harvard and enjoyed a privileged upbringing, he'd adjusted amazingly well to his new station in life. In fact, it seemed to suit him better, his mother used to say. Rather than working as the CEO of the family company and attending Broadway openings and Lincoln Center charity events, he'd taught American Lit at NYU for most of his career, and had just recently retired, speaking here and there when invited.

Otherwise he lived a quiet life in Brooklyn, visiting his favorite bakery every morning, reading the newspaper, or with his nose in whatever obscure book he'd picked up from the used bookstore on the corner.

But whereas his father had experienced life on both sides of the fence, young Ryder had spent his youth with his fingers fused to the fence links, staring longingly at the skyline across the river. Driven not only to recover his family's longstanding wealth and status, but to up the ante on both counts.

And at thirty-six he'd done all that and more.

"And that's the third time you haven't answered me." His father chuckled quietly then put his arm around his son's shoulders. "Ask the experienced, not the learned."

Ryder offered a half grin. His life had been filled with quotes from one source or another. Mostly his father had been trying to convince him that it wasn't how much he had in his pockets but the love he held in his heart that was the true measure of a good man.

Ryder had in turn spent most of his life ignoring that advice.

"Just some things going on at work," he said.

"Anything you'd like to share?"

"No, no."

"And here I thought the problem might be a woman." The senior Blackwell drew to a stop near the edge of the boardwalk and squinted out at the sparkling Atlantic. "You know, one of your mother's biggest regrets was that she never got to enjoy a grandchild."

"If I remember correctly, you were the one to say that I probably would never have children."

"That's because you have to find a good woman first. And you move too fast to catch bad women, much less good ones." He looked at him. "Up until recently I at least hoped you'd make an effort at continuing the Blackwell name if just for legacy's sake."

"I thought you didn't buy into any of that."

"I don't. But you do. Me? I'd just like to have a grandson or granddaughter who I can teach to play chess. Or at least know that my son, my only child, will finally learn what it means to know love."

"I know love. I had it with Mom. With you."

"And when I'm gone?"

Ryder also stared out at the ocean. "Are you planning on a trip I don't know about?"

"No. But it's something that's been on my mind a lot lately."

"I told you it was a bad idea when you retired—"

"I was forced out, Ryder. There's nothing more irritating than a rambling old man who can't find his notes."

"So teach somewhere here. At a Brooklyn school."

"My teaching days are over." They began walking again. "Besides, if I couldn't teach my own son, tell me what impact I'd really have on other's children."

It wasn't like his father to talk about death in such a direct way. And Ryder wasn't sure how to take it. While he'd heard other parents talk to their children about the impending visit from the Grim Reaper, even if that visit was some twenty to thirty years in the future, his father had never been like that. There were too many topics to discuss, politics to cut through.

"A wiser man, perhaps, might have figured out early on that the way to teach you was to misteach you."

"How do you mean?"

"If I had encouraged you, no insisted on, you rebuilding the family fortune, you would have rebelled and done the opposite. Had I told you having a wife and children would only saddle you down, you probably would be married fifteen years now with three kids."

Ryder chuckled. "Reverse psychology. But you're leaving out that I would have seen through such a ruse. Besides, you could never have done it. It goes against everything you are. Everything you taught me to be."

"But you're still not married."

"Why don't you travel, Pops? You and mom always talked about wanting to travel."

In fact, he'd arranged a month-long tour of England, Scotland and Ireland while his mother was still well enough to travel.

"I'm too old for the hassle. Besides, that was your mom's and my dream. Without her…well, without her it wouldn't be the same."

And one day, perhaps soon, Ryder would be faced with life without his father in it. And for the first time he accepted that it wouldn't be the same, either.

5

THE FOLLOWING FRIDAY everyone around Ryder had officially admitted defeat. But Ryder refused to raise the white flag.

He stood at the windows of his office staring out from his elevated spot at the buildings of Manhattan spread out before him like a giant's handful of mismatched dice. Somewhere out there was the woman who had set his sheets on fire, then outwitted him. And he intended to find her. Whatever it took.

He turned back to his desk and the telephone book he had opened to with the listing of detective agencies in the tri-borough area. Being in Brooklyn with his father last weekend had given him a couple of ideas by reminding him that he hadn't always been standing at the top of the mountain. He'd gotten a raw view from the gutters looking up, as well. After a four-year stint in the marines, he'd received his degree from

Columbia, then had emerged onto the social scene using his family name as his passport with which to rebuild the Blackwell empire. Within six years, he'd sat at the helm of the first company at which he'd worked. Two years after that, he'd bought the company and taken it private and had been expanding the business ever since.

And he hadn't gotten where he was now without getting his hands dirty from time to time. And the mystery woman made him want to thrust both hands directly into the black dirt.

Ryder noted the name and address of a Brooklyn detective agency then picked up the phone. Sometimes it took a fellow gutter rat to find another one in the maze that was the criminal underworld. He picked up the phone and placed the call.

THE BROOKLYN detective agency was little more than a small storefront that could have easily have been a travel agency or a take-out restaurant, not unlike the other businesses around it. The furniture was old, but the place was clean. And P.I. Kylie Capshaw had the tough exterior of someone who'd spent more than a few years foraging around in the gutters, both as a result of the hand life had dealt her, as well as to succeed as a woman in her chosen profession.

"Mr. Blackwell. A pleasure." She said, extended her hand.

"Ryder, please," he said, returning her firm shake. She was dressed in jeans and a T-shirt and well-worn cowboy boots he suspected were steel-toed and capable of doing a fair amount of damage should anyone cross her. And she looked like the type who wouldn't hesitate to do that damage.

"Slumming it, huh?" she questioned, taking two mugs out of a metal desk drawer then crossing to a coffeemaker.

Ryder glanced at his Lagerfeld suit. He hadn't thought about changing his clothes to take the late-afternoon meeting. "In a manner of speaking."

"So tell me," she said, sitting down behind the old metal desk covered with paperwork. She took a bottle of Bailey's from a different drawer then poured the Irish cream into the coffee and handed him a cup. Ryder took it then watched as she sipped hers. "How do you think I'll be able to help you where others haven't been able to? Because I get the feeling that you're not here for a personal matter you don't want others to know about. Am I right?"

"Spot on."

"Who've you been to?"

He told her.

"Ah. The Big Three." She raised her brows. "And they haven't been able to get what you want?"

"No. While this is a white-collar crime, a blue-collar criminal committed it."

"And your reasoning is that it takes a blue-collar gal to find a blue-collar criminal."

Her words weren't so much as a question as they were a statement. "Yes," Ryder answered simply.

Kylie grinned. "Then it looks like you've come to the right place...."

BETWEEN Seline's legs vibrated one of the most powerful machines built by man, and something she'd been craving ever since sneaking out of Ryder Blackwell's bed the week before. The custom black Ducati 999R Xerox motorcycle with a Testastretta 143-hp engine gave her a sense of freedom not even a car could afford her. And as she ran it down the empty roads in rural southwest Wisconsin, the roar drowning out all other sounds, the air whipping around her black leather-clad body, she felt like a hellcat demon on a mission.

That is, if she ignored that there was no real mission, to rid the brand of Ryder's touch from her skin.

It had been nine days since she'd pulled one

of the biggest cons of her career. Yet a sense of a job incomplete tailed her like a state trooper with his siren blaring. Returning home usually calmed her, allowed her distance from her last job in order to concentrate on what needed to be done to ensure her security and to focus on the next con. But not this time. This time, her mind ceaselessly returned to Blackwell & Blackwell. Or more specifically to the man who sat at the helm.

She popped the clutch and further gunned the engine, nudging the speedometer needle up past a hundred.

Her father Angelo had once told her that grifters subconsciously knew when their time was up. That they sense when they'd made a fatal mistake, then come home to find the authorities waiting for them. But somehow she didn't think that was the case here. While she'd had to push up the timeline of her con by a day, and had left a couple of loose ends dangling, she and the money were ultimately untraceable.

Which brought her right back to Ryder himself.

There was a really good reason why she never got personally involved on a job, beyond it not being a professionally shrewd move. But she didn't want to think about that. Not now. She wanted to focus on the future instead.

In fact, that's why she was out on this hour-long ride toward Chicago. To clear her mind of the cobwebs draped there by Ryder Blackwell…and the lessons of her past so she could look to tomorrow.

Before long two lanes turned into three then four and Seline was officially on the outskirts of Chicago. She slowed her speed and drove straight downtown, toward a bakery she'd passed during a previous ride that had looked intriguing. After she'd parked, secured her helmet to the bike and straightened her skin-tight leather jacket, she stepped inside Natale's Bakery on Taylor Street. The Italian sweets shop was just what the doctor ordered, if only for the minute it reminded her of home in New York and the family she'd been forced to leave behind there years before.

A frazzled-looking, attractive woman at one of the tables called out, her words mingling with the bell that jangled as Seline entered, "Hey, Izzie. What do you know about computers?"

Seline guessed the curvy woman with long dark-brown hair on the other side of the counter was Izzie.

After acknowledging Seline, she answered the other customer's question, "Well, I don't know how to find any naked pictures of Heath Ledger, and I haven't figured out how to send a death-ray to spammers, but I do the Web site for the bakery."

"I hear ya."

Seline lowered her sunglasses to eye the café's menu.

"So you know how to enlarge pictures?" the woman at the table continued. "Other than ones of naked movie stars?"

Izzie grinned. "Yeah, give me a sec." She looked at Seline. "What can I get you?"

Seline placed her order for an espresso and asked if there were any fresh cannoli.

"Sorry, Lilith took the last."

She looked over her shoulder at the woman getting cannoli crumbs on the laptop she was bent over.

"Will that be all?"

Seline nodded and paid her then, watching as she came out from behind the counter to stand next to the other woman.

"What do you need?" she asked.

Lilith jumped at Izzie's sudden appearance, and then laughed. Seline understood the response. She'd been living on the edge for so long, any loud sound threatened to push her over the side.

"I need a close-up of this guy's ring."

Izzie leaned toward the computer and squinted. "It's pretty big already."

"Not big enough."

Izzie sat down and slid the laptop toward her. Seline stepped imperceptibly closer, watching as Izzie's fingers flew over the keypad with confident ease, but when she turned the screen back toward the other woman the picture was distorted, connected blobs with no detail.

"That won't work," Lilith said.

Izzie shrugged. "You need a higher resolution picture."

Her friend grunted. "How can I get a higher resolution picture?"

"Where'd you get the first one?" Seline asked. Computers were second nature to her, her partner in crime in a manner of speaking.

Lilith looked at her. "Newspaper Web site."

"They'd use a lower resolution there so the page will load faster. They'd probably only use high res in the actual printing process."

Lilith frowned. "I don't have any contacts at the paper. I don't think they'd give access to their archives to just anyone."

Seline arched a brow and grinned. "Do you want access?"

"Most definitely."

Seline put her coffee down on the table and threaded her fingers together to give them a stretch. Lilith scooted around to give her room, but she simply leaned over the machine and worked standing up, her eyes darting periodically outside Natale's plate-glass window.

"Nice ride," Lilith commented about the Ducati.

Her fingers didn't slow. "Gets me around. Who is this guy, anyway? Don't tell me you're trying to figure out if that ring is a wedding band and he's the asshole you've been dating for the last three months."

Lilith nearly spat out what Seline guessed was cappuccino. "Ew."

She nodded in approval. "So he's not your lover."

"Say that again and I'll dump the dregs on you. He's a jerk I'm investigating."

"A jerk?" Seline asked. "What makes him different from every other man on this planet?"

"Good question," Izzie muttered. With no other customers in the shop and, Seline guessed, closing time quickly approaching, she'd taken to wiping down the tables of all their remnant stickiness. Lilith looked impatient as Seline accessed a number of remote, unconnected servers and then circled back to what she wanted to do, shielding the laptop from any trace that might be run back to it. She suspected she was being overly cautious, but in her line of business, caution kept you free.

"Name one guy who isn't a jerk," Seline said, swiping her tongue over her lips as her concentration deepened.

"Mac Mancusi," Lilith whispered.

"You know Mac?" Izzie asked, apparently familiar with the name.

Seline mistyped a word and had to correct it, the obviously Italian name distracting her. Maybe returning to the bakery wouldn't be a good idea.

"Biblically," Lilith said.

Izzie's eyebrows shot up. "No kidding? You and Mac? Wow. I can't picture the two of you together."

"You won't need to. We won't be together much longer."

"You're dumping him?" Izzie was clearly disappointed. "You're right, you know, Mac's not a jerk. He grew up just a few blocks from here. Our families know each other. I'd think any woman would love to catch a good, honest cop like him."

Seline stopped her work. "You're sleeping with a cop?"

Lilith pushed the laptop closer. "I'm sleeping

with him, not married to him," she insisted. "Trust me when I say that my definition of right and wrong varies from his by huge degrees. Keep working and your next ten espressos are on me."

Seline definitely couldn't return to the bakery, no matter how good the coffee and cannoli. She covered her uneasiness with a smile and returned to her task. "I won't be around that long, but thanks for the offer."

"Add her to my tab," Lilith instructed Izzie. "Any time she stops in, coffee's on me. What's your name?"

"Seline."

With a nod, Lilith told Izzie to give Seline free rein of her coffee tab.

"Does that mean you're actually going to pay it someday?" Izzie asked, an amused grin tugging at her full lips.

"Soon. I swear."

Lilith tapped her fingers impatiently on the table, stopping when Seline gave her warning glare.

Finally, she cracked the code to access the newspaper's computer—you would think programmers would learn that the word *God* was the first backdoor password a hacker tried—and did a search for photos that fell within the dates of the one Lilith was interested in. "Don't get ahead of yourself. I haven't got it…wait…ding, ding, ding. We have a winner."

Lilith clapped enthusiastically. "I had a feeling you were up to the task."

"You would," Izzie quipped.

Seline stood back, wondering what that meant. She took in Lilith's flowy top and pentagram charm, thinking that she looked a lot like the woman who'd read tarot cards down the street from where she'd grown up.

Lilith appeared to hesitate as she stared at the ring on the man in the photo's hand. She took a deep breath, blowing it out slowly as if willing herself to remain calm.

Seline eyed her. "Is that what you need?"

Lilith saved the image to the hard drive, e-mailed it to someone, and then shut off the machine and tucked it into her bag. "Unfortunately, yes." She stood and extended her hand to Seline, who, after a moment's hesitation, gave it a strong shake. "Thanks for your help. If you ever have need of a psychic, look me up. Well, in a few weeks when I'm back on the job." She patted the laptop case. "I think I just found my golden ticket back to gainful employment. Izzie, thanks for the sugar boost and the wi-fi."

Izzie waved. "Anytime."

Lilith weaved through the tables and chairs until she reached the door. The bell jangled before Izzie called out, "Lilith!"

Lilith turned.

"Don't be so quick to write off a great guy like Mac," Izzie said, her voice tentative, as if she couldn't quite believe she was offering romantic advice. "Maybe you and he can find a way to make it work, even if you think there's no way it ever could."

Humph. Seline had always been one to trust her instincts over her heart. If your gut told you something, you were wise to heed it.

She thought of Ryder and the impossibility of anything working between them and then banished the thought.

"Here," she said, putting a hundred-dollar bill on the counter. "For her tab. I sense that she needs the money more than I do. And I don't have to be psychic to figure that out."

"Thanks." Izzie sounded surprised.

Seline smiled, picked up her coffee and then took that as her cue to leave. Never stay anywhere long enough for them to get to know you. While it sometimes left her longing for something more, she knew she had to make certain tradeoffs in life. And this, unfortunately, was one of hers.

6

AN HOUR and a half later Seline turned onto the long, private drive that wound around five acres of lush, sloping land before finally leading to her house set up on a low hill in the midst of open land, the security gates behind her clanging shut. She set a leisurely pace with the bike, taking in the grounds. A part of her enjoyed the landscape. Another looked for flaws in the security.

Often was the time when she looked around and thought, damn, what a great effin' place. I must be doing pretty good.

This was one of those times. And she hoped soon it would really become home.

She pressed the button to open the fifth and farthest door on her multi-car garage and rode the bike inside, then cut the engine.

"Jeeves?" Seline called out when she entered the house from the garage. There was no answer. She hung her leather coat on a hook and shook out her dark hair…hair that was a shade darker than her regular color as a result of the dye it had taken to cover the bleaching she'd used to impersonate Carol Lambert.

Her steps slowed then stopped altogether when she called out again to no response.

Someone was here…

Seline hugged the wall then reached for the switchblade tucked into the back pocket of her leather pants. A quick flick of her wrist and it was ready to go.

Jeeves was always aware when she returned. It was the noise she made on those occasions, he said. In this case, the sound of her Ducati engine would have been more than enough of a heads-up.

Yet he hadn't responded to her calls.

Shit.

Seline remembered the feeling earlier. Recalled the advice from her father that she'd sense when her time was up. When she'd played her last ace and the law was about to slam down around her.

But even facing the unusual silence of the house, she didn't think that was the case here. And she generally wasn't into self-delusion.

She turned the corner into the kitchen. A pot of water was boiling on the stove. She slunk around the corner into the hall leading to the large foyer. Empty. She stepped out into the open doorway to the sitting room and spotted the reason for the silence.

Ryder Blackwell sat in one of the wing chairs in front of the fireplace, hands casually folded in his lap, his grin telling her he'd been thinking about her at least as much as she'd been thinking about him.

Albeit she'd guess for different reasons....

"HELLO, Carol."

Ryder relaxed in the comfortable chair that would look at home in any one of his three posh residences within the United States. He was exactly where he'd planned to be for the past nine days. Confronting the woman who had conned him in more ways than one. But this time the power was fully in his hands.

"Or should I say Seline?"

Late-afternoon sunlight glinted off the blade she held as she sighed and dropped it to her side.

"Christ, Ryder. What in the hell do you think you're doing?"

He raised a brow as he watched her skillfully close the blade then tuck it into the back pocket of her tight black leather jeans.

Ryder took her in from head to foot. While she

looked nothing like the woman who had worked at his firm or graced his bed, he'd known instantly it was her. Would have known it if it were pitch black and they were in a roomful of people.

Her hair was dark-brown now instead of blond. And the tough biker style suited her in a way that business attire had not.

He hadn't fooled himself into thinking that he understood anything about the woman even now pouring a splash of bourbon into two crystal decanters. The thick thud of her boots sounded against the Aubusson rug as she crossed it and held one of the glasses out for him to take.

She didn't say anything as he accepted it, downing her own. She stared at him, her gray eyes darkened by widening pupils as she wiped the side of her full mouth with the back of her hand then held the tumbler against her white T-shirt-covered chest.

"Jeeves?" she said, focusing her attention on the fireplace mantel rather than on Ryder.

"Yes, ma'am." The man he'd convinced to let him in appeared in the doorway. Even though he was dressed in black pants and a white shirt, Ryder got the impression he would have looked equally as comfortable in a vested butler's suit.

"Bring us a tray."

"Right away, ma'am."

Ryder allowed his attention to drift back to the woman standing within arm's reach. The scent of fine leather teased his nostrils along with a trace of coconut and the outdoors. When he'd first raced her on the streets of Manhattan, he'd had no idea about the woman in the Audi. But after having spent an erotic night with her, he didn't find her appearance now that much of a stretch.

She was a chameleon, changing her colors at will and blending in wherever she went. Surely, it was part of her job. But was he seeing the real Seline Sanborn now? Or was this merely another facet of her diamond-hard shell?

"Do you have any idea what you've done?" she asked quietly.

Ryder considered the glass that he had yet to drink from. "Funny. I'm here to talk about what you've done."

She rested her left hand against the mantel then looked down at him, her expression serious. "I'm going to ask you a question. It's very important how you answer it."

Ryder stared back at her.

"How did you find me?"

"I'm not without my resources."

Seline dropped her head and closed her eyes. "Okay, I conned you, you found me, I'll give your money back. But that's not what's at issue here. I need to know what resources you used to uncover my true identity."

"Like, are the authorities aware of your whereabouts?"

She didn't respond or move. And, oddly, he got the distinct impression that that wasn't what she was talking about.

"Answer me, Ryder. This is more important than you can know."

He didn't say anything, if only because this wasn't exactly the way he'd imagined this going down.

He wasn't sure what he *had* envisioned, but it was closer to her running in the opposite direction or trying to sweet talk him. Not matter-of-factly stating the series of events and offering him his money back as though this was a business meeting, then demanding he answer questions.

He put his glass down on a table and then stood, walking a few paces away to lessen the impact of her nearness.

"I want you to answer a few questions for me first."

She turned toward him, her eyes dark and dangerous. “Shoot.”

“Why Blackwell?”

She had her hands behind her back and was leaning casually against the large fireplace. He was reminded that she had a knife in her back pocket. “Why *not* Blackwell?”

“So the hit wasn’t personal.”

“I learned a long time ago not to mix business with pleasure.”

“Then what happened between us was business then.”

She smiled. “No, that was pleasure.”

Ryder held her gaze.

“The business end of the con was done.”

He watched as she pushed from the fireplace and slowly crossed to stand in front of him. She appeared to be staring at something on his shoulder, allowing him to gaze at her face without restraint.

Damn, but she was beautiful. Her skin was flawless, aside from a small scar above her right brow that merely added to her attractiveness rather than detracted from it. She wore little makeup, but her eyes didn’t need it, not with lashes as thick as branches and a generous mouth that could fuel enough fantasies to last the rest of his life.

"So now you answer my question," she said, focusing on his eyes. "How did you find me?"

Damn it all to hell, but he still wanted her on a physical level he couldn't ignore. Her proximity brought to life every part of him, left him longing to kiss her lips and snake his arms around her slender waist and pull her tight against him. Take up where they'd left off.

"Where would you like it, ma'am?" Jeeves appeared next to them with a silver tray filled with teacups and scones and clotted cream and jams.

Seline closed her eyes. "Remind me to talk to you about your awful sense of timing, Jeeves."

The butler grinned at her as if he believed his timing was perfect as he put the tray down on the table near the long sofa. "Yes, ma'am."

Just like that they were alone again.

And Ryder became doubly aware of how very close she was.

And did something he definitely hadn't planned to do. At least not consciously.

He kissed her.

THERE WAS a time when Seline might have used sex in order to get what she wanted. A time well before she learned how very dangerous such a prospect could prove.

But it hadn't been her who had initiated the kiss, it had been Ryder. And his mouth on hers felt better, hotter, than any kiss had a right to.

She pressed her palms against his chest to push him away. But when they met the solid wall, her resolve faltered. His tongue against hers, his fingers at the side of her neck, felt so damn good. Within an instant the house around her faded to black, the questions surrounding his presence disappeared, leaving only the sound of his ragged breathing and the thump-thump of her heart.

He groaned. And she pushed him slightly away.

"I thought that was supposed to be my move," she whispered, gazing up at him.

He cracked a grin. "By all means."

She lingered for a moment longer then turned away from him, walking toward the sofa where she sat down and poured the tea. He stood where he was for long ticks of the grandfather clock in the foyer and then followed her.

"Nice place," he said, clearing his throat then accepting the tea she offered.

"I liked it." Seline sat back, well aware of the contrast she made in her black leather against the floral sofa. She crossed her legs and swung her booted foot.

"You used the past tense."

"I did." She sipped the tea. "Because I'll have to leave now that I've been found."

"Because I've found you."

"Because you have no idea the can of worms you opened when you walked through that door."

She watched him grin. He didn't have clue one what he'd done. And she couldn't blame him. In fact, she gave him a lot of credit. She'd lived at the manor for over three years without being uncovered. Yet this one man had somehow found her in a little over a week.

She'd known sleeping with him wasn't a very good idea. Men like Ryder had egos as large as…well, as large as hers. They fed on challenges and she'd posed a challenge to him. Not just on the financial end, although she was sure that had stung him. No, rather they relished themselves in the role of love 'em and leave 'em bachelors and they didn't cotton to having their own behavior turned around on them.

She rested her elbow against the back cushion so she could look at him more fully. "I'd forgotten your background."

A chip in his armor.

"Marines, studying at Columbia even as you fought to make your way up the business ladder.

A ladder that once bore your family's name on a golden ring but that had collapsed under your grandfather's weight before you were born. Little-known associations with some shady characters."

Everything about him tensed.

"It seems I made a grave miscalculation."

"Seems that you did."

There was a sound outside on the grounds. Ryder heard it as well, but he appeared to be more interested in her start at it. Which meant she'd just revealed her own chip.

Casually putting her cup down, Seline stepped to the front window and looked out. A visiting gardener had just put down a wheelbarrow full of annuals he was about to plant around the front shrubs. She hadn't known she was rubbing her arms or that Ryder had joined her until he spoke.

"You're spooked."

Seline considered him long and hard. "You have no idea...."

7

RYDER TRIED to penetrate the tough exterior of the enigmatic woman before him.

She avoided his gaze and stepped around him. “If you’ll excuse me a minute, I’d really like to get out of these clothes and wash up after my ride.”

Ryder reached out and grasped her arm before he knew that’s what he was going to do.

She stared at him. “Do you really think I’d try to bolt after you’ve somehow managed to find me?”

“I think exactly that.”

“Fine,” she said, smiling. “Then feel free to follow me.”

Ryder wasn’t sure what he was leaving himself open for, but staying behind in the living room waiting for her return wasn’t even a remote option for him.

Jeeves was in the foyer as they passed. “Shall I arrange for dinner, ma’am?”

“You hungry?” she asked Ryder.

"No."

"Just leave a tray of sandwiches and finger foods, Jeeves. Then you can retire."

"Yes, ma'am."

Ryder got the impression that the two shared more than a mistress-butler relationship. It was something in the way Jeeves looked at Seline. But he couldn't figure out the connection. Friends? Did he help her with her cons? He didn't know. But he didn't think it was a good idea to underestimate the other man, nonetheless, despite how amused he'd been when Ryder had shown up at the door.

He watched Seline's leather-clad bottom lead the way up the winding staircase, then followed her down the hall to a room at the far end. She opened the door then turned toward him.

"Surely you don't plan to watch me change?" she asked, batting her eyes in a way that he might have bought nine days ago.

"That's exactly what I had planned."

She stared at him for a long moment, then walked inside the room. "Have it your way."

"That's exactly the way I intend to have it." Ryder closed the door after himself then looked around.

Various shades of white were everywhere,

with a throw pillow and chaise here and there in red velvet, probably placed so as not to completely blind the room's inhabitant.

Seline went to a closet and began to shimmy out of her black leather jeans. Ryder crossed his arms and openly enjoyed the view. She wore a pair of skimpy purple panties that hugged her rounded bottom to perfection. And those legs… He'd seen how long they were during their night together, but still the sheer length and curve of them threw him. Legs like that on a woman as beautiful as Seline Sanborn ought to be illegal.

He caught the ridiculous thought and grinned.

Seline reached inside the closet for a silky white robe then stepped into what he guessed was the master bath. She began to close the door.

"Oh no you don't." He caught the door before she could close it.

Finally he appeared to get a reaction from her other than cool control. "Knock it off, Blackwell. I'm not going to let you watch me take a shower." Then, just like that, the irritation was gone as she smiled. "Not without paying."

"Don't you think I've given enough already?"

She stepped aside. "Go ahead. Take a look around. No windows. Nowhere for me to go aside from back into this room."

Ryder examined the well-appointed bathroom with its steam shower and hot tub and was sorry that he didn't have an excuse to watch her. The thought of suds skimming her wet flesh was definitely a turn-on.

He looked at his Rolex as he stepped back into the bedroom. "You have ten minutes."

TEN MINUTES were more than enough for Seline to be well away from Ryder Blackwell.

She turned the lock on the door, switched on the shower, then moved the decorative screen away from the far wall and considered the secret passageway hidden in the ceramic tiles. Then she sighed and sat heavily down on a dressing-room chair, staring at the invisible entrance. Truth was, she didn't want to go.

She told herself it had to do with her need to find out how Ryder had uncovered her name and location, but she knew it was more than that. It went well beyond her reluctance to leave this house behind without a backward glance.

Simply put, Ryder Blackwell intrigued her in a way no man had been able to do in a long, long time.

She recalled Jeeves' knowing expression downstairs and suppressed a groan. It was just like her butler to invite Ryder inside—he kept telling her it was long past time she had a man in her life. She always told him that he was more man than she'd ever need, but the quietly homosexual Brit merely grinned at her and said that he didn't swing that way.

She stared at the secret doorway again, then looked over her shoulder at the door on the other side of which Ryder waited. She supposed it was enough for now to know that she could escape if she had to. While she always had at least three exit routes in any situation, she also had the added advantage of this being her home court. She knew every inch of the place up and down.

And if need be she could leave it faster than Ryder could use his considerable skills to bring her to orgasm.

So she moved the screen back into place along with the chair and took a quick shower, then exactly when Ryder knocked on the door to tell her that her ten minutes were up, she opened it and flashed him more than a dirty smile.

AN ALARM went off in Ryder's head as he stood looking at Seline in her slinky robe, the ends of her dark hair damp and leaving wet spots on the front…right where her breasts were. Her areolas were clearly outlined and her slightly protruding nipples made his mouth water with the desire take his fill of them.

"Happy?" she asked.

Happy wasn't the word for it. Certain parts of his body were downright ecstatic with her wanton display. Especially when his attention moved south to where her robe didn't quite close in the front, baring her cleanly shaven womanhood to his hungry gaze.

She leisurely pulled the robe more tightly closed, blocking his view, then moved toward the bed. "So, Ryder, you haven't told me yet whether you have been in contact with the authorities."

"No. I haven't told you." And he didn't plan on telling her, either. Although he figured she could guess that he hadn't.

So he'd wanted…no, needed to see her reaction when she realized he'd found her. He figured he could always call in the proper authorities if it came down to it.

Only as he watched her move around the intimate confines of her bedroom, it wasn't so much about what was down, but rather what was up. Namely his desire to show her exactly how much frustration she'd caused him over the past week and a half. How much he'd wanted to get even with her one moment, to just plain wanting her, period, the next.

He'd never felt anything quite similar before. The money Seline had swindled would have been a clear deal-breaker in any other context. But somehow he was currently having a problem connecting the crime to the criminal.

It could be the dispassionate nature of the act itself. She hadn't stolen from him because of revenge. Or because she was desperate. In fact, she hadn't stolen from *him* at all, but from Blackwell & Blackwell. And while it might seem that he and the company were one and the same, they weren't.

And he was just now coming to understand how very true that was.

What Seline had done was nothing more than a financial transaction. Not unlike what he might do to business competitors himself. Hold up a big contract here, pull strings to deny a bank loan or scare away investors there—what he did on a day-to-day basis could be argued to be along the same lines.

The difference lay in that what he did was viewed as business as usual. What she did was a prosecutable crime.

He blinked, just then realizing that she was

sitting on the bed applying lotion to her smooth skin. And he was so occupied with his thoughts he hadn't noticed.

Or rather his mind hadn't noticed. His body was fully aware that her nearly bare body was nearby.

He pulled a chair closer to the bed and sat down, stretching his feet to rest against the end of the bed, crossing his hands over his abdomen.

"So business must be good," Ryder commented, looking around the room, though time and time again his hungry gaze returned to her glistening skin, made softer still by the lotion she rhythmically applied to every inch.

"Can't complain. You?"

He shrugged. "I have a complaint or two, but nothing I can't handle."

Her hands slowed and she looked at him under her fringe of lashes. "Oh?"

"Mmm."

She finished with the lotion then lay back against the pillows, looking at him suggestively. Her right leg moved provocatively over the other, her slender foot rubbing the inside then the outside of the other calf. "Mind sharing exactly what you plan to do?"

"Yes, I do mind."

She tugged on the end of the belt holding the robe closed. "Too bad."

"Isn't it just?"

The belt untied and the robe gaped slightly open, revealing the flesh between her full breasts. "I think it's a pretty safe bet that the law isn't involved."

Ryder found it suddenly difficult to swallow. "Yet."

She tugged on the edge of the robe, causing the material over her right breast to fall away. He took in the taut puckered nipple. "Dependent on..." she led, her voice growing softer.

"Dependent on how this goes?"

"And what's 'this,' exactly?"

"The next few minutes."

He saw her tense slightly, but just as quickly she appeared to regain momentum as she orchestrated the baring of her other breast.

"Are you saying if I sleep with you, you'll leave?"

He blinked up into her eyes, which were inscrutable.

Seline abruptly sat up and pulled the robe closed. "Screw you, Blackwell." She strode toward the hallway door.

Ryder rose to his feet and caught her around the wrist, pulling her to him.

"Let me go."

"Not until I get what I came here to get."

"If that's sex—"

"It has nothing to do with sex."

Well, that wasn't entirely true. But at least it didn't in the way she thought it did.

"I came here for some answers."

"Right."

Ryder allowed his gaze to travel over her. He was certain that she probably knew at least a dozen ways to escape his grip. Yet she stayed where she was, perhaps allowing him to think he had the upper hand.

"Why did you sleep with me, Seline?"

"It seemed like a good idea at the time."

"Did it?"

"No, actually it didn't. But I wanted to anyway." She swung her long hair over her shoulder and glared at him. "As you probably already figured out, I'm a bit of a risk-taker."

"But sleeping with me put more at risk than I'm guessing you usually do."

She stared at him for a long moment as if trying to piece together the puzzle of his reasoning. "Are you thinking I slept with you because I felt more than desire?"

Ryder broke eye contact, damning himself even as he did so.

He cleared his throat then fought to maintain his gaze. "I'm saying that on a level you may currently be reluctant to acknowledge, you knew that if you slept with me you'd make your con personal. That I would come to find you."

"Yes, but trying and actually finding are two different things."

What might have been her next words fell silently between them.

Until now.

8

UNTIL NOW.

Seline stared back at Ryder, inordinately aware of how heavily her heart beat against her ribcage. For a moment she'd forgotten that men like Ryder didn't come to be where they were because they allowed fundamental desires to get in the way of their goals. He hadn't come here for sex. He'd come for answers.

And the sheer thrill associated with finding an unfindable woman.

She wasn't aware of what changed between them in that one moment. But she did know that it had changed. She was back to the time she'd originally given up fighting her attraction to him and instead had given herself over to emotion.

Did he have any idea how he affected her? She searched his eyes even as the hand at her wrist began to caress instead of grip. No, she suspected he didn't.

However, she could see that he responded to whatever attraction existed between them as powerfully as she did.

"I thought you said sex had nothing to do with this," she murmured, even as her gaze moved to his mouth, longing for him to kiss her.

"It didn't."

"You used the past tense."

"That's because it no longer applies."

She met him when he bent to kiss her, her hands immediately going to his hair, her body arching against his. His groan filled her ears as she swirled her tongue around the inside of his mouth. He tasted of bourbon and desire. Like temptation personified.

Her robe disappeared first, followed quickly by his slacks and shirt and briefs. He nearly tossed her to the bed, where she bounced against the mattress as he bent over her. His hands claimed her breasts, his lips her mouth. She wrapped her legs around his waist, wanting and seeking. When he didn't immediately deliver, she rolled him over and straddled him, sitting upright, her sex in direct contact with his.

"Condom," he said.

She reached into the nightstand drawer and

pulled one out, but held it in her palm without opening it.

Ryder openly watched her, curiosity hiking one dark brow.

Seline moved her hips so that the long, hard length of his erection was sandwiched between her swollen labia. Ryder's pupils grew by degrees, nearly overtaking the electric blue of his eyes. She could tell it was taking all his willpower not to buck his hips so he could enter her without protection. She slid down the length of him again, pausing so that the tip rested against her tender bud. She was so hot for him a powerful shudder ran through her. Her juices covered him, lubricating the harmless bit of foreplay.

Rather than sheathing him with the latex, she dropped the condom to the top sheet then leaned over, putting her breasts in close proximity to his face. He took full advantage, curving his fingers around one of the sensitive globes then sucking her nipple against his tongue. Her reaction was such that she nearly couldn't concentrate on what she wanted to do. Nearly. She undid the white satin cord holding the wispy white canopy curtains back, then leaned to the right to get the other one there. Then she grasped his hands and lifted them high above his head, kissing him deeply.

"I'm the one who's supposed to be punishing you," he murmured, watching as she tied first one of his wrists to the bedpost, then the other.

"Who said I was punishing you?" she asked.

Even as she said the words, she knew there was a dark place within that demanded he acquiesce to her wishes. Allow her the control that his mere appearance at her estate had ripped from her.

Finally satisfied that he couldn't free himself without doing some damage, she wriggled her bottom back upright, considering his impressive male physique.

God, but the man was stunning. She flattened her palms against the well-defined muscles of his chest, then shifted them slowly over his collarbone and shoulders, then down toward his stomach. Springy light hair tickled her fingers as she worked her hands back up, bending to lave his flat male nipples with her tongue.

His erection throbbed between her legs. She tipped her hips forward, then back, then slid down his legs until her mouth was parallel with his distended flesh.

She watched with hooded eyes as he swallowed thickly. And the instant her mouth closed over the head of his arousal, he strained his neck and groaned.

Seline guessed it wasn't often that Ryder Blackwell gave up control. And while a part of her wondered why he was doing so now—after all, it would be all too easy for her to get up and leave him tethered to her bed while she made her escape—an even bigger part of her wanted to stick around and see why.

She grasped his thick width in her palm, moving her fingers down until the back of her knuckles met with his swollen sac. Holding him upright, she flicked her tongue over the straining flesh, tasting herself on him, tasting him as his own liquid beaded on the mushroom head. She moved her mouth down until she covered the hood then applied suction. His hips bucked against the mattress, forcing another inch inside her mouth even as he pulled at his restraints, the evidence of his coming climax making her hotter yet.

And she was nowhere near done.

Squeezing her fingers more tightly against his girth, she nudged her hand up, then down, mimicking the movements with her mouth…up and down…up and down…

With her free hand, she weighed his balls, not

about to leave them out. Ryder's deep groan told of his appreciation.

She sensed his impending orgasm and quickened her actions, then removed her mouth, watching as his semen exploded from him, his hips bucking violently against the mattress.

Seline then set about cleaning him all up.

RYDER HAD NEVER BEEN that big on receiving blow jobs. Quite frankly, he enjoyed being the one in command when it came to sex. But Seline's expert ministrations were giving him cause to rethink his entire take.

He tried to move his hands to cup her face and draw her up for a kiss, only to be reminded that he was bound to the heavy four-poster bed. As if the burning chafing of his wrists hadn't been enough.

It seemed that the woman lapping his penis with her tongue was introducing him to all kinds of firsts.

He watched as his semi-aroused flesh began to grow rock-hard again.

Seemingly satisfied, Seline lifted her head, sweeping her long dark hair to the other side of her face even as she straddled his hips again, giving him a clear view of her nude womanhood as she settled over him.

Dear Lord, the woman was determined to be the death of him.

"Untie me now?" he rasped.

She smiled and kissed him, the taste of both of them on her tongue. "Not just yet."

He watched as she finally tore open the foil packet with her teeth and sheathed him with the condom. Then she reached her fingers between her thighs and parted her swollen flesh. Ryder swallowed hard at the sight of the pink, tender pathway as she slowly slid down his engorged length.

For long moments he could do little more than lie there trying to gather his wits about him. His lungs were frozen, his every muscle tense. He tugged on his restraints again at the same time as she moved.

Ryder was mesmerized by the sight of her straddling him. Her face was an artist's rendering of bliss. Of a woman who not only wasn't afraid of sex, but knew how to thoroughly enjoy it. Her breasts heaved. Not as a result of her movements, but rather her quick, shallow breathing. Her skin glistened with moisture and that dark hair…that thick dark cloud framed her face as she slid back, then forth, her stomach muscles clenching as she did.

He longed to touch her. To caress her breasts. To clutch her hips. To roll her over so he could thrust into her as deep as he would go. The fact that he couldn't had an interesting effect on him. He felt on the verge of climax and frustrated by turns. He'd raise his hips to meet her and she'd move slightly away, only to slide back over him again, her sweet essence coating his member.

He heard her deep intake of breath and watched as every part of her seem to tremble. Her hair, her breasts, her stomach. He thrust his hips upward, going even deeper, and she moaned.

And he blasted right over the precipice with her.

The loud crash of broken glass sounded appropriate to him, so he didn't make much of it. Until he saw the shocked expression on Seline's face.

She rolled quickly away.

Ryder looked behind him at where the glass window had completely shattered. Something crashed to the floor in the room and he jerked as holes appeared in the opposite door and wall.

Bullet holes.

He opened his mouth to speak but Seline was quickly unbinding his hands.

"Follow me!" she shouted over the sounds of breakage around them.

She slid over the side of the bed to the floor

and he followed, gathering his clothes as he crab-walked toward into the bathroom. The bullet holes climbed the door as he passed, showering him with splinters.

"Haul ass, Blackwell!"

Where? Where could they possibly go inside the bathroom?

No windows. He remembered having checked the room out before she'd showered.

Still, the fact that someone was shooting at them didn't leave a lot of options. Was there only one shooter? Or was another making his way through the house even now?

He quickly dressed in his slacks and pulled on his shirt, watching in silence as Seline moved a chair and a changing screen, then pulled open a hidden door.

"Go!"

Ryder didn't need to be told twice. He had to stoop to fit into the short opening, but there was plenty of room to maneuver. Seline followed, pulling the door closed behind her and driving home a series of locks. It was pitch-black until she switched on a flashlight then passed him, leading the way through a maze of dark path-ways, picking up small black bags along the way.

He couldn't hear the gunshots anymore, but

whether that was good or bad, he couldn't be sure. If there was no sound to mask their movements, could the gunman or men be listening for their progress?

Finally Seline pulled to a stop in front of him. She shut off the flashlight and he heard rustling. Then she opened up another door, revealing that she had dressed in black clothing she'd apparently found in one of the bags she'd collected.

"Here," she said, shoving a nickel-plated 9mm pistol at him.

Ryder blinked as she jumped the three feet down into what seemed to be the garage. She made a beeline straight for the Ducati he'd watched her ride up on earlier.

She was about to start it when her gaze snapped up to meet his. "Are you coming? Or would you prefer to wait around for them to catch up with you?"

Ryder stuffed the pistol into the back waist of his slacks then jumped. The tiled floor was cold under his bare feet as he quickly buttoned his shirt.

"Move back. I'm going to drive."

"Over my dead body."

Gunshots sounded on the other side of the garage door.

"What about Jeeves?" he asked, deciding not

to argue with her just then and climbing onto the seat behind her.

"He can take care of himself." She started the bike. "Besides, somebody has to stay behind to destroy the house."

"Destroy…"

The bike lurched at the same time she pushed a button, popping open a small opening in the garage door. A door they flew through.

Seline made a sharp left, angling them nearly parallel with the cement driveway, then leveled out and hit the gas, the powerful Italian engine growling beneath them as she zigzagged down the long drive, past two dark SUVs.

Ryder looked over his shoulder to find that one of the vehicles was turning around to give chase.

"Hold on," Seline said.

Then she veered off the main road, negotiating a path through a tangle of vegetation he half suspected had been placed there to give the motorcycle an advantage over, say, an SUV.

Jesus, he thought, tightening his grasp on her when the cycle went airborne just as the house behind him exploded, giving the sun a run for its money in the brightness department. Just what in the hell had he gotten himself into?

9

"YOU'RE HIT."

An hour later, Seline stopped at an out-of-the-way gas station in northern Illinois that still had old analog pumps and an old man manning the register, with nary an expensive bottle of water on display anywhere.

She looked down at where she'd absently tucked her right hand inside her leather jacket and drew it out. Blood coated her fingertips. "It's nothing," she said. "A flesh wound."

She'd been shot twice in her life, but that didn't automatically qualify her for expert status on gunshot wounds. However, she knew enough to understand that her continued mobility and endurance an hour after the hit meant that her wound wasn't too serious.

"Do you have your cell phone?" she asked Ryder.

"It's in my briefcase back at your place."

She fished around in the backpack tied to the bike and tossed a cell his way. "Make arrangements to get yourself back to New York. I'm going to clean up."

Without sparing him another glance, she walked to the station office, got the restroom key that was attached to what seemed like the trunk of an oak tree, then let herself into the ancient bathroom off to the side. Not bothering to lock the door, she shrugged out of her jacket, careful not to jostle her right shoulder too much, and considered the damage in the scratched mirror.

Damn.

She poked around. As she'd suspected, it was only a minor wound. But it had put a hole through her shoulder and might have nicked her clavicle in the process. She took off her black tank top, soaked it with hot water, then squeezed it out over the wound, cringing with pain as she cleaned the blood from her skin so she could get a better look. A wave of dizziness hit her and she leaned against the chipped porcelain sink for support.

"Who in the hell *are* you?"

She didn't bother opening her eyes. She'd heard Ryder enter the unlocked room. "Someone you should never have gotten involved with."

"I knew that the first night," he said.

She stared at him.

"But that doesn't change the fact that I chose to get involved anyway." He took the tank top from her and wrung it out. "Turn around."

She did as requested, clenching her teeth against the dizziness that refused to go away, barely aware that she was naked from the waist up.

"Gunfights a normal part of the job for you?" he asked quietly, gingerly patting her shoulder with the tank top then rinsing the fabric out again.

"Not normally."

"But you have been involved in them before."

It was more of a statement than a question so she didn't acknowledge it.

"You're right," he said after long minutes. "The bullet appears to have traveled clean through."

"Nice shoes," she said, noticing that he wore an old pair of work boots.

"Thanks. I gave the old geezer a ten spot for them."

"His?"

"I hope not. His feet were smaller than a ten-year-old girl's. He got them out of the garage."

Seline moved to get iodine and gauze from the bag she'd brought in with her.

"Let me. While it doesn't appear that you've lost a lot of blood, you're pale as a communion wafer."

She cocked a brow at his description.

Within minutes he'd neatly dressed her wound then handed her a white tank top that was packed with the kit.

"Not bad," she said, examining his handiwork before carefully putting the top on. "Do this often?"

"Once or twice in the military."

"Ah, yes. The marines. Bosnia."

He grimaced as he threw away the wrappings.

"No, not there." She took out a plastic bag. "We should leave as little as possible behind in case they come this way."

"*They* being?"

She didn't answer, just stuffed her bloodied tank top and the wrappings into the bag, then tied it up, cleaning the sink and the floor around her feet with ammonia. Even if Luminol picked up a blood trace, the evidence would be unusable so long as she covered it all.

"Did you make the call?" she asked, leading the way from the bathroom with both bags in tow. She gave the station attendant the tree trunk back, paid for the gas she'd filled the bike with, then walked toward the waiting Ducati.

"No."

She swiveled toward him. "Look, Ryder, you

being with me isn't a good idea. One target is harder to follow than two."

She secured both bags to the bike.

"Go back to the city. Surround yourself with security. Lay low until everything blows over." She mounted the Ducati. "It's me they want, not you."

He grasped her right arm, causing her to wince in pain. "Who in the hell are *they,* Seline?"

"It doesn't matter. What does is that your innocent game of cat and mouse led them straight to my doorstep." She caught his wince and briefly bit her bottom lip. "Go home, Ryder."

"And if I refuse?"

She stared at him. "Why would you refuse? This is my problem, not yours."

"Yes, but if it's true what you said, that I'm the one who led the gunmen to you, then I'm in this as far as it goes."

"Not if you leave now."

He looked around. "Where would you have me go?"

She fished the cell from his front pocket, flicked it open, then shoved it in his direction. "With your resources, you should be able to get a 'copter here to pick you up in a matter of minutes."

"I'll do that on one condition. That you come with me."

"Not an option." She started the bike.

He climbed on the back.

"What in the hell are you doing, Blackwell?"

"Going with you."

She revved the engine several times but didn't move. "Get off or I'll force you off."

"Goddamn it, Seline. Either you come with me or I go with you. One or the other. You choose. But I'll be damned if I'm just going to let you ride off into the sunset."

She squinted to the west, finding that, indeed, the sun was setting in a fiery glow over the horizon.

"Red sky at night, thief's delight. Red sky in the morning, thief take warning."

She recalled the twist on the old sailor saying that her father had repeated a few times.

But he'd had no way of knowing that she would be right where she was in that moment, with a stubborn, handsome male on the back of her bike refusing to get off.

She gunned the engine, half hoping he'd fall off the back. But he'd anticipated her move and barely blinked at her in the rearview mirror.

DOWNTOWN Chicago was the next stop. Even though only an hour and a half had passed since the first bullet had shattered Seline's bedroom window, Ryder felt as if it could have been a month and a half. He climbed from the bike only after Seline had cut the engine and removed the key, looking around at the packed parking lot of a bar named Jazzy's. Did Seline crave a stiff brew?

He noticed she was a little slow getting off the cycle.

"Are you okay?" he asked, steadying her.

"I'm fine." She gathered various items from the bike, including the garbage bag from the gas station, and headed in the opposite direction from the bar entrance. He followed.

"You'll want to go the other way," she said.

He looked over his shoulder.

"You'll find at least three hotels to check into until you can make arrangements to return to New York."

"And you?"

She stared at him as she continued walking. "We already discussed this."

"Yes, we did. And I made my stand clear."

No matter how bizarre the past hour and a half had been when compared to his normal life, he wasn't a man who cut and run at the first sign of trouble. While he'd had no way of knowing how heavy the baggage Seline Sanborn carried was, he'd known there would be some. She'd stolen a cool three-quarters of a million from his company. That alone indicated complications.

Of course, he hadn't exactly expected to sleep with her again, either. If asked to guess how he'd saw things going down when she'd returned to her estate earlier, he'd have said would run more along the lines of, "Hello, I found you," and a call to the proper authorities to enjoy watching her be arrested for the crime. After he got his money back.

How far away that all seemed now.

More specifically, hot sex, a gunshot wound, a manic motorcycle escape and a massive explosion ago.

Items of that nature had a way of putting a different spin on things.

Survival.

"One doesn't fight wars," his father had once quoted to him. "One survives them."

He'd shared the wisdom the night Ryder had told him he'd signed up for a stint in the marines.

The elder Blackwell was as pacifist as they came and he hadn't been pleased with his son's decision to go into the military. But Ryder's grades hadn't been high enough to earn him a scholarship to Columbia, his school of choice, and since his father couldn't afford the tuition and he wasn't about to take on a ton of student loan debt, the military and the GI bill emerged a solid option.

Of course, neither he nor his father could have anticipated Somalia or Bosnia or Kosovo.

He'd seen far more action than he'd anticipated. And lost two close buddies as a result.

He wasn't about to leave a man behind. Even if this man was a woman. Who had stolen from him.

"I can have both of us in a safe house within a hour," he said to her back now.

She laughed.

He rounded her, forcing her to stop and consider him. "I'm serious, Seline."

He noticed a flash of something in her eyes. Surprise? Gratitude? Whichever it was, the expression that followed soon after told him she was going to turn him down flat. "Thanks, but no thanks."

"Your activities at Blackwell & Blackwell need never be mentioned."

"And just how would you explain what happened at my house?"

"The ultimate in home invasions? Mistaken identity?"

She smiled then circled him to continue walking. "Not going to happen. First," she said, holding up a finger, "you'll have to involve the authorities." She raised a second finger. "Second, whichever channels you used to locate me have already led them to me. How long do you think it'll take for them to find me again? Third..."

He walked at her side. "Third?"

She looked at the sidewalk ahead of her. "Third, while I appreciate your show of whatever outdated act of chivalry you think you're performing, I prefer to work alone."

And with that, Ryder suspected Seline had put her finger on exactly the reason why he couldn't, wouldn't walk away. Simply because he recognized himself in her. Not in her actions or her being a moving target for something bigger than he could currently wrap his mind around. But the fact that they were both loners, used to depending on themselves and themselves only in order to get something done.

He'd heard of opposites attracting. But loners? Was it possible that the recognition alone was enough to draw him to a woman he'd known he had no business getting involved with even before getting shot at? To feel a connection to her that transcended all common sense and rationale and compelled him to do something so outside his normal M.O. as to be almost ridiculous?

"Are you still here?"

He grinned at her. "Get used to it. Because I don't plan on going anywhere anytime soon."

10

HER GODMOTHER had once claimed that Seline was a stupid-man magnet. Put her in the middle of a street and every stupid man within a five-block radius would find his way to her.

And despite all prior evidence to the contrary, it appeared Ryder Blackwell was as dumb as a bag of rocks.

She shook her head as she walked, turning off the main drag, going up two blocks, hanging a right, another left, then navigating an overgrown alleyway that ran between businesses and houses until she came to a one-car garage that was in dire need of good lighting and a paint job. Using a key she found under a loose board to the right of the door, she let herself in, grimacing when Ryder followed. Her shoulder ached like nobody's business and she could do with a massive infusion of sugary liquids and sleep. The last thing she needed was a curious greenhorn with illusions of being her knight in shining armor hanging around.

Especially if she was the one who was going to be doing the rescuing.

Swiping cobwebs out of the way, she walked around to the front of an old 1969 Chevy SS Camaro Z28 that was more a bondo special than the navy blue with white stripes it originally had been. She unplugged the battery charger, took off the contact claws and reattached the engine cables before closing the hood.

"Watch it."

Seline had known exactly where Ryder was—standing off to the side staring at the powerful engine—before she'd closed the hood.

"Yours?" he asked as she climbed between the wheel.

"In a manner of speaking."

He climbed in the passenger seat. "Like Carol Lambert's identity?"

She turned the key in the ignition, the roar of the engine making conversation impossible. Even if she'd been interested in offering it.

She gunned the engine a couple of times, then climbed out and counted four rusted old coffee cans to the right and three down on the dusty shelves. Pulling a can down, she fished through the three plastic bags of IDs there, found the one she wanted, emptied out the contents then put her current IDs inside, closed the can and put it back on the shelf with the other.

"Jesus, you have this down to a science, don't you?" Ryder said quietly, looking over her shoulder.

"Comes with the territory."

She started to open the garage door, wincing at the strain it put on her shoulder, then gladly stepped aside when he offered to do it for her. She backed out into the lane, and he began to close the door again.

Without a moment of hesitation, she gunned the engine and roared down the alley, leaving Ryder behind.

HE SHOULD HAVE seen that one coming.

Ryder watched the cloud of dust rise up to envelop the one glowing streetlight in the alley and shook his head.

Then he ran full out into the yard between the garage he'd just closed and the next, the overgrown vegetation slightly impeding his progress as he moved. He jumped over two low fences and emerged onto the street just as Seline turned the corner. She squealed to a stop mere millimeters away from where he stood, blocking the road that was down to one lane given the cars parked at both curbs.

She revved the engine and lurched forward, the front bumper nudging his knees.

Ryder met her gaze through the window even as he fought to catch his breath.

He'd have been in sorry shape had she chosen to turn the other way. No amount of running would have allowed him to catch up with her.

But thankfully his luck was good and she had the choice of running him over, letting him in or backing up.

The third option was taken away from her when another car pulled up behind her and the driver lay on the horn.

"Christ. Get in, already," she said.

He climbed into the car. His head snapped back when she hit the gas.

"That wasn't very nice."

"I was trying to do you a favor."

"Yeah, well, don't do it again." He pulled some sort of vegetation from inside the hem of his pants. "I probably ran through poison ivy."

He looked over to find her grinning.

"That's not even remotely funny."

"Humor is relative."

"You find my running after you amusing?"

"I find the thought of you with poison ivy slightly funny, yes."

"Yeah, well, just so you know, you're the one who's going to have to apply the calamine lotion."

And just like that Ryder found himself sharing a smile with Seline Sanborn that had nothing to do with their situation or her stealing from him or trying to leave him behind, and everything to do with the connection he could sense forming between them.

It was his reference to the future.

He guessed it wasn't often that Seline could look beyond the next few hours, much less look forward to them in the company of someone other than her butler.

Of course, he wouldn't have dared crack such a joke in the company of any of the women he'd dated over the past couple of years. Not that he'd classify what was happening as a date by any stretch. But…

Before long they were on the highway heading west. A half hour into the trip, Ryder found his gaze was still on her. He found it incredible that even without makeup and with much of the color drained from her face, she had to be the most fascinatingly beautiful woman he'd ever met.

His gaze dropped to her posture; she sat stiffly.

He lightly touched her shoulder and she winced. He pulled back the jacket to find her T-shirt showing blood.

"You're bleeding again."

"I'll live."

"I'm glad you're confident."

She gave him a long look.

"I think we're safe for the time being. Pull over and let's change the dressing and get you some fluids."

Surprisingly, she did as he requested.

After getting something to eat, several bottles of mineral water and a cooler with ice in which to put them, they returned to the car, both of them reaching for the driver's side door handle at the same time.

Ryder won.

"Let me take the next shift," he said. "Do you have a blanket or something in the trunk?"

"There might be something."

She must have been feeling worse than she was letting on because she didn't fight him when he took the keys from her hand. He moved to the trunk, pulled out a plastic-encased pillow and blanket then opened the driver's door, sprang the seat release and placed both items in the back seat.

"Get in."

She did as asked, stretching out as best as she could with the pillow behind her head. Ryder unfolded the blanket and placed it over her legs, feeling an odd nurturing sensation.

When was the last time he'd had to take care of anyone? Never, he realized.

"How do I know you won't take me back to New York?" she asked, wincing even as her eyes drooped closed.

"Because you're going to tell me where to go. Outside hell, that is."

She managed a small smile. "Stay on 66 heading west."

"Until?"

"Until I tell you not to."

He had begun to put the driver's seat upright when she grasped his hand.

Ryder paused. Her skin felt cold against his as he looked into her eyes.

"Ryder, I…"

He didn't help her out. Merely waited to hear what she had to say.

"Thanks."

It was more than her hesitation that told him that she wasn't used to thanking anyone, and what was usually a simple sentiment touched him.

"Don't mention it."

He righted the seat then climbed into the car. If her words and the fact that she was allowing him to take the lead had him feeling a bit cocky, he wasn't worrying about it.

He found the highway on-ramp and set out in the direction she'd indicated, trying to keep from looking at her sleeping face in the rearview mirror more than ten times a minute.

SELINE woke up with the sun across her face, her shoulder throbbing and her head feeling as if it was the size of a watermelon. The first thing she realized was that the car wasn't moving. The second was that Ryder was nowhere to be found.

She quickly moved to a sitting position and looked around. Arkansas. It had to be. And they were stopped at a rest area. She turned her watch around on her wrist. After noon.

Had she really slept for over fourteen hours in the back of a moving car? And had Ryder really driven all that way without stopping to sleep?

"Good, you're up."

Ryder held a cup of vending-machine coffee out to her. She took a deep pull then grimaced. "Like a little coffee with your sugar and cream?"

"That's not mine, it's yours. I figured you could use the sugar." He held up another cup. "Mine."

She moved to press the seat release.

"Whoa, where are you going?"

"Bathroom would be nice."

"Oh." He opened the door and held the seat for her, helping her climb out.

Seline gingerly stretched each of her muscles.

"How do you feel?"

"Like shit warmed over."

He chuckled. "You this cheerful every morning?"

"Yep." She started in the direction of the bathrooms.

"You need any help?"

"That's not where I was shot."

"I meant with redressing your wound."

She turned back, took the supply bag from him, then turned back again. "Thanks."

"Don't mention it."

"I won't again."

She threw a smile over her good shoulder to find him shaking his handsome head.

And it was handsome, wasn't it? Even sleep-deprived, with a good deal of stubble on his jaw and his hair wind-tousled, Ryder Blackwell looked almost more attractive to her now than he had before. He'd rolled up his sleeves past his elbows and had left the tails of his shirt out, his soiled slacks looking absurdly fitting against the oily work boots.

She imagined him in a pair of tight-fitting jeans and a T-shirt and found her mouth watering.

Stop it, Seline. At the first opportunity you've got to find a way to dump him.

First off, she'd been so out of it last night, she had no idea if he'd been in contact with anyone. If so, the men on her tail might be close to catching up with her even as she peed.

If he hadn't called anyone…

She swallowed hard, ranking that possibility up there with being just as dangerous as the gunmen. Men like Ryder Blackwell didn't have a selfless bone in their bodies. Oh, yeah, they were good in bed, so long as you could stand them, and they cleaned up well, but they would drop a dollar into a blind man's cup a hundred times without ever really noticing the person holding the cup was blind.

What Ryder was experiencing right now had everything to do with adrenaline and nothing to do with common sense. And as soon as he woke up from his bout of temporary insanity, he'd head straight back to his cozy, insulated life in New York and leave her high and dry.

It would be safer for her in the long run to just speed the process up for him.

The key lay in exactly how and when to do it….

11

"SO TELL me," Ryder said from the passenger's seat. "How much money did you take that would warrant someone wanting you dead?"

Seline had driven over the Texas state line into New Mexico and heat rose in waves from the barren landscape around them, the impending dusk doing little to lower the high temperatures. The air circulating through the open windows helped dry the sweat coating her face, but didn't stop rivulets rolling between her breasts and down her back.

It was hotter than Hades and Ryder wanted to talk.

"Aren't you tired?"

She could feel his gaze on her and knew he was probably grinning. "No."

The loud hum of the engine would have kept most from attempting conversation. But not Ryder. Not that she could blame him. If their roles were reversed, she'd be looking for a little info herself.

"If they had wanted me dead, I would be dead."

She looked to find his right brow raised, waiting for her to give him more. She didn't.

"Money?"

"You could say that's part of it." She lifted her good arm and wiped her T-shirt sleeve against her forehead.

"The rest?"

"You always ask so many questions?"

They'd stopped awhile back for dinner at an out-of-the-way greasy spoon. He'd tried to pump her for info then, as well, but she'd quickly eaten her meatloaf and left as soon as she was done, forcing him to leave half his uneaten food behind.

"Is there anything else you'd suggest we do?"

Seline gave him a long look. The open invitation on his face was almost laughable. Almost. If only a part of her didn't respond in kind. A longing that started deep in her stomach and spread quickly north and south, sparking awareness that while personally she didn't know this man all that well…in bed, oh, in bed she knew too much.

He returned his attention to the road and

leaned his elbow on the door. "So you think I led these guys to you."

A statement of fact rather than a question. "I know you did."

"Funny, because I know I didn't."

"Come on, Ryder, you probably had a team of people looking for me. People who have contacts beyond you."

He shook his head. "In the beginning, yes I did. But they couldn't draw a bead on you."

She waited.

"It was an independent low-rent P.I. out of Brooklyn who found you. And only she and I were privy to the information."

"Then someone was following you."

"On the off chance that I'd happen to pay you a visit?"

"They're very determined."

"And I was very determined that I wouldn't be followed."

"Perhaps the Brooklyn P.I. was persuaded to share the info."

"Possible, but not probable. The high-end agencies I originally hired couldn't find you. What were the chances that she would?"

"Good point." She let her foot up slightly on the gas when she realized she was speeding. Not a good idea to get pulled over right now. "Which leads us back to your being followed."

"Did you see an unfamiliar car in your driveway?"

No, she hadn't. A car would have triggered suspicion before she'd entered the house.

"I drove a rental from O'Hare, pegged your estate, then parked at the edge of the driveway of one of your neighbors and put the hood up. Then I walked to your place."

"Quite a hike."

"Yeah, but worth it."

She remembered walking in to see him waiting for her. Recalled the moment of pleasure combined with dread. Pleasure that she could stop fantasizing about him. Dread that if he could find her, so could the others.

"You know, sleeping with me again probably wasn't a good idea," he said. "Once, a guy can overlook. Twice and he might begin to imagine a relationship."

Seline laughed. Not a surface giggle, but a gut-deep guffaw that left her coughing and shoulder throbbing.

Ryder's grin told her he liked her response.

"What, do you think only women can be romantics?"

She stared at him, the laughter filling her chest and staying. "There's nothing romantic about the sex we had, Ryder."

"Considering the sex, a guy could be persuaded differently."

"Ah, I see. Along the lines of, 'the way to a man's heart is through his stomach.'"

"Something like that."

"I might buy that if I didn't know more about you."

He moved so that he was partially facing her. "And just what do you think you know about me?"

"First," she said, holding up a finger. "You're a serial dater."

"Not unlike yourself."

"I don't date. I indulge in a series of one-night stands."

"The difference being?"

"Point granted." She raised another finger. "Second, you're so focused on your career that women and marriage rate low on your list of priorities, much less romance."

"Again, like you."

She narrowed her eyes. "And what do you think you know about me?"

He shrugged. "I didn't say I knew anything.

But you pointing out what you think you know about me is allowing me a bit of insight into you."

"Pop psychology."

"Perhaps. But true nonetheless, I'm guessing. I don't think your choice of careers is exactly conducive to much of a personal life outside your job. Which makes the finger you point at me accusing me of being a workaholic my number one, and the other fingers in your hand are also pointing back at you."

She looked to find that her hand was positioned in the way he'd outlined. She gripped the steering wheel.

"Third," she said, forgoing any more hand gestures on the grounds that they might incriminate her. "I don't think there's a woman out there that can live up to your high expectations."

Seline concentrated on the road, passing a large RV that was traveling five miles under the speed limit. After she'd moved back into the right lane she looked at Ryder to find him thoughtfully silent. "What, no crack about how I'm the same?"

"Did you just call me a snob?"

"Maybe."

Rather than taking offense, he appeared to be giving the possibility some consideration.

She wasn't used to that. And couldn't say

whether she would have given anything he said the same weight.

"My father says the same thing," he said quietly.

Father. Instantly Seline imagined a man twenty years or so Ryder's senior, essentially an older version of him with graying hair and that one cheek dimple that he used often when he smiled.

"He doesn't say I'm a snob so much as he's afraid I'm too choosy." He looked out the window. "He mentions grandchildren a lot."

"Being an only child must have its drawbacks."

"I didn't say I was an only child."

She stared at him.

"Oh." He ran his fingers through his thick dark hair. "Pre-con research. What do they call that, anyway? Pre-con recon?"

"Funny."

"Yeah, well, I'm not very amused right now."

And for some reason Seline couldn't pinpoint, it bothered her that he was bothered.

"I have two older brothers," she found herself offering. "We were all raised by our father."

She had his attention and he no longer looked bothered. Which was a good thing in her book. No matter what it might have cost her.

"Your mother?"

"My mother left the three of us on our father's doorstep when I was four and took off for parts unknown. Yours?"

He seemed surprised by her answer. "She was married to my father for twenty-five years before dying of breast cancer fifteen years ago."

"I'm sorry."

"Thanks."

The car fell silent for a stretch. A stretch that Seline used to reflect on her brothers and father who she hadn't seen in years and missed terribly.

"So where did you pick up your trade?" Ryder asked.

Seline shifted in her seat, regretting the instant she did because it made her more aware of her sweaty state.

What did she tell him? That her father had been one of the more successful conmen in New York City when she was growing up? That when she was twelve the law had finally caught up with him and he'd spent the next eight years at Riker's? That where she'd grown up gangsters and con artists and criminals and prison time were accepted aspects of life? That she'd pulled her first con when she was thirteen with her brother, netting her a cool grand? That despite her father trying to keep her from the life, she had enjoyed the rush of pulling a con too much to go back?

That her choices had ultimately demanded a price higher than she could have ever imagined? A price she was still paying and always would?

Seline didn't know what to share, so she shared nothing.

"Touchy subject?" he asked.

"Complicated." Too complicated to explain to a guy she'd had sex and little more with. Twice. "How about you? I mean, I understand that Blackwell used to be a big name about town before you were born, but what made you want to get it all back? To work toward the goal at the expense of all else?"

"At the expense of what?"

"I don't know. A wife. Kids. Normal family stuff."

"I consider my life normal."

She smiled. "I guess it all depends on your definition of normal then, doesn't it?"

He got her point and smiled back.

"Maybe you're right. Maybe we are more alike than either of us knows," she said. "I mean, it's not beyond the realm for you to pull some under-handed stunts to get a competitor to sell or to force them out of business or play rough with the union to get them to take fewer benefits or lower pay."

"The difference is that what I do is legal."

"That's because suits like you make the laws."

"Are you trying to say that what you do is legit?"

"What I'm trying to say is that I've never conned anyone who couldn't afford it. That I've never personally hurt anyone. I bet you can't say the same."

He looked out the window again. "But at the end of the day I don't get shot at."

Seline winced.

So Ryder gave as good as he got out of bed as well as in it. She could respect that.

"So do you plan to tell me where we're going?"

Seline had been so distracted by their conversation that she'd forgotten that she had planned to dump him long before now. As it stood, she was only three, four hours, max, away from her destination.

When was the last time she'd been distracted to such a degree? She couldn't recall. And it both baffled and intrigued her that Ryder had been the one to do it.

"You'll see," she said, giving herself over to the fact that she didn't want to dump him. Not just yet. She was interested in knowing what made the man tick. What made him track her down then go on the lam with her when it would have been smarter and easier for him to return to his regularly scheduled life.

And if some small part of her was actually beginning to like him, well, she wasn't going to admit it to herself much less to him.

12

AT AROUND 1:00 A.M. just outside Albuquerque, New Mexico, Seline pulled the car to the side of a long, empty road, slid her seat back and settled in for the night. Ryder did the same. And despite thinking he wouldn't be getting much sleep knowing Seline was within touching distance, he dropped off and didn't awaken again until after seven the next morning. He got a chance to see to business, and wash his face with bottled water before Seline was ready to go again.

Ryder had flown into Albuquerque in the past, but he couldn't remember seeing much of the area, probably because he'd been busy in the limo that had taken him from the airport to the hotel and to various meeting places, either on his laptop or on his cell following up on other business matters even as he'd traveled to one. But now that he was without limo, laptop and cell, he had nothing better to do than take in the distinct landscape around him.

That wasn't entirely true. He'd prefer to talk to Seline some more, but she'd fallen silent and had refused to be drawn in further, answering his questions with a simple yes, no or maybe if she answered at all.

That was fine. While there weren't many people he could share silence with without being uncomfortable or wanting to fill the void, Seline was proving to be one of them.

Maybe because when they talked, she gave him something to think about during those silences.

"Beautiful, isn't it?" Seline said as if half to herself.

Ryder looked at her. "Yes it is."

"Have you been out—" She caught the way he was looking at her and stopped. "Oh."

Ryder smiled to himself and looked back out the window.

Instead of taking the route into Albuquerque as he'd expected her to, she veered north toward Santa Fe, an area he definitely had never visited. He watched as the landscape gave way to smaller haciendas with tiny yards bursting with flowers. She exited the highway and drove for another half hour before finally pulling up in front of a guardhouse. Ryder looked behind the gate at the houses there, half expecting to find another estate the size of the one she'd had in Wisconsin.

"Hi, Gerry," she said to the guard. "I have a guest visiting."

"Name?"

"John Black."

"Very good, Miss Smith."

The gate lifted and they were allowed entrance into what looked like a modest subdivision. The houses were newer, but they were small, with plenty of privacy and set back from the street.

"Smith?" he asked.

"Yes. Sally Smyth, with a *Y*. Oh, and in case you should have opportunity, you don't want to get too friendly with the neighbors. You're more than likely to find yourself staring into the double barrel of a shotgun."

"If it's all the same to you, I think I've had enough of being on that side of a gun to last a lifetime."

"That's how the residents here feel. Some of them were abused wives, some parents of molested children where the spouse was the offender, others are crime victims who couldn't find a sense of safety anywhere else. A lot of them had no choice but to move here from all across the country."

"And you fit in where?"

Seline looked at him, her face fresh and open and nonjudgmental. "I play a small role in helping them achieve that safety and secure them jobs they can do from home." She gestured toward what appeared to be a community center. "We have our own elementary school, health and child care clinics and a staff of no fewer than fifty armed security guards."

Ryder couldn't take his eyes from her. "Sounds like a self-contained city."

She smiled faintly. "Something like that. There are nearly seven hundred and fifty residents, many in apartment complexes a little farther up the road. And we have a waiting list of at least a thousand."

He raised his brows at that. "I'm surprised you're telling me this."

"Me, too." She took a deep breath as she negotiated narrow streets that were empty of cars but full of kids. "But I figure if you ever change your mind and want to have me arrested, this may make it a little more difficult for you." She looked at him. "And how do *you* give back to the community, Mr. Blackwell?"

Now that was a question he hadn't been expecting, mainly because he was still trying to digest what she'd just told him.

Here she was, a con artist who attracted

gunfire and she had a hand in funding a safe haven for others. The contrast was stunning.

He said quietly, "The company makes its share of charitable contributions."

"I'm sure. But I'm not asking about the company. I'm asking about you. And don't try to make them sound like one and the same, because I'm not buying it. Companies like yours make the donations for PR and tax-write-off purposes."

"What would you have me do?"

Seline shrugged as she stopped the car so a boy of about five could get a ball that had bounced into the street. The kid's mother followed him to usher him out of the way, her wary gaze securely on Ryder.

"You could volunteer as a big brother. You used to play varsity basketball, how about coaching at a community center?"

He'd half expected her to say something along the lines of "why not create your own mini-city?" Instead, her suggestions were on a much smaller scale. And more hands-on.

"Hi, Jan," she said to the woman who was still looking at Ryder from where she now stood on the curb. "How's Jason coming along?"

"Better. He's sleeping through the nights now. Thanks for asking, Sally."

They spoke for a couple of more moments then Seline continued on down the road.

"Do you know everyone here?"

"Not everyone. My job," she said, giving him a loaded glance, "doesn't allow me to spend the time here that I'd like. But since I bought into the place six years ago, there's been an in-residence panel—the majority of whom came here like most everyone else—that oversees everything."

The con artist with the heart of gold.

Ryder rubbed his chin, just then realizing that he probably looked like a homeless guy. No wonder the mother had looked at him suspiciously, no matter that he was with Seline…or Sally…or Carol…

"Is Seline your real name?"

She merely smiled at him.

"This is it."

She turned into a long drive meandering back from the road over a large plot of land. The house was a one-story adobe house with a three-arch porch from which hung planters of vivid flowers. Large terra-cotta vases stood on either side of the door. The place looked airy and comfortable and, considering the size of her sprawling Wisconsin estate, very small.

A fiftyish woman who could have been of

Mexican or Native American heritage opened the door and stood wiping her hands on an apron. Seline parked the hot, dusty Camaro and climbed out and Ryder followed suit, the sudden stillness a bit of a shock to his road-weary body. He eyed the climbing sun. He'd had a long day before flying to Chicago and driving the rental to her Wisconsin estate, in addition to the two-day road trip they'd just taken. And it was a good long shower and sleep that he craved now.... He watched the gentle sway of Seline's bottom in her black jeans. Among other things.

Ryder closed the passenger door and followed her up to the porch.

"*Hola,* Señora Sally."

"*Hola,* Gurtza," Seline said, giving the other woman a quick, hard hug.

"I came the moment you call. I'm almost done readying the place now."

"Thank you, Gurtza. Whatever isn't done can wait. Why don't you go home now—I'll stop by in awhile."

"Very well, Señora Sally."

The older woman took off her apron and Seline accepted it with a smile, watching as she walked to a pickup truck and pulled from the drive. Within moments there was nothing but the sound of crickets and a nearby water fountain fashioned from terra-cotta vases in a small courtyard he could see through the open door. He and Seline were completely alone.

"Come on. I'll show you to the guest bedroom," she said, leading the way inside.

Ryder took in the sparsely but tastefully decorated living and dining areas as he passed. Ceiling fans whirled, and patio doors were opened to the courtyard that seemed to be in the center of the house, the point around which the entire house revolved like a wheel. He didn't feel air conditioning but it was comfortably cool inside.

"Guest room?" he asked as she stopped outside a door.

"I figured you'd want to get a shower. And since I do, too, this is the most obvious solution."

They'd stopped at a department store yesterday and he'd picked up a few items of clothing and shaving gear, feeling awkward that she had to pay for them even though it was likely with money she'd stolen from him and his company.

"Another option would be to shower together."

Seline smiled at him and then folded the apron over her arm. "I hope you're happy with your accommodations, Mr. Blackwell."

Ryder leaned against the wall and crossed his

arms, watching as she walked away from him. Every time he thought he had the provocative woman pegged, she'd do something completely unexpected.

While he couldn't be entirely certain, he thought he detected a New York City accent from time to time. Especially when she was getting heated up on a topic, like when they'd discussed the possibility of his being to blame for her uninvited, gun-toting guests back in Wisconsin. But how did a New York girl end up not just with a place in New Mexico, but the whole secure compound they were in? He considered that she could have gotten involved in the community as a result of her own need to hide from time to time, but that somehow didn't fit. While her job required that she disappear every now and again, he figured that there were at least a thousand different ways she could do that, with a fraction of the cash she'd obviously invested here. A thousand cars parked in garages across the country each with their own coffee cans of identifications she could rely on to get her to her next destination.

Which made him even more curious about her. Had she been an abused wife? A violent crime victim?

While none of those titles seemed to fit Seline, neither had he imagined the street racer he'd first spotted in Manhattan, and slept with as Carol Lambert, was a thief about to con his company out of nearly a million dollars.

She'd long since disappeared down the circular hall. Ryder shook his head, pushed from the wall, then went into the guest room to get that shower that would, he hoped, help him think clearly now that the immediate danger of their situation was past.

TWO HOURS later, Seline stepped out of the shower in the master bedroom. After drying herself and attending to her wound, she left her damp hair hanging free over a nightshirt that brushed the tops of her thighs and plain white cotton underpants, and moved around the kitchen eating a light meal and drinking iced tea that Gurtza had left brewing in a jar in the New Mexican sun.

She then sat down at the table and picked up her cell phone, taping a pen against the pad she'd gotten from out of a drawer, the laptop at her elbow switched on, the browser pointed to three different nationwide crime-tracking Web sites and the Wisconsin newspaper closest to her estate.

Correction: former estate.

"Seline." Jeeves answered her call on the first ring.

She'd called him on the road, asking after his wellness and the status of the estate. The areas of the house she had needed "cleaned" were gone, fireproofing having protected her cars and leaving about seventy-five percent of the residence still intact...and bringing a hundred-and-ten percent interest from the local law-enforcement community that had managed to chase one of the SUVs toward Illinois, where they'd lost it.

"What's going on?" she asked him now.

"About the same as the last time we spoke."

She'd suspected as much. While Jeeves was her point man in Wisconsin, he wasn't plugged into New York, which was just the way she wanted it. She liked keeping the various aspects of her life compartmentalized. Kept things simple.

Her current cell phone had an ID block on it and Jeeves didn't have the number. So she told him she'd call him in the morning and rang off, turning toward the laptop instead.

Twenty minutes later, she craned her neck, listening for sounds from the guest room. Nothing.

She'd expected to find Ryder waiting for her when she got back from Gurtza's place. Surely he'd heard her return?

She clicked on a link in the browser, then scanned the Web site. There was an expanded piece on the estate fire in the local Wisconsin paper, but it said nothing about her beyond reporting that the owner was away at the time of the incident and couldn't be contacted.

The second part, at least, was true.

Seline shut the browser window and got up from the table, heading in the direction of the guest bedroom, her curiosity getting the better of her. Ryder was sprawled across the king-sized bed wearing little more than a towel around his hips. He'd obviously showered, but hadn't shaved, probably opting to stretch out for a minute on the bed first.

She hesitated in the doorway, her hand on the knob as if to close the door and allow him privacy. But a more primal part of herself, brought on by their trip westward and by what had transpired in the past hour or so, spurred her to step farther into the room instead.

I just want to see his face, she told herself. *Then I'll go and let him sleep*.

She drew even with the bed. His face was

turned in her direction and he was snoring quietly, a long shadow created by the morning sun slanting through the narrow window crossing his cheek. Her breath snagged in her chest. He looked so rugged yet so vulnerable. Like a mischievous boy at the end of a long night of being naughty.

Unable to stop herself, she moved closer until she could sit on the edge of the bed. It had been a long time since she'd watched a man sleep. She reached out and brushed a lock of his hair from his brow. So handsome.

Before she knew she was going to do so, she scooted until she lay next to him, facing him, wanting to just look at him. Trying to crack the exterior of the man she'd spent the past two days straight with. What kind of father would he make, she wondered? Would he be hands-off, choosing work over spending time with his kids? Or would he insist on being involved in every aspect of their lives?

She recalled Ryder mentioning his father and his parent's lament of not having any grandchildren to spoil. She smiled softly and cuddled a little closer to his long, lean body. She must have shifted the mattress enough to alert him to her presence, because without awakening, he rolled onto his back, the towel around his hips dropping off, and he absently reached for her and curved her body against his side.

Seline didn't need any more invitation than that.

13

RYDER had no idea how long he'd been asleep, but he was surprised when he awakened to Seline curled up next to him, her arm draped around his chest, her leg hooked over one of his.

He swallowed and allowed his eyes to adjust to the dim light from the open bedroom door. Was it night? It seemed the logical conclusion. But surely he hadn't slept all day?

When he'd emerged from the shower earlier, he'd gone in search of Seline, and had been mystified when he'd found her bedroom empty, her shower dry, and the Camaro absent from the driveway. He couldn't figure out where she had gone. Hadn't they driven two days straight to reach this house? What was so important for her to do that it couldn't wait until she'd had a shower and eaten something?

He'd intended only to rest a bit and listen for her return. Obviously things hadn't gone as planned and she'd not only come back while he was asleep, she'd climbed in next to him and dropped off to sleep herself.

He swept away a strand of her dark hair that clung to her chin and stared down into her beautiful face. Then he leaned in and did what he'd been longing to do since they'd left Wisconsin: he kissed her.

SELINE grew aware of a slight pressure against her mouth. A pleasurable, hot pressure. She lazily blinked open her eyes to find Ryder's intense face mere millimeters away from hers as he leaned in to kiss her again. She reached up and entangled her fingers in his hair and sighed up into him, welcoming the feel of his mouth on hers.

There was something decadent, primeval about being wakened from a dead sleep by a sexy man's kiss. And given the darkness and her sleep-clouded mind, she found it all too easy to give herself over to sheer desire. For the feel of his tongue against hers. His hard body pressing insistently into her softer one.

Ryder groaned lightly at her touch and the return of his kiss, gently spreading her thighs so he could position himself between them, resting his forearms on the bed on either side of her head. He brushed her hair back repeatedly, alternately kissing her deeply, then drawing away to gaze into her face in the soft light. Warmth suffused her inside and out. Desire. Need. And an intimate connection that somehow transcended both.

That reflection caused Seline's breath to catch in her throat. She'd thought she'd known romantic love before. She knew other forms of love, like that between a parent and a child. But this… What she was coming to feel for Ryder was oh so different. Frightening and exciting all at once. Overwhelming and empowering.

Common sense dictated that she not read too much into her passion-fogged thoughts. After all, she hadn't known him for that long. But another part observed that they'd shared more in a few days than many people did in a month or even six. Their time together definitely eclipsed whatever dates she'd managed to go out on in the past few years.

Besides, the risk taker in her demanded that she see whatever was happening between them through to the end. Not only see it through, but boldly welcome it and embrace it.

Ryder bent his head and kissed her again, lingeringly, tenderly. And she leisurely kissed him back, aware of the deep thrum of her heart, the languidness of her limbs. She felt that she could kiss him, just kiss him, like that for hours. The sign of affection was strangely as intoxicating and satisfying as physical release. He shifted between her thighs and she moaned. Okay, *almost* as satisfying.

It felt as if hot coals that had been burning inside her burst into flames at the not-so-innocent touch, threatening to consume her with red-hot need. She grasped his bare shoulders, reveling in the feel of his rock-hard muscles even as she widened her legs to allow him a closer meeting.

His erection pressed against the white cotton of her underwear, the sensation innocently erotic. When she'd chosen the panties, she'd done so thinking they wouldn't be having sex. Not tonight. Not after all that had happened and all that had yet to come.

Only this wasn't mere sex, was it? What Ryder seemed to be offering went far beyond that.

He cupped her breast through her T-shirt, squeezing her engorged nipple so that it tightened further. Then he leaned back and grabbed her shirt by the hem, stripping it over her head before bending to take that same nipple into his mouth.

Seline arched her back, encouraging his attentions and the ripples of sensation that went with them. He licked her breast yet she felt the movement of his tongue against the core of her, and grew increasingly aware of his erection pulsing against her swollen sex through the white cotton.

Restless to feel his flesh against hers, she reached for the elastic top of her panties, shifting to push them down then off the rest of the way with Ryder's help.

He seemed to pause above her, his silken hard-on resting against her slick opening.

Seline swallowed thickly. "Condoms…"

She didn't have any in the house. There had never been any cause to stock them since he was the first man she'd ever brought back here with her.

And she knew that he'd used the last of whatever supply he'd carried in his wallet.

She wanted to scream and cry simultaneously.

And it appeared he felt the same.

"I can withdraw," he said against her neck where he was kissing her.

Seline's hands rested at the small of his back, sliding over his hard rear then back up again, knowing that he was putting the ball fully in her court.

But she wanted both his balls in a place that didn't have anything to do with a sports arena.

She reached down and cupped his thick length in her palm. Amazing that such a minor part of the human anatomy could inspire such a tremendous reaction.

Her heart expanding in her chest, she positioned the head against her center, the flesh-to-flesh contact igniting a shiver along her skin.

He didn't move, so she did. Rocking her hips upward, she took an inch of him in, the small action robbing her of breath and saliva. He groaned and grasped her hips, as if prepared to immediately withdraw for fear of orgasm. She held still, watching him, then gasped when he sank into her to the hilt, filling her to overflowing.

Sweet Jesus…

The molten quality of the blood running through her veins seemed to make her heart work overtime in order to pump it through. She experienced an odd weightlessness in her womb that spread outward until it encompassed her entire body. He moved, slightly withdrawing, then thrusting deep again, heightening the unfamiliar feelings.

Seline realized she was trembling all over, and as she stared into Ryder's eyes she saw that he was fiercely trying to control himself and their unprotected union. His teeth were clenched, his jaw granite. Sweat beaded across his brow and his biceps bulged where he held himself rigidly above her, as if needing to watch her. To take in her every expression. To take her emotionally as well as physically.

Another deep stroke that coaxed a low, trembling moan from her throat. Then another. And before she knew what was happening, Seline threw herself head-first into the most phenomenal orgasm she'd ever experienced.

Or what would have been had Ryder not completely withdrawn and pressed his penis against her lower belly, his hot seed spilling over her quivering skin.

AN HOUR LATER Ryder sat across the open kitchen/dining area across a rough-hewn pine table from Seline, plates of food between them that they picked from with their fingers and with rolled fresh...what had she called them? *Sopaipillas.* She'd put out skinny glasses for tequila, but after knocking one back Ryder went for his water glass instead.

"So where did you go earlier?" he asked quietly.

Had he not been watching closely, he might not have noticed the slight hesitation in Seline's hand as she took a bite of guacamole-laden *sopaipilla.* But he had noticed. Not just that, but the slight blanching of her skin. Otherwise, she appeared unconcerned with his question.

"I had to go see someone."

"Anyone I know?"

The side of her mouth curved upward. "I don't think so."

"Male or female?"

Another hesitation. "Female."

She finished off her food, brushed her hands together, then refilled their water glasses from a pitcher.

The only light came from an overhead fixture that cast a warm orange glow over the table.

"Been a while since you've paid the phone bill?" he asked, stuffing another *sopaipilla* with refried beans, cheese and lettuce.

"No, I disconnected it from the box outside when I left."

At least she was honest. "Why?"

"Because I don't need you tipping off anyone so they can follow us here."

"I wasn't followed."

She ignored his statement. "Tell me, Ryder. What are you still doing here?"

Now there was a question. He slowed his chewing, thinking over how to answer her. Hell, he needed to answer the question for himself.

What *was* he still doing with her? Surely he should have left a long time ago. Probably back in Chicago when she'd pointed toward the hotels in the opposite direction to that she'd been walking. But he hadn't. And he still didn't want to leave.

"I don't know," he said finally, holding her gaze.

She nodded. "I suppose that's fair considering that I don't know why I haven't forced you to leave."

He grinned and sat back. "And how would you go about doing that, exactly?"

She propped her chin in her hand. "Not the whole me-Tarzan-you-Jane bit?"

"No. I wouldn't do that. After all, it was you who saved my bacon in Wisconsin." Ryder shrugged. "Never mind that you're the one who slapped it into the frying pan to begin with." He sipped his water. "You didn't answer my question."

"How I could force you to leave? Simple. I could have asked the guard at the gate to remove you from my car."

He was amused. "Here I thought you were going to outline the weapons you have stashed all over the house."

"Then there's that."

"You didn't have anything on you when you crawled into bed with me earlier."

She slowly shook her head. He got the distinct impression that she wasn't only thinking about literal weapons, but those of the emotional variety.

He could relate. He felt…strange, somehow. Altered by the sex they'd had tonight. Her musky sweet scent combined with his filled his senses and he was still semi-hard. Which was coming to be a regular state for him when in her presence.

"So what happens from here?" he said.

Her eyes darkened as she considered him. "Now you go home."

He grimaced, deciding it best not to say that option wasn't anywhere near the table, much less on it. "And you?"

"I…well, I put together the con of my lifetime. Not for money or revenge, but to save my life."

The wall phone gave a shrill chirp. Both of them stared at it, jarred out of the moment of levity her words had inspired.

Seline got up and answered just as Ryder heard the loud crack of something that could have been a firecracker in the distance…or a gunshot.

"Hello?"

A moment later, Seline dropped the phone and ran toward her bedroom. "They've found us."

14

SELINE'S adrenaline shot to new levels as she quickly dressed in jeans and a black T-shirt in her bedroom, then pulled out the armoire and gave the upper right-hand corner a smack so that a compartment opened up to offer a selection of arms.

Ryder was buttoning up his jeans and wearing a similar black T-shirt as he joined her. She chose a 9mm Glock and drove an ammunition clip home, then slipped the firearm into a double holster she'd fastened across her shoulders. She then picked up a matching Glock and did the same on the opposite side.

"You may want to lay low for this one," she said. "I can't guarantee I can look after you this time."

What she didn't say was that it was because she had others to attend to as well as him. One special person in particular.

"Using a round-about route, head to the community center we passed on the way here. There's a safe room there."

"Safe room, my ass." He pulled a 9mm from the selection, then followed it with a sawed-off shotgun. He fastened an ammo belt snugly around his hips, and loaded it with shells. "I've never run from a fight in my life. And I'm not going to start now."

Seline paused for a heartbeat, looking into his handsomely determined face.

"In fact, maybe *you* should head for the community center."

That made her laugh unexpectedly as she closed the armoire, shoving it back against the wall. "Stay close on my heels."

She led the way out the back door, hitting the lockdown button once they were outside. The gate guard's words echoed in her ears.

"They were asking for Seline Sanborn. And then they unloaded on the shack like there was no tomorrow. I'm sorry, I couldn't stop them."

Little had the gunmen known that the guard shack was made of reinforced steel and bulletproof glass so that if something like this happened, the guard could get the word out to the other seventeen armed guards on the perimeter and at similar stations within the compound. As well, an alarm would go out to the other thirty-two off-duty guards to report immediately.

Crouching to make as small a target as possible, Seline ran to the house next door, then to the next one, scanning the area as she went. Behind her she watched Ryder do the same.

It was said that once a marine, always a marine, and Seline had to agree in Ryder's case. All he needed was camouflage paint and clothes to make the image complete. He was deliberate and vigilant, his entire demeanor exuding a sense of confidence that made her feel safer somehow.

She started to move on to the next house when she felt two things simultaneously: Ryder jerking her closer to him and the spray of adobe as a bullet hit the wall where she'd been standing.

"Down!" he quietly ordered.

She hit the ground so hard she ended up with a mouth full of dirt. Before she could grab her gun from her holster, Ryder was aiming the sawed-off shotgun and firing, hitting his target twenty feet away with unerring accuracy.

The shooter went down and she was yanked up by Ryder who, just like that, took the lead, pulling her after him.

A part of her wanted to balk at the macho maneuvers. She was used to working alone, taking care of herself.

A bigger part of her was glad she had a partner with whom to share the reins. A competent partner who had just, how had he put it? Saved *her* bacon, putting them about even by her estimation.

She easily met him stride for stride, stopping when he stopped, moving when he moved, the synchronicity of their actions not lost on her, even if she did question her own abilities just now.

That's what happened when your emotions were attached to your job…

"We need to cross the street," she whispered.

"It's safe here," Ryder responded.

"Yes, but what we're running toward is that way."

RYDER HAD THOUGHT their main objective was to remove themselves from the compound posthaste. He'd believed they were running away from something—namely the gunmen who had skillfully invaded the community—rather than toward something.

But as Seline once again took the lead he realized he'd been wrong.

Most human mysteries, he'd discovered, either weren't worth the original attention, or once uncovered revealed an aspect of someone you'd thought you knew that you didn't want to see. Like the whiz-kid accountant who had worked for him for nearly ten years who hadn't really been a kid…but, as they all found out, had a sexual predilection for them. Or his first college girlfriend, a pretty young woman sworn to save herself for marriage, who'd gotten an STD because she'd slept with everyone in his class, it seemed, but him—including the prof.

Then there was the financial assistant who would sneak out during lunch, generating gossip that she was having an affair, when she'd really found a private spot to feed the pigeons that no one else knew about. Or the janitor who had locked himself into the office of one of the executives. He'd been suspected of casing the place for a future theft; it turned out he had been taking his lunch break in there so he could catch a sports event on cable.

But Seline…

Ryder got the definite impression that her mystery might fall solidly into both categories at once. She likely had secrets that would surprise him but probably shouldn't. And ones that might make him wish he'd gone back to his safe, stuffy life in New York the first time she'd ordered him to.

He noticed she was leading him in a circuitous route, and silently commended her on her tactical instincts. She'd have made a great marine. That is, he thought as he appreciated her curves in her dark attire, if those working with her could keep their minds on the task rather than on her backside.

Finally, they approached a house that was dark and appeared abandoned.

"This is it," she said, rounding the place then looking left and right before unlocking the back door.

Their shoes scuffed against the kitchen tile as she slipped through a hallway into a living room. Holding the shotgun upright and at the ready, Ryder scanned the other rooms they passed. It appeared no one was home.

Seline stopped and he covered her back as she moved a picture frame and entered a code into a keypad. A portion of the wall opened, revealing a six-by-five safe box. Inside were two shadows. One he identified as Gurtza. The other he couldn't make out.

"It's me," Seline said, dropping to her knees.

The other shadow launched itself into her

arms. A child, he realized. A little girl of no more than seven.

"Mommy, Mommy! I thought you'd never come. Are you here to save us?"

AN HOUR LATER, in the cramped confines of the old pickup truck Gurtza had been driving earlier in the day, Seline sat between her and Ryder, cradling her daughter in her arms. Rosalina had long since fallen asleep, as had Gurtza for that matter, leaving her with a silent Ryder for company. In fact, after hustling the seven-year-old and Gurtza into the truck, then telling Ryder to head south, she hadn't uttered a single word to him. Although the questioning gazes had been countless.

Ryder couldn't seem to keep his eyes off the sleeping little girl, who hadn't always been sleeping, but had instead bugged Ryder about who he was and where they were going and whether or not she could climb into his lap.

The answer to the last question had been no and had come from Seline herself, the tone of the one word drawing her companions' stares.

"So that's who you'd gone to see." Ryder finally broke the silence.

Seline nodded, brushing Lina's hair from her face.

Lina had her head on Seline's lap, her legs on Gurtza's, and while she looked uncomfortable as hell, she slept like a baby.

Ryder shook his head. "You know, there's got to come a time when you don't knock the air from my lungs."

She smiled and looked out at the dark southern New Mexican landscape as the truck hit a bump and rocked from side to side, the old struts groaning.

"How old is she?" he asked.

"Seven."

He looked at her. "Were you married at the time?"

Seline bit on her bottom lip then shook her head.

"But her father knows she exists."

A statement rather than a question. So she didn't answer.

"And your chosen career, as legally dangerous as it may be, isn't the reason you had her stashed away at the compound?"

"No."

"Anyone I know?"

How did she answer that? While she was certain that Ryder didn't know Mario Trainello personally, being a New Yorker, she was pretty sure he'd be familiar with the name.

A name she didn't intend to share just then.

"Am I driving to Mexico?"

"Yes. Gurtza and Lina will get on a bus just on the other side of the border."

"Another safe house?"

"In a manner of speaking, yes."

"You're not going with them?"

She shook her head again, her heart breaking at the thought of being away from her daughter for another extended amount of time.

She looked down at the sleeping face, tears welling up in her eyes.

There had been a few sweet months when it had just been her and the little girl she'd named after her maternal grandmother. The instant she'd known she was pregnant, Seline had headed up to British Columbia and rented a small place near the Strait of Georgia. Months had passed and she'd grown bigger, decorating the tiny nursery and waiting for the arrival of her baby. Just hers. No husband. No father. No boyfriend.

And when Rosalina was born...she'd felt as if the sun had finally broken out from behind the clouds that had always shadowed her life.

While she hadn't enjoyed anywhere near the financial resources she had now, she'd had enough to see her through the first year of Lina's life.

Then Trainello had discovered she'd had his

baby, and that peaceful time she'd had with her daughter had been shattered. She'd taken measures to make sure Lina would remain safe...always. Even if that meant that she couldn't play an ongoing role in her life.

"It must have been difficult for you all these years."

Seline's gaze cut to Ryder's face. They passed a gas station and the lights illuminated his features enough to see the sincerity in his eyes.

There had been several times over the past few days when she'd experienced moments of kismet with Ryder. When he'd looked at her and she'd truly felt she was being seen. Felt his understanding and empathy and experienced a connection as firmly as a caress.

But this was the first time she felt as if she'd had her breath stolen from her.

"The men back there...and in Wisconsin... they weren't after you, were they? They were after your daughter."

Seline shifted uncomfortably, the moment of affinity gone as she snapped back into protective-mother mode. Lina mumbled something in her sleep and then rolled over, Seline's help guaranteeing that she didn't hit her head on the dash or accidentally kick Gurtza.

"Her father?"

"Look, Ryder, I appreciate everything that you've done. But that's about all the questions I'm prepared to answer at this point."

A couple of miles disappeared under the truck before he said, "Why do I get the feeling that's the last question you're going to answer ever?"

Seline stared into his handsome face, her chest growing tight even as the impending sunrise brightened the horizon just beyond his arm to a deep purple.

Why, indeed?

15

RYDER SAT quietly in the passenger's side of the truck as Seline pulled into a parking lot that joined a small motel and a greasy spoon just west of Odessa, Texas. It was after noon and four hours had passed since they'd dropped Lina and Gurtza off at a bus stop in Ciudad Juarez just over the border into Mexico. As the little girl had waved at Seline, he'd watched as the woman who ranked right up there with some of the strongest people he knew seemed to fold in on herself, and he was filled with an incredible need to protect her. To use his considerable resources to shelter her and her daughter. Take care of them. Allow them to live their lives together.

And he had every intention of doing just that. With or without Seline's cooperation.

With or without any future involvement with Seline.

She shut off the truck engine and climbed out,

heading for the restaurant instead of the motel she'd parked in front of.

"Don't you think we should check in first?" he asked, closing the truck door.

She didn't answer.

They'd stashed their arms behind a cactus just north of the border, and then had picked them up coming back, the hardware now locked in a toolbox in the back of the truck bed.

Ryder shook his head and followed Seline, moments later sliding into a window booth across from her.

For the first time since early that morning, it seemed, she met his gaze head-on.

"This is where we part ways, Ryder."

He blinked at her. He'd had a feeling that this was coming, but, still, hearing the words was like taking a steel fist to the stomach.

He didn't quite know how to respond. He merely read the determination in her metal-gray eyes.

Finally, he reached out and took her hands in his. "I can help you, Seline. If you let me. I can call New York today, now, arrange to have you and Lina and Gurtza flown somewhere safe, guarded 24/7. I can see to it that the person trying to hurt you is stopped."

He drifted off. Not because he didn't have anything more to say, but because Seline was shaking her head. "No, Ryder, you can't. You have no idea what's going on here. Do you think money can really solve this? Money, I have."

She slid her hands from between his and a waitress took that as a cue to place two water glasses in front of them and ask if they wanted coffee.

As soon as she was gone, Seline continued. "You're an unknown quantity, Ryder. Ever since you entered my life, everything's been turned upside down. I can't let that happen anymore."

Was she blaming him for what had happened in New Mexico? Just as she blamed him for what had gone down in Wisconsin?

"I'm not even going to ask you who you called in Santa Fe. It doesn't matter." It seemed to take her extra effort to swallow. "If you want to help me, then leave. Go home. Go back to New York and forget I ever existed."

"I can't do that."

Her gaze sharpened. "I'm sorry, but I can't let you do otherwise. I can't continue to put myself…my daughter at risk for you."

"Damn it," he said, more forcefully than he'd intended. "I'm not to blame for what's going on.

The sooner you accept that, the sooner we can figure out what's really happening and stop it."

She abruptly got up, left a five-dollar bill on the table, then strode from the restaurant.

Ryder followed.

He shouldn't have been surprised when she knocked on one of the motel-room doors and it swung open to reveal Jeeves and two other people parked in front of computers. But he was. While she'd made a couple of brief phone calls from the road since this morning, something like this took orchestration. An effort he'd apparently missed.

"You look like hell," Jeeves said to her.

Seline ignored him. "Do you have the bag?"

He handed her a duffel and she handed it to Ryder who still stood in the door.

"What's this?" he asked, weighing the bag in his hand.

But Seline had already turned her attention to the people around her. A young woman had on a headset and was working a phone line. A young man was searching for something on the Internet that Seline examined over his shoulder.

And Jeeves stood staring at Ryder as though he was an uninvited encyclopedia salesman who had just been asked to leave.

He unzipped the duffel an inch to find wrapped stacks of one-hundred-dollar bills.

He jerked back as if physically pushed. "I don't want this," he said, tossing the bag to one of the two double beds.

Seline looked over her shoulder. "It's your money."

"I don't want it back."

Jeeves chuckled and Ryder glared at him.

The other man held up his hands. "Hey, don't look to use me as your punching bag, mate."

Ryder followed his gaze to where he had, indeed, curved his hands into fists as if itching to bury one into the smug houseman's handsome face.

Instead, he leaned against the open door frame and crossed his arms, planting himself.

A moment later the room went silent but for the tinny sound of a voice in the woman's earpiece and the beep of the other computer as it pulled up another document. All eyes turned toward him.

Seline stood straight and crossed her own arms, indulging his desire for a stare fest.

Finally, she grabbed his arm and pulled him outside, snatching up the duffel as if it was an afterthought. She slammed the door shut behind her then shoved the bag into his chest.

"Leave, Ryder. You're no longer welcome."

She dug into her pocket for the truck keys.

"Here. Take the truck. Drive to Abilene and catch the next plane out. Or have your personal jet come pick you up, I don't care. Just don't lead anyone else to me."

"I haven't led anyone to you."

"Who did you call from Santa Fe?"

Ryder gritted his back teeth together. "I didn't call anyone. You disconnected the line. Remember?"

She turned to go back into the room. He dropped the duffel and keys and grasped her arm.

"There's one way to figure out if what I'm saying is the truth."

She waited.

"You're right. I did make a call. From the neighbor's house."

Seline looked angry enough to hit him.

"I called Coleman's wife's cell. A number no one would be monitoring."

"You underestimate those on my tail."

"Then tell me who it is."

She didn't.

"Look, all you have to do is call your people in Santa Fe. Find out which house they went to first."

"What will that accomplish?"

"If they went to your house, well, then, my call isn't what brought them there. If they went to the neighbor's..."

"I don't need to call anyone. I already know you're to blame."

"Check it out."

"Go home, Ryder," she said.

The quiet tone of her voice stopped him in his tracks. The statement wasn't said in anger or reproach or accusation. Rather in that one moment she looked as crushed as he felt at the thought of leaving her to fend for herself.

"Please," he said, cupping the side of her face with his hand. "One phone call. Check it out."

She shook her head. "I'm sorry...."

Then she turned and disappeared inside the room and closed the door behind her.

RYDER didn't plan on going anywhere.

Checking into the motel room next to Seline's, he went about setting up a network of his own. He called a cell company in New York and arranged to have four new cell phones in the name of a subsidiary of his company delivered to four different people: the first to Coleman, the second to his secretary, the third to his father out in Brooklyn. And the fourth to the P.I. he'd used to find Seline.

A fifth cell phone he arranged to have delivered to him at the motel via a carrier two-and-a-half hours away in Abilene.

Once it arrived, he set about finding a way to convince Seline that he hadn't been followed. But without her assistance, his chances of doing that were nil.

He talked to everyone, assuring his father he was all right, and checking to make sure his company was still viable via Coleman, then giving him and his secretary a set of instructions that had nothing to do with the company and everything to do with Seline.

Finally, he called the P.I. and after receiving assurances that no one had coerced or beat any information out of her as to the whereabouts of Seline, he asked her to check a little further into her background. Namely, to unearth who else wanted to find her…and who the father of her child was.

The sun was visible through the west-facing window when the answering call came in.

He picked up the cell. "Blackwell."

"Just the man I'm looking for," Kylie said.

"You got the information."

"I got the information and then some."

"Tell me."

"Are you sitting down?"

He told her that he was.

"Carol Lambert aka Seline Sanborn's real name is Annette Agostini."

She paused and Ryder waited, running the name around his head.

Then it dawned on him. "Of the New York Agostinis? Part of the Venuto crime family?"

"That would be it."

He hadn't been sitting, but he did so now, collapsing to the edge of the bed as if his weight had quadrupled.

The Venuto family was one of the most powerful Mafia families in New York City. Not a day went by without a mention of one of their members being arrested or turning state's evidence or floating in the East River after a pair of cement overshoes turned out to be incapable of keeping them at the bottom.

"Jesus…"

"You can say that again," Kylie said. "I nearly got myself killed when I asked a few questions at the wrong time and in the wrong place earlier tonight.

"Anyway, she's not solidly connected. Rather, her father is the younger cousin of the big don, given more to penny-ante cons than to any real involvement in the family business."

"Define *penny-ante*."

"A few thousand here and there, sometimes tens of thousands. One con brought in over a hundred thou, but that's the one he served a dime for so when he was paroled, he went back to the smaller jobs." Ryder heard paper rustling and imagined her turning the pages in her handheld notebook. "Annette, I mean Seline, has two older brothers, also in the biz, Sergio and Paul. The con biz, not the mob biz, although the older one was known to dabble in his younger days—until the big boss's second son felt threatened and ordered a hit that crippled the guy for life."

"Some family."

"You can say that again. Anyway, Seline was tempted to follow in her dad's footsteps after he was put away and when brother number two figured out that using a fresh-faced eleven-year-old could help him land some pretty good cash. He coached her on how to pretend she was lost in Central Park and appeal to well-heeled passersby, thereby gaining their trust and easy access to their handbags and wallets, and he took her to the track where she could convince gamblers that her father had left her behind. By thirteen she was pulling cons on her own, with a couple of juvie convictions for selling fake newspaper subscriptions and items from those school magazines that were never received."

Ryder had a hard time reconciling what he was hearing. While he was proud to possess his own share of street smarts, he'd never seen the streets Seline had grown up on. Or rather the dark alleys full of hulking shadows that could hide unimaginable dangers or provide protection if you knew how to use them.

The picture Kylie painted for him fit the woman he was coming to know. And made him feel that much more protective of her.

"So the people after her are the result of a con gone bad?"

"I wish it were that simple," Kylie said. "You said that she's got a seven-year-old daughter, right?"

"Yes."

"Well, I don't think I need to explain the birds and the bees to you, so just as Seline's the mother, you know there's got to be a father. And in this case, the father is Mario Trainello. Also known as the Train.

"Seline's daughter isn't just an average little girl, she's a Mafia princess to a father who can't have any other blood children after an unfortunate accident on the job. A child he very much wants to claim—completely."

RYDER couldn't be sure how long he'd sat in that same position on the edge of the bed staring at nothing and thinking about everything. But when he looked at the clock it was past six. He stepped to the closed curtains and parted them to find Jeeves walking by along with his two friends, apparently going to the diner for a dinner break.

Which meant that Seline was by herself in the other room.

As soon as the threesome was well inside the diner, Ryder left his room and made his way next door. He tried the handle to find it unlocked, then knocked briefly before opening it.

Seline sat on the edge of the bed, her knees pulled up to her chest as she talked on a cell phone. He noticed that she'd changed into a fresh pair of jeans and a tank top. She eyed him warily as she dropped her voice.

"I'm glad you're having fun, sweetie," she was saying, closing her eyes. "Give the phone back to Gurtza, okay? I love you."

There was something vulnerable in the intimate exchange between mother and daughter. Especially in light of the new information he'd unearthed. Ryder pondered whether his parents could have put him in the hands of someone else for his own wellbeing.

Or whether he himself was capable of such a selfless act.

After discussing monetary matters and where Gurtza planned to head next with Rosalina, Seline finally closed the phone. But rather than address Ryder, she laid her cheek against the pillow of her knees and closed her eyes, not saying anything at all.

SELINE was aware of Ryder walking across the room and sitting next to her even though neither of them had said anything. Despite her best attempts at objectivity, her pulse leapt at his nearness and she felt a bone-deep gratitude that he hadn't left. Although, lord knew that if he had treated her the way she had treated him…well, she would have hitched a ride to the closest town if that's what it took to get away.

"They're okay?" he asked.

She knew he was talking about Lina and Gurtza and she nodded with her head turned away from him, hot tears stinging the back of her closed eyelids. For the next few days Gurtza would move around, never staying in the same place for more than twelve hours straight until Seline told her differently. But her daughter was well and even viewed the traveling as an adventure of sorts. A vacation after spending the past few years at the compound with few trips outside, because to do so was a risk Seline hadn't been willing to take.

Of course, she didn't kid herself that Lina's hunger for travel would last long. Even a seven-year-old would grow tired of moving around so much and begin to long for an uninterrupted period of time to replant her roots.

That's why it had been so important to her for her little girl to have her time at the compound, even if it meant that it couldn't be with her.

She felt Ryder's hand on the back of her neck and to her surprise a thick sob escaped her throat. She hadn't been aware of its existence and was even more saddened at the evidence of weakness. But when Ryder pulled her into his arms and held her to his strong body, a maelstrom of emotion ripped from her chest. She clutched him almost desperately, helpless to stop herself from baring her soul to the man holding her.

She'd lived for so long in an emotional vacuum, separated from her daughter, from her family, that she felt as insignificant as a butterfly in the face of a hurricane. She craved connection beyond all else. Intimate, personal connection. With her daughter. With Ryder.

Of course, it didn't help that she'd done as he'd asked earlier and discovered that he'd been right. He hadn't been to blame for the attack on the Santa Fe compound. The armed men had made a beeline directly for her house, the neighbor's from where Ryder had made his one phone call all but untouched.

She clutched him more desperately. "None of this makes any sense." She laughed without humor. "Not to me, and I know all the details. You…"

He kissed her lingeringly on the forehead then the nose, using tissues he took from a box on the nearby nightstand to gently wipe away the dampness from her face.

"Me…I'm just waiting for you to let me all the way in so I can try to help you make sense of it." He curved his finger under her chin and lifted her mouth to his, kissing her softly. "They always say two heads are better than one."

And six heads were better than two.

Seline thought of Jeeves and Joan and Earl at the diner and forced herself to sit up lest she be discovered in a position of weakness.

"One of the biggest mysteries here is…why

are you sticking around?" she asked, squinting her tired eyes to stare at him. "I thought maybe stumbling across my location was a way to break up the monotony of your life. Rather than skydive, you jumped right into the mess of my life by way of excitement."

"Yes, but when I skydive, I usually have a back-up chute."

She smiled, then stopped. "Why then?"

He looked altogether too sober. And so damn handsome that she was determined to remember the expression on his face in that moment forever.

"Did it ever cross your mind that I might care about you? Care about what happens to you?" He shook his head. "No, don't ask me why. I couldn't tell you that beyond saying something stupid like, 'Why is the sky blue?'"

"Because of the way our atmosphere reflects sunlight."

"Smart ass."

She sat up straighter. "If what you say is true, and you're sticking around because you care about me..." She trailed off, uncertain where she was going with the statement. Oh, she knew Ryder was drawn to her. Just as surely as she knew she was connected to him in some sort of mysterious way that she couldn't begin to explain, either. They were fused together by need and extraordinary circumstances.

"Well, then, you must understand that there is no future beyond now," she said quietly.

16

HOURS LATER, back in his room, with Seline soundly asleep on top of the double bed behind him, the ratty bedspread leaving a crease on her smooth cheek, Ryder stood at the window going over what she had said to him earlier. Trying to make sense out of her words, and his gut-deep reaction to them.

Never had he felt so conflicted. So torn between what he'd spent his life convincing himself that he wanted…and what he wanted now.

Namely Seline. At any cost.

"Come on, Ryder," she'd said earlier, looking at him as if it was the most important thing in the world to make him understand what she was saying. "You're all about tradition and building a bridge to the future that'll last for generations of Blackwells. I'm…I'm a ghost. I'll never be a soccer mom or belong to the PTA or bake cookies for the school bake sale. If I entered a church, the place would probably spontaneously combust. I don't exist on paper. And I can never exist on paper if I hope to keep my daughter safe."

But she existed to him. More than any other person in his life.

"Can't you see?" she'd asked. "There can be no future for you and me. Can never be any *us*. There's you. There's me. Then there's Lina. And my first priority will always be to take care of my daughter."

He'd told her he knew why, though he hadn't needed to. And even though telling her what he'd uncovered might tempt her to slam the door shut on him all over again, question his loyalty and trustworthiness just for having sought out information on her, never mind finding it, being honest with her had been more important.

Besides, the details didn't matter. Not to him. While the situation was more dire than he could have ever imagined on his own, it was dire with or without names.

The knowing merely increased his desire to play the role of protector, not detract from it. With or without her cooperation.

Ryder rubbed his forehead. It was after 4:00 a.m. central time, which meant it was 5:00 a.m. eastern. Before too long, everyone would be up and back to arranging the con they'd begun carefully piecing together like a complicated puzzle. He'd gotten the feeling they were leaving him out of some details, but he was relieved to be included at all and didn't question them.

He heard rustling and guessed Seline was shifting in her sleep.

Moments later, her soft voice broke the silence, "I checked up on Santa Fe like you asked."

Ryder turned from the window. The way she was positioned, he wondered if she'd gotten any sleep at all, or whether she'd been working everything out in her mind just as he'd been doing.

"You're right. Your phone call wasn't the tip-off."

He experienced a relief so complete he suddenly felt exhausted.

"Come here," she said, scooting over on the bed then patting the spread next to her. "Lie with me for a while."

Ryder crossed, took off his boots, then climbed in beside her. She immediately curved her bottom against him and he draped his arm across her hip, pulling her closer still. The rattling of the old air conditioner filled the room along with cold air and he shuddered, breathing in the fresh scent of her hair even as he gritted his back teeth together.

Whatever it took, he intended to prove to

Seline that she did exist. Maybe not as Annette Agostini anymore. But as Seline Sanborn.

And if he had anything to say about it, perhaps one day as Seline Blackwell.

TWO DAYS LATER, the five of them were in Trenton, New Jersey, having taken a private jet that Ryder had chartered, and they were staying in a rundown rental house in a seedy part of town where the police were known to be scarce, and the mob even scarcer. Control central was in the upstairs master bedroom, with a wall of monitors and three computers tuned in to the cameras that had been placed in carefully chosen areas.

"Okay," Seline said after taking a deep breath then clapping her hands. "Let the games begin."

All the chess pieces were in place and the con that wasn't for money or an adrenaline rush but rather for the lives of Seline and her daughter, Lina, went into play.

Ryder stood off to the side, content to let everyone do their jobs. He leaned against the doorjamb, watching as the view on his father's button camera flickered to life, then he heard his voice. "Testing, one, two, testing."

"You're coming through loud and clear,

Number One," Jeeves said into a microphone. "Now, go ahead and buy a newspaper from the corner kiosk, keeping the front of the Trainello house in view as you do so. But don't wander too far away from the waiting taxi in case you need to give pursuit quickly."

"Roger that."

Ryder rubbed his chin, amused that his father had not only volunteered to take part in the con, but that he was doing so as if he'd been running them all his life.

"Number Two, are you live?"

"Depends on your definition of the word."

Seline smiled briefly. "You're fine, Earl. Just follow the script and you'll be done before you know it." She looked at a monitor that fed through a roof camera across the street from Trainello's Brooklyn brownstone.

"I'd feel better if I were wired."

"They'll check you before you get a foot in. And if they find anything, that'll definitely test your definition of the word *live*."

"Not funny."

"Take a deep breath, Earl. You'll be fine. By the way, have I told you how good you look in black?"

"That's comforting. Maybe my mother can

use the suit to bury me in, you know, if it's not filled with too many holes."

Ryder stood upright and walked further into the room where another camera was focused on...was that a Burger King wrapper?

"What are they doing?" he asked.

Jeeves looked into the monitor then pushed a button for a microphone. "Number Three, what's going on?"

The Burger King wrapper disappeared, giving a clear view of a car's dashboard and the street beyond again. "Me and the guys were hungry."

"You couldn't have waited twenty minutes?"

"The food will be gone in two."

Jeeves cut the voice feed. "Actors."

Seline had decided to go with four aspiring actors for the second act of the con and had supplied them with two Crown Vics—cars that Ryder didn't want to know how she'd obtained—and outfitted them in black suits with black ties and mirrored sunglasses.

They thought they were playing a practical joke on a friend of Seline's for his birthday.

If everything went down as planned, they wouldn't have to learn differently.

As Seline had said when they'd begun outlining their options in Texas, they were at a distinct disadvantage in that none of them could play a key role because they'd be identified off the bat. And while she didn't like using outsiders, she had no other choice.

"Is this a go yet?" Ryder heard Earl ask. "I'm starting to sweat. And I don't think real FBI agents have sweat glands. It's in the contract or something."

Seline looked at Ryder, then at Joan and Jeeves. "Anytime you're ready, Earl."

"That would be never."

"Go."

"Going. Over and out."

They heard a click, indicating he'd shut off his cell phone.

All of them stood stiffly in front of the two monitors that would show Earl's movements. He was spotted by the roof cam and stepped into Ryder's father's button cam the instant he pulled up to the curb in his own dark-blue Crown Vic. A pause, then he climbed out of the car, looking every bit the FBI agent. Well, aside from the way he stretched his neck before looking up at the brownstone. He mounted the steps and rang the bell. Ryder's father's button cam bounced slightly as he walked nearer the house to get a closer view.

The door opened. Earl exchanged words with the armed goon who looked up and down the street before patting him down then stepping aside to let him in.

Seline let out a long breath, accenting all their feelings. "Now we wait."

Until Earl reemerged there was little else they could do.

His duty, simply, was to act like an agent looking for a quick buck. A buck he hoped to earn by tipping Mario Trainello off that Seline aka Annette Agostini had turned state's evidence and was going to testify against him. And to notify Trainello that agents were on their way to the house now to arrest him.

Stage one of the con: With an imaginary noose hanging above his head, Mario would have to abandon his search for her, and instead look for ways to save his own hide.

"Shall I head for the taxi?" Ryder's father asked.

Ryder reached for the mike. "Yes."

"Not yet," Jeeves said, but Ryder had already cut the sound.

Ryder stared at the other man. "It'll take him at least five minutes to reach it. He doesn't move the way he used to."

"If he gets in too soon, he could tip our hand."

Seline looked between the two men. "Let the order stand."

"The Train's door is opening," Joan said.

And just like that, two goons hurried outside and down the stairs, very obviously armed, looking up and down the block before motioning behind them that the coast was clear. Then Mario himself emerged and hurried for the Mercedes that roared up just as he hit the curb.

Ryder looked at his father's button cam. He had just climbed into the back of the taxi. "Have him follow the Mercedes, Dad."

"I know."

Ryder smiled as his father played secret agent. Maybe everyone was born with a desire to push the boundaries at least once.

"Number Four, where are you?" Seline asked, referring to another car parked up the block and positioned to follow Trainello when he bolted.

"Right on his tail."

"Where's Earl?" Seline asked, reaching for the control for the roof cam.

"He hasn't come out yet."

"His car's still outside in plain sight."

Ryder watched as another goon came out and got into the Crown Vic.

"Shit."

Seline picked up her cell.

Ryder said, "Give it a minute. Maybe they're waiting to see if the agents show before they let him go."

Seline held his gaze for a long moment and then nodded. "I hate not being on the scene, not being in control."

He smiled at her and curved his fingers over her shoulder, feeling the steel-like strength beneath her T-shirt. "It's going to be fine."

"Should I tell the actors it's a go?" Joan asked.

Seline turned around. "Yes."

Ryder looked around the room, curiously finding one person suddenly missing. "Where's Jeeves?" he asked.

Seline's gaze darted about then she called out. No answer.

On the monitors two Crown Victorias pulled in front of Trainello's place at opposing angles. Doors opened and the four actors paid to look like FBI agents got out, drawing fake weapons and charging the brownstone.

But Ryder was more concerned about Jeeves' disappearance.

17

"HE'S GONE," Joan said.

Seline felt suddenly sick to her stomach. Jeeves had been with her for over two years, and she had only just come to completely trust him in the last few months. Relied on him, especially, over the past couple of days. Mostly because of what had been happening. But she also recognized that her growing need to trust Ryder had extended to others in her life as well. Including Jeeves.

His absence now told her how very wrong that instinct had been.

"Abandon base," she said, her voice cracking. "Now," she said with more conviction.

"But what about the monitors? The equipment?" Joan asked.

"Grab the radios, nothing more."

Ryder grasped her shoulders. "What's going on?"

She briefly shut her eyes. "All this time, I thought

you'd been the one to lead Mario to me in Wisconsin. Then in Santa Fe. Instead it was Jeeves."

"How can you be sure?"

"Where is he?"

Ryder's frown frightened her further.

They both watched on the monitors as the actors hired to play apprehending FBI agents knocked on Trainello's door, then went inside, coming out moments later empty-handed. Stage one accomplished.

Not that it mattered. The mission had been highly compromised. In fact, Seline now knew that she was a part of someone else's con. Jeeves'. And by extension, Mario's.

Ryder grabbed the mike and found the button for Number One. "Dad, abort the mission. Repeat, abort."

"What? I can't hear you—"

Static. Ryder watched the button camera go dark as the taxi his father was in entered the Brooklyn Tunnel.

"We need to move. The best I can figure is we have five minutes," Seline said breathlessly, helping Joan gather what they could into small duffel bags.

"It takes longer than that to get from Brooklyn to here."

"Trainello has people here. And if Jeeves is involved..."

"If Jeeves is involved, then they'll be waiting for us the minute we leave the house."

They hurried down the stairs to the first floor, but didn't open the front door.

Aside from the electric feed in the upstairs bedroom, the power had been cut, and the house was already dark since the sun had set. Seline couldn't tell shadow from person.

"What now?" Ryder asked.

Seline pushed the button to dial Earl's cell phone. She didn't like that they hadn't seen him come out of Mario's place even after the FBI actors had swept the place, supposedly for birthday boy Mario.

After she got dead air, a strange busy signal sounded.

"Damn. I think they have a cell jam on us."

"Are we in trouble?" Joan asked.

Seline and Ryder looked at the young woman as if just seeing her for the first time.

The sound of heavy footsteps came from the front porch, made by someone not even trying for quiet.

Seline found herself being yanked by Ryder into another room. There was a curtained window off to the side. He hurried her and Joan to it just as the front and the back doors of the house rattled ominously.

At the same time as the intruders crashed inside, Ryder broke the locked window, then lifted Seline over the sill until her booted feet hit a narrow sidewalk overgrown by weeds. He quickly followed after passing Joan through the window.

"They're going straight upstairs."

Which erased whatever doubt she may have had about Jeeves' innocence.

"No," she said when Ryder started toward the front. "We'll have a better chance going the back route."

"In the front we can hit the neighbor's porch and scramble out that way."

"Lead on."

He did and she wasn't surprised to find that he was right. The neighbor's porch was positioned in such a way that there wasn't a direct line of vision from the front of the rental house. He hoisted her up along with Joan, then followed, and all three crawled across to the other side and down and over the ground there until they came to the next porch. On house three, Ryder edged his way inside the open door, scaring a woman who was handing her husband a beer where he sat in his recliner. Two children under five sat in front of the television.

Ryder held his hands up, even though there was a gun in one of them. “There’s no reason anyone has to get hurt. Is your car in your garage?”

“Yes,” the wife said in a high-pitched voice.

“Where are the keys?”

The wife looked at the husband. He didn’t move.

“Harry!” she shouted. “Give them the goddamn keys!”

“All right, all right. Stop your nagging.”

Ryder took out a roll of bills and peeled off what had to amount to two thousand. “Look for more in your mailbox soon. Until then, tell the police you think two teenagers made off with your car. But wait an hour before you call.”

The man accepted the money, then the woman snatched it from him. “How much more?”

“A lot.”

Harry gave him the keys.

“You stay here,” Ryder told Joan. “It’ll be safer this way. Have some coffee in the kitchen with…” He looked at the wife.

“Margaret.”

“With Margaret. Lay low until the sirens die down, then disappear for awhile.” He handed her a fistful of money even though Seline had already paid her well for her services.

Joan nodded and hugged Seline. "Be careful."

"You, too."

Seline took the keys from Ryder and led the way to the door to the garage. The car was an old Ford that was more rust than metal, and when she started it up, the garage immediately filled with exhaust smoke from its lack of oil. Worse, they were probably heard at the house three doors up.

"They're going to spot us."

"Well, then," Ryder said, reaching across her to fasten her seatbelt buckle. "You're just going to have to lose them, aren't you?"

TWENTY MINUTES later they sat in a strip mall parking lot, Seline having lost the car that had given chase. Ryder sat quietly next to her, considering all that had happened. He had finally gotten through to his father via his cell, but it didn't sit well with him that the old man was now a known target because of Jeeves. He'd ordered him to have the taxi take him to Grand Central so he could catch a train for Boston, Detroit, D.C.—it didn't matter, just so long as he paid cash for the ticket and got out of the city now. Ryder couldn't be sure what Mario would do once he figured out Seline had slipped through the cracks again.

The one high point was that Earl had called Seline a couple of minutes ago. He'd managed to use a fire poker against the distracted goons at Mario's place and get out the back. He was told to do the same thing as Joan: disappear for a few days, longer if he could swing it.

Ryder looked over at Seline, who kept pushing Redial on her cell, her face unnaturally pale in the light given off by the streetlamps.

A strange busy signal sounded again.

"Let me try," he said, reaching out for her cell. She reluctantly gave it to him, but rather than try to use her phone, he entered the numbers into his, with the same result.

"Maybe Gurtza's somewhere where there's no service."

Even as he said the words, he knew they'd prove little comfort to a worried mother.

A mother who had told the wrong guy where her daughter was. Not the exact location—not even she knew exactly where Gurtza was traveling. She did, however, have a rough idea.

And so did Jeeves.

"So what do you think the plan was?" he asked, suspecting he knew the answer, but needing to fill the silence. He had too try to wrap his brain around what had gone down in the hopes of figuring our where they went from there.

"Find Lina. Kill me." She looked at him. "That's always been his plan."

"Drastic."

"Yeah, well, he knows if he leaves me alive I'll always try to get my daughter back."

Ryder stretched his arm across the seat and gently grasped her shoulder. The muscles beneath her T-shirt were tensed into steel balls.

"You know, we could always move forward with the con."

She jerked to look at him. "What are you talking about? There is no more con anymore."

He swallowed hard. "The next step was for Earl to tell Trainello the address of the safe house where you were being held."

"A safe house that was a set up to trap Mario." She sighed heavily. "But thanks to Jeeves, Trainello knows that there was no safe house because there was no turning state's evidence."

"You could always make it real."

She stared at him as if he'd just lost a few of his marbles.

And maybe he had. Maybe it was stupid for him to suggest that a woman who was used to operating on the darker side of the law turn to the law for help.

Or maybe it was the smartest idea he'd had.

"What did you plan to do once you had Trainello, anyway?"

"Get him to confess to certain deeds then turn the tape over to the authorities."

"A tape that would have been useless without a live witness to testify."

"The tape would have been his confession."

"The law's a sticky business. There's no guarantee that the charges would have stuck. Even if the authorities decided to bring charges."

"Then there's the media."

Ryder nodded. "I get that part. But news like that only stays news until the next scandal or natural disaster or a politician's misstep."

"Are you telling me I should really consider turning state's evidence?"

"I'm suggesting that it may be your only option now that your hand's been tipped."

Seline bit her bottom lip. Whether it was to keep herself from lighting into him, or to keep from crying, he couldn't be sure. But he gave her the room she needed to let her decide.

"There's another option…"

He squinted at her. "Go on."

"We could show up at the safe house and take care of the situation ourselves."

"Define *take care of*."

She looked at him.

She intended to kill Trainello.

He rubbed the back of his neck.

He couldn't blame her. He'd only lived a short time with the knowledge of Trainello's existence, and he wouldn't mind seeing him dead.

But wanting to see someone dead and actually playing a part in making that happen were two entirely different things.

"That would be akin to suicide, walking into something like that. We're two. Trainello's goons can easily number a dozen."

She didn't blink.

"What happens to Lina if something happens to you?"

"Gurtza will take care of her."

He wasn't surprised by her answer. He'd known from the start that she was the type to sacrifice everything for a cause. And for her daughter, she was willing to lay down her very life…and offer up his in the process.

She started the car back up.

"Where are you going?"

"To get us some better wheels."

That hadn't been the answer he'd been looking for.

But he did know that whatever Seline decided, he was in. Until the end.

18

THREE HOURS later, Seline was crouched down in the shadows outside an old abandoned warehouse. She'd often laughed at B movies that had included scenes set just like this. There was too much room, too many open spaces, too little safety.

But after having been trapped inside three houses in a row, she'd quickly come to appreciate the setting.

Rather than set things up at the fake safe house as had been planned, she and Ryder had decided to set things up here. They'd spent two hours booby-trapping the place, stashing back-up weapons, wiring up the equipment they had managed to salvage from the failed con.

Then, ten minutes ago she'd accepted the latest call from Jeeves, who'd been trying to contact her since shortly after they'd escaped from the Trenton property in the old Ford. And she listened to him explain that he'd heard a sound and when he went to investigate, he'd been taken hostage by Trainello's goons.

Ryder had motioned for her to play along, but she hadn't been able to. She'd told Jeeves he could screw off and to tell Trainello and his gang that they could meet her at the warehouse in half an hour.

Of course, she fully expected them to be there in a third of that time. And she was ready for them.

She caught a glimpse of Ryder closing his cell phone, his attention on a spot she couldn't see in the distance. Her heart lodged firmly in her throat. She'd gotten him to agree not to call in the FBI.

So who had he called? He'd already arranged everything with his father.

Shit, shit, shit.

She moved back into the shadows before he looked her way in case he suspected she'd seen him.

A long time ago she'd come to expect the unexpected. But certainly even she had had more than her fair share of surprises over the past week. She deserved a break, didn't she?

She squinted up into the cloudy sky. Then again, maybe this was God's way of making her pay for her crimes, no matter that the people she targeted hardly missed the money she'd taken. The mere act of taking something that didn't belong to her was a crime. Technically.

Just how high of a price was she going to be asked to pay?

Seline swallowed hard. Whatever it was, she'd pay it. No price was too high to guarantee the safety of her little girl.

A car pulled up into the cracked and weed-choked parking lot some hundred feet away. She grabbed her 9mm and switched off the safety.

Ryder's hand rested against her wrist, pushing her arm down.

"These are the good guys."

Good guys? There were no good guys.

Ryder motioned for the car to pull inside the warehouse and park off to the side behind a wall of empty loading pallets. And when all four doors opened and her two brothers, her father and a cousin got out, Seline's knees nearly buckled.

"Is that my little girl?" her father asked, pinning her with his steely gaze.

Seline met him halfway and stood looking at him.

"What's this I hear? You're in trouble and didn't think of asking us for help?" he asked.

She looked down, admitting that she hadn't considered calling her immediate family, if only because of the extended Mafia family to which they were connected.

A part of her had wanted to keep them safe by keeping them out of this. Another part wasn't afraid to put them in a position of choosing between her and their own lives.

Her father hugged her and she nearly lost it.

It had been three years since she'd last seen him and her brothers. She pulled away to look at the two other men in question. The last time she'd seen her older brother Sergio, he had been in a wheelchair and had been expected to remain in one for the rest of his life. Instead he stood in front of her on half crutches. She hugged him, then turned toward Paulie, embracing him and then her cousin Vinny right after.

"How… I mean, why…"

"I called them," Ryder said unnecessarily.

Somewhere in the back of her mind she knew that Ryder had to have been the one who contacted her family. She just couldn't figure out how he knew how to get hold of them. Or why he would.

"I thought we could use reinforcements."

Another three cars pulled into the parking area

in quick succession and Sergio motioned for them to follow his lead, parking inside the warehouse.

And just like that they weren't two, but eighteen.

"Reinforcements, my ass," Seline's father said. "Get out of the way or you two might get hurt."

IT HADN'T BEEN easy keeping Seline in the dark as to his plans. But Ryder knew that he couldn't have allowed the two of them to face Trainello and his men without more firepower.

He just hadn't figured how much firepower his spur-of-the-moment call to her father would scare up.

"You Ryder?" the elder Agostini said.

The man was a couple of inches shorter than he was, but easily made up that difference in girth, his build stocky and solid.

Seline had told him that her father had never really played a role in the family business. He'd chosen running cons over gambling and prostitution and protection rackets.

All Ryder knew was that he wouldn't want to run across Seline's father or either of her two brothers in a dark alley.

"That would be me," Ryder said, offering his hand. Angelo Agostini took it and squeezed to the point of pain. Pain that Ryder refused to show him. "Glad you could make it."

"Make it? You should have called me before now. Had I known what was happening, I could have stopped this a long time ago."

"This isn't any of your concern, Papa."

"The hell it isn't," he said, looking over to where Seline was strategizing with her brothers on where to place everyone. "You're my little girl. And that little girl of yours is my granddaughter. I don't give a shit who her father is, both of you are my blood. And by trying to spill it, Mario might as well have shot at me."

Her younger brother cocked a brow at Seline. "And we all know how Dad feels about being shot at."

Ryder didn't know the details, but he got the hint.

And if he hadn't, the sawed-off shotgun the elder Agostini pulled out of the trunk of his car would have clued him in.

"How long we got?" he asked.

"Five minutes at most," Seline said.

"Well, then, enough of this lollygagging about. We've got a job to do."

And just like that, everyone scattered to take their places.

Ryder and Seline retreated to the back of the warehouse where they'd already mapped out a position behind an old safe that had been tipped over, and away from any doors a car could drive through and catch them unawares. They had clear sight of the parking lot and any approaching vehicles. And had at least three direct escape routes.

Not that he thought they'd be needing any of those.

"I can't believe you called my father," Seline said softly beside him.

He made out her beautiful profile in the dark. "I had to call somebody."

"Yes, but my father? Do you know what might happen?"

"I'm not sure, but I'm guessing that if Trainello doesn't give up the ghost, he's going to become one."

"Along with us, maybe."

Ryder nodded. "Along with us, maybe."

Her lingering kiss surprised him. She'd been in full combat mode since they'd relocated to Trenton and had begun implementing the failed con. The demonstration of affection rocked him back on his heels.

"Knock if off, you two," her father said from

the shadows somewhere behind them. "We can look into a ceremony after we wrap this up."

Ryder raised his brows. "Ceremony?" he whispered to Seline.

"Welcome to the family."

IN THAT one moment, Seline felt more confident than she had in hours that the situation might sway in her favor. She gave the roof of the warehouse and the sky beyond a brief glance and offered up thanks. She couldn't believe Ryder had called her family, but, boy, was she ever glad that he had. While she was concerned for their safety, their mere presence gave her back the strength that had been lanced out of her by Jeeves' betrayal.

The sound of a car—correction, the sound of many cars—then headlights cut through the dark warehouse as a line of vehicles made its way through the parking lot toward the warehouse. The lead car stopped just short, causing the others to stop behind it. And just as it had happened with her family minutes earlier, doors opened, bodies spilled out and weapons were cocked and aimed.

"Mario," Seline called out. "Why don't you come inside? It's long past time you and I had a talk."

All heads turned toward a car door that had remained closed. Then, finally, it opened and Mario climbed out.

It was the first time in six years that Seline had seen him up close and personal. All she could feel was contempt. And regret.

She felt Ryder's presence close to her side.

Mario walked with four of his armed goons inside the warehouse then stopped just inside.

"Where are the freakin' lights? I can't see a goddamn thing."

As planned, her brother triggered a single lightbulb that hung a few feet in front of Seline and Ryder, although they were still in shadow.

Mario shielded his eyes. "Where you at?"

Seline moved to step forward and Ryder grabbed her with his free hand. She looked at him for a long moment, then he removed it.

She stepped a few inches forward. Not enough to be directly in the light, but she was partially illuminated.

Mario grinned, making her skin crawl.

"Annette, baby. You haven't changed a bit. Still the hot piece you always were."

"Wish I could say the same of you," she said between clenched teeth.

The conversation that sounded more like two

people having a chance meeting on the street than deciding the life of their daughter made her pulse quicken further.

She noticed the cockiness in his swagger as he moved closer, stepping as much into the light as she was on her end.

"So…how's Rosalina? My daughter?" he asked.

He may have grinned, but his eyes shot shards of sharp glass.

"Safe. And away from you. Two things I intend to make sure are always the case."

He tsked. "Come on now, Annette. As her father, I'm entitled to see my daughter."

"Take your beef up with the courts."

He chuckled along with a couple of his goons. "Call me stupid, but I don't think the courts and me would see eye to eye on this matter."

No, the families of New York served as their own judge, jury and executioners. And she was high on Mario's wish list of those he wanted executed.

Seline's gaze went to another man who had stepped up out of the shadows to stand next to Mario.

Jeeves.

"What?" Mario asked, putting his arm around

Jeeves' shoulder and giving a pat. "You look surprised to see my cousin Gino from England." He chuckled. "Didn't know we had any family from that part of the woods, did you?"

"No, I didn't. Did you check his credentials?"

Mario looked at her then at Jeeves. "Didn't have to. His mother is one of my mother's long-lost cousins. Remembers when the family came over to visit when little Gino here was knee-high to a grasshopper."

"More like student to Hannibal Lector," she said.

Jeeves chuckled.

"What I meant is, are you sure he's your cousin?"

Mario started to answer, then stopped, taking a long look at Jeeves instead.

"What are you looking at me for, mate?" Jeeves said with a grin. "The woman's trying to mind-fuck you."

"Am I?"

Seline knew the family and its interactions well. Given that they existed in a vacuum outside the law, trust was at a high premium. And the saying, "you're innocent until someone accuses you" was coined in her neighborhood a long time ago.

"What do you know?" Mario asked her.

She shrugged as if it was of no-never-mind

to her. "Enough to know that he worked for me for two years and I never completely trusted him. How long's he been working for you, Mario? For the family? Your father know how deeply you let him in?"

Mario threw back his head and laughed. "I think you're right, Gino. She is trying to mind-fuck me." His tone hardened as he took out a Glock and pointed it at her. "Just like she fucked me seven years ago when she disappeared with my daughter."

"If I remember my history, it was you who screwed me, Mario," Seline said, taking out her own firearm and pointing it at him. "Literally. By raping me."

19

RYDER'S adrenaline shot well beyond any watermarks from previous runs. Mario had raped Seline? Or was she trying to further undermine his position? Ryder couldn't be certain. What he was sure of was that he didn't like the thought of the pig having his paws anywhere near Seline, either invited or otherwise.

"Rape? You called what happened between us rape?" Mario asked, looking too cocky for Ryder's comfort. "I call what happened love."

Seline squeezed off a shot, grazing Mario's shoulder but otherwise leaving him unhurt. The warehouse filled with the sound of metal against metal as guns were cocked all around. Mario's guys aimed their guns first at Seline, then everywhere else, trying to figure out how many people hid in the shadows with their guns trained on them.

If Ryder had had any doubts about Seline's accusation, he didn't now. She wasn't one for random violence.

Mario had raped her.

And Ryder wanted to kill him for it.

"Oh, come on, Annette. You know you wanted it. You were begging for it."

Ryder caught Seline's arm before she could squeeze off another round, this time aiming for more dangerous territory.

"Who's this?" Mario asked. "You new loverboy?"

Loverboy. Such an antiquated word and reference. Had someone told him that a man his own age had used it, he would have questioned their sanity. Even in this tense situation, he had to suppress a smirk.

"It doesn't matter who I am," Ryder said. "What does matter is what happens from here."

Mario looked around at his men. Then he smiled. "Look who thinks he's calling the shots."

Ryder wanted to let Seline shoot him.

"Is it true, Mario?"

An unfamiliar voice echoed through the warehouse. But while it was unfamiliar to Ryder, apparently it wasn't to everyone else present. Jeeves took a couple of quick steps back as if afraid he might be caught in the crossfire. And Mario himself looked suddenly nervous, even releasing the hand that clutched his grazed shoulder.

"Father?"

Ryder was aware of two people approaching the light at once. One came from behind him and was Seline's father. The other came from behind Mario, and he guessed it was no other than Don Giovanni Trainello himself, the head of the Venuto crime family.

Seline looked at Ryder. He resisted the urge to shrug but he was sure his own surprise was written there for her to read.

No, he hadn't arranged this. He'd merely called her father for backup. Angelo must have called Mario's father, hoping to defuse what had escalated into a very dangerous situation.

"Is what she said true, Mario?" Don Giovanni said, coming to stand next to his son. Even though he was a good five inches shorter, and thirty years older, the power he exuded couldn't have been stronger had he worn a sign announcing he was The Don.

"Of course not, Papa," Mario said, laughing nervously. "Who you gonna believe, your son or some two-bit slut?"

The Don smacked his son with an open palm, the sound reverberating off the aluminum walls.

"You kiss your mother with that mouth? You show some respect when you're talking about the mother of my granddaughter. A child through whom runs the blood of the Trainello family."

Ryder sensed Seline's growing tension before he noticed the way her hand tightened around her 9mm. For a second he'd believed that this might be all resolved with a brief conversation. Now, he was afraid that more power might be put behind Mario's efforts to take Seline's daughter.

He'd tried to protect her. Instead, he might have put her in deeper danger…along with Rosalina.

The Don crossed to stand in front of Seline. "Is she a good girl?"

"What do you think?" Seline's father asked, stepping up to stand next to her. "She's smart and she's beautiful. Just like her mother."

Giovanni nodded. "Please…accept my apologies on behalf of my ill-mannered son. And for any wrong he might have perpetrated against you and your family."

Seline didn't respond, so her father did. "Apology accepted, Don Giovanni."

The Don nodded again, then, after a long moment spent staring into Seline's face, he turned and walked back into the shadows.

Both sides still had their guns pointed at each other, and Ryder waited for someone to take the first shot. Or rather the second.

"Mario, go home. Now. And call your dogs off the mother of your child. No child should be raised without its mother."

"But, Papa—"

"Now."

Mario glared at Seline and her father, looking as if he might disobey his father's order. He finally turned and stalked from the warehouse back to his car where he waited for someone to open the door for him.

Within moments, Mario's goons had disappeared back to their own cars, the long line taking turns backing up so they could turn around.

And just like that, a violent situation was defused, leaving Ryder to wonder whether or not he'd just imagined the entire episode.

And pondering just where, exactly, he and Seline went from here….

IT TURNED OUT that they went nowhere. Because no sooner had everyone left than Seline herself had disappeared.

Two days later Ryder stood in his top-floor office staring out at Manhattan…and couldn't drum up the enthusiasm that it took to remove a paper clip from a sheaf of papers on the Stanton deal.

"Uh-oh," Coleman said from behind him. "I'm not sure I like that look."

Ryder glanced at his second in command over his shoulder. It had been over forty-eight hours since the party had broken up at the New Jersey warehouse, time he'd used to try to reinsert himself back into his regular life. The problem was, nothing quite seemed to fit anymore. Including Coleman's familiar observation.

"Edit that," Coleman said, sitting up and putting his own papers on the desk in front of him. "I don't think I know this expression."

Ryder sighed and turned from the window. "Forget facial expressions for a minute, John, and answer something for me."

"Shoot."

Ryder winced at his friend's choice of words. "How did you know Jenny was the one for you? I mean, the woman you wanted to marry and spend the rest of your life with?"

Coleman looked momentarily surprised by the question. Apparently he'd been expecting something of a business nature.

But it didn't take him long to sit back in his

chair, cross his ankle over his knee and grin. "Simple. I knew the moment I figured out I couldn't live without her."

Ryder nodded, put his papers next to Coleman's, then shoved his hands deep into his pockets.

He'd suspected as much. But in Coleman's case, he hadn't had to hire a P.I. to look for his woman. Twice. Hadn't had to wonder if she was safe, or whether or not he'd see her again.

He knew Seline too well to know that finding her again wouldn't be easy. She was the type who didn't make the same mistake twice. And even though the Trainello family—or rather, Mario "the Train" Trainello—was no longer looking for her or her daughter, he doubted that would make much of a difference to the protective mother. She'd disappeared from the face of the earth as effectively as if she'd caught a ride on the next space shuttle.

He rubbed the back of his neck.

"Coleman, I want to sign the company over to you."

John blinked several times. "Stanton?"

"No, Blackwell."

His friend looked as if he'd been jerked back by an unseen hand. "And why would you want to do that? You've spent your life building this company. It's in your blood. It's your legacy."

Ryder smiled slightly at the description. All that had applied and more…B.S. Before Seline.

Now…

Now all he could think about was getting out from under his responsibilities to spend his time trying to find her.

And when he did…

He'd have to cross that bridge when he came to it.

He didn't kid himself that convincing her into any sort of long-term relationship would be easy.

But he couldn't do anything less.

"I'm not talking about giving you the company, Coleman. I'm suggesting that you step into my shoes as CEO." He fingered through the papers then laid his palm against them. "Hell, you practically run the company now as it is."

"Only in your absence."

"Even when I'm here."

Coleman looked down. "Yes, but without the pressure of official responsibility."

"Are you saying that makes a difference?"

John stared at him for a long moment. "Does this mean a pay increase?"

Ryder laughed. “It means a considerable pay increase.”

Coleman got up and thrust his hand across the desk. “Then you’ve found your man.”

20

AS SOON AS the airplane reached cruising altitude and the seat belt sign rang off, Seline released the mechanism and then pulled her legs to her chest in the plush first-class seat. Outside her window, New York City was no more than a blurry outline quickly being left behind.

And she felt as if the thin tether to the heart she'd left there was being stretched to its breaking point.

Two days. That's how long it had been since she'd last seen Ryder's handsome face. Enjoyed his wide, one-dimple grin. Reveled in the feel of his large hands branding her soft flesh. It seemed a lifetime ago. And it would extend to be a lifetime because she could never, ever hope to see him again. To do so would only add salt to the raw wounds leaving him had rent.

But leave him she had. While Don Giovanni had called a cease-fire in her standoff with Mario, she didn't kid herself into believing it would last for long. No, she fully expected Mario would soon figure out he could gain a new ally by turning to his father for help in obtaining legal and physical custody of his granddaughter, the seven-year-old born with the curse of Trainello blood. Which meant that she would have to double up her efforts to protect Lina.

And the first way to do that was to cut all ties with everyone in her life, much as she had done years ago. Only now that list of people included Ryder Blackwell.

A small sound escaped her throat and Seline was surprised to find herself crying.

Never had someone outside her immediate family affected her in such a deeply personal way. In the days she and Ryder had spent together, she'd learned how to trust again. Had relied on him as surely as she relied on her own limbs. And had learned that despite the titanium wall she'd erected around her heart, she was capable of falling in love.

It hadn't been easy lying low the last couple of days while she'd methodically closed every one of her accounts, pooled her resources, then created fresh fake fronts so she could redistribute her monies into more secure accounts. It had taken her being in the city to do that. And being in the city meant that Ryder was never that far away from her. In thought or reality.

Just one last time, her heart had pleaded with her.

But there could be no more times. She'd played out her hand where Ryder was concerned. Aside from not wanting to further hurt herself, it wouldn't be fair to Ryder, either.

A flight attendant neared her chair and she turned to face the window, pretending to sleep even as her shoulders trembled from the tears she was incapable of keeping at bay.

"Miss, I'm sorry, but something's wrong with this gentleman's seat. Do you mind if he takes the free one next to you?"

She minded. But there was little she could do about it. She waved her hand without looking to indicate her approval then edged her sunglasses down over her damp eyes.

"May I offer you a tissue?"

Not the voice of the attendant.

A tissue was held out over her shoulder. Seline slowly took it, the familiar scent of lime filling her senses.

She jerked around to face the man in the seat next to her.

Ryder…

RYDER hadn't known if he'd made the right decision until he saw the tears streaking Seline's flawless cheeks and witnessed the unguarded warmth in her gray eyes when she saw him.

Oh, the decision to act on P.I. Kylie Capshaw's information was right for him. He hadn't known if it would be right for Seline. After all, she wouldn't have disappeared if she'd thought their being together was a good idea.

"You're going to have a rough ride ahead of you, son," his father had told him when Ryder stopped by to tell him what he had planned. "I never thought I'd meet someone more stubborn than you, more driven than you. Then I met Seline."

Of course, his father was correct. He and Seline weren't opposites, they were almost painfully alike. He suspected it would more times than not emerge as a challenging aspect of their relationship.

To his surprise, Seline launched herself into his arms. He quickly braced himself so that they wouldn't end up on the aisle floor, then wrapped his arms around her, holding her close and pressing her body to his.

This...this sensation of completion. That's what he'd been after. And, he guessed, it was what everyone sought without knowing that's what they were looking for. And it was something you could only find with one other person in your lifetime.

Now that Ryder had found his, he wasn't about to let it go.

"How…? Why…?" Seline pulled slightly back to gaze into his eyes. A fleeting smile flickered over her strikingly beautiful face. "Never mind."

"You didn't think I'd just stand back and let you walk out of my life, did you?"

She looked down and he realized that she had thought exactly that. Or maybe hoped for it.

But it wasn't what she had wanted. Ryder knew that as surely as he knew his own name.

Threading his fingers through the hair over her ears, he drew her closer, leisurely tasting the salt from her tears on her lips, drinking deeply from her hot, slick mouth.

After long moments that left them both more than a little hot and bothered, Seline cleared her throat, smiled at him, then sat back in her seat, grasping his hand tightly in hers on the armrest.

And they both stared out at a future that wouldn't be traditional, wouldn't be expected, but would be theirs.

Epilogue

Chulucanas, Peru, near the Ecuadorian border, three months later

RYDER stood on the sweeping terrace of an old Spanish villa shaded by palm trees, taking in the stunning panorama from the top of the highest hill in the Piura highlands. The South Pacific sparkled like a polished blue jewel to the west, lush, untouched greenery to the east. To the untrained eye, it would seem the large house was unprotected. And that's the way he wanted it. While the compound was guarded by an obscene amount of security, not one of the countless cameras could be seen as they blended into the natural surroundings.

"Check."

The girl's voice pulled his attention down a shallow bluff to another shaded terrace beneath the one where he stood. Off to the right Lina and his father played chess in a small garden alcove, the elder Blackwell scratching his head as he considered the eight-year-old's latest move. Gurtza looked up from a nearby loveseat where she sat cross-stitching.

"Actually, Miss Rosalina, I believe that's checkmate."

Ryder smiled. His father had finally gotten the grandchild he'd wanted to teach his favorite game to, and much sooner than he had expected. While Alan Blackwell had supposedly come down for a brief visit, he'd been there for over a month, and Ryder hoped he'd decide to stay longer. If the growing bond between him and Lina wasn't enough to keep him there, then Ryder suspected the longing gazes he caught him and Gurtza exchanging when they thought no one was looking might.

"Well, good evening, Mr. Black."

Ryder didn't move, his hands casually tucked into the pockets of his white linen pants, the hem of his matching shirt flapping in the light, balmy breeze. But his smile spread from the outside to the inside, igniting a warmth that had as much to do with love as sexual desire.

He slowly turned. Seline stood in the open balcony doors of the villa wearing a black bikini top and a red wrap around her hips. And, as it always did, his heart dipped low in his chest.

This was his bad girl. His passion. His heart and soul.

"Good evening, Mrs. Black."

If he found it amusing that he'd spend the better part of his life trying to prove that his name meant something, then had so easily cast it aside in order to help protect the women he loved, he wasn't saying. He preferred to focus on the here and now.

Seline was here. And apparently she wanted him now.

Seline crossed to him and curved her arms around her husband's neck, reaching up to rub her cheek against his then kiss him lingeringly. He pressed her closer and she closed her eyes, breathing in the scent of him, reveling in his nearness. She blinked open her eyes to see her wedding ring throwing off shafts of light from the sinking sun. While Ryder had spent a considerable chunk of change on the set, she'd have been just as happy with a plastic one out of a gumball machine. Either would be worth more than every payoff she'd ever reaped from her career as a con artist...put together. He thrilled her every night and every day, both in bed and out. And he was building a connection with her child while at the same time wanting to know when she might want another.

Together they'd created a safe haven for their new family and had found ceaseless passion in their bedroom.

A bedroom she had arranged for them to spend an entire, blissful night in alone.

Ryder kissed her so deeply he took her breath away.

"Shall we join the others?" he asked huskily.

"Actually, we're not expected until brunch tomorrow, Mr. Black." She opened the top buttons on his shirt then trailed her fingers inside. "That is if you'll do me the pleasure of being my date tonight."

His bright blue eyes sparkled at her, and his one cheek dimple came out to play. "I couldn't think of anything else I'd rather do, Mrs. Black."

He swept her up into his arms and she held tight, pressing her mouth against his hot neck. "Oh, and if we happen to have a little extra time, there's this…job I'd like to discuss with you."

Ryder carried her into the room and used his foot to close the balcony doors. "Trust me, Seline, there won't be any extra time…."

* * * * *

Wait! The wide ride's not over yet…
There's another bad girl on the way!

Don't miss: Stripped
by Julie Elizabeth Leto

Available next month,
wherever Mills & Boon® books are sold.

CALL ME WICKED

BY

JAMIE SOBRATO

Dear Reader,

I've loved witches ever since I first read Anne Rice's Mayfair witch novels as a teenager. There's just something about powerful women with a hint of supernatural mystique that captures my imagination. Stir in elements of the dark, sensual and forbidden, and my romantic mind runs wild.

I hope you enjoy my take on witch lore in *Call Me Wicked* – a world where tattoos can come alive, anyone could be a witch or, conversely, a member of a secret witch-hunting society. Best of all, it's a place that is unknowingly on the verge of a supernatural revolution.

You can find out more about me and my upcoming books at www.jamiesobrato.com. There you can also e-mail me or participate in my often-gratuitous blog discussions. I'd love to hear from you!

Sincerely,

Jamie Sobrato

JAMIE SOBRATO

writes for Mills & Boon® Blaze® and lives in Northern California. She is not a witch. She does, however, long for a few supernatural powers, such as the ability to make mean people disappear, and/or the power to turn wheat bread into chocolate. Until she hones those skills, she is content to write about the supernatural in fiction.

To Annelise Robey, the coolest agent
in the known universe

Prologue

"SHE IS ALMOST MORTAL."

Beneath the table, the little girl's ears perked up. The elders were talking about her again. They always forgot she was there.

"It's true, Lauren is the weakest of us all. In another generation, there may be no more witches," her mother said, her voice sounding strange. Not sad, as she should have sounded, but kind of flat and bored, like when she said there was no more honey for the tea.

Lauren sat very still at her mother's feet, under the ebony dining table with its clawed feet and carved legs, and she practiced being invisible. It was her favorite thing to do when the elders were around, and they were so easy to fool with all the big important business they were always busy doing—talking about the quality of grapes or the export of the wine or the upcoming harvest.

"If it weren't for the other child, this generation might have been spared. They are all weakened in their powers, nearly indistinguishable from mortals."

The girl tried not to smile. She had the gift, whether the elders knew it or not. She was just as much a witch as any of them, but she knew how to hide it. She knew how much they disapproved of the children practicing their gifts, so she and her siblings and cousins did it in secret. They snuck out into the vineyards or into the hills to see who was the most powerful, who had learned to move a rock with their mind or make the rain fall hard from the sky. And they had agreed never to tell.

Lauren could sometimes see in her mind things that hadn't happened yet. Prescience, she had once heard her mother call it, because her mother had the same gift, though like the rest of the elders she had sworn never to use it on purpose. Her mother tried not to be powerful.

The grown-ups were not talking about Lauren anymore. Now they were talking about the grapes again, and she didn't care about the grapes, so she closed her eyes and tried to see something that had not happened yet.

It didn't take long. First came a burst of white light behind her eyes, and then came the pictures so clear she felt as if she was living them. She could see a man with brown hair and a woman with long black hair. The woman felt very familiar to her. They were scared; she could feel it. They were running from someone or something. There was sand and darkness and cold wind and the sound of the ocean. A gunshot rang out, and the woman fell to the ground.

In a flash the scene was gone again.

Lauren was shaking. She covered her mouth to keep from crying out and being discovered. She had never seen a person shot before, had never had a vision so scary. She did not know what it meant, but she hoped the woman who was shot would be okay.

Her heart continued to race long after the vision had passed. She willed the shaking to stop, and again sat still, hoping the fear the images evoked would go away, and after a while, it did.

Lauren would not let her gift die the way the elders wanted. She wouldn't live hidden away and afraid all her life. Not when they had her little sister, the most powerful witch ever born, living amongst them, playing with them, reminding them of what they might be if they used their gifts instead of hiding them away.

And when they were grown, there would be a time when witches would never have to hide again. Lauren had seen it happen in her mind.

1

Lauren Parish did not intend to die today.

Death was nowhere on her to-do list, and yet here she was, crouched on the fire escape outside her bedroom window, cold wind snaking up her night-gown and her heart pounding wildly in her ears. Four stories up, with two men in black tearing through her apartment and muttering Czech words she could not identify, death didn't seem such an unlikely scenario all of a sudden.

Five minutes ago, she'd been sitting in bed flipping through research notes for a presentation due next week, when an image had flashed in her mind. She saw two men standing at her door, using some kind of tool to pick the lock. When her hearing, more acute than that of mortals, caught the slightest sound of metal against metal at her front door, she'd turned off her bedside lamp, dropped the notes, and scrambled to the window, her only escape. She was easing the window shut again when she heard the men enter the apartment.

It hadn't been the first time one of her visions

had proven useful, but it had definitely been the most opportune.

She barely had enough room to keep herself out of sight of the window on the small landing, and she had to either go up or down. Her breath was coming out in quick shallow gasps, and her legs quaked beneath her. She wanted to cry, but she wouldn't. She had to summon whatever strength she possessed to stay calm, to escape.

She knew without thinking twice who the men were, and she knew their intent without a doubt was to kill her, or take her to be interrogated and then kill her.

Neither choice was remotely appealing.

So this is what it felt like to stare death in the face. It was a fear she hadn't been struck by since childhood, a fear her ancestors had held close and nurtured, a fear she'd foolishly let slip away in her comfortable life—in her disdain for what had always seemed to her generation as the elders' cowardice.

The men only had to feel the still-warm bed where she'd been sitting to know that she'd been there, that she was hiding somewhere close by. She glanced up and saw that her crazy upstairs neighbor was home, but the woman would call the police before she'd let Lauren climb in her window.

She looked down and could see no light coming from the window directly below. The apartment was occupied by a young couple who had a cat they let go in and out the window, and if she was lucky, the window would be open now.

Ever so slowly, she peered into her bedroom again and caught sight of one of the men standing beside her bed, doing exactly what she feared he'd do. Her heart flip-flopped. When he ran his hand along the sheet where she'd been sitting, she held her breath and eased herself slowly toward the ladder.

The old metal fire escape was creaky, and even a cat scaling it had a tendency to sound like a herd of buffalo. Lauren didn't have a chance. Why couldn't she have been born with some really cool power like the ability to shape-shift? Now would have been a great time to transform into a mouse.

She moved as quickly as she could, eased herself down the ladder with a minimum of noise, and stopped at the neighbor's landing. The window, as she suspected, was ajar six inches. But when she tried to push it up farther, she saw that a piece of wood had been nailed into place to prevent the window from opening any wider.

Lauren muttered a curse and glanced up. From above, she could hear her own window opening. She sucked icy air into her lungs and shivered, then pushed up hard on the window. It wouldn't budge. She noticed the wood window frame was rotting, and she had to decide whether to keep trying to get into this window or take the risk of going another floor down.

Above, if they were looking down at her now, they'd see her. She felt a burst of adrenaline, and she stood up, kicked the window frame with all the strength she could summon, and felt the satisfying give of the wood against her heel. Broken glass pierced the top of her foot, but she didn't feel pain, just the warmth of blood.

The men upstairs had to have heard. She broke away a few large shards of remaining glass and eased herself quickly through the opening, where she thankfully found an empty bedroom. She ran to the front door, flung it open, and kept running.

Downstairs, out the door, into the street, through the alley, toward the apartment three blocks over where she could only pray her best friend was home.

Her nightgown didn't protect her from the cold October air, and the cut on her foot was beginning to throb with pain, but she ran, faster than she'd ever run before, her bare feet slapping cold pavement—across streets and around cars and past buildings and up stairs until she was pounding on Macy's door.

When the door opened a moment later, she saw her friend's worried face, and she collapsed into her, into the apartment, then she spun and slammed the door shut. Locked all the locks. Caught her breath.

No one had followed her closely enough to see where she'd gone, she was pretty sure of it. But only now did she feel the weight of guilt that she had possibly led those murderers right to Macy's door.

"Lauren! What happened? What's wrong? Are you okay?" Macy was holding her at arm's length now, taking in her half-naked appearance, her bare feet, the bloody gash.

Lauren heaved a few deep breaths, but said nothing. Macy didn't know Lauren's true identity. No mortal knew.

"Oh my God, your foot! Let me get something," Macy said, hurrying to the bathroom. "Should I call 9-1-1?" she called over her shoulder.

"No!" Lauren eased onto the floor, leaned against the door, fearful now of not being near enough to an exit should she need one.

This was not the first time Lauren had been forced to hide from assholes who had a thing against witches. Once when she was a kid visiting her extended family in Brittany on the coast of France, the house had been raided by the witch hunters, and she'd been forced to hide in the forest for days with her cousins.

She'd grown up in hiding, and she'd been lectured a thousand times about the dangers of being a witch in a world of mortals. But all things drift toward complacency, and even the gravest dangers cannot loom large in one's mind for long when at a distance. There had not been many raids in California during her lifetime—certainly not enough for her to worry about. The Parish family—they'd changed their names from Beauville to Parish when her grandparents had moved from Louisiana to the Napa Valley in the thirties—had been very good at hiding.

So what had changed? Why her? Why now?

She didn't have to consider the questions for more than a second. The CNN interview had done it. It had aired for the first time early this morning. The witch hunters apparently worked fast.

Her mother had been furious, had called her on her cell phone that afternoon to tell her she was a fool and a traitor, had told her she'd put the entire family in danger for the sake of her own ego.

But Lauren hadn't believed her. She'd grown so complacent and secure, smug even. She hadn't seen any harm in doing the interview to talk about the study she'd headed up, the results of which were making news all over the world now. She'd believed the witch hunters weren't really a threat anymore, that most of the zealots among them had died out and that any remaining ones weren't really interested in a battle that was centuries old.

Lauren had been wrong. Her inconsistent and troublesome ability to foretell the future had not warned her far enough in advance. Instead, it had waited until danger was at her door.

Macy returned carrying a towel and a first aid kit. She knelt on the oak plank floor beside Lauren's foot and began tending to the wound. "Is this glass?" she said, gently picking it out as Lauren winced in pain.

"Yeah," she said, looking at her friend instead of the cut. "I had a little accident. I can't really tell you what happened, okay? Can you just trust me and promise not to say a word to anyone about this?"

Macy peered at her with concerned brown eyes. She looked so safe, so surreal here in her warm, familiar apartment, her long blond hair still wet from a shower. "You're scaring me, Lauren. What the hell's going on?"

"I have to disappear for a while, okay? And you can't tell anyone you saw me tonight. You can't act like you know anything at all."

"About what? What are you talking about? Is someone trying to hurt you?"

"I just need you to loan me some clothes, and maybe your car if you can spare it. And some money, just enough to get me away from here."

Lauren's mind raced now, forming a plan. She'd always known what she had to do if she was ever found out. But the logistics of getting to her cousin Sebastian in L.A.—how to get clothes and money when she was chased out of her apartment wearing nothing but a nightgown—were never discussed by the elders.

"God, Lauren, this is crazy. You know you can tell me anything, right? You can trust me."

Macy was wrapping her foot in a bandage now, securing it with tape.

"It's not that simple. And I swear I would tell you if I could. Just trust me on this. As soon as I can, I'll give you the whole story, and this will all make perfect sense, and you'll understand why I'm protecting you by not saying anything."

Macy regarded her seriously. "What about Griffin? Should I not tell him you've been here either?" Griffin was Macy's fiancé.

Lauren shook her head. "Don't tell anyone."

"I think you need stitches in your foot. Can I at least give you a ride to the emergency room?"

She looked down at the bandage. "No. I'll have to have it looked at somewhere else, not here in the city."

Her friend sighed heavily. "Okay, I'll give you whatever you need. You can have my car. I'll just tell Griffin I had to put it in the shop for repair."

"Thank you so much, Macy. You're saving my life right now. And whatever you do, don't go to my apartment. In fact, don't even let on that you know me if anyone asks."

"This is just too weird," Macy said as Lauren followed her into the bedroom. "You're acting like a criminal or something."

It's way worse than that, Lauren wanted to say, but didn't. "Don't worry, I'm not, I swear. When I'm able to explain, you'll understand."

Macy wouldn't have believed the truth anyway. What mortal could without some kind of solid proof? They needed to see milk being curdled on the spot or corpses raised from the dead to believe a witch was in their midst. Not that real witches did any of that stuff, but stereotypes died hard.

Lauren's foot throbbed now, yet she could walk on it with little trouble. Wearing shoes might be a different story, though.

But she had to get out of San Francisco, and she had to do it fast. She wasn't sure if she'd ever be able to come back. At that thought, tears stung her eyes, and when Macy glanced back and caught the stricken look on her face, she halted in her tracks in the doorway to the bedroom.

"Lauren," she said, and took her friend into her arms.

Lauren awkwardly allowed Macy to hug her. She'd never been much for the whole cheek kissing and hugging friends thing. But slowly the gesture comforted her enough to relax into the embrace.

She wasn't the one who broke into tears about anything, ever. She was the scientist, the medical researcher who viewed everything through the cool, impartial lens of science. She was the icy intellectual, the one people relied upon for the harsh, unvarnished truth. While her gift of prescience may have been unpredictable, she'd always relied on her intelligence to solve any problem. She didn't do *this.*

Not cowering. Not weakness. Not falling apart.

She didn't realize right away that she was crying hard, that sobs racked her chest, until she heard Macy murmuring soothing sounds.

And then Lauren stopped. She calmed down, silenced herself, pulled away, wiped her face.

Macy stared at her with concern. "Are you sure you'll be okay to drive? Do you need me to give you a ride somewhere? I'll take you wherever you need to go. I'll drive you all the way to Mexico if—"

Lauren was shaking her head before Macy even stopped speaking. "No, it's not safe for you. I have to go alone."

She nodded. And after a pause she said, “Okay, let’s get you packed then.”

“You’re not expecting Griffin to stop by any time soon, are you?”

“Not too soon—he’s hanging out with Carson tonight actually.”

“Oh.” Carson. Great.

Carson McCullen, Lauren’s most recent mortal lover, was a man she had been trying to avoid at all costs for the past two months.

It wasn’t easy to take a mortal as a lover. For one thing, it was a practice strictly forbidden by the elders. Not that forbidding anything ever stopped the witches of Lauren’s generation from doing whatever the hell they wanted, but this particular forbidden act had its unique complications.

Mortals, with all their weaknesses and sexual limitations, tended to get, well…addicted, when they had sex with a witch. Witches were so much more sensual creatures, so sexually superior, that having sex with one tended to ruin the average mortal for all future encounters of the nonsupernatural variety. And so while Lauren tried her best not to do mortal men, occasionally her appetites got the best of her.

It wasn’t easy limiting herself to sex with other witches. For one thing, she was related in some distant or not so distant way to most of the ones she knew—urk!—and for another, witches were forbidden from congregating together in public, so every interaction had to be on the down-low, which got to be a drag real fast.

She tried to be good, and she often traveled abroad to find lovers, but occasionally she grew weak and took a mortal.

Carson was one of those instances.

And entertaining him for that weekend in Vegas had been a favor to Macy, too. She couldn't very well have turned down helping her best friend, not when she was horny as hell and in need of a weekend getaway to boot. So she'd spent one blissful weekend rocking Carson's world, and ever since, he'd been trying to track her down.

To his credit, he'd been an unusually talented mortal lover. She'd never met anyone before who'd satisfied her so thoroughly. But she knew the only way to cure his addiction now was to stay as far away from him as she could. It was the kindest thing to do.

She watched Macy filling an overnight bag with clothes for her, and she glanced at the clock. It was half past eight. She could be in L.A. before morning.

Far away from Carson, which was good, but also far away from her job, her friends, her entire life. Far away from everything she held dear.

But the fear that lurked in her belly told her she had no choice. She had to run as fast as she could, and she had to do it tonight.

2

"HEY, ISN'T THAT LAUREN?"

Carson McCullen nearly spewed his beer across the room when he spotted Lauren Smith's face on the plasma-screen TV. He hadn't seen her in two months, not since the scorching weekend they'd spent together in Las Vegas. And now there she was, being interviewed on CNN Headline News, while he and his best friend, Griffin, gaped at the TV.

"I thought her name was…"

"Lauren Smith," Carson filled in.

But no, her name wasn't Lauren Smith. Right there at the bottom of the screen, the text said her name was Lauren Parish, medical researcher at San Francisco Pacific University.

He blinked as the facts settled themselves in his brain.

That would explain his inability to track down Lauren Smith, who did not work at Western Airlines the way she'd claimed. Aside from one unpleasant phone conversation, they'd had no contact since Las Vegas, in spite of Carson's crazed urges to see her again.

He had never been addicted to a woman before. He'd been infatuated, enthralled, aroused, in love and in lust, but addicted? No.

Then came Lauren, a woman he had not been able to stop thinking about for the past two months, a woman who'd possessed him so thoroughly, he was willing to make a complete ass of himself to have another chance with her.

Some more words came flying at him from the TV. Words like *sex* and *reduced IQ* and *weakened recall skills.* He grabbed the remote and hit the rewind button—thank God for TiVo—then listened all over again as Lauren talked about the study she'd apparently conducted, which proved that sex really was responsible for making people stupid.

Or in her words, *sexual orgasm led to a temporarily reduced intellectual capacity in humans.*

What the hell?

He cast a disbelieving glance at Griffin lounging on the other end of the couch. Griffin, who'd been in Vegas that weekend, and who'd met Lauren "the flight attendant" Smith, as well. In fact Griffin's very own fiancée, Macy, had helped perpetrate the lies about her friend.

"Dude," Griffin said, shaking his head. "I'm as stunned as you are. I had no idea."

The woman on TV, although she looked identical to the Lauren Carson had spent that frenzied weekend making love to, didn't sound much like her. This Lauren was clearly a brainiac, with a vocabulary to rival Webster's and a look that only whispered sexpot. Sure, she was still sexy, but her blatant sensuality was hidden behind an austere black blazer and top, trendy little black-rimmed glasses and a severe bun that tamed her long dark hair and made her look less like a Goth Angelina Jolie and more like the object of someone's kinky dominatrix school mistress fantasy.

When the interview ended, Carson backed up the segment again and watched a third time. "I don't freaking believe this. She's the same woman, right? We're not imagining this, are we?"

Griffin shook his head. "They even said she's right here in San Francisco. I can't believe Macy didn't tell me…."

"Oh hey, don't let this come between you two. You know how women are—she was probably sworn to secrecy or something."

"So are you gonna stop jonesing over this chick and go find her now?"

Carson hesitated, but he knew the answer in his gut without saying a word. Hell yeah. He was going to find her, and he was going to find a way to get another chance with her, whomever she really was.

Lauren Parish, medical researcher at San Francisco Pacific University?

Not at all who she'd led him to believe she was. He wasn't sure whether to be amused or pissed off. Sure, Las Vegas was a town where people lied about their names and behaved in ways they wouldn't in their everyday lives, and with any other woman, Carson would have let it go.

But this woman—she'd gotten to him. She'd worked her way under his skin, and he'd barely been able to function, he craved her so badly. This woman—this woman he'd fantasized about constantly, wasn't the woman he thought he'd been with at all.

He'd tried to imagine her true identity, pictured her sitting in an office somewhere, or even working as a flight attendant for some other airline than the one she'd told him. But he'd never imagined this. He paused the screen with Lauren's image on it. No doubt it was her.

She was a scientist. A scientist who'd discovered sex's dirty little secret, according to CNN.

No wonder she'd lied about her profession. Had she been experimenting on him? Testing him to see how dumb she could make him in one hot weekend? Or had she been as hot for him as he had been for her?

"So do you think she was like, experimenting on me?"

"What do you mean?"

"You know, that weekend, all the, ah, bedroom activities. Do you think she was testing out her hypothesis on me or something?"

Griffin laughed. "I think she'd lose her standing in the scientific community if her research methods involved Vegas hotels and alcoholic beverages."

"I guess," Carson muttered, not feeling very convinced.

"Hey, medical researchers have to get laid, too. I'm sure she was into you."

Carson stood and went to Griffin's desk, opened the Web browser on the computer, and navigated to a directory Web site, then typed in Lauren's correct name and city. A few seconds later, an address he didn't recognize popped up, and he read it aloud to Griffin.

"Hey, that's like three or four blocks from Macy's place."

Carson stared at the address. He could hardly believe he now had a way to see Lauren face-to-face again. This woman who'd wrought wonders on his body and haunted his fantasies was only minutes away.

Why did it matter so much that he try one more time to have a second chance with her? In his gut he knew without a doubt...

She made him feel alive. In his entire wild-child life, he'd tried everything and done everything. He'd begun to fear his picture appeared on UrbanDictionary.com beside the word *jaded.* He'd started to believe there was nothing left in life that would thrill him, nothing that would ever truly excite him again.

There were downsides to growing up a spoiled upper-middle-class brat, having the cushy house in Woodside and the mom who drove the Mercedes wagon, the Brazilian nanny and the Christmases in the Tahoe vacation house with the million-dollar views of the lake. Carson had had it too easy. He knew this about himself, and he knew he'd taken it all for granted.

Whatever he'd gotten in life, he'd gotten by coasting, because he'd always been too busy chasing after the latest thrill or the latest honey to give a damn about anything else.

Until Lauren. Not only did she make him feel alive, but he had a feeling she could make him care about something again, and he wanted to find out if he was right.

"I was being all eco-conscious and took the Muni over here. Do you know if it stops in that neighborhood?"

"Are you for real?" Griffin said. "You're just going to go over there and drop in on her unannounced?"

Was he?

"Yeah," he finally said. "I think we had such a strong physical connection, if she sees me face-to-face, she won't be able to slam the door on me."

"You're going to wait until daylight, though, right? You know, so she doesn't call the police on you and have you arrested for stalking her?"

Carson glanced at his watch. "It's only eight-thirty. Not too late to drop in for a friendly visit."

"If you're determined to make an ass of yourself, I can give you a ride just to witness the spectacle. I'm spending the night at Macy's anyway."

Carson clicked Print on the Web browser, and a few seconds later Griffin's printer spit out Lauren's street address. He folded up the sheet of paper and put it in his pocket.

He was vaguely aware that his behavior had left the realm of normal and entered might-be-mistaken-for-a-lunatic territory, but he was having a hell of a hard time caring about appearances right now. Not when he had a chance to see Lauren again.

"Okay, man, let's go."

Fifteen minutes later, they were parking outside the address. He stared up at the building where Lauren lived and felt a pang of desire hit him like a brick wall. God, how could he want a woman so badly who apparently didn't want him? He wasn't sure he wanted to explore any answers to that question, so he took a deep breath and got out of the car.

Before shutting the door, he leaned down to look at Griffin and said, "I can catch the Muni back home if you don't want to wait."

"I wouldn't miss this for the world. I'm sitting right here."

"What if she invites me in?" Carson said, realizing he sounded a little too pie-in-the-sky hopeful.

Griffin laughed. "Come back out or call me on your cell to tell me to go. Until I get the word from you, I'll be here."

He sat back in his seat and cranked the stereo, and Carson slammed the door.

He climbed the stairs to her apartment two at a time, his heart racing and his mind whirling around the fact that he was about to knock on her door, possibly about to see her again. Finally.

He hadn't even brushed his damn teeth. Pausing at the top of the steps, he dug around in his wallet and found an emergency piece of gum tucked into one of the credit card slots, unwrapped it, and popped it in his mouth. Much better. He couldn't meet the woman of his erotic dreams with dog breath.

But when he arrived at Lauren's door, he found it ajar. He knocked tentatively, waited, then when he heard no sounds coming from within, he stepped inside.

A coatrack lay across the floor at his feet, and all around the wreckage of the apartment suggested something was seriously wrong. Papers, pillows, toppled furniture and the various items of everyday life were strewn about, cluttering the floor. Either Lauren was allergic to housework, or someone had trashed her place.

His chest tightened.

Where was she? He stepped over some books that had been knocked off shelves and went to the bedroom, where a similar state of disarray prevailed. A window gaped open next to the bed, and cold air poured in. Had someone broken into the apartment via the window?

Had Lauren been home? Was she hurt, or worse? His gut clenched at the thought.

No one was in the bathroom, either, nor the kitchen when he peered into it. Something was seriously wrong, and his brain was only starting to catch up to the facts. Careful not to touch anything unnecessarily and damage evidence, he eased Lauren's front door closed, then ran back downstairs to Griffin's car.

Griffin was staring at his PDA when Carson pounded on the driver's side window. He frowned and lowered the window.

"What's wrong?"

"I don't know what the hell's going on, but Lauren's place is trashed, and she's not home."

"You went in?"

"The door was wide-open. I think we need to call the police or something."

"That's crazy. Let me call Macy first and see if she's heard from Lauren." He hit a couple of buttons on the PDA, then held it to his ear.

A few seconds later he was talking to Macy, explaining the situation, then listening, then saying "Oh" and "Uh-huh."

He hung up and stared at Carson again looking as if he'd just received news that Elvis was actually alive and hiding out in the trunk of his car.

"What's going on?"

"I'm not sure, but I think my girl has lost her mind."

"Griffin, what the hell is going on?" Carson demanded with a little more force as his stomach coiled itself into a bigger knot.

"She said we shouldn't call the police, and that we need to get out of here as fast as we can. That we have to make sure we're not followed, before going to a gas station three blocks north of here. Lauren is supposed to meet us there."

Carson looked around, wondering who it was that might follow them. And why the cloak-and-dagger routine? Lauren was going to meet them? Lauren was there with Macy right now? This was all too weird to even wrap his brain around. He felt as if all the key facts were missing, and yet at the same time, his pulse quickened at the thought that Lauren was only a few blocks away, out of his reach...but not for long.

He had to shake himself to remember the fact that she was in some kind of trouble.

He got in the car, then Griffin started driving in the opposite direction and making a few turns to shake off any possible tail before finally heading north. The entire time Carson watched out the rear window to make sure no one was trailing them. As they were pulling into a gas station out of the shadows on the side of the building emerged the woman he'd been aching for months to see.

She was more stunning in real life than he remembered. She had a strange, cool, sexual energy about her that made her seem almost otherworldly. Not like a mere mortal, but like some sex goddess come to Earth to bring to life his every fantasy.

Her long black hair draped her shoulders and

chest, framing a face so ethereally pretty, he had a hard time looking away from it. She was tall—at least five-nine and the only woman he'd ever been with who could look him in the eye when she wore heels—and her body was lean and catlike, with a few lush curves thrown in to make things even more interesting.

She motioned for them to park, then she climbed into the backseat, all the while her gaze only brushing past Carson, barely acknowledging his presence. Her spicy-sweet scent wafted over him and his cock went hard instantly.

"Drive," she said by way of greeting. "Fast."

3

LAUREN HATED HERSELF for getting caught without a plan. She didn't want anyone else involved in the danger she faced now, but already three innocent mortals had been pulled into it.

"Where are we headed?" Griffin asked as he glanced at her in the rearview mirror.

"Macy's going to let me borrow her car, but I wanted to talk to you two first. She's going to meet us at Stonestown Mall."

"Going shopping?"

"Not exactly," Lauren said, not wanting to give away any more information than necessary. "I'm sorry I can't tell you what's going on. I'd really appreciate your not asking me any questions right now."

Carson was sitting sideways, watching her over the back of the passenger seat. He seemed shocked to see her again, and if she hadn't been so damn scared, she might have been able to summon some surprise herself.

"I saw you on the news," he said.

"What were you doing at my apartment?"

Lauren finally remembered her seat belt and buckled herself in as the car turned a corner.

"I wanted to say hi."

"How'd you find me?" she asked, her stomach queasy.

"The magic of the Internet. It was easy once I had your real name from the CNN interview."

Apparently The Order had found it easy, too. Or was she being paranoid? Was it possible the men who'd broken into her apartment had just been run-of-the-mill meth addicts looking for something to steal?

Her brain couldn't dwell on a single thought for long. One thing she'd had hammered into her relentlessly her entire life was that there was no such thing as too much paranoia where The Order was concerned.

"You went to my door and knocked?" she asked Carson.

"Yeah, but the door was open. I looked inside and saw that the place was empty, and then I left. Why?"

"Did you see anyone, or did anyone see you?"

"I don't know."

"Griffin, did you stay in the car or go to my apartment?"

"I stayed in the car."

The witch hunters had been known to leave surveillance equipment behind after they invaded a witch's residence, and they very well could have video footage of Carson now.

"When are you going to tell us what's going on?" Carson asked.

She covered her face with her hands and sighed. This was all too much, too fast. She would have to take Carson with her. He wouldn't be safe in San Francisco.

"Just give me some time to think," she muttered.

Lauren's heartbeat didn't return to normal until they were well out of her neighborhood. That damn study. It had endangered not only her, but her friends, and Carson. How had she been so stupid?

Why hadn't she paid more attention to the elders' warnings?

Lauren had spent most of her adult life too busy working toward her career goals to worry much about clan politics and fear. Her intelligence was stronger than her unpredictable gift of prescience, so she'd gone with her greatest strength, graduating summa cum laude from Stanford with a Master's in human biology, then taking a much-sought-after position at a major university, where she'd gotten involved in sexuality studies.

Her entire adult life, aside from a minor rebellion at the age of eighteen, had been normal and free of danger. It had made her get sloppy.

The guys in the front seat had fallen into an uncomfortable silence, probably trying to decide whether Lauren needed to be hauled to the nearest police precinct or mental hospital, rather than the mall.

Traffic was light, and in fifteen minutes they

made it to the mall parking lot. Lauren had already warned Macy that they had to do a quick exchange of cars and not linger talking.

When they pulled into the lot beside Macy's car, Lauren leaned forward and said, "Carson, I need you to come with me, okay?"

He gave her an odd look, but shrugged and said, "Sure."

"Griffin, Macy's going to get in the car with you. I want you and Macy to leave, be careful to make sure no one's following you, and don't ever go back to my apartment again." She held his gaze until he nodded. "Carson and I will be in contact again as soon as we can, but don't worry if you don't hear from us for a while."

Carson's expression was growing more concerned by the second. "Um, any minute now would be a good time to tell me what the hell's going on."

"You'll have to let someone at your office know that you won't be in for a few days—at the least."

He looked at her as though she'd lost her mind. "Just as soon as you tell me what's going on."

Lauren bit her lip, but said nothing. If she'd been smart, she would have come up with some great cover story to not alarm them all so much.

"Let's get in Macy's car, and then I'll explain."

Carson did as instructed, exiting Griffin's car without any more protest. Good thing he probably would have walked through fire to get some time alone with her.

Outside the car, Lauren gave Macy a quick hug, took the car key she offered, and waved goodbye to Griffin. Once in the car with Carson, they watched as Macy and Griffin drove away.

"We have to find a pay phone. I think there's one on the other side of the mall," she said as she started the car.

"I've got my cell phone—you can use that," Carson said.

"No, it's not secure enough."

"Are you like a spy or something?" he asked.

"I wish it was that simple."

The mall parking lot had emptied out at this time of night, and the remaining cars were clustered around the restaurants that stayed open late. Lauren spotted a pay phone and pulled over near it.

The farther she got from the invasion of her apartment, the less real it felt. She could have almost convinced herself it had only been a bad dream, except for the gash on her foot that was still aching.

She looked over at Carson in the passenger seat and allowed herself to really take in his presence for the first time, now that they were alone together.

His wavy brown hair had grown since she'd last seen him, brushing his collar, and he now sported a five o'clock shadow that hadn't been there in Vegas. He was tall and substantial with his wiry, athletic physique and his broad, rock-hard shoulders.

He wore a black turtleneck, black leather jacket, and a pair of faded jeans that fit him so well they would have driven her to distraction at any other time. A pair of black Doc Marten's completed his look, which was the sort of carefully planned casualness that said he cared about his appearance but didn't want to look as though he was trying too hard.

"So do I get the scoop now?"

"I need to make a phone call or two, and then I'll explain everything as best I can."

In truth, she needed more time to decide how much information she could risk giving him.

He studied her. "Sex makes us dumb, eh?"

"Don't worry," she said. "I wasn't experimenting on you in Vegas. I promise."

"That's reassuring to know, I guess. But it doesn't explain why you've gone to such lengths to avoid me."

Lauren shrugged. "I just wanted a weekend fling. I though you did, too."

"Am I allowed to change my mind?" he asked with a cocky little half smile.

"Is that the real reason you came to my apartment? To interrogate me about why I'm not really a flight attendant named Lauren Smith?"

"I came to visit because I wanted a real explanation. Well, that and a chance to see you again."

Then this was his unlucky day. "You'll probably wish we'd never met by the time I explain everything."

"I'm all ears."

"I'll be right back. Just let me make these calls." She fished some quarters out of Macy's storage compartment and exited the car.

Outside, in the cold night air, she felt exposed and vulnerable. With shaking hands she inserted some quarters and called her mother.

Now her hands shook? Not a half hour ago when she was fighting for her life, but now that she had to face the wrath of her mother…

The phone rang five times before someone picked up. “Parish residence,” the maid answered.

“It’s Lauren. I need to speak with my mother right now.”

“I believe she’s retired for the evening.”

“Wake her up. It’s an emergency.”

“One moment please.”

Lauren scanned the area, but no one looked suspicious. The patrons of the nearby restaurant were absorbed in their own lives, paying no attention to her. She glanced toward the car and caught Carson’s eye. His expression inscrutable, he watched her as she watched him, and she got the feeling he wasn’t nearly as calm as he looked. She couldn’t blame him.

A moment later her mother’s voice came on the line. She had a remarkable ability to never sound as though she’d just woken up. “What is it, Lauren? Bette said it was urgent.”

Lauren took a deep breath. “The Order found me. I’m not sure how, but I think it must have had something to do with my TV appearance.”

Silence, and then, “How did you get away? Where are you now?”

"That's not important. I need to figure out how exactly they found me."

"I hope you understand now why we should shun the spotlight—"

"This isn't the time for lectures. Of course I understand."

"You know, you bear a remarkable resemblance to your great-grandmother, who was, of course, killed by The Order. Maybe that's how they recognized you."

"But that was over a hundred years ago."

"They don't forget. And I'm sure they keep photos of all known witches on file for occasions like this."

The truth sank in, and Lauren felt her dinner churning in her stomach, threatening to rise up into her throat. She steadied herself against the pay phone, pressed her forehead to the cool metal surface of its frame.

Her stupid moment in the spotlight would lead to her own doom. Now that she'd been ID'd by witch hunters, she'd spend the rest of her goddamn life on the run, fearing death at the hands of The Order, never safe.

"Lauren? Are you there?"

She wasn't sure if she'd missed anything her mother had said. Only now she realized her ears had been filled with a hissing sound that was subsiding as she gained control of herself again.

"I'm here. I didn't realize…I mean, I forgot about my great-grandmother."

"Well, you've made quite a mess of things, haven't you?"

"I'm going to disappear for a while."

"Yes, I imagine so. You'll need to enlist Sebastian's help."

"I'm not sure he will. There's a mortal involved, and I have to protect him, too."

Again, silence filled the line, and then her mother expelled an exasperated sigh.

"Don't tell me you've been consorting with—"

"I'm not going to talk about this right now. I have to go. I just wanted you to know what's happening, why I've disappeared," Lauren blurted, filling the line with words. "I love you, Mom. Bye."

She hung up the phone, knowing she was risking her mother's considerable wrath by doing so. But getting to Sebastian for help was more important than her mother's temper tantrum. He'd been her closest childhood friend, and maybe based on that old allegiance, he might consider helping a mortal, too.

Or not.

Lauren stared at the receiver resting in its cradle as she tried to remember Sebastian's number, which she'd been forbidden to write down. It had been over a year since she'd seen him, many months since they'd spoken on the phone.

Slowly, the numbers came to her. She inserted more coins, then dialed and waited. After a few rings voice mail picked up. His recording sounded in his unmistakably laid-back style. She'd never once seen him get flustered, shaken or perturbed.

He was the epitome of cool, unlike her right now.

"Hi, it's me..." She hesitated, then decided not to say her name as she realized leaving any specific details might be too dangerous. With luck Sebastian would recognize her voice. "I'm coming for a visit, and I'll be there before morning. Don't call my cell phone, though—it's not safe. I'll find you when I get there."

So she had no choice but to go to Sebastian's club in West Hollywood and hope like hell he wouldn't send her and Carson away. Because if he did, she had nowhere else to turn.

She hung up the phone and wondered belatedly if it had been a mistake to leave a message at all. Her paranoia was growing by the second.

She glanced around again, but there were no shadowy figures lurking about, no one staring in her direction. Well, except Carson.

How to tell him? And *what* to tell him?

As a child, she'd occasionally imagined revealing the truth about herself and her family to a mortal. She'd imagined their reaction, their awe at the powers she possessed, and she'd gotten a thrill from it. But that was before she'd been old enough to fully understand the inherent dangers of the truth.

Lauren hurried back to the passenger door since Carson had switched to the driver's seat and got in. He studied her.

"Well?" he said.

She had no idea how to tell him. She took a deep breath and said, "What I have to say you probably won't believe. But it's really important that you believe it anyway."

He drummed his fingers on the steering wheel, as if doing so was a response in itself.

"Okay, so what is it?" he finally asked.

"Another thing—I need to know that you're trustworthy. If I tell you this thing, it's a secret you'll have to keep your whole life. You can't ever tell anyone. If you do, lots of people could die, including you."

His expression was growing more alarmed by the second. "You can trust me."

Based on Macy's and Griffin's adoration of Carson, she was almost sure she could take his word for that.

"Just so you know, I don't have any choice but to trust you. And you don't have any choice but to keep this secret. Since you might have been spotted in my apartment, the people who are after me are going to want to kill you, too."

He looked outraged. "Who's trying to kill you? What kind of trouble are you in? Lauren, please tell me what the hell's going on."

"Just slow down. It's going to take a while to explain everything."

He expelled a ragged breath. "I've got all night."

The words had never crossed her lips before, and saying them aloud was an act so foreign, she almost couldn't do it. She looked Carson in the eyes, swallowed her fear, and said it.

"I'm a witch."

CARSON HAD OFFICIALLY heard it all now, and he would have laughed except Lauren looked dead serious.

A witch? "Is that a PC way of saying *bitch,* or do you mean you're like one of those goth people who goes around trying to cast spells and stuff."

"Neither," she said.

And he listened as she explained. As she talked, he drove south toward the highway, and before she'd finished explaining, they were passing through San Jose.

Carson half believed her and half suspected she was suffering from an undiagnosed case of schizophrenia. He asked questions here and there, but mostly he listened in amazement to her elaborate tale of ancient witch clans and secret orders of witch hunters and genetic differences between witches and humans, and how she didn't cast spells but she did have some kind of supernatural power.

By the time she was done, they were several hours south of San Francisco, well on their way toward the underground safe house Lauren claimed they were headed to in West Hollywood, and Carson's head was spinning.

"I know this all sounds crazy, and you probably don't believe me," she said. "But I appreciate your trying to understand."

"I admit I'm a little suspicious about your sanity," he said.

"Do you remember how awful you felt after you left Las Vegas? Probably like you were coming down off a high and going through withdrawal symptoms?"

"Yeah, how'd you know?"

"That's what happens to mortals who have sex with witches. You get addicted. That's why you couldn't leave me alone and couldn't stop thinking about trying to get in touch with me again."

"Addicted?"

Lauren nodded. "Not to brag, but mortals tend to find sex with a witch by far the best sex of their lives, and the chemicals released during orgasm are so intense they create an addiction."

That certainly explained a lot.

"So, let's say I tentatively believe you. How long will I have to stay at this place in L.A.?"

Lauren stared at him, looking grim. "I don't know," she said. "It depends on what my cousin says when we get there. He's the expert on evading the witch hunters."

"Is it okay if I use my cell phone now to leave a message at work that I won't be in for a while?"

"Yes," she said. "Go ahead. Just say you've had a family emergency. But don't leave any information about where you are or where you're going."

Carson did as instructed. There was a big meeting he'd miss tomorrow, and someone would have to fill in for him there. Not to mention the rest of his jam-packed schedule for the week. But as he explained the situation to his boss's voice mail box, he felt a sense of excitement filling his chest.

Why the hell would he care about missing some boring-ass meetings with ad agency clients when he could be running off to L.A. with the woman of his fantasies?

And, he realized, he actually wanted to believe Lauren's story. It had everything his life was lacking—danger, intrigue, mind-blowing sex….

Carson had always felt like a trapped animal in his buttoned-up workaday life, and now, for the first time he could remember, he was feeling as though someone had finally opened up the cage and set him free.

4

SOMEWHERE ALONG I-5, they stopped at a rest area and traded seats so that Lauren could drive. Carson finally must have given in to exhaustion and fallen asleep, he realized as he woke up at a stop light. He'd asked for Lauren to let him drive again whenever she got tired herself, but she insisted she was so hyped up on adrenaline there was no way she could sleep, and she wanted him to rest if he could.

"Where are we?" he asked as he stretched and yawned.

Outside, it was still dark.

"We're almost there," she said. "My cousin operates a network of safe houses for witches in trouble, and his center of operation is on the edge of West Hollywood. He runs a nightclub located in the lobby of a hotel. Hopefully he'll have room for us at the hotel."

Lauren turned into a parking garage, parked the car then turned to him. "My cousin Sebastian may be hostile toward you. Just stay calm and take my lead, okay?"

"Should I be packing a weapon or something?"

"No, but try not to let him get to you. He's like my brother, and aside from the fact that he dislikes mortals, he won't be thrilled with the relationship I've had with you."

"I promise I'll stay cool," he said.

They got out of the car and took an elevator up to a darkened nightclub that was still busy even at what must have been past the legal closing time.

Carson followed Lauren along a dim corridor lit by eerie red lights. They passed one person after another who stared at him as if he were the most unwelcome person they'd ever encountered. He was beginning to get a complex.

"Friendly bunch," he muttered to himself, but Lauren overheard.

"They consider this a mortal-free zone. They can sense you're not one of us."

"Should I get a pointy black hat and a broom?"

Lauren ignored his bad joke and led him into an open area in the noisy nightclub, where the deafening bass of house music set the beat for the pulsing crowd of bodies on a large dance floor. Carson took in the industrial-goes-Goth decor, and the great mass of people, and he wanted to get the hell out. Instead, he continued to follow Lauren as she wound through the throng toward the bar that sat on one side of the club.

The bar was full, but she whispered something into the ear of a man sitting at the end, and he grabbed the hand of the woman next to him and they vacated their seats without looking back.

Weird. Had she cast some kind of spell on them? No, she'd said real witches didn't do that kind of stuff.

They sat and the bartender spotted them immediately. A smile transformed his face when he recognized Lauren, but a moment later when his gaze settled on Carson, his expression turned to cold suspicion.

Lauren leaned over and said to Carson, "That's my cousin. Just let me handle him."

Carson didn't have time to respond before the man rounded the corner of the bar and swept Lauren up into a hug. When they parted, he said, "Cousin, it's been too long."

"Yes," she said. "It has." Then she turned her gaze to Carson. "Sebastian, this is my friend Carson. I'm sorry to be blunt. Did you get my voice mail message saying I was coming for a visit?"

"Come to my office," he said, and they were up again and following him beyond the bar, through a door marked Employees Only and down another long dark corridor, its walls painted black, until they reached an unmarked door. Sebastian let them in.

The office was spare and dimly lit, equipped with a desk, a couple of visitors' chairs, a couch and a black wall unit with sleek black doors that Carson imagined hid some interesting secrets.

Sebastian leaned against the edge of the desk and crossed his arms over his chest. For the first time, Carson took him in as more than another tall, hostile witch.

Or since he was a guy, did that mean he was a warlock? Could men be witches?

Sebastian looked a little like Lauren. At least they shared the same stature, bone structure and hair color. His hair was long and pulled back in a ponytail. His eyes were a haunting, inscrutable gray-green, an odd color against his pale skin. It made him appear otherworldly…as he pretty much was.

On his left hand and arm was a disturbingly realistic tattoo of a sleek black raven, and on his right shoulder was the start of an elaborate patterned tattoo that must have covered at least part of his shoulder and ended halfway up his neck.

His gaze, fixed on Carson with open intensity, seemed somehow connected to the piercing eye of the raven on his hand and forearm.

"Sebastian, I know Carson is mortal, but I need you to put that aside and listen to me."

"I don't help mortals," he said evenly, his gaze finally settling on Lauren.

"There's an exception to every rule, right?"

"Tell me why I should make an exception."

Carson listened as Lauren recounted the story of the men who'd shown up in her apartment, her suspicion that The Order had found her because of the CNN interview, Carson's stumbling upon her apartment and her fear that he, too, was now at risk.

"You don't know if the men saw him?"

"No. I can only assume they planted a camera in my apartment and are probably watching it now. We've heard of that happening, right?"

Sebastian nodded. "Yes. You can't go back there."

"I'm worried about my other friends, too. One of them drove Carson to my house. And after fleeing my apartment, I ran to a friend's house—"

"Both humans?"

Lauren nodded, her gaze fixed on the raven tattoo now.

Carson glanced down at it and could have sworn that he saw it move, but when he watched it further, he saw nothing. All this hocus-pocus crap had his mind tripping out.

"Your friends in San Francisco should be fine. And him," he said with a dismissive gesture to Carson, "you should never have brought him here."

"I know he's supposed to help me, Sebastian," Lauren said, then hesitated. "I had a vision."

Carson blinked at this news. Was she telling the truth? Had she really had a vision about him?

Sebastian was glaring at Lauren now. "You are saying too much."

"He knows everything. That's the other reason I need you to help him."

"I don't protect mortals," he said. "You know I don't, and you shouldn't be asking me to."

"I have as much reason as you do to feel that way," she said.

"You're the one consorting with them."

"You're starting to sound like one of the elders," she said in a tone of voice that let Carson know that was just about the worst accusation she could make.

Sebastian glared at them both.

"You were with me in the forest in Bretagne," Lauren said, and then she started speaking urgently in French.

Carson tried to follow the words, but his one year of college French didn't get him anywhere near understanding what she was saying. He watched her face, the cool intensity of it, and he watched Sebastian's expression transform ever-so-slightly from impenetrable to perhaps willing to relent.

The uncaged feeling that had possessed Carson earlier was settling now into a sense of vague uncertainty. He wasn't sure he wanted to glimpse real freedom, only to have it snatched away before he'd had the chance to taste it. Did he want to be confined here to Sebastian's compound? Or was he intoxicated by the idea of being on the run with Lauren, destination unknown?

He was a fool, he realized, if he thought his lame little sense of adventure mattered at all in the face of Lauren's life being in danger.

"One night," Sebastian finally said when she stopped. "I'll find a place for you for one night, and then you have to get him the hell out of here."

But when he looked at Carson again, his expression said something different. His expression was—

and Carson didn't think he was overstating things here—murderous.

Carson found himself in a staring contest with Sebastian now, neither of them willing to blink, neither willing to look away. But then some movement from the man's hand caught Carson's eye again, and when he looked down the raven tattoo was gone.

LAUREN COULDN'T SHAKE the feeling of doom that had settled on her when she'd been arguing with Sebastian. Without his cooperation—and for more than just a night—they were screwed.

She had not been a visitor in her cousin's world since the age of eighteen. She remembered it all, the freedom, the sense of living authentically. But by the end of that rebellious summer when she'd run away from home and toyed with a life of living underground as a real witch—instead of being the repressed, half witch she lived as now—she'd succumbed to Sebastian's advice that she was far too intelligent and talented to not do something important with her life.

Her cousin had only one room left in the building, a bedroom with one bed and a cot he'd had brought up by an attendant with the understanding that Carson would sleep on it. World-weary as Sebastian was, he could be a little old-school about things on occasion.

"You look like you're seeing a ghost," Carson said as he sat down on the edge of the bed.

Lauren snapped out of her survey of the hotel room with its minimalist furnishings and its air of quiet where she'd spent that summer so long ago, hiding out from the world, a temporary rebel.

"I guess I am. A ghost of my own life, anyway. I was here once before."

"This isn't your first time running for your life?"

Lauren shook her head. "That's not why I was here. I was just running away from my overbearing family back then. Fresh out of high school and refusing to go along with their plans for me."

She sat down on the edge of the bed and winced at the throbbing pain in her foot. She didn't want to risk going to a hospital, so she'd either have to have Sebastian sew up the cut, or hope it healed well enough on its own. She was too tired to think about it right now.

But then she thought of the broken window glass, and how she must have left her blood behind on it. The witch hunters could sample her DNA from the blood, and they'd know for sure that she was a witch. But no, they didn't even have to do that, she realized. They'd surely take a hairbrush from her bathroom, and have all the evidence they'd need to kill her stuck in the bristles of her brush.

"Is your foot going to be okay?"

"Yeah, it's nothing." She hoped.

"So…you ran away to Hollywood and…?"

She shrugged, her gut twisting at the thought of a life she hadn't had the balls to live out back then.

"And nothing. I had a head full of stupid ideas, and I eventually realized I should be doing something productive with my life, so I gave in and went to Stanford just like Mother wanted."

"I hate to bring this up now, when your cousin is probably eavesdropping outside our door, but what the hell was with that tattoo on his arm. Did that thing—"

Lauren cut her gaze at him so sharply he went silent. Her heart pounded in her ears.

"Did it what?"

"Nothing. I was probably just seeing things. I'm delirious from exhaustion."

"Tell me what you think you saw," she demanded.

She'd never met a human who could see the movement of a witch's tattoo. She herself had a tattoo that did not move, but it was on the back of her neck, always hidden by her hair unless she chose to show it to someone.

She'd heard of humans who had witch blood, and who could see the supernatural even though they had no special gifts themselves, but it never would have occurred to her that Carson might be one of those humans.

"That raven. I swear it was looking at me. And then it was like it moved or something, and then it was gone."

"Are you sure?"

"I thought you saw it, too. I noticed you looking at it when it moved."

He'd definitely seen what she had. Did this mean he had witch ancestry?

Lauren took his large, perfectly shaped hands into hers. She turned them over so that she could see his palms, both wanting it to be true and yet knowing it would make no difference. Even if he had a bit of witch blood, he was still off-limits to her according to the elders. He was still human.

"You're not about to read my palms, are you?"

"No," she said, studying them intently.

"Then what the hell are you doing?"

"Could you shut up for one minute?"

Carson went silent.

The lines of his palms intersected, like human palms, but two of the major lines did not intersect with any others—one of the marks of witch blood.

"Pure-blooded humans cannot see the supernatural in action," she finally explained when she looked up at him. "You are not pure-blooded."

"What does that mean?"

"One or more of your ancestors was a witch."

His eyebrows shot up. "So I'm still wondering, what the hell does that mean?"

She shrugged. "Not much. You're human, but you might show an occasional witch trait, like the ability to see Sebastian's tattoo move."

Carson's expression rested somewhere between amused and freaked-out. "This is getting weirder by the minute."

Lauren didn't know how to break it to him, but it

was going to get a lot weirder before they were all done, she feared.

"I know it's a lot to take in at once—"

"And why the hell did your cousin look like he wanted to kill me?"

Because he probably did, but she didn't think it would be very wise politically to point that out at the moment. Somehow, she needed to find a way to get Sebastian and Carson on a cooperative playing field, and Carson was going to be the easier party to persuade.

Maybe Carson's bit of witch blood, if nothing else, would soften Sebastian up with regard to helping him.

"Sebastian has seen too much. To say he's jaded would be a serious understatement."

"He has a grudge against mortals?"

"You would, too, if you spent your life trying to save witches from the wrath of them."

"So he basically operates an underground railroad for the witch community. Can't he tell I'm a friend?"

"The witch hunters are subtle and have managed to infiltrate witch circles enough times to make Gandhi suspicious. Sebastian is only doing his job by being hypervigilant."

"Vigilant is one thing. Looking like he wants to rip my head off is another. I don't care how powerful a witch he is, I'm not going to sit around and let him treat me like dirt."

"I'll talk to him. It might help that you're not a

pure-blood. It's actually kind of rare for a human to exhibit any witch trait."

"What's up with that tattoo, anyway? Why'd it disappear?"

"Sebastian is a shape-shifter. The raven can act as his eyes when he needs it to."

"Wow. Pretty cool talent to have."

"Trust me, I'm envious."

Carson leaned back on the bed, shaking his head in disbelief. "I thought I'd seen and done it all."

"You haven't seen the half of it."

"I guess that shape-shifting thing must come in handy during sex, huh?"

Lauren winced. "I try not to imagine my cousin having sex."

"You haven't been with any shape-shifters?"

There was that one guy in Paris, but Lauren thought it better not to mention such things to mortals. They tended to get intimidated.

"No. Against the rules. I've probably had more mortal lovers than witch lovers."

"And you see the future?"

Lauren nodded, not sure how much more she wanted to reveal about herself. It was a new sensation, this telling her secrets to humans thing. It was beyond strange. And although it was kind of liberating, it was also scary.

"Occasionally, I have visions." She'd briefly explained in the car earlier that she had premonitions, that her ability to predict the future on occasion was what set her apart from a mortal—along with her superior senses and heightened sexual abilities—but she had been purposely vague.

"And I'm in them?"

"I was lying to Sebastian," she lied.

No sense in giving Carson all the information. And she knew it wouldn't do any good for him to know he'd inhabited more than a few of her dreams and fantasies. It was no surprise he'd turned up in a vision, too.

Well, except… The surprising part was that her vision of him had happened before she knew him. Twenty-something years before she knew him, when she had been a little girl.

Lauren hadn't realized right away when she met Carson that he'd been the man in her vision. It had taken a recurrence of the vision last week, identical to the one she'd had as a child—and had had on occasion every few years or so since—of a man and woman running scared on a beach in the half darkness, for her to understand a least some of its significance.

The couple was her and Carson.

"Why'd you lie?"

"He trusts my visions. It was a way of getting him to let you stay at least for tonight. I'll have to do some more convincing to make him understand why he has to help us both."

Carson had his arms behind his head. He looked tired, like a guy who hadn't expected to get swept up in someone else's life drama on an otherwise dull

Tuesday night. Lauren felt a pang of guilt now for the first time. She had been so caught up in worrying about keeping them both alive that she hadn't stopped to consider how screwed this situation could make Carson's life.

How screwed it *would* make his life, because there really wasn't any turning back now.

His gaze half-lidded, he asked, "How do these visions of yours happen?"

"Sometimes I can will one to happen, and sometimes I can't. I can close my eyes and try to see some event from a different moment in time—usually the future, but sometimes I can get a vision from the past that I didn't witness. Sometimes it happens, but sometimes it doesn't."

"There's no rhyme or reason to it?"

"Witches are usually at their most powerful as children. Unless we practice and learn to harness that power, it fades with time. So as a kid, I could control it more than I can now."

"Why didn't you practice more?"

"I did practice as much as I could, but it was forbidden by the elders."

"Who are these elders you keep talking about?"

"It's our way of referring to the generation in power. They enforce the rules that have been handed down from antiquity, and they make new rules based on their own feelings about our time. The ruling generation is strictly opposed to the practice of our gifts."

"Wouldn't that help you defeat the people who

want to kill you, though, if you could do your supernatural stuff?"

"They took the opposite strategy. Practicing our gifts can draw attention and therefore can make us more vulnerable to being detected, so the elders decided to stop using their gifts generations ago. Mine was the first generation anyone can remember who decided to resist that rule."

"Why did you?"

Lauren stretched out on the opposite side of the bed, her tired body finally giving in to the need to relax. "Two things—my sister, and a vision I had."

He frowned, obviously perplexed by her cryptic answer.

"What was the vision?"

"I can't tell you right now," she said, her voice revealing her exhaustion, but when she saw his disappointment, she added, "but I will eventually."

"What about your sister? I didn't even know you had a sister."

She thought of pointing out that they knew almost nothing about each other. A shared Las Vegas fling may have taught them about each other's bodies, but their lives were still a mystery.

The thought of Carson's body caused her gaze to roam over him, and even now, she felt a warm buzz between her legs. They'd been amazing together. Explosive. Unforgettable.

And she had to get her mind as far away as possible from that particular train of thought.

She needed to adjust to the reality that she'd tumbled a few steps down on Maslow's Hierarchy of Needs, and now she was supposed to be in survival mode, not I-need-to-get-laid mode.

"I have a younger sister named Corinne. She's the most powerful witch alive, far as anyone knows, and she gave the younger generation the will not to suppress our powers completely. So we practiced in hiding. Even so, most of us have seen our powers fade over the years."

"How about Corinne's? Have hers faded?"

Lauren shook her head, a chill tingling along her spine at the strength of her sister's power. "Not one bit. She's amazing when she is disciplined about what she's doing."

"Why can't she just wipe out the witch hunters then?"

"I have no doubt she could, if only it were that easy. Corinne is still young, and quite the rebel. She's got a lot to learn about discipline before she'll be truly effective."

"So, you each have some different gift—what's hers?"

"She can command the natural world around her. The wind, the weather, fire, water, even animals will do her bidding."

"Wow. That's intense."

"We were once out hiking around in the hills near our family's house, and we accidentally wandered into the territory of a mountain lion. I froze in terror, but my sister just stared into the animal's eyes until it lay down and let us go without even the slightest aggressive gesture."

"But she can't do that kind of thing remotely?"

"No, she has to be within sight of the animal or element she wants to influence."

"Must be kind of hard, living in the shadow of such a powerful sister."

Lauren smiled. "I've never thought of it that way. She's my baby sister, three years younger than me. We grew up taking care of each other in a weird way. My mother was lost in her own world."

"So she wasn't the affectionate type?"

"She's a bitter, fearful woman. She never wanted to be a witch. She's always wished she was human, and while I don't blame her, I also don't see the point of ruining your life wishing for a different one."

"So she never practiced witchcraft?"

"Never. She is in charge of the family winery, and I think she was always horrified that my sister and I embraced being witches. It made us foreign to her."

"What about your father?"

"Witch families don't often include patriarchal figures in the way mortal families do. It's considered perfectly normal to have children with or without the paternal father sticking around to help raise the kids."

At the thought of kids—or more precisely the activity that made them—Lauren let her gaze roam over Carson's body. She wanted desperately to reach out and touch him, to forget everything else and ease the aching they both had to be feeling.

Running for her life wasn't supposed to make her horny. Her body wasn't supposed to be channeling her excess adrenaline into her libido. But it was. Then a wave of guilt hit her, because she'd endangered Carson's life, pulled him into a situation for which he had no coping skills, and here she was thinking about sex instead of thinking about the gravity of the situation.

"Do you even know your dad then?" Carson asked, jarring her out of her thoughts.

"I do. He lives in France, and we've visited him a few times. He's actually bisexual—which is pretty common among male witches—and living with a man now. I don't think he was ever comfortable with the idea that he had children with my mother. It wasn't exactly his style."

"Do witches live longer than humans?"

Lauren frowned. She'd never considered the matter before, oddly enough. "Sure, I guess so. I mean, I had a great-great-grandfather who lived to be like a hundred and five, but other than that, normal life spans."

"So back to the men thing. Where do they fit into the witch culture?"

"We grew up around uncles and grandfathers and such. It's just more casual, less structured as to who is a father figure for whom. I was close to one of my uncles—my mom's youngest brother Adrien who is an artist—and I guess he was like my father figure."

"Adrien Parish the San Francisco artist?"

"You know of him?"

"I saw one of his shows recently—the biomorphic cement installation pieces. Impressive stuff."

"He's amazing. Funny thing is, for the sake of the clan he's always tried not to achieve any kind of success or notoriety. He's made his art as unsellable and weird as possible just to stay out of the limelight, and that's what has started to bring him into it."

"I was given the assignment of finding a good piece of art for the lobby of the ad agency where I work. That's what I was doing combing the galleries. His stuff was definitely too weird for corporate America."

"So you got the big Bronson and Wade promotion, I heard. Congratulations."

"Pretty crazy when I wasn't even competing for it. Lucky for me Macy and Griffin left the agency."

Lauren smiled. During the infamous Vegas weekend Macy and Griffin had been competing for a promotion to Creative Director at the same advertising agency.

Instead of taking the prize job, they'd fallen in love, and decided to leave the agency to form their own firm. They'd been happy with the decision, even with all the stress and uncertainty of starting a new business at the same time they were starting a new relationship with each other.

In the aftermath, Carson had gotten the promotion, and Lauren had spent the past few months avoiding him at all costs. Now here they were, locked in a room together with nowhere else to go.

Life was crazy.

When she looked over at Carson again, she could see that he was struggling to stay awake. Under any other circumstances, sexual tension would be crackling between them, and knowing the two of them, they'd have been rolling around sweating and exchanging body fluids by now.

But these were no ordinary circumstances. It was nearly four in the morning, and their lives had been turned upside down, inside out and tossed against the rocks for good measure. They were both exhausted, and scared, among other things.

Likely they'd exchange body fluids again some other time, but not tonight. Lauren would have liked to think of herself as capable of maintaining an extra measure of self-control, for Carson's well-being, because the more he had her, the less other women would satisfy. Too bad she knew she couldn't. She wanted him almost as much as he wanted her, and soon enough, she would have him again.

She would have no choice. Her desires had been denied for too long.

Just when she thought he was asleep, he asked, his eyes still closed, "What does it feel like to have a vision? How does it happen?"

She tried to figure out how to describe it. She

closed her eyes and imagined. "I feel like I'm in a trance, like I'm concentrating really hard on something and I can't look away from it. And the images appear in my head."

"Tell me the truth. Was I really in one of your visions?"

She was so tired, the very act of closing her eyes had put her on the edge of a dream state, and she answered with her guard down, "Yes, we were in trouble. Running together on the beach, our lives in danger. That's how I know I have to protect you."

But she didn't tell him the rest. She didn't tell him that she had two kinds of visions, ones that came to her with a startling clarity—those were the ones she knew were real, that she couldn't change—and ones that came to her like a dream, fuzzy and weird. The second kind were always changeable. They were her chance to alter the future, to make a choice about her fate or someone else's.

She couldn't alter her and Carson's fate, though. She'd only had that one crystal clear vision of him, filled with a sense of fear, of impending doom. She had the burden of knowing he would witness her death on that cold beach at night. It had taken her years to understand that she was the woman in the vision, and that she'd been shown the moment of her own death.

Not exactly cheery news to walk around with, but she'd learned some things were bigger than herself. And she believed her death would serve an important purpose.

She was drifting off to sleep when she felt Carson take her hand in his. Her eyes fluttered open at the movement, and she saw him stretched out next to her, his hand holding hers. Not exactly the physical contact she'd been aching for, but still…nice.

Nice enough to chase away her fear for a little while.

This, she knew, might be the last time they'd ever feel even a little safe together.

5

HER MOUTH WAS ON HIM.

Kissing, licking, teasing. First his neck, then his shoulder, his bicep, his forearm, his fingers.

Oh yeah, his fingers. She was sucking them as if they were…

And then, his belly. And lower still. His cock strained, aching for the same attention. She didn't disappoint. Her hot wet mouth took him in, sucking gently, and he buried his hands in her silky hair and gasped at the mind-blowing sensations.

Carson could not remember when he'd wanted a woman so badly. "Lauren," he murmured. "Man, I've missed you."

Her fingertips trailed up his inner thigh, then over his balls, and she gripped him, massaging as she worked that magic with her mouth.

And then in an instant she was on top of him, straddling him, her naked, hot flesh only inches away. He grasped her hips, thrust into her tight, wet folds, realizing a moment too late that he hadn't bothered with a condom. He felt too damn frenzied to care.

This was the thing he lived for at this moment—being inside of Lauren, claiming her, having his way with her until she melted like butter on his cock. Until he spilled into her the way he'd fantasized about countless times in the past few months.

Their bodies slapped together as he thrust his hips and she moved in time with him. She was far better than he'd remembered. She felt too good to let go of again.

He was lost, and found, all at once.

Quickly, she reached her climax, and he held her heavy breasts in his palms and kissed her as she came. Her body contracted around him, wet and sated. He held her until she calmed, and then he thrust into her more fiercely than before. In a frenzy, he moved without thinking. Only feeling.

Over and over, again and again, until he, too, felt an orgasm coming on so strong he was powerless to slow it. The sensation hit him like a wall of water, and he rode it to its sweet, delicious end, overcome with the pulsing contractions.

More kissing, more caressing, more limbs tangled together. She was beside him, then under him, always against him—because he'd never let her get away.

He was delirious with the joy of finally having her again. So delirious he could feel tears on his cheeks, and he was not the kind of guy who ever shed a tear....

Carson opened his eyes, and he saw only the gray darkness of early morning. His eyes were dry. He was still dressed. His cock was hard and straining against his jeans. His mouth was parched and tasted bad. Lauren was not beneath him, but rather, as indicated by the sound of her breathing, she was on the other side of the bed.

Their hands were the only parts of their bodies still touching.

He whispered a curse to himself and ran his free hand over his face. He needed a shave, he decided as he yawned and stretched, finally letting go of Lauren.

He'd dreamed that entire episode. *Dreamed* was putting it mildly, though. It had been the most vivid, intense dream of his life. He rarely had sexual dreams anymore, and this one took the prize. For sure.

He felt as if he really had just had sex, his body was so full of sexual energy.

Then he noticed that Lauren wasn't sleeping soundly. Her breathing was fast and shallow, and growing more so. She was starting to move around on the bed. He sat up on his elbow and watched her in the darkness.

Her face held a slight tension, and her lips parted as she moaned softly and arched her back. Carson's dick strained harder.

Could she really have been experiencing the same kind of dream he had? Was this some kind of supernatural witch thing, to share sex dreams?

It took every ounce of his willpower not to unzip

his fly and mount her as he watched her moan and writhe. Her breath grew even shallower, until it sounded as if she herself was about to come.

Sweat broke out on his forehead, and he could feel himself leaking in his jeans.

Should he wake her and make love to her?

No, she wouldn't want that.

But watching her dream like this was the most erotic thing he'd seen in a long time. He wasn't sure how much more of it he could take before he'd have to get some relief.

He didn't have to wonder any longer. Her body tensed against the bed, her back arched harder, and she cried out the same way he remembered her sounding in Las Vegas when she came.

He watched, tortured, as the orgasm overtook her and her breathing slowed, then, finally settled to silence.

"Christ," he muttered, nearly insane with desire, and her eyes fluttered open.

She appeared disoriented for a moment, and then her gaze fixed on him.

"What…?" she said, her voice raspy.

"What just happened?"

"Yeah?"

"From my end, it looked to me like you came in your sleep."

She sat up on her elbow, frowning, and shuddered.

"Actually," she said slowly. "I did."

"Happen often?"

"No."

"I had a pretty erotic dream myself. Starring you, as a matter of fact."

She looked at him curiously. "You did?"

He nodded. "I don't think I got the grand finale you got, though," he said as he looked down at his erection.

"Wow."

"Is that some kind of witch thing? Shared erotic dreams?"

She lay back down and sighed heavily. "Um, yeah, I guess. I never thought of it as strictly a witch phenomenon, but I suppose it is. Maybe you were able to experience it because of your little bit of witch blood."

"Any idea how often this kind of thing happens? Because, you know, if we have to stay in close quarters and aren't allowed to touch each other—"

"We might go insane," she filled in.

"Well I will. I mean, at least you got yours in your dream."

She laughed and covered her face. "I don't know how often it happens. I think it's sort of a side effect of pent-up sexual energy."

"Great. I've got more than my share of that right now."

Carson dropped heavily onto his pillow, his cock stiff as ever, and the thought of going into the bathroom to take care of himself about as appealing as taking a sledgehammer to the problem.

This was going to be one long-ass stay at the Hotel Hell.

SEBASTIAN PARISH KNEW more than most people that trying to lose one's troubles in the flesh of a woman was a risky prospect, at best. For one thing, it might not have been a popular notion in the postmodern world, but as far as he could tell, women were by their very nature the embodiment of trouble. So even if one care might be forgotten through sex, a whole new storm of problems would be brewing.

But every once in a while, he would try again. Even now, with the pretty girl in the torn jeans and black tank top kneeling before him, his cock in her mouth, he knew he was doomed to fail.

In the dim morning light, he watched her red lips against his skin, watching her head bob back and forth as the sensation of her wet tongue and lips against him caused tension to coil inside him. He should have had an orgasm by now.

She'd been working on him for maybe a half hour, and while he was enjoying himself vaguely, he feared he wasn't going to come. But he didn't have the heart to tell her to stop, either. After working all night and into the morning, he should have been going to bed. The sun had risen, and this girl, left over from the crowd of revelers, had wandered into his office.

She was one of the lost ones. They came from everywhere, having heard he was powerful and that he provided a safe haven for witches who had nowhere else to go. He tried his best. But he felt lost, too, and he grew weary being everyone else's rescuer.

Who would rescue him? Certainly not this girl, with her probable drug habit and her reckless eyes. But somehow he had become the protector of every witch like her, the lost generation who'd been waiting for the powerful to rise up and lead them to a better life, free from fear.

Her mouth on his cock, he was not such a great protector. But he could see it in her eyes that she wanted to give him something back, and some heartless part of him wanted to oblige her in this small, selfish way.

Maybe... Maybe if he could close his eyes and imagine a different woman, a different set of circumstances...

He did. His breath quickened as he brought to mind the image of the woman he'd never wanted to love but who'd nonetheless haunted his dreams for months now.

Maia. Why did she always appear in his fantasies this way, when he wanted so badly to forget?

But it was Maia. Always Maia. He imagined her curly mane of hair, her impetuous smile, her small white teeth, her tiny, perfect breasts, her torso that snaked against the sheets, silky and warm beneath him.

Maia.

His breathing quickened more, and as he imagined plunging himself between her legs, imagined her here in this office with him, he felt his release coming. Faster, closer, almost there. Then, the rush of release, blinding white pleasure for a few moments, until it was gone.

He looked down at the girl, who was not Maia, and remorse flooded his chest, wiping away that momentary euphoria. This girl, like so many others, was nameless to him. Her dark brown hair was not Maia's, her slight, lovely body was not Maia's, and her warm, wet mouth was not Maia's.

A deep, crushing regret settled on his chest, and he nearly gasped for breath. But no, his lungs still worked, as did most of his other major organs. It was his heart, he suspected, that had died. Otherwise, how could he have done what he'd just done?

He stepped back from the girl as she stood and smiled coyly at him. She took a step closer, pressing her body to him, to kiss him, but he grasped her arms and said, "I'm sorry."

He leaned in and brushed her lips lightly with his, then set her aside. He tucked himself back into his jeans and zipped his fly.

"What?" she said, her eyes wounded.

"I shouldn't have."

"Oh." She had probably heard the stories, that this was what he did. That he never let anyone in, that he used women, that he was incapable of real intimacy.

But still, even with the rumors that floated around

the club about him, there were always women willing to offer themselves up as the one who might get through to him, who might reawaken his dead heart.

None could, yet he didn't always have it in him to turn them away.

"I'll go," she finally said, when he made no move toward her.

He nodded. "I'm sorry."

"Whatever." She opened a compact and checked her blood-red lipstick, which, remarkably, was only a little smeared.

A man with a heart would have taken her into his arms and kissed her, drawn her down to the desk and made love to her. But Sebastian wasn't that man and everyone knew it.

That knowledge didn't make him feel any less ashamed.

His physical need overcame him regularly, turned him into something he didn't want to be, but the need was still there. Always there.

"I'll go," she said, turning toward the door. "I have to work tonight."

Sebastian watched silently as she left the office. He'd given her a job serving drinks at the club a week ago, and she'd spent the time since stealing glances at him every chance she got. It was the burden he had, being a shape-shifter, knowing what people did behind his back. He always saw. He always knew, whether he wanted to or not.

A moment later, the door closed, and he was alone. On the wall, the clock read 8:10 a.m. And he thought of his cousin. She probably needed to sleep longer, but he doubted she'd really be asleep.

He went into the bathroom and cleaned up, and as he did so, he caught sight of himself in the mirror. He was starting to look like death. Like an addict, though he never used the drugs that some of the weaker witches used to mask their pain at being outcasts.

But sometimes it wasn't a drug or a disease that drove people close to death. Sometimes, he knew all too well, it was simply pain.

His eyes had gotten hollow, with purple shadows beneath, and he'd lost weight, giving his bone structure a disturbing prominence. His long black hair had gotten limp and greasy, and always looked that way no matter how often he washed it. It draped his shoulders like the cloak of a dead man.

And yet he had other things hc needed to focus on besides his own self-indulgent pain. Lauren was in trouble. Lauren, whom he'd adored since childhood, whom he loved more than a sister. They'd grown up with the common bond of knowing death could seize them any moment they made a wrong move—a bond made all the stronger by the fact that they'd chosen to tempt fate by rebelling against the elders' rules.

He left the bathroom and headed upstairs to the room where he'd deposited Lauren and the mortal a few hours ago. He needed to talk to her while the mortal was still asleep. His anger flared at the thought of Lauren consorting with such an obviously smug, useless asshole.

Sebastian knew his cousin was too good for a mortal, but what could he say?

He'd have to think of something. He could not risk the danger of allowing a mortal to remain in their midst.

He stood outside the room about to knock on the door, when she opened it. She startled at the sight of him, then gathered her wits and covered her mouth with her finger to urge him not to speak. Over her shoulder, Sebastian could see the mortal still in bed sleeping.

Mortals were lazy—another of the ways they were inferior to witches, who only needed a few hours rest each day.

She closed the door behind her, and when they'd made their way down to Sebastian's office, she finally spoke.

"I need you to help Carson, too, and for more than just a day," she said, cutting straight to the issue.

She knew him too well. Sebastian bit his tongue. It wouldn't do any good to argue at the moment.

"Sit," he said, nodding at the chair across from his desk. "Tell me what you know about this mortal."

"First off, he's not totally mortal. He has some witch blood. I can see it in his palms."

Sebastian stared at her, unimpressed by the news.

"So what if his great-great-great-grandmother was part witch. He's still mortal."

"And he's also part witch. Our blood runs through him, too. Keep that in mind."

He shrugged. It didn't really matter to him. Anyone who'd grown up as a normal mortal knew nothing of the fear and persecution that came with being a witch.

"He's totally innocent, Sebastian. He's a friend of my best friend, and I know for a fact that he's not out to get us."

"How do you know that?"

"I just know. He's appeared in one of my visions, and I have the absolute feeling that he's someone I need to help me—and that I have to help him, too."

"I don't help mortals, Lauren."

"Do it for me."

A sick feeling settled in Sebastian's gut. He thought of the other mortals. Three had shown up here in the past two years, and he would have to tell her about them.

"The underground isn't the safe haven it once was, I'm afraid."

Lauren's eyes grew startled. "What do you mean?"

"I'm afraid The Order may be infiltrating. Three times, I've had mortals show up here in the past two years, and they were all one of them."

"Witch hunters? Found their way here? How?"

Sebastian shook his head. "I wish I knew."

"So what happened? How did you find them out?"

He said nothing, but she glanced at the raven tattoo on his arm and understanding dawned on her expression. "You saw."

"I don't know where they came from, or how they found us, but they did."

"But…what did you do?"

His gaze dropped to the surface of his desk. The truth many of their generation overlooked was that in facing down The Order, they had to also face that they had to kill, or be killed.

He leveled his gaze at her again. "I took care of the situation."

"You…"

"Killed them."

The color drained from her face. "But it's forbidden."

"A lot of what we do is forbidden. If we agree to break one of the rules of the elders, we are silently agreeing that it's okay to break them all, are we not?"

She leaned over and put her elbows on her knees, and covered her face with her hands. She wasn't crying, but he knew she was reeling. So was he, in his own way. It felt good somehow to hand the burden of his secret over to someone else, even if only for a moment.

"God, Sebastian. How did you— Where did you—"

"It's better if you don't know."

"Maybe the more important question is how they found this place. We have to figure that out."

"*We* don't have to do anything. You're on the run from The Order, so our first priority is keeping you safe from them. Let me worry about the other stuff."

"I'm such a goddamn fool," she said, and this time her voice broke, and she began to cry.

"We all are, in our own way."

"I'm sorry. I didn't realize I'd be endangering you by coming here."

"It's okay. It's my job to protect you," he said, but something in his voice sounded flat.

Dead.

She pulled herself together and wiped away the dampness in her eyes. "I can take care of myself," she said. "You have your own problems to worry about."

"Don't start talking like that. I'm not going to let you go off on your own and get yourself killed."

"I'm responsible for Carson's safety, and I won't let him down. So if you're not going to help him, too, I have no need for your help."

"You'd really let a mortal come between us?"

"It's not as simple as that, and you know it."

"It is, Lauren. We're family. Nothing, especially not some punk-ass mortal, should stand between us."

"He's a friend."

"More than a friend," he said, his gaze pinning her with his accusation.

"Yes, he's been my lover in the past."

He didn't feel jealousy, exactly. He thought of Lauren in the same way he would think of a sister. But he did feel a surge of protectiveness for her that verged on the irrational.

"Why?" he asked.

"You know why."

"I don't sleep with mortals."

"You've got access to a lot more witches than I do. You're surrounded by them. I, on the other hand, am surrounded by mortals every day."

He tried to put aside his distaste at the idea long enough to imagine himself in her situation. All he could imagine was being celibate. He didn't have the slightest desire for inadequate mortal flesh.

"I guess I'd have to be in your shoes to understand."

"You've seen the worst of humanity. You have a lot more reason to hate mortals than I do."

"Perhaps that's true."

"I worry about you. I think you let the hate consume you. You don't look so good, you know."

Sebastian thought of his own grizzly reflection and couldn't disagree. "Thanks, cousin."

"I mean, you look tired, and thin."

She didn't know about Maia. No one knew.

"What is it?" she asked.

He said nothing.

"The killings…are they weighing on you that much?"

He shook his head.

"Something else then…girl problems?"

He said nothing again, but her expression said she knew that she'd nailed the truth.

"Who?"

"You don't know her."

"What happened?"

"One of the mortals—she led him here. He was her lover, and she came here for protection, but she didn't realize he was the one she needed protecting from."

"So you killed the guy."

"I did, and she hated me for it. She thought I was a monster after that."

"Where did she go?"

"I had to send her away. Gave her a new identity, helped her get started in Miami. I haven't heard from her since."

"But you fell in love with her?"

Sebastian stared at the black, scuffed surface of the desk again. "I don't know why. I just looked at her and thought I saw my home."

"She didn't return the attraction?"

"In a weird way, I think she sort of did. Which made her want to get away from me even more after what had happened with the mortal."

"She thought you were motivated by jealousy."

He nodded. "Maybe I sort of was. But I had to kill him, regardless."

"What was her name?"

"Maia," he choked out before it could catch in his throat. He hadn't said her name aloud in a long time.

"I've never seen you like this over a woman. How long has it been?"

"Eight months."

"It'll get better," she said, but her eyes still looked worried.

"Don't worry about me. Right now we need to think about where you should go."

"Given my choice, I want to stay here with Carson."

"No. That's out of the question."

Lauren leaned forward in her chair, resting her elbows on her knees again, and she looked at him the way she did when she wasn't going to change her mind.

"You need help right now, and I can help you."

"No, you can't."

"Maybe what we need is to lead the guys who are after me right here, so we can capture them and get information about The Order. This could be the opportunity we've been waiting for."

"I'm not going to risk your safety like that. Someone else can be a decoy, but not you."

"My visions have been getting more frequent. Corinne thinks that means something."

Sebastian wanted to argue further, but at the mention of Corinne he went silent. His little cousin, of any witch on Earth, would know.

"What else did she say?" he finally asked, but he was torn between feelings of dread and curiosity.

The curiosity, he understood, but the dread gave him pause. Why? The answer came to him in an instant. All these years of hoping and looking forward to the uprising, he'd never considered the very real possibility that they might not succeed in it. He'd never considered that Lauren's vision of their future might be wrong, or that they had all their hopes pinned o a pipe dream.

He'd never considered it, and he wouldn't start now. They had no choice but to succeed.

6

OCCASIONALLY, LAUREN envied the power her sister's name evoked. Mention of Corinne Parish was enough to send any witch of her generation into reverent silence. But with that considerable power came a huge burden, one Lauren didn't envy at all. She'd never aspire to be the savior of an entire generation.

And as a big sister entirely too familiar with Corinne's personality, Lauren wasn't sure she wanted that burden to fall on her wild, impetuous younger sibling, either. But it was the way it was. It was the way it had always been.

Corinne, for her part, didn't seem to mind. She was too headstrong and full of herself to slow down and consider the weight of her burden or think about the consequences her every decision had.

Lauren stared into Sebastian's bloodshot eyes, and she knew she absolutely was not going to leave him here alone. He needed her help, whether he realized it or not, and she was going to find a way to give it.

"Corinne said she was beginning to feel like it was time. Like the season was coming."

"The season?"

"That's how she's started describing the uprising."

He nodded. "Makes sense, I guess."

Corinne's ability to control nature was stunning to the uninitiated. She could command the weather to change in an instant, shift the ocean tides, summon the wind, bring the animals to heel at her side. Hers was the rarest of powers among witches, because in harnessing the natural world, she could increase her own strength until almost nothing could stop her. An awesome power in the hands of someone who tended not to think before acting. This was compounded by the fact that the purity and intensity of her gifts were at levels higher than any witch anyone could remember.

The elders only had an inkling of how strong Corinne really was. If they'd known the truth... Lauren could not allow herself to think about what might have happened.

On top of her other activities, Corinne had a sense of intuition that was uncanny. While all witches were intuitive, Corinne could take any situation and foresee its logical conclusion more quickly than anyone Lauren had ever known. When her little sister said something was going to happen, it happened.

"What else did she say?"

"Only that I should keep myself ready to act, not go too far."

"So that's why you really want to stay here? You think Corinne will want us all together when it starts happening."

It. The event they'd all been fantasizing about their entire lives.

"Yes," Lauren said. "She will."

"We've been living on the edge for so long, it's hard to believe the revolution we've been waiting for might finally happen."

"Tell me about it. I feel like it's become this unattainable dream. Despite wanting it so much, I've almost accepted it will never really happen. Now even the suggestion that it's imminent freaks me out a little."

Sebastian nodded. "Have you ever tried to imagine how it will go down? What our lives will really be like after?"

"I've always imagined that we'd experience real freedom to be truly ourselves… But maybe that's a little naive."

"Why do you say that?"

"Because in my mind I too often skip over the hard part—the actual uprising. I don't know how it will go or how long it will take."

"Your vision only told you it would be successful, right? No other details?"

Lauren nodded. "Yeah. I saw us celebrating victory against The Order." It had happened so long ago without recurring that the image was fuzzy to her now.

And she sometimes worried that, because it had not recurred, it was perhaps a faulty vision, that her longing for a successful uprising had sparked it rather than insight into actual future events. But she could not let those fears dissuade them from what had to be done.

"I've thought about how to defeat The Order. We'd have to infiltrate it and bring it down from within, but they're worse than the CIA when it comes to security."

"No easy task, that's for sure. How would witches get in without being detected? I guess we could use mortals but how could we trust that The Order didn't brainwash them?" Lauren sighed. "I don't doubt we can do it, but it's such a huge maneuver it overwhelms me."

"I hear you, but we have to hope Corinne will be up for it. Even if the rest of us aren't."

"You're right," Lauren said. She did want to believe they had a future in which they could live openly as witches without fear.

It occasionally struck her as odd to think of her baby sister launching a revolution—especially a baby sister as out of control as Corinne. Lauren was too familiar with the varied aspects of Corinne's personality—too often had witnessed her being impulsive or selfish or stubborn—to see only the leader who would guide them to victory. But then again, they'd know Corinne would take charge since their childhood. The basic plan they'd hatched in the hills near the vineyards under the cypress trees had never changed in all these years.

Sebastian studied Lauren intently before seeming to come to a decision. "Only because you say your vision includes the mortal, I will let him stay here for now. But the first time he crosses me or takes any unnecessary risk, I will remove him. His life doesn't matter to me."

Lauren's stomach clenched at his words. Sebastian had changed since she'd seen him last. Something in him had hardened. And even though his earlier confession should have warned her, she now fully understood he was capable of things that she was not.

"Thank you," she said. "I owe you my life."

At least she had time to figure out how best to aid Sebastian, how best to protect Carson and how best to help defeat The Order. For the first time since she'd heard the men outside her door, she felt as though she had some tiny measure of control.

And with this reprieve Sebastian had granted, she knew she walked a fine line where Carson was concerned. Now, more than ever, she had to deny her desire for him so as not to piss off Sebastian and give him justification to *remove* Carson. Lust and concern for him battled within her. She only hoped that Carson did nothing to tip the lust advantage because she wasn't convinced she could resist him.

CARSON WOKE UP with another raging, rock-hard erection. Or perhaps the one he'd gotten earlier had never gone away. Entirely and frustratingly possible.

At least he hadn't been plagued by any more unfulfilled erotic dreams. A guy could only take so much.

He stared down at his dick straining against his jeans and struggled to think past his sexually charged state to remember where he was and why he felt as though he needed to sleep for another ten hours or so.

There was also the simultaneous need to piss. An ache so deep he felt as if he hadn't gone to the bathroom in ages.

He blinked in the morning light, and as soon as the fog began to lift from his brain, he remembered why his erection was so damn urgent. Lauren. Lying next to him. He looked over at where he thought she would be, but no one was there.

The rumpled cover and pillows on the other side of the bed told him that his night sleeping in the same bed with her hadn't been a cruel dream, but the room was silent. When he turned his head, he spotted a note on her pillow.

Be back soon. Gone to find breakfast. LP.

Her handwriting was small and exact, the writing of a scientist. Not a flight attendant. Man, he must have been blinded by sex that weekend to have ever believed that she was anything but a brilliant researcher. If he'd bothered to look past her hot bod and actually listened to her, he would have known she was way more intelligent than she pretended to be. But no, he'd been too focused on getting her on her back—and against the wall, and straddling him—again that he hadn't seen the holes in her story.

Before his mind replayed a selection of his favorite steamy memories from that weekend, Carson got out of bed. He stumbled across the room, his tired body not quite ready yet to give up its fight to get some rest, and made his way to the bathroom where he relieved himself. Then he stretched, splashed some water on his face, and went back out to the bed to take stock of his situation.

He'd slept in his clothes, which were now rumpled but probably good for wearing another day. Besides, he had nothing else to wear. The room had a phone, but no television or computer. He did have his cell phone, too, although he'd been instructed not to turn it on or call anyone.

So he was stuck here until Lauren returned. And he was still damn tired. He stretched out on the bed again and closed his eyes, figuring he'd probably need all the rest he could get if they had to be on the run again soon.

But his mind wouldn't quiet down. He wasn't sure what to make of all the witch stuff—the magic and the secrets and all that—but he wasn't finding himself feeling all that skeptical, either. And it did explain why Lauren was so much more thrilling to him than any mortal woman.

Because she wasn't mortal.

He laughed to himself at the thought.

Then a sound at the door silenced him, and he sat up on his elbow as Lauren reentered the room. She looked refreshed in the morning light, in a way that Carson distinctly did not feel. Her skin was luminous, her eyes bright as she took in the sight of him.

"Hey," she said. "I brought breakfast."

He then noticed the two bags in her hand. She crossed the room, and on the table next to the window, she took out two covered cups of coffee and two pastries.

"You went out?"

She shook her head. "Sebastian brought us some stuff."

"You talked to him?"

"Yes, he's agreed to let us stay here for now, until we have a better plan."

"But what does that even mean? Do you have any way of catching the guys who are after you?"

Lauren sipped her coffee and frowned. "I have some memory of what they look like. I think I'm going to put all the information into a computer database that we have about The Order, including physical descriptions of those men."

"Maybe you could get an artist's rendering of them."

She nodded. "Sebastian can draw very well. I'll ask him to do it."

Carson took a bite of his pastry, a chocolate croissant, and realized for the first time how hungry he was.

"So what else can we do? We can't just sit here. Can't you get the police involved or something?"

She already said no to calling the police last night in the car, but he couldn't help asking again. It just seemed insane that there were murderous thugs after them, and they had to battle them on their own.

"No, we never involve the police," she said, as if it were perfectly logical not to.

"Doesn't Sebastian have some idea of what you should do? I thought he was the big protector guy."

"He would have me take a new identity and leave the country, but he's overreacting out of protectiveness."

"I want to help, however I can," Carson said.

Lauren frowned. "For now, we just sit tight and stay out of sight. I'll keep talking to Sebastian until we have a better plan."

Easier said than done. Carson thought of his erection, which was back in a big way now that Lauren was in the room, and the crazy-lucid dream they'd shared last night. He craved her just as strongly as he had before, only now there was all this intrigue and danger and denial that should have been tempering his libido.

But his dick didn't care about witches or witch hunters. His dick only cared that Lauren was in the room, and that she was the most arousing woman he'd ever met, and that the dream he'd had last night was a vivid reminder of how amazing she was in bed.

He smiled. "I'm sure we'll think of something to do."

"SHE WON'T BE EASY to catch."

"No, she's left San Francisco by now, I'm sure."

Lars Klein stared out the window of Lauren Parish's apartment at the gray San Francisco day. Fog hung low in the air, giving the afternoon a chill and a damp scent of sea air. They'd combed every inch of the apartment twice, considering every bit of information a clue to the witch's possible whereabouts.

The video camera they'd left behind when they'd pursued her had given them the image of a man entering the doorway of her apartment for a moment, but nothing else. They didn't know if he was a witch or a mortal, and they had no idea who he was to Lauren Parish.

His partner Noam was reading files on the computer, making note of names and addresses.

Lars did not hate witches. His purpose in life was to kill them, but not to hate them. His father, and his father's father, and all the Kleins who had come before, had been witch hunters. He had been born into the calling, so to speak.

He'd been raised in the secret society known only as The Order, and for as long as he could remember, he had been taught that his purpose in life was to rid the world of witches, because they upset the natural order.

Some tried to claim it was a battle between good and evil, or a struggle between morality and immorality. The truth was simply a matter of keeping nature in balance. That was the ultimate purpose of The Order, as Lars saw it, and anything more was a bastardization of the truth.

"She's been careful," Noam muttered. "I'm not finding much in the way of personal contacts on her computer. Just food delivery places, a dry cleaner, crap like that."

Lars turned from the window and surveyed the disheveled room. They'd torn the place apart, and by now, it seemed they'd found everything they were going to find.

"She could be across the border into Mexico now, or on a plane to Europe for all we know."

"But we're assuming she's one of them," Noam said as he closed the laptop. Lars watched as the younger man packed it in a case to take with them.

"I think it's a safe assumption. She fled faster than any mortal would have, and she didn't call the police."

Not that it would have made a difference if she had. The Order had been evading the police's lackadaisical eye for too long to find them even the slightest deterrent to their mission.

"The family resemblance thing has been a false lead before."

"Lauren Parish has the eyes of a witch. There's

something hard in those eyes that I've never seen in a mortal. It's the hardness that comes with the knowledge that one has power over other people," Lars said.

"Let her goddamn powers save her now."

The two men gathered up the last few things they wanted to take from the apartment, then slipped out. Their plumbers' uniforms were a safe decoy in case they ran into any neighbors, but they exited the building without being spotted.

Five minutes later, they were sitting in their van, studying a map of California.

"There's one obvious place for a witch to go in this state," Lars muttered, as he eyed the southern portion of the state.

"L.A."

Lars nodded. "West Hollywood. If she's anywhere..."

"I'll bet she's there."

They'd only recently begun to crack the underground network that seemed to exist around the famous neighborhood that was known more as a place to look for stars than anything else. What was hidden beneath the glitz and tourist bustle was a labyrinth witch haven.

Gaining access to it without getting killed was a challenge in itself, but The Order was making progress. The Order didn't have the advantage of supernatural powers, but the most skilled of their hunters, Lars among them, had keen senses of intuition that could detect witch from human. It helped that witches often had distinctive physical beauty that set them apart from humans. But mostly The Order relied on traditional spy methods to seek out the witches, and when necessary, DNA testing to positively identify them. The Order was experimenting with technologies that helped them differentiate the electro-magnetic fields that were created when witches used their supernatural powers.

This generation of witches had proven to be their first real challenge in centuries. Instead of cowering, some of these younger witches had chosen to fight back. More frequently than ever before, members of The Order had been killed trying to track down their prey.

Who had done the killing, they didn't know. They only knew that they were getting close to something big, and it would take skill and patience to find the truth.

Lauren Parish, with her carelessness, might lead them right where they needed to go, if they were lucky. And Lars, for all his years of witch hunting, had come to know that luck was always on his side.

To be a hunter was to understand when he had to let go of reason and rely on the senses, to follow his animal instincts just as quickly as he followed his intellect. Lars, born of The Order, was above all else a hunter.

He would hunt down Lauren Parish, with her cold, unrelenting beauty and her steely eyes, and he would take her. He would show her just how little power she had, and then he would rid the world of her for good. His cock stirred at the thought.

They headed toward 19th Avenue, which would take them south, out of the city, and he could only suspect, closer to their prey.

7

THE NIGHTCLUB WAS EMPTY, but a Nine Inch Nails song still pumped from the speakers, and overhead strobe lights flashed. Lauren had never lain down on the dance floor, and she was surprised how clean it was, how smooth and shiny.

But then Carson was on top of her, mounting her, and she forgot about the floor against her naked flesh. She gasped as he penetrated her, stretching and pushing into her where she ached most. Wrapping her legs around his hips, she pulled him closer until he filled her all the way.

"Closer"... That was the name of the song playing, she recalled in a haze as he claimed her mouth and thrust his tongue in.

She dug her nails into his hard shoulders, and she returned his fierce kiss with her own. Her muscles were coiling so tightly around his cock, it was all she could do to hold on to the edge without letting herself come so soon.

So fast. It was happening so fast. They were sweating...a pool of it forming between her breasts, and on her belly. His sweat and hers, mingled together.

He felt too good inside of her. So good she couldn't imagine this ending, couldn't imagine letting go.

Why were they on the dance floor? And where was everyone? The questions faded as he pumped into her faster.

She watched his face, dark and intense, his gaze locked on hers, never looking away, and she wondered why she'd wanted to hold off. She couldn't imagine saying no to this ever again.

So what if they were lost? So what if their lives were ruined? So what if they died tomorrow, as long as they had each other right now?

Inside her, his cock grew stiffer, harder, and he pressed deeper into her as he neared climax. He was hitting her in just the right spot…so right…so good…she was almost there…

He cried out as he spilled into her, and she let herself go with him. She came hard, her body overcome, her every nerve stimulated.

And then she was in a dark room. Lauren blinked, looking around. The hotel room. The clock radio read 5:00 a.m.

Her body was drenched with sweat, and between her legs, she was aching, throbbing, just on the other side of orgasm. She took a deep breath and sank heavier into her pillow.

What the hell?

It had all been a dream? Again?

Damn it.

She looked over at Carson, who was breathing fast, stirring in his sleep, his left hand grasping at the sheet and his brow furrowed in concentration. He must have been having the dream, too, and she wanted in the worst way to wake him up and make that dream a reality.

No.

She had to be good. Had to practice restraint. Had to keep her eye on the matter at hand. Dealing with The Order. That was her purpose in life now, wasn't it?

She wiped at the sweat on her forehead, and then she decided she needed a long, cold shower. But she couldn't risk waking up Carson and making this night even more difficult to get through.

So instead, she rolled over, putting her back to him, and closed her eyes, praying she could make the rest of the night without dreaming.

LAUREN'S EYES had started to glaze over as she sat at the desk, keying in information, trying her best to distract herself from Carson. It was their second day stuck inside Sebastian's hotel, and their second day recovering from a night of intense erotic dreams. She wasn't all that accustomed to having orgasms in her sleep, and the experience was oddly unsatisfying. It left her aching for sex in a way that normal desire did not. It was a bone-deep kind of aching.

Carson had been in the shower for a while now, and when he came back into the bedroom and stood near her, the ache intensified even more. The fresh, clean smell of him had lust pounding so hard in her veins she almost didn't hear him when he spoke.

"Where did you get the computer?"

"Borrowed it from Sebastian."

"What are you doing?" Carson said as he peered over her shoulder at the computer screen.

She wanted to grab him and screw him like an animal. She wanted his mouth on her body, on all the places that were throbbing.

"I figured if we're stuck here, we might as well be doing something productive, so I'm entering all the new information I have into the database we have about The Order."

"You know how to do that?"

"I'm a scientist. I know a few things," she said. "But it's really as simple as keying in data—nothing complicated."

"Right. I keep forgetting you aren't actually a flight attendant."

He poked her in the ribs, and she laughed even as her body responded to the physical contact. But a pang of guilt hit her in the stomach. She really regretted the lies she told mortals, but something about Carson made her crave honesty. "I'm sorry for lying to you," she said. "I hope you can understand now why I had to."

"Sure. Besides, it was Vegas. I'm the fool for

even thinking you'd give me your real name. I think I was thrown off because Macy was involved, and I didn't think she'd have any reason to lie to me."

"You were right about that. But that's best friends for you. Even if she didn't agree with me lying to you, she never questioned me about why."

"Will you ever be able to tell her the truth?" Carson said, pulling up a chair at the desk beside her and watching as she typed.

She felt another pang of guilt. What was it with these mortals lately? "I'd like to but I doubt it. At least not any time soon."

"Not until after the uprising?"

"Right."

She was a bit surprised she'd told Carson about the witches' plan to stop living in secret and let the world know they existed for real. But then again, she'd been so desperate to distract him—and herself—from thoughts of sex, she would have said just about anything.

Part of her desperately wanted to sleep with him again—apparently the part that controlled her dreams—while another part of her felt a crippling fear of pissing off Sebastian by sleeping with Carson in this place and giving him all the reason he needed to get rid of Carson. Plus there was that issue of sexual addiction. Right there was a chance—albeit a small one—that he'd be able to return to his normal life. If she seduced him again and he became obsessed all over, he would probably stop at nothing to see her again. And now that The Order most likely knew of his connection to her, he would lead them right to the witches' doorstep.

Still, having Carson this close was a distraction, to say the least, and she could tell their physical closeness had a strong effect on him, too. She wanted to back away, to make things easier on him, even while she wanted to forget all the reasons they shouldn't be together.

Lauren glanced back at the computer screen, at the sobering information about The Order, and reminded herself why they were here. Not for sex, but to save their lives.

Carson may not have understood yet how much the course of her life would be altered from now on, but she did. She was losing her old life. Now that she'd been identified, the chances that she could return to her life were remote. She couldn't let herself think about it too much or she'd be overcome with rage and sadness. Until the uprising, she'd have to build a new network of friends and lovers, seek out a new occupation, find a new reason to exist. And it would include defeating The Order.

If she was able, she'd also make sure Carson could return to his old life. But that had to be a secondary goal now.

"I can't believe such blatant racism is happening in America today, right under everyone's noses."

Lauren looked at him, and she had to resist the urge to lean in and kiss him. That he could grasp the root of the issue so quickly and not get sidetracked by the distraction of the witches' supernatural powers said a lot for him.

"Our powers do complicate things," she said. "It gives people more to fear."

"Fear comes from ignorance, though," he said. "Don't you think that if everyone understood your powers, they'd be more tolerant?"

"I wish, but the Salem Witch Trials weren't that long ago."

"Yeah, but those were the freaking Puritans doing the persecuting. What do you expect?"

She smiled. "That's why most of us witches live in large, liberal cities now. We figure if we're ever found out, we're more likely to be accepted as normal."

"I'm sorry you have to live like this. The more I think about it, the angrier I get."

Lauren turned away from the computer and studied his expression. "You're serious, aren't you?"

"What? Of course I am."

"Thank you for caring. I have to admit I never expected a mortal to give a damn one way or the other."

"Then you're not giving people enough credit. I'm sure there are lots of us who will care."

"It's hard to think that way, since history has proven otherwise."

"We live in more progressive times now. There will always be narrow-minded people, but I'll bet whenever you finally come out of the closet as a race, you're going to meet with more acceptance than you might expect."

She shook her head. "I can't imagine. The Order has made it hard for us to feel anything but paranoia."

"Those bastards need to be brought down. I'll do whatever I can to help."

"It wouldn't be fair to get you more involved than you already are. You'd be in even more danger."

"It should be my choice whether or not I want to put myself in danger for a cause I care about."

He looked and sounded dead serious. Lauren found herself reeling from the rush of emotion toward this man. During that weekend when she'd taken him in every conceivable way, she would have never expected him to have this sense of outraged justice, never expected him to volunteer to slay her demons. The heroism in his words humbled her and moments passed before she was able to speak past the tightness in her throat.

"Why do you care so much?" she asked.

"I care about what happens to you, for one thing. And for another, I can see you're a whole race of people in trouble. Why wouldn't I care?"

She shrugged. "You barely know me." Her answer served as a reminder. She needed to rein in her spiraling emotions. He was a mortal. She was a witch. Their lives were in danger. There was no room for sex or, God forbid, romance in this situation.

He went silent and seemed to be staring at a spot on the desk that wasn't there. She desperately wanted to reach out and touch his strong jaw. She couldn't help imagining what that soft brown stubble would feel like against her face, her breasts, her belly....

The aching between her legs was too much, demanding attention, demanding release. She shifted in her seat, trying to will her thoughts back to safe territory.

When he finally spoke again, he said, "I guess racism is more of a hot-button issue for me than I realized. I had to think for a while to figure out why."

"Why is it?"

"I dated a woman for a few years in my twenties. We were in love, and we were getting serious about each other. I was thinking of proposing to her, actually."

"What happened?"

"My parents disapproved of the fact that she was African-American. They were friendly enough to her when they thought she was just another girl I was dating, but when I told them I was thinking about getting married to her, they flipped out."

"Wow, I'm sorry."

"I tried not to let their opinions affect me, but I have to admit, their reaction made me hesitate. Then she found out about my parents' feelings and she broke up with me."

"That must have been rough." But Lauren felt a secret pang of relief that he hadn't gotten married in his twenties, because then she never would have met him.

Except, their meeting had gotten him into trouble with her. She knew she wasn't supposed to be glad to have Carson around. It was just kind of hard to remember why when she wanted to do him so badly.

"As far as the relationship went, breaking up was for the best, I guess. We were young and dumb, and probably wouldn't have gone the distance. But I've always been ashamed that I might have let my parents' racist opinion sway me even a little."

"Don't be too hard on yourself. You probably hesitated because you knew what a difficult life you'd be bringing her into, with in-laws who didn't like her. And what would that have meant for any kids you might have had? It would have been hard on them, too."

"None of that is any excuse. I promised myself I'd never be swayed by racism again, and maybe that's why I feel so strongly now about your cause…and you."

Lauren considered his words. None of it was any excuse? Had she been trying to justify to herself why she didn't want to deal with the complications of getting more involved with Carson?

She didn't want to think about their relationship now. The layers upon layers of problems they were dealing with were all making her head hurt.

Carson shifted his leg, and it bumped against her, sending a chill through her body that was far too intense for a mere brushing of body parts. The screaming of her libido overshadowed their present situation and reminded her that she seriously needed to get laid.

"So do you get along with your parents otherwise?" she asked, hoping to distract herself from any more thoughts of sex.

But Carson was studying her, and he didn't answer right away. Instead, he said, "When I brushed up against you, you reacted, didn't you?"

"What do you mean?"

"Your nipples got hard."

She glanced down at her traitorous nipples. "It's a little cold in here."

"It just suddenly got cold when my leg bumped you?"

Lauren rolled her eyes. "Oh stop."

"You're hot for me. Admit it. Those sex dreams we've been sharing aren't cutting it, are they?"

She tried not to laugh but failed. "I told you that witches are highly sensual. We're more sexually responsive than mortals."

"I noticed. I suspect you've gotten to come the past two nights, while all I've gotten is rock-hard."

"And yes," she admitted before she could stop herself. "I am very attracted to you. That doesn't hurt."

Or it did. Or something.

"You're crazy if you think we can stay cooped up in this hotel room without having sex."

"I'll make sure Sebastian gets you your own room as soon as one's available."

"If you want me to stay in this crazy-ass place, we're sleeping in the same room."

"What is that? Some kind of threat?"

Carson shrugged, his eyes sparkling with mischief. "Maybe."

"Are you saying that if I don't sleep with you, you won't stay within the safety of Sebastian's protection?"

"Not exactly, but now that you mention it, yes. That's what I'm saying."

"That's not fair," she said lamely.

"I'm sorry. I'll give you a bit of time to consider my offer. How's that?"

She glared at him but said nothing, and unlike other mortals who might have cowered under her cold glare, Carson simply smiled as if he knew he'd won the battle before it had even gotten started.

CARSON WAS STARTING to learn how to push Lauren's buttons, and he was having far too much fun with his newfound knowledge. If he was going to be tortured by agonizingly good sexual dreams at night without getting any satisfaction from them, he needed to find some kind of entertainment for himself during the day.

When he'd seen Lauren working at the laptop, it reminded him that he hadn't once thought about work since he'd arrived in L.A. His work, which he'd once claimed to be his all-consuming passion and his reason for not getting involved with anyone, hadn't even crossed his mind.

Admittedly, having a woman as gorgeous as Lauren around was a good way of giving a guy a brand-new all-consuming passion. But still, he was the creative director of a major ad agency. He was supposed to be running the show, and he hadn't even spared a thought for the job.

That was when he knew he didn't really give a damn about his work. And for a moment he felt without purpose, as though his life had been an elaborate forgery.

"To answer your question about my parents, no, we don't get along much anymore. I don't think I ever forgave them completely for their reaction to my girlfriend back then."

"You have any siblings?" Lauren said as she stood and stretched.

He tried to focus on her words, but instead the sight of her long lean torso distracted him. Her little black top pulled up as she stretched, exposing the pale smooth skin of her belly above the waist of her jeans. He wanted desperately to touch her there, to slide his tongue over her. She followed his gaze and then tugged her top down in a hurry.

"Behave yourself," she said with a little smile.

"What did you say?"

"Siblings. Do you have any?"

"An older brother and a younger sister. They're both closer to my parents than I am and still live within a few minutes of the family McMansion in Woodside."

"The family McWhat?"

"McMansion—you know, one of those stucco monstrosities that everyone around here seems to aspire to own. A big-ass house with too many bedrooms and too many bathrooms and a pool in the backyard."

"Oh right. I forgot you were a spoiled little rich kid like me."

"Your family strikes me as old money. Mine's all new money from some smart real estate investments my dad made back in the seventies."

"Yeah, the wine business has been in my family for centuries," Lauren said. "First in France and now here. I guess that counts as old money."

"I would think with all that money would come some power to defeat The Order," Carson said.

The amount of anger he felt toward an organization he hadn't known existed until a few days ago surprised him. Pure outrage filled him to think that there were people dedicating their lives to hunting down and killing people like Lauren.

She shrugged. "You would think, but I guess the thing about the witch clan is that we've had to live in fear for so long, we've let the fear control us."

"I guess I can see how that would happen. Like you said, witch hunting isn't exactly a new thing."

She regarded him curiously. "Why aren't you afraid of us?" she asked.

Good question. Carson wasn't sure he knew the answer, but in his gut, he just knew Lauren wasn't someone to fear. Her cousin Sebastian, however, was another matter entirely.

"I've always believed in trusting my gut about people, and my gut tells me you won't harm me."

"Your gut hasn't really dealt with the supernatural before, though. And, I haven't harmed you. Remember that obsession thing."

He shook his head. "Whatever that was it didn't hurt me. I could sense from the start that there was something different about you, something that set you apart from other women."

"Well, thank you for trusting me. It makes things a little less complicated, at least for now."

Carson watched her walk across the room and peer out the window, and his entire body ached to follow her and take her into his arms. He wanted to throw her on the bed and bury himself in her the way he had in the dance floor dream, until all the damn aching stopped.

Sadly he also knew that probably wouldn't go over very well at the moment. Soon enough though, he'd convince her, damn the consequences.

He wasn't afraid of a big bad addiction, not if it meant having Lauren in his bed again. Now that he was beginning to understand how little he was missing his job—how little he was missing his entire life, actually—he realized he had nothing to lose by going after Lauren with everything he had. A woman as amazing as her overshadowed everything else he'd thought mattered to him. She made the rest of it seem as meaningless as it really was.

8

HANGING AROUND with a bunch of witches was driving Carson to drink. He and Lauren weren't allowed to go out anywhere, and, since she had yet to take him up on his not-so-subtle offers of sex, their only entertainment was the nightclub. Which was where he sat now, feeling the slightest bit out of place.

Sebastian wasn't helping matters. As he served drinks, he took every opportunity he had to glare at Carson as if he wanted to snap his neck. Enough was enough already. Finally, while Lauren was in the restroom, Carson decided to confront her cousin.

Sebastian set the drink Carson had ordered in front of him, letting some of it slosh onto the bar, and his expression challenged Carson to say something.

"What's your problem?" he asked casually.

"You," Sebastian answered.

"Look, man, I appreciate your letting me stay here. I know you're only doing it as a favor to Lauren—"

"I don't want your thanks, mortal. I want you the hell away from my cousin."

"That's her choice, don't you think?"

The raven on Sebastian's arm fluttered its wing, and Carson glanced down at it.

"You're lucky you have a drop of witch blood, or I would have already killed you for sleeping with Lauren."

The fact that Sebastian's tone was chilling, without a hint of rage, made his words seem more dire. Carson grabbed his courage with both hands, refusing to let this guy get the advantage. "Is that a threat?"

"Call it whatever you want. Just understand that if I have the chance, I will not hesitate to take your life." And with that, Sebastian turned on his heel and went to the other end of the bar.

Carson watched him and sipped his drink, his male ego urging him to jump over the bar and settle their dispute with his fists. But he knew he was on shaky ground, in a nightclub full of witches with supernatural powers. The odds were not in his favor so there wasn't a hell of a lot he could do.

He downed the last of his Johnnie Walker Black and winced at the familiar, smooth burn as it went down. Not even the best whiskey—or Sebastian's promise of retribution—could rid Carson of the intense need that got worse every time Lauren was near. How the hell was he supposed to stay in that tiny room with a woman who was the best kind of addiction, and yet never get to fulfill his need? Absolute insanity.

He watched her return to the bar, where she stood at the far end talking to her jerk-ass cousin. Just watching her mouth and his cock went stiff in his jeans again. Something had to give—preferably Lauren, and preferably tonight.

No more of her goddamn excuses, and to hell with Sebastian's threats. He was either going to have Lauren hot and willing underneath him, or he was outta here.

A sly-looking blonde watched Carson from a few feet away, but he kept his expression blank and turned his attention back to Lauren. She stopped talking to her cousin and caught his eye, then came toward him.

"Hey," she said when she'd made her way through the growing crowd. "You're still here."

"The thought of going back to the room isn't exactly thrilling. I'd rather put up with your cousin's glare than stare at those four walls."

"I'm sorry. I know it's easy to go stir-crazy all cooped up here. And don't worry about Sebastian—I'll handle him."

"If he's got a problem with me, I'll be glad to take it up with him outside."

Her mouth went flat. "Spare me the testosterone show, okay?"

"Sure, as soon as your cousin stops looking at me like he wants to kill me."

Lauren leaned in close, her gaze cool and piercing. "My cousin is one of the most dangerous witches you will ever meet. I suggest you give him as wide a berth as you can."

"Or what? He'll kill me? Or is that just what he wants me to believe?"

She said nothing, and he could tell she was choosing her words carefully.

"You really think he'd do something crazy?" he finally asked.

"I don't know what he'd do."

"I think it's time for me to get the hell out of here. I'll take my chances with the assholes who chased you out of San Francisco."

"No," Lauren said, as if that settled the matter. "You will stay here."

"Look babe, I'd love to stick around and see if your cousin will murder me in my sleep, but the truth is, if you and I aren't going to be happening, I've got no reason to stay here."

"The Order will kill you, Carson. They'll torture you and then kill you."

"That doesn't make any sense. Even if they do figure out who I am, torturing or killing me will only bring the police. Because, unlike your elders, my friends and family won't hesitate to go to the authorities. I can't see it happening." He didn't want to sound dismissive of something that Lauren was so serious about, but he honestly didn't believe The Order would track him down. The threat certainly wasn't as strong as the one Sebastian had issued.

"Carson, I'm serious. They will be after you."

In his entire vaguely pointless life, Carson had

never faced actual death. There'd been that car accident in college, but he'd never seen the collision coming. He'd simply woken up in the hospital afterward, in some pain but happily unaware that his car was totaled.

And now, the prospect of death still seemed so far removed from his reality, it was absurd. People didn't get tortured and killed by secret witch-hunting societies in modern-day California.

"And I'm serious. I'm out of here first thing in the morning." He'd try to persuade her to join him and, even if she didn't, he'd figure out some way to lend his support to the witches' fight against The Order.

Lauren sat on the bar stool next to him and a mojito appeared before her. She picked up the glass of clear mint-laced liquid and took a long drink.

"Is this about me? Is it getting too hard to be around me?"

"No, *I'm* getting too hard to be around you." He eyed his own crotch meaningfully, and Lauren's gaze followed his down to his zipper, where his cock was pushing to get out.

She sighed. "Damn it. I'm sorry."

"If we're not going to sleep together, I have to get the hell out of here."

"Is that another ultimatum?"

"Yes."

"If we sleep together, things are going to be more difficult for you."

"How so?"

"You know how—the addiction will become more intense."

"I don't think it gets any more intense than the rock-hard erections I'm walking around with all freaking day."

She shook her head. "It does, I promise. It gets worse."

"So let me take the risk."

She closed her eyes, and he admired the thick black lashes resting against her cheeks. She was exquisite in a way few women were. Not so much because of some outlandish beauty, but because she looked as rare as she was, like some bird you might only spot once in your lifetime and spend the rest of your life craving the sight of again.

He knew what craving Lauren felt like. He'd spent the weeks after Vegas almost in a cold sweat with wanting her again. His dreams had been filled with the erotic sensation of sliding into her, feeling her clench around him. Her scent, her taste, her touch had haunted his days until he'd have given everything he owned to have sex with her just one more time.

So, yeah. He knew the risk in sleeping with a witch. He knew and he still didn't care about the consequences.

When she opened her eyes again, she nodded. "You're sure you want to take that risk?"

"Yeah."

"You'll stay here with me as long as I ask you to?"

"Yeah," he lied. Even with Lauren's body to distract him, he wasn't sure how long he could tolerate her creepy cousin, but he would stay as long as it made sense to do so.

Despite his pressing urge to get the hell out of here, he was beginning to realize he didn't have much to go back to. Something about being with Lauren made his life in San Francisco feel empty and pointless. She had a cause she was personally committed to. Even the work she did as a scientific researcher had purpose and meaning. What did he do? Come up with campaigns to persuade people to part with their hard-earned cash for crap they didn't need or want. Some purpose.

Her gaze turned dark, and he could see a desire in her eyes as clear as what he felt in himself. So she had it bad, too. All thoughts of life purposes fled as he relished getting her naked again. She might have thought avoiding sexual contact was in his best interest, but he knew differently. The only thing he needed was her—over and over until his lust was gone, addiction or no addiction.

And having spent a few years in college dedicated to the pursuit of getting high, he knew what it meant to be addicted. He was the kind of guy who knew how to embrace excess.

And he knew how to go too far.

LAUREN KNEW IT WOULD BE extremely difficult for Carson.

But when faced with the choice—give him a

brutal addiction, or let him walk into the hands of killers—what could she do?

And to make the choice even more obvious, she wanted him as badly as he wanted her.

When she was near Carson, she could barely resist touching him, tasting him, clinging to him and devouring him. She had not felt this way about a man before—not quite in this way. Not quite so desperate.

"Come back to the room," she said, and she led him away.

She didn't dare touch him where Sebastian might see. There was always the risk that Sebastian, with his all-seeing talent, might spy them anyway. If he did, there would be some kind of hell to pay.

But with this situation, no matter how they looked at it, there was going to be hell to pay.

As soon as they were behind the closed door of the room, she pulled Carson to her and kissed him with the absolute yearning she'd been feeling for days.

His tongue plunged into her mouth, caressed hers, as he moaned and roamed his hands over her body. Lauren pressed him against the door and unfastened his pants, found his cock beneath his boxers, grasped it through the thin fabric.

"Damn," he whispered. "I've missed you."

He dipped his head down and bit her neck, licked her shoulder, pushed her breasts up and kissed the tops of them. Then he turned her and pinned her against the door where he had been a moment before.

Lauren closed her eyes and concentrated on the feel of his hands and mouth against her. She'd craved this sensation for so long and now she reveled in it. He tugged at her skirt, baring her thighs to the cool air, an exquisite contrast to the heat consuming her. Without warning, he dropped to his knees, and pulled her panties down. For a few moments he just looked at her, his eyes feasting on her with such intent her insides contracted with sharp longing. She wanted to spread her legs wider, tempt him with even more of her flesh. Finally she could feel his hands moving up her thighs, and his fingertips scarcely touching her pussy, teasing her.

She gasped and squirmed closer, chasing those elusive fingers.

And then his lips and his tongue were there, caressing her, stroking her. Warm liquid sensation. Hot tingling pleasure. Heaven.

Lauren leaned against the door and opened herself to him, her breath quickening. He held her hips as he licked and sucked at her clit, torturing her and edging her closer to the brink of orgasm with every second that passed.

It had been too long for her. She hadn't taken a lover since she'd been with Carson three months earlier. Three long months of denial, of wanting him but thinking she'd never have him again. To have that hunger satisfied now was nearly more than her senses could take.

"Stop," she whispered, not wanting to come too soon, feeling herself getting close.

"Mmm," he moaned as he continued to pleasure her.

"No," she laughed, trying to squirm away but failing. "I want this to last longer than a minute."

He stopped and looked up at her. "Trust me, this will last all night if I have any say in the matter."

She sighed and decided it was time to take control of the situation. Lauren lifted her foot up and pressed the stiletto heel of her sandal against his throat. "Don't make me get rough with you."

His eyes locked on to her sex, revealed so clearly in this position, and she almost came from the erotic expression on his face. "You'd really stab me with your shoe?"

"Would it turn you on?"

"Maybe."

"Then maybe I would."

His gaze traveled up her torso to her face. "I dare you."

Instead, she kicked him gently, just enough to make him lose his balance and fall backward. A moment later, she was on top of him on the floor.

"Don't take it personally," she said as she hovered a few inches from his lips. "I don't want to come so fast."

"I'll make you come at least a dozen times. You know me."

"I know me, too. I want to take it slow. This is dangerous stuff, this addictive sex, you know."

"Seems like everything in my life is dangerous all of a sudden," he whispered.

His gaze half-lidded, he looked drunk, and she didn't know if it was from the whiskey he'd been drinking in the bar, or from her, or both. She'd guess both.

Lauren tugged off her clothes, and straddled Carson again wearing nothing but her heels. Being naked while he remained clothed with only his pants undone should have made her feel overexposed. Instead, she felt the thrill of power and control as his gaze roamed her assets and his hands slid over her body. She leaned down and kissed him long and deep as he grasped her breasts and tugged at her nipples, and that tugging went all the way to her core. She moaned into his mouth, then rocked her hips against his, stroking her sex along his hard cock, but not allowing him in.

"I want inside you," he said.

"You have protection?"

He pulled his wallet out of his back pocket, and Lauren took the packet from him, tore it open with her teeth and took out the condom. She sheathed him, and mounted him in one smooth thrust of her hips.

Having him buried deep inside her, she thought, should have relieved a bit of her craving. Instead it coiled tighter, made her feel more desperate, more needy. She began riding him at an urgent pace, her gaze locked with his as he held tight to her waist and thrust in time with her. He looked as desperate as she felt.

"Don't stop," he gasped. "Don't ever stop."

She couldn't have if she'd wanted to.

She watched his face rapt with pleasure, savored the feel of him bringing her closer and closer to orgasm, and she knew they'd be here all night, satisfying their cravings, making up for lost time.

She wanted to memorize every inch of him, commit him fully to memory and live right here in this moment for as long as she could.

She rocked faster against him, her body tensing as she watched his own body tense.

And as she felt him reach orgasm, she gave in to the sensation, as well, crying out at the jolts of pleasure that shot through her. It went on until the intensity was almost too much to bear, and then it subsided, leaving her spent.

Lauren collapsed, gasping, on the floor, her skin damp with sweat and her body tingling. Carson stretched out long beside her, and pulled her leg over his hip.

"It's been too long since we've done that," he said, looking even more drunk now but sounding completely sober, if a little breathless still.

"Yeah." She stretched, closed her eyes and inhaled his scent.

And at the same time it had been not nearly long enough, because their absence from each other's bed had not cured Carson of his need for her. Next time they parted ways, it would be much, much more difficult for him. And maybe for her, too, given how well their bodies worked together and how powerful their chemistry was.

She winced at the thought of what he would go through, the physical and emotional withdrawal, the lifelong disappointment of never feeling such pleasure again. The weight of guilt settled in her stomach, now that she was satisfied enough to think more clearly.

"I'm sorry," she said. "I shouldn't have done that to you."

He laughed. "Oh yes you should have. And you should have done it sooner, so what the hell are you apologizing for?"

"I just meant, it will feel worse when we're apart again."

"You're already planning our breakup? Why don't we stick around for a while and start driving each other crazy before we start thinking about splitting up?"

Because she would be dead soon—her vision dictated it. But she would not tell him that. Not yet.

"Under normal circumstances, sure, that makes perfect sense. But in case you haven't noticed, we are enduring the most abnormal of circumstances."

"Oh right," he said, mock-surprised. "You're a *witch,* and I'm supposed to get all addicted to you because I'll never have sex even remotely as good as this again in my life."

"Don't be a smart-ass. You know how you felt after Las Vegas. Do you really want to endure that feeling times ten or twenty? Or worse?"

"I can't even imagine."

"I've been through it with someone once before."

"And what? He went insane and jumped off the Golden Gate Bridge because he couldn't have sex with you anymore?"

"Something like that."

She didn't want to explain the whole story. She'd only been nineteen, and she hadn't quite understood the gravity of her power over humans yet.

But he persisted. "Tell me what happened."

"I had a mortal lover my freshman year of college. We dated for about six months until my mother caught wind of what I was doing and told me she'd stop paying my tuition to Stanford if I continued."

"So you broke up with him then?"

"No, actually, I dropped out of college for the rest of the semester and messed around with the guy for a while longer."

"And where's the part about him going crazy when he loses you?"

"He dropped out of school, too. But we eventually burned out on the relationship because it was too intense. I broke up with him, and it was a downward spiral for him after that. I feel like I ruined his life."

Lauren didn't think about Kyle often, and she didn't tell people about him. He'd been this disastrous event in her life that she'd carefully skirted for years—for so long that talking about it now seemed surreal, as if she was recounting something that hadn't really happened.

"You ever hear from him anymore?"

"No. A few months after we broke up, he tried to commit suicide. And after that, he joined a 12-step program for sex addicts, and that was the last I ever heard about him. I'm not proud of the fact that I nearly ruined his life."

"So, these elders you mentioned—they forbid you from ever having sex with mortals? What happens if they find out what you're doing with me?"

"They could banish me from the clan, or have me killed."

"What?" Carson sat up on his elbow and stared hard at her. "Killed? For having sex?"

Lauren shrugged. "They're hard-asses. What can I say?"

"Can't they get put in prison or something for killing people?"

"Witches have had centuries of practice at hiding things. The police are the least of our worries."

"I guess so, if you have to worry about your own family killing you."

"Let's don't think about that, okay? It's a worst-case scenario."

Carson sighed, but said nothing more.

Lauren slid her hand across Carson's belly, lifting his shirt in the process, and admired the contrast of their skin colors, hers pale with the slightest pink undertones, and his light golden brown. "Where do you get so much sun living in the city?"

"I go out hiking and biking a lot on the weekends. Mostly trails in Marin where it's sunnier."

"Ah. Must be a good stress reliever after doing the daily grind all week."

"Yeah, it is. I try to get as far from the job mentally as I can on the weekends."

"I've watched Macy survive that world all these years, and I don't know how you guys do it. I think it would kill me."

"Your job can't be all that low-stress. Medical research is pretty competitive, isn't it?"

Lauren shrugged. "Not in the same way."

"How'd you ever decide to do a study on whether sex makes people dumber? I mean, isn't that kind of a no-brainer?"

She smiled and traced her finger along the little trail of hair that led down toward his cock fully exposed now with his pants down around his ankles. "I had a vision, actually."

"A vision of what? People doing stupid things after orgasms? Putting their shoes on the wrong feet and stuff?"

"No, actually, it all started with the side effects I noticed my lovers experiencing."

"You mean guys were acting like dumb-asses over you? That shouldn't come as any surprise."

"I thought it was a phenomenon worth exploring, anyway, and as I was thinking about it one day, I had a vision that the results of the study would be groundbreaking news. So I got started with it."

"It just seems like such an obvious thing. Do we really need a study to prove it?"

"That's what science is for—to explain the processes that make our world work."

"I guess," Carson muttered and pulled her closer. "Next time, could you do a study about how many orgasms it's possible to achieve in one day?"

"I think we're well on our way to finding the answer to that question. Besides, there isn't going to be any *next time* for me as far as my work goes."

"Oh right. I guess you can't just get a job as a scientist somewhere else?"

She shook her head. "I pretty much have to get myself a new identity now."

"Wow, that really sucks. Won't you miss your old life?"

"Of course I will, but it's not like I have a choice in the matter."

One thing Lauren had learned to accept along with having the gift of prescience—there were far fewer choices in life than anyone ever liked to believe there were.

She closed her eyes and allowed her body to drift toward sleep. Savoring this moment, right now, was the only choice she was sure she could make.

9

LAUREN SAT ON THE EDGE of Sebastian's desk and watched as he scrolled through image after image of suspected Order operatives. She had some shaky memory of the men she'd seen in the vision outside her door, and Sebastian wanted her to point out if any of the men in his database looked like the ones she'd seen that night.

So far, no luck.

"Where is the mortal?" Sebastian asked.

"Carson. His name is Carson. He's probably sitting in the room, bored out of his mind. I don't think he's going to be able to stay here much longer."

"He's lucky I haven't kicked his ass out into the street."

"I don't think he sees it that way. And if you kick him out, I'll leave, too."

He continued to scroll through photos and sketches, and Lauren thought she recognized a sketch that popped up on the screen. "Stop," she said. "That one." She stared at it, trying to recall the image that had come to her before.

One of the men had been tall, in his forties maybe,

with short dark hair and a receding hairline—nearly bald on top. She remembered his eyes best, which were cold and blue.

"He looks familiar?"

"Yes, maybe..." She studied the drawing, but it was impossible to tell if the eyes were the same in the black-and-white sketch. "We don't have a color version of this?"

Sebastian shook his head. "No, and no information on this guy, either, other than that he was heard speaking Czech."

"That matches what I heard in my vision, too. I think that's one of the men."

"Let's keep looking and see if you recognize the other one." He continued to scroll.

"What happens if we figure out who these guys are?"

"Then I will make a special point to track them down and kill them myself."

"Sebastian..." She hated hearing her cousin talk that way.

"You know the uprising can't happen without blood being shed."

"I guess I never thought of it that way. I'd hoped there would be a public outcry from the mortal community against our persecution."

He cast a scornful glance at her. "Don't be naive."

She blinked. Sebastian never talked to her that way before. He'd always been kind to her. He'd always made her feel loved.

"What's happened to you?" she whispered.

She was looking at him now, instead of the photos. She wasn't sure she wanted to identify the men, if it meant her cousin's hands getting soiled with more blood.

He leaned back in his chair and regarded her wearily. "Maybe I sold my soul," he said. "Or maybe I never had one in the first place."

"You had me fooled," she said. "The Sebastian I know has both a heart and a soul."

"You had me fooled, too, cousin. I never thought I'd see the day when you were more loyal to a mortal than you are to me."

She reached out and took his hand, and she looked him in the eye, hoping to reach that place she used to know so well. "It's not about loyalty. It's about doing what's right. I love you, but I have a duty to protect Carson. It's my fault he's in this mess."

"You're going to have to lose that moral conscience if you want the uprising to succeed," he said.

"No, you're wrong. We can't have our freedom at any cost. We have to achieve it justly, or not at all. Otherwise we're simply a version of The Order."

"Is it just that we have to live in hiding, in fear of persecution?"

"Wasn't it Gandhi who said 'An eye for an eye makes the whole world blind'?"

"Spare me the bumper sticker philosophy, Lauren. This is the real world, where we will die if we aren't careful."

They stared at each other, neither willing to back down. An awful feeling settled in Lauren's gut. Was she being naive? She'd never considered the real cost of their freedom. She'd never made herself look hard at that problem, and she'd never asked herself before if she could live with the answer.

For the first time she could remember, she wished she'd never had a vision of an uprising, or a victory, or a sense that they should have ever strayed from the elders' rules.

She suddenly longed for her old life, which was so simple by comparison—her old life, where she knew all the rules. Now it appeared they had to make each rule up as they went along, and she wasn't sure she was up for the task.

LARS DETESTED Los Angeles, but he held a special distaste for West Hollywood. As he and Noam walked the streets of the neighborhood that probably held more witches than any other place on Earth, he could not help but look at every face and try to sense if they were mortal or witch.

And the more beautiful the face, the more suspicious he was about their true identity. It was a cruel joke that witches were more physically beautiful than mortal women, as if their physical appearances were designed to fool and distract normal men.

"You want to stop looking for a while and get some lunch?" Noam asked, glancing at his watch. "It's getting to be that time."

"I saw a sandwich place down the block. We can go there."

They headed in the direction of the deli, and five minutes later, they had each ordered lunch and were sitting at a table waiting for their food.

"Two days and no luck. What do you think that means?" Noam asked.

He was too young and impatient. He would have to learn that the hunt never ended, so there was never a need to be in a hurry.

"I think it means we haven't found Lauren Parish yet."

"What if she's not here?"

"It's like always—if we have enough patience, we'll find what we seek."

Noam's gaze followed a thin, beautiful blonde along the sidewalk as they stared out the window. "You ever slept with a witch?" he asked.

Lars did not know how to answer. While it was officially forbidden for a member of The Order to have sexual relations with witches, it was also commonly accepted that many among them took liberties with their captives before they killed them.

He was torn between wanting to warn the boy about his firsthand experiences with the addiction that came along with having sex with a witch, and wanting to brag that he had indeed taken some of the most beautiful women in the world before killing them.

He chose his words with care. "I'm sure you've

heard rumors of the pleasures that come with taking a witch."

Noam nodded. "Sure. It's all the trainees talk about almost."

"It's been a long time since I've been a trainee. In my time, we didn't dare discuss such things out in the open."

"I guess we've gotten bolder over the years."

"Once you've had a witch, mortal women will feel inadequate to you," Lars warned.

Noam made a whistling sound and shook his head seemingly in appreciation. "I can't wait."

"Shh. Don't say such things so boldly."

"Hell, nobody around here even knows what we're talking about," the kid said, now in his native Czech.

Lars responded in Czech, as well, to be safe. "It's a dangerous addiction, worse than any drug."

"So you have had sex with witches?"

"Many times."

And now he could not even make love to mortal women. His cock wouldn't even get hard for them. It was shameful to admit, but true.

"Then you can't go around telling me not to do it."

"I can at least warn you that you will regret it," Lars said, but he knew the lure was too great.

It was the shameful secret of The Order, that many of its members were addicts. Some had even dared in the past to hold their witch concubines hostage so that they could continue to enjoy the physical pleasures of them. But that had proven too dangerous, and now, as far as Lars knew, the policy was to kill every witch captive.

Their sandwiches arrived, and they went silent as they ate. Then Noam broke the silence with, "What's so great about it? How do they make you get addicted?"

"It's impossible to describe until you experience it. I think that's why so many of us are unable to resist the temptation, and why some of us have died trying to have that pleasure."

"Damn," Noam muttered. "Pussy worth dying for…"

His time would come soon enough. Lars would let him have his way with Lauren Parish if he so desired—after Lars was through with her of course.

"I've heard some of the prostitutes here are really witches," Noam said. "You think we could, you know, check it out?"

"I don't want to waste time with such pursuits."

"Couldn't we consider it another way of finding witches? You know, if the sex is that great, then they must be a witch?"

Lars sighed. "Maybe tonight, if we have no luck this afternoon."

"Hey," Noam said, pointing at a man across the street. "Is that the guy we saw on the camera from her apartment?"

Lars stared at the man, then withdrew from his

chest pocket a photo that they'd produced from the video footage. The man on the sidewalk wore a baseball cap, dark glasses and had the start of a beard, but he had the same brown hair and the same bone structure as the man from the video.

"Let's check him out," he said coolly, and they stood quickly and left the deli. From the opposite sidewalk they followed the man as he headed west, and when he made a left at the next corner and disappeared out of sight, they started across the street. But traffic was heavy, and Lars noticed too late the red Mercedes coming toward them.

The car screeched to a stop, but not before it bumped against Noam and sent him sprawling. Lars's first instinct was to leave the kid behind and run after the man. But when he looked down and saw that Noam wasn't getting right up, he paused.

The kid was his responsibility, and one rule he would never violate was abandoning his apprentice. He knelt beside the kid, who was wincing as he tried to bend his leg. "Are you okay?"

"Yeah, I think so," he said as he grasped his knee. "Just a little scraped up."

"Let me help you up and let's make sure you can walk."

The driver of the Mercedes, a woman in her fifties, looked horrified as she got out of the car.

"Don't worry, ma'am," Lars called out. "He's fine."

The last thing they needed was filing a police

report or making a trip to the hospital. Lars knew how to splint a leg himself, if worse came to worst.

"Come on," he said to Noam as he stood up. "You steady on your feet?"

He nodded.

"If we hurry, we might still catch up to the guy."

Noam took a few tentative steps, dusted off his pants, and said, "I'm fine."

The two men crossed the intersection and broke into a jog as they hit the sidewalk again. Around the corner, the man they'd spotted earlier was nearly a block away now, and they ran to catch up, slowing down only as they came close enough to draw attention from him.

On the next block, he paused at a store window and eyed some lingerie on a mannequin, then continued on.

"I'll grab his wallet if I can, and you keep following him to see where he goes," Lars whispered to Noam.

He nodded his agreement, and then hung back as Lars hurried ahead. He pretended to bump into the man, and as he'd practiced hundreds of times, he slid his fingers quickly into the rear pocket and withdrew the wallet in one fluid movement.

"I'm sorry," he said as he passed by, trying not to make eye contact.

Lars tucked the wallet into his pants and continued on. When he'd reached the safety of their van, he sat in the driver's seat and inspected the contents of the wallet. The driver's license said the man's name was Carson McCullen, and his home address was in San Francisco.

They had found the man they were looking for, and they were one step closer to Lauren Parish.

Fifteen minutes later, Noam returned to the van.

"Where did he go?" Lars asked.

Noam looked sheepish. "I guess my leg wasn't as fine as I thought it was. My knee gave out and I had to stop and let it rest for a minute. I lost him."

"Damn it! He's the man from the video. He lives in San Francisco. You just ruined our freaking chance of grabbing the witch today."

"Well, why the hell did you leave me alone?"

"I thought you could handle it," Lars said, tossing the wallet at the kid.

But the truth was, he'd been careless. No more. From now on, he would leave no stone unturned, and he would not leave the job of a professional to a mere baby.

CARSON HAD SPENT five solid days indoors, and he had been going stir-crazy. He was an outdoor kind of guy, and far as he could remember, this was the first time in his life he'd spent this much time inside.

Lauren was a pretty damn good reason to stay indoors, but when she was busy conspiring with her cousin Sebastian, it left Carson bored as hell. He hadn't seen any harm in going out for a quick walk around the neighborhood, especially when he'd never even *seen* the neighborhood before—and the sunshine and fresh air had been well worth what had seemed like a small risk. However, he knew he was in big trouble when he saw Lauren's face upon arriving back in the hotel room.

"What the hell did you do?" she said coldly.

"I just wanted to go for a walk. I'm so damn sick of being stuck in this place, I couldn't stand it anymore."

Her eyes widened. "You went for a walk. In broad daylight."

"Last time I checked it wasn't a crime." He took off the stupid hat and sunglasses that had been included in the parcel of clothes Sebastian had had delivered for him, and tossed them on the dresser. "At least I wore a disguise."

"Oh yeah, that hat and glasses transformed you into an entirely different person."

"Look, I wanted to experience normal life for a half hour. I'm getting a little tired of being locked up in freak world, where everyone but me has at least one tattoo and a supernatural power."

"How about talking to me? Do you realize what you've done?"

"I went out and enjoyed the sunshine. I saw some people who aren't witches. It felt good. I'm not so stir-crazy now. Big freaking deal."

"It is a big deal. You have no goddamn idea."

"You know, you ripped me out of my everyday life, took me away from my job and my friends and told me there was this whole underground world I didn't know about and now I have to live in it. And you expect me to just sign up for the whole damn vacation to hell package without a second thought?"

She glared at him and said nothing, her arms crossed over her chest.

He flopped onto the bed and sighed, feeling guilty now. "I'm sorry, Lauren. I'm not used to being inside all the time. I'm the outdoorsy type. I need fresh air regularly or I start going insane."

"So go up on the rooftop deck! Don't go out walking around West Hollywood when we've got people who are hunting us down!"

She slammed her fist against the wall for emphasis, then winced at the pain of it.

"Don't you think maybe you're being a wee bit paranoid? There are thousands of people on the street out there, and we're hundreds of miles south of where you last came in contact with the witch hunters."

"I told you, there are rumors that The Order has a network of people here now because they've figured out that witches gravitate to this area. Witches have been disappearing recently."

The guilt twinged stronger. He hadn't intended to put Lauren in danger.

"I'm really sorry," Carson said. "I won't do it again. I promise to follow all the rules from now on."

"Don't you dare let Sebastian know you went out, or he'll be furious. I'll have to tell him…" She appeared to be thinking. "This is bad," she said, running her hand over her face.

Carson resisted rolling his eyes. He was getting the slightest bit tired of having to live under Sebastian's rule, but he said nothing because he was responsible for this particular incident.

"Aren't you maybe overreacting a little? Do you really even need to tell Sebastian?"

"I'm going to have to tell everyone, damn it! The whole place is going to have to be put on alert, with heightened security."

"Shit," he muttered.

"Knowing Sebastian, he won't let anyone out of the building for the next month after he hears this."

"I didn't realize how big a deal it would be."

"Did anything strange happen while you were out?"

"Not a thing," Carson said, but at that moment he noticed the lack of an uncomfortable lump in his rear pocket that was normally created by his wallet.

Then he recalled the man who'd bumped into him. He reached around and felt his pocket, and realized nothing was there.

Damn it. He kept his expression neutral, not sure if it was worth alarming Lauren over.

"What are you doing?" she asked.

"Just looking for the package of gum I bought while I was out. Guess I dropped it."

No, there was no sense in worrying her. She was already on edge about every little thing, and maybe he'd left his wallet somewhere in the room. Or maybe it had fallen out here in the hotel. Yeah, and maybe little elves had come and taken it away.

He had to be sure his wallet was really stolen, though, before he risked freaking Lauren out. Hearing that he'd lost it to a pickpocket might have put her off the deep end.

10

WITH NOTHING ELSE TO DO and no one allowed to so much as breathe in the direction of the outside world now, Carson and Lauren tended to hang out at the club every night, where the other witches displayed varying degrees of hostility about his presence, especially since the leaving-the-hotel incident.

He'd gotten enough scathing looks and disgusted glares to last him a lifetime after Sebastian ordered the entire place to go on lockdown and forbade all witches from setting foot outside. One guy had even attacked Carson in the elevator, slamming him up against the wall and clenching his hand around Carson's neck, but Lauren had stepped in and explained how Carson hadn't understood the gravity of leaving the hotel.

A woman sidled up to the bar next to Carson and waited for the bartender to notice her so she could order a drink. When Carson glanced at her, she smiled wickedly.

"Stupid human," she whispered. "You're lucky to still be alive."

And she was right, apparently. He was. He finally understood that.

How Lauren heard the woman's words over the loud music in the club was beyond Carson, but she had. "Shut the hell up," she said to the woman, who glared at Lauren for a second, then turned and walked away.

Lauren took Carson's hand and tugged him toward the dance floor, so he downed the last of his scotch and let her lead the way. In the darkness of the pulsing crowd, she was all he cared about. He could ignore the weird vibes from the witches surrounding them when she was in the room.

He pulled her close right before they reached the dance floor, and said, "You are stunning."

She smiled coyly back at him. "So are you."

He watched her ass in the skimpy white fringed dress she wore. In a sea of dark colors, she stood out like a vision from heaven. And it enticed him all the more that he knew she was anything but.

The way she moved was so natural, so fluid, so full of raw sexuality, that when she found a place for them among the other pulsing bodies and began dancing, there was no point at which her walking had stopped and her dancing started. She turned to him, her hips swaying to the techno-tribal beat of the music, and her gaze was heavy with what he had come to recognize as desire.

For him.

Amazing.

He started dancing with her, against her, their bodies moving in time, and the heat of the bodies all around them immediately drenched him in sweat. Carson ignored the feel of his clothes sticking to his body and let the music entrance him along with Lauren.

She was nothing like he'd originally thought, months ago in Las Vegas. And yet she was. It was as if he was watching her shed the trappings of her buttoned-up life in the real world and let herself become who she really was, here in safety among the witches.

She was his addiction and his cure, all rolled up into one irresistible package.

She leaned in close and asked, "What's wrong? You look distracted."

"Nothing," he lied. "I guess I won't ever get used to being the lone mortal in the room."

"Don't worry," she said into his ear, barely audible over the music. "They'll get over it."

"I don't belong here," he said.

"I'll decide that. You belong here as long as I'm protecting you."

He bristled at the thought, but said nothing. He had his male pride, but he knew better than to go around puffing it up in front of a woman like Lauren. The truth was, he wanted to be protecting her, not the other way around. He wanted to kill any bastard that would dare harm her, but he didn't exactly feel equipped yet to navigate the world of witches and witch hunters effectively.

After all, it was a world he hadn't even known existed most of his life.

But the fact remained that he would do anything he could to keep Lauren safe. He would learn all about her world if it meant he could somehow help her.

He placed his hands possessively on Lauren's hips as she danced, and he let his mind drift to more base thoughts. Of their bodies moving together not here on the dance floor, but somewhere more private. Somewhere free of these goddamn stifling clothes.

She pressed herself against him and felt his erection. Her gaze dropped for a moment to his crotch, then traveled up again to meet his. "You want to get out of here?"

"We just got here."

"It's hot as hell in here," she said. "Come with me. I know someplace we can cool off."

Five minutes later, they were away from the deafening dance music and the stifling crowd of witches. They'd gone up four flights of stairs, through a door marked Employees Only, and out onto a rooftop deck with an utterly amazing view of the city.

"Wow," Carson said as he took in the lights, the night sky and the Hollywood sign on the distant hillside.

"Yeah. Welcome to my favorite place in Hollywood. Sebastian doesn't tell anyone about it. It's his own place to escape from all his responsibilities."

"Will he mind us being here?"

"No, I'm one of the few people he'll let come up

here any time. Besides, he's busy with the club tonight. He won't even know we're here."

Carson surveyed the deck. Right in the middle of it was an outdoor fireplace, and a bed with an outdoor canopy over it. "I guess we know what goes on up here, huh?"

Lauren shrugged and headed for the fireplace, which was a minimalist glass cube with a small fire pit in bottom. A flick of a switch brought flames to life. Instant fire.

"Cool," he said.

"I doubt Sebastian brings women up here," she said. "But he does sleep up here sometimes. He likes the outdoor air."

"What? Your cousin's celibate or something?"

"No, but he's very private, and he doesn't let many people get close to him. It's part of his way of protecting the witch clan. To be a protector, he has to be inaccessible, I guess."

"To make sure the wrong person doesn't get too close to him?"

"Something like that."

"Have any of those witch hunter guys ever infiltrated this place?"

"Yes," she said, but he heard some hesitation in her voice.

"What happened?"

"They were found out," she answered, and he had a sense that he shouldn't ask any more questions about the subject.

He came up behind Lauren and pushed the thick curtain of her dark hair aside, then kissed the tattoo on her neck. "Does this mean something?" he asked, tracing the design with his finger.

"It's Celtic. I can't tell you what it means, but it represents the essence of my power, if that makes any sense."

"It doesn't, but I'll take your word for it," he teased, then kissed her there again, this time letting his lips linger.

His hands found their way up her rib cage to the heavy curves of her breasts, and he massaged them slowly, his cock aching as he felt her nipples harden.

His addiction to her was growing by the day, by the hour, by the minute, and he was helpless to control it. When he thought of living a day without making love to Lauren, his stomach went sour.

In the firelight, her tattoo looked especially luminous, as if it were somehow alive separate from her. He thought of the raven tattoo on Sebastian's arm, and he didn't doubt for a moment their supernatural powers.

"What happens if a mortal falls in love with a witch?" he asked.

Lauren turned to him, gazing at him with dark, unfathomable eyes. Even the firelight didn't lighten them. "I don't know," she said.

"Is it like selling your soul to the devil?"

"Witches aren't evil," she said.

"I know that, I just meant—"

"None of the stereotypes you've ever heard are true. We're not the brides of Satan. We don't ride broomsticks or wear pointy hats, and we don't go around stirring cauldrons or casting spells."

"I'm sorry, I didn't mean to insult you."

"It's okay. I get touchy about the subject."

"Where do you think all those stereotypes came from?"

"I'm sure some of my ancestors did some of that stuff. I mean, people used to cook in cauldrons. And both witches and nonwitches alike attempt to practice black magic. It doesn't have anything to do with being a witch, though."

"So all the myths were invented by people who were afraid of witches."

"Perhaps. Over the centuries, The Order had plenty to do with demonizing witches and making the public afraid of us."

"Why?"

"Like you said before, it's a form of racism, just like Hitler attempting to eradicate the Jews or the Turks massacring the Armenians or the KKK trying to scare blacks out of the South."

"Yeah, I see what you mean."

"Our battle is a lot more ancient than that. It's been going on since before recorded history, as far as we know."

"Amazing that it's been kept secret all this time."

"It hasn't always been. There were times in history when witch hunting was more acknowledged by the public, the Salem Witch Trials being the most recent example. But The Order has managed to keep themselves mostly a secret from the world. That's their talent—even better than us—that they know how to stay hidden."

"Maybe the key to stopping them is finding a way to make their actions public."

"But that would mean making ourselves public, as well. It's a tricky thing. We have to choose our time."

"You seem to have some idea when that time is."

"Not exactly, but I know someday that things will change for the better. Maybe not when I'm around to witness it, but someday."

A chill went up Carson's spine at her words. "Of course you'll be around to witness it. Don't sound so doom and gloom."

He cupped her chin in his hand and tilted it up so she had to look him in the eye, but she said nothing. She simply stared at him, her gaze still unknowable to him, filled with something like sadness.

"What is it? Have you had some vision about yourself?"

Her lips parted as if to speak, but she said nothing.

"You have, haven't you?"

She smiled, but it looked forced. "What I'm having a vision of right now is you and me on that bed, naked. Think you can accommodate me?"

"Are you trying to bewitch me to distract me from the subject?"

"Call me wicked," she said, smiling still. "I won't deny it."

She slid her hand down his belly, and her fingers traced the head of his cock through his pants. He expelled a gush of air as she gripped him and massaged gently.

"You're wicked," he said. "And I love it."

She unzipped his fly and pushed him until he was at the edge of the bed, then sitting on it. She took his dick out of his boxers and knelt between his legs. He was aching as he watched her long, delicate fingers encircle him.

Then she dipped her head and took him into her mouth, and he felt a jolt of satisfaction as real as if he'd just taken a hit of the world's most powerful drug. Perhaps he had.

She ran her tongue up and down the length of him as he watched her, disarmed by her beauty and her skill with his body. He didn't think, for as long as she was in his life, he'd ever stop being amazed at what it was like to be with her. Perhaps that was the addiction talking, but one thing he knew about this addiction—the pleasure was the most real thing he could imagine.

There was nothing artificial about it.

She took him all the way into her mouth again, and he moaned at the sensation of it, closing his eyes and letting the whole experience become about the feel of her mouth on his dick. As she worked his body, he felt the pressure building within himself, and he had to find the willpower to stop her. But she knew his body too well—right before he reached the edge of orgasm, she stopped and smiled sinfully up at him.

"You didn't think I'd let you have all your fun now, did you?" she whispered, barely audible above the street sounds and the distant bass of the club music below.

"I was going to stop you," he said, smiling, but he wasn't sure he could have summoned the strength.

He tugged her up from the deck, found a condom in his wallet and put it on as she crawled onto the bed next to him.

Then she was kissing him with an eroticism that almost took him back to that edge. She straddled him, her dress bunched up around her waist, and the sight and feel of her pussy on him was too much pleasure to bear. He lay back, gasping raggedly, as she began riding him. His hands on her waist, he didn't even have the strength to guide her.

He was simply helpless under her spell.

LAUREN WAS BEGINNING to suspect there was no such thing as a single orgasm with Carson. She'd already come once, only minutes after they'd started making love. She hadn't exactly intended to, but the sensation of his body inside her, along with the night air, and the firelight, pushed her over the sensory edge into a realm of pleasure she couldn't control.

But now he was lying on top of her, his weight a delicious pressure and he moved inside her, and she felt herself building toward orgasm again. It was rare that she could come in the good old missionary position, but Carson's cock fit her so perfectly, he rubbed all the right places.

"That's it," she gasped into his ear, and then he covered her mouth in a long, desperate kiss.

He was getting close, too. She could feel the tension in his body building, as the thrusting of his hips grew more urgent, and all she could do was wrap her legs around him and hold on. She stared up at the stark white canopy above them, and she imagined she could see stars.

Except there were rarely stars of the celestial variety visible in Hollywood. The smog was too thick, and the city lights too intense. Rather, what she saw was the way Carson made some kind of magic with her body, a magic she wasn't capable of on her own.

She grasped his wide, firm shoulders as he braced himself on his elbows, and with a final few thrusts, he spilled into her, just as her body contracted around his cock in a second orgasm that was more intense than her first. She cried out at the delicious sensation of it, gasping as he gasped.

When she opened her eyes again after the rush had passed, she saw him staring at her, his brow damp with sweat, his gaze softened from pleasure.

He eased himself down and kissed her again, this time slowly, tenderly, his tongue brushing lightly against hers.

"You," he murmured against her lips.

"What about me?" she said when he pulled back.

"I want to stay in this bed forever with you. Think your cousin will mind?"

She smiled. "Likely he will mind. In fact, we'd better get out of here before too long or he'll come up here and find us."

"And then there'll be hell to pay."

"If it were just me, no, but with you, he's a bit touchy."

"I'm not used to being so thoroughly hated."

"Don't take it personally. It's not really about you, anyway."

"He couldn't possibly like the thought of you sleeping with a mortal."

Carson slid off her, pulled off his condom and dropped it over the edge of the bed into a wastebasket next to the nightstand. Then he returned to her side and pulled her tight against him.

"Don't worry about what he would or wouldn't like. My life is my own, and I decide who I do or don't sleep with."

"Do you think he'd do anything violent to enforce that no sex with mortals rule?"

Lauren gazed at his chest, in love with the firm curves of it, the flat brown nipples, the smooth skin. She didn't want to answer his question, but maybe shielding him from the truth wasn't exactly fair.

"Sebastian has changed since I knew him as a

kid. He scares me now. I don't think he'd harm me, but—"

He sat up. "But you think he'll harm me."

"Don't overreact. I'm probably being paranoid. It's sort of an unspoken thing that some of us break the sex with mortals rule and don't talk about it. Because of my history, the consequences could be harsher."

"Isn't death kind of a harsh punishment?"

"It's a stupid, archaic rule, and that's why I don't abide by it. It has its value, at least as far as protecting mortals from addiction and protecting us from any negative consequences of such an addiction. But as far as mating goes, it's wrong to keep us so limited."

He didn't look satisfied.

"Look," she said, "I'm a scientist. I know there isn't any permanent physical harm that can come from us sleeping together. Genetically, at least, if we were going to produce offspring, we'd actually be giving them a strong advantage. So at least in theory it's a good practice."

"Then why do you look worried?"

"I'm not worried," she lied. "The elders are superstitious and old-fashioned. Modern science doesn't mean much to them in the face of ancient traditions and rules."

"Lauren, I couldn't live with myself if something happened to you because of me." His expression had gone deadly serious, and she could see he was speaking from the heart.

"I feel the same about you," she said, but his words kicked her in the stomach.

She thought of her vision, of the two of them on the beach, in danger. He would survive, and she would not. How would he live with that? Maybe she needed to tell him the whole truth.

It was wrong to keep hiding it from him.

Lauren sat up and grabbed her dress from the side of the bed, then tugged it on. When she was covered, she sat on her knees and regarded him seriously.

"Listen, there's something I should tell you. This might sound awful, but I know how my life ends."

He blinked. "What are you talking about?"

"I've had a vision of my own death. It's common to those of us with the gift of prescience. Some gift, huh?"

He shook his head. "Why are you telling me this? Are you saying it happens soon or something?"

She didn't usually talk about her vision. It was, at the very least, a downer, and at worst, a major conversation-killer even among witches. Besides, she didn't like to think about it.

"I'm telling you because you're there when it happens."

"Hell no," he said, scowling now. "I'm not going to stand by and watch you die. Are you crazy? Your vision must be wrong."

She held up a hand to silence him. "Please," she said. "Just listen."

"But…" He was shaking his head in disbelief.

"I know it sounds really shitty, but you have to remember that there are some things in life we have no control over. I wasn't sure whether I should tell you this. It seems almost too cruel to bring up."

"Then why? Your vision must be wrong. Don't you have wrong ones sometimes?"

"Not like this. It's a recurrent vision, and it never changes."

"What happens?" For a moment, he stopped looking and sounding like the brave, strong man he was, and she caught a glimpse of the scared little boy he once might have been.

She looked away, appalled at herself for doing this to him. It wasn't information that anyone deserved to have. The way he looked, it was as if he really cared about her, as if he were here because of something much stronger than an addiction.

It was wrong and cruel for her to hope for that, or encourage it. It would only lead to more pain for him, if he really cared about her.

She looked back at him, and she realized at that moment exactly how big a wall she'd built around herself. She'd tried to keep herself from caring about him because she could never trust that he was with her for anything more than his next fix. And maybe that's really all it was. But the stricken look on his face made her consider that he did actually care about her. Or could care. And maybe she wanted him to.

No, scratch that. She did want him to care. There was no doubt.

He'd scaled her wall, and she had no idea how to get him out of her heart now.

"I shouldn't say any more. I'm sorry for bringing it up," Lauren said and tried to climb off the bed, but Carson grabbed her arm and held her there.

"You can't just drop a bomb like that on me and not give me any details. I need to know what you saw so we can stop it from happening."

"There's something I've learned from having visions," she said. "Fate is strange. There are some elements of it we can change easily, and there are other parts of our fate that no matter how much we try to avoid them, our destiny twists back around and happens anyway."

"That's bullshit. Tell me what's supposed to happen."'

She was surprised by the roughness in his normally laid-back, no-worries voice. Surprised enough that she finally said it. "We're running on a beach at night, running from someone, and I get shot."

He sighed heavily. "So we simply don't go to the beach. That's not too hard, is it?"

She shook her head. "Remember what I said about fate. It's a tricky thing."

"What makes you think I don't get shot?"

"It's a vision of my death, not yours. You'll escape. I know that much."

"Lauren, I'm not going to stand by and watch you die. There has to be something we can do about this."

"I've been seeing my own death since I was a little kid. It's not exactly a surprise to me anymore."

He was shaking his head, his brow furrowed, looking as if he'd just received some news he couldn't accept.

She felt like scum. Lower than scum. She should not have told him. She hadn't anticipated how awful it would feel to share the news of her death with the person who would witness it.

"I'm leaving then. If you're supposed to die, then I have to get the hell away from you. We can't ever see each other again."

Lauren stared at her own hands, trying to think how to convince him that it was useless to fight this fate, that they might as well enjoy themselves until the end came. But when she looked up at him, she could see that his eyes were full of grief, that he needed to feel as though he was doing something to help her.

"I really do appreciate your concern," she said. "But maybe the very act of your leaving would be what draws us back together and leads to my getting shot. Do you see how that could work?"

There was a sound from the entrance to the rooftop deck, and they both looked over at the same time to see Sebastian standing in the way, staring at them in complete disgust.

"What the hell are you doing?" he said so low Lauren was sure she was the only one who'd heard.

Carson, next to her, was still naked, and she could

see now there was no way Sebastian was going to be okay with a naked mortal on his bed with her. She'd been stupid to take the risk of bringing Carson here.

"I'm sorry, Sebastian," she said. "We shouldn't have come up here."

"No, you shouldn't have."

"I wanted to get some fresh air, and I didn't think you'd mind if we came up here for a bit to escape the nightclub crowd. But then things got out of hand, and—"

She stopped when she realized she was explaining too much, and Sebastian wasn't even looking at her. He was glaring only at Carson now, so that she wasn't even sure her cousin had heard her.

"We'll go," she said.

Then he looked at her with a coldness she'd never seen before. "The mortal will not be leaving here alive."

11

IF THE MORTAL WOULD BE the witness to Lauren's death, then it was the mortal who had to die first. Then, Sebastian reasoned, his cousin's vision of her death on the beach could not come true. She might never forgive him for killing her lover, but she would get to live out the full length of her life. That mattered more to him than forgiveness.

Sebastian reached into his boot and withdrew the knife from his ankle holster. "Lauren, you have to leave now," he said coolly.

She must have caught the glint of silver metal in the firelight, because she was staring at the knife now. "No," she said. "Sebastian, don't."

His cousin moved so that she was between him and Carson, but it would only take a few quick moves for him to be in position to throw the knife. He only needed one good throw, and the mortal would be as good as dead. A knife in the heart, or the side of the throat, or the eye—three easy spots to bring death. He'd been practicing knife-throwing since childhood, and he'd never met anyone who could match his skill.

"Lauren, move out of the way," Carson said. "This is between me and your cousin."

"Don't be stupid," she said. "You can't sacrifice yourself for me. It's not going to change anything. I'll still die when it's my time."

"I'm not going to let you get killed on my behalf," Carson said, standing up from the bed and crossing his arms in some kind of ridiculous challenge to Sebastian's knife.

"At least your mortal lover has some courage," Sebastian said. "Let him exercise it so he can die like a man."

He caught Lauren's movement from the corner of his eye, and then he realized she was digging something out of her purse. He heard the click of metal against metal.

"I'll shoot if I have to," she said, and he looked over to see she was aiming the same small gun at him that he'd made her take yesterday to protect herself.

"You've got your loyalties confused, cousin," he said, turning his attention back to the mortal.

Carson glanced over at Lauren's gun, apparently dumbfounded. "What the hell are you doing with that?" he said.

"Sebastian gave it to me for occasions like this," she said quietly. And then to Sebastian, she said, "My loyalties lie with the innocent, which you are not."

He laughed, but he didn't think anything was funny. He thought of the way he'd spent his life defending the family, protecting every goddamn witch who had come into his life, and he felt nothing but sad that his dearest cousin would now think of taking him out over a useless mortal.

He could end it right here. He could throw the knife, and save Lauren's life. If she killed him, then at least all the freaking pain would be gone.

"I'd rather die than leave you to the hands of The Order," he said, "So go ahead and shoot me when I throw this. I don't give a damn. You'll be doing me a favor."

Her expression was cool and even, but if he knew her at all, he knew she wasn't so sure of what to do.

"I just want to say one thing," Carson said. "Why don't you both save yourselves some trouble having to dispose of dead bodies. I was about to leave anyway."

Sebastian eyed the naked man who'd just been lounging on his bed. "Yeah, looks like you were on your way right out the door."

"I don't want to see Lauren die any more than you do. I'll do anything I can to keep her from coming to harm."

Out of the blue, he felt a moment's sympathy for the mortal. He was simply a weak, powerless man who'd fallen into Lauren's web. It was, after all, she who should have known better than to be sleeping with a mortal. "I'm listening," he said without lowering the knife.

"I'll leave and never come anywhere near Lauren

again. If I stay away from her, then there's no way she can die on the beach with me, right?"

"Sebastian, you know you need to be alive to help Corinne when the uprising begins. You're a part of that destiny. I don't want to shoot you and hurt the clan's chance for that freedom…but I will if I have to."

He regarded his cousin curiously. "You care about this mortal that much?"

"I do," she whispered.

Sebastian looked at Carson, and he felt a moment's sympathy for Lauren, who now knew what it was like to want someone she couldn't have. Just the way he wanted Maia, and would never have her.

He was silent as he considered the words on the tip of his tongue. Then he dropped his hand with the knife to his side. "Go," he said to Carson. "Before I change my mind."

The mortal eyed him suspiciously, and Lauren didn't put away her gun. She kept it leveled at Sebastian, as Carson gathered his clothes from the floor and dressed. A minute later, he edged past Sebastian, his gaze pinning him with no small amount of hostility. He got credit, at least, for having balls, and for caring enough about Lauren to get the hell away from her.

When Carson had disappeared through the doorway, Lauren finally put away her gun.

"I'm hurt, cousin. You put a mortal above a family alliance."

She looked at him for the first time with pure, unabashed disgust. "I don't know you anymore, Sebastian. I don't know what happened to you."

Then she followed the mortal out the door, and Sebastian stood on his rooftop deck alone, staring listlessly at the fire. After a while, he went to the edge of the bed and sank onto it. The knife slipped from his fingers onto the deck.

He didn't know what had happened to himself, either. Somewhere along the line, he suspected that bearing the weight of the supernatural world on his shoulders had turned him into a broken man.

"DON'T GO YET," Lauren said. "Let's talk about this first."

Carson turned to her, and for the first time, she realized her hands were shaking. Could she have really shot her own cousin, her blood, someone she'd loved for as long as she could remember?

She feared she could have.

"I'm causing nothing but trouble. Knives, guns, visions of death. It's time for me to get the hell out of here and leave you alone."

"No," she said. "First we have to talk."

Carson pulled a phone book out of the desk. "I need to find a rental car place, and then I'll be out of your hair."

"I'm sorry about Sebastian," she said. "I'm not sure I'll ever forgive him for what he almost did."

"He's just trying to protect you," Carson said. "I

can't blame him for that. I'd probably try to kill me, too, if I were in his shoes."

"You men and your goddamn egos. When are you going to realize it's not all about what you want, all the time?"

"What? You think your death will be for the greater good or something? You think I should stand by and watch it happen without trying to stop it?"

Lauren saw the anguish in his eyes and her words caught in her throat. It felt good to know he cared about her so much, so quickly. Perhaps it was only his addiction coloring his feelings, but some part of her wanted very much to believe his emotions meant something more profound.

She was a fool.

"Thank you for caring," she said, "but I do believe my death is part of something bigger. I believe it's the event that galvanizes my sister's energy and begins the uprising." This was the first time she'd articulated the greater significance hidden in her vision.

"If your sister is so powerful, why can't she save you?"

Lauren sat on the edge of the bed, suddenly feeling tired of having to explain the nature of fate. "I wish I could answer that, but maybe you'd just have to know Corinne."

"What does that mean?"

"She's all power and no discipline. Sort of like a loose fire hose when she tries to make anything happen."

"Then how is she supposed to be the leader of this big uprising?"

"She needs something that forces her to grow up and accept her destiny. She's not mature enough. She believes it, but she also thinks it's all a big game, and she's simply the one who wins."

"Can't you just tell her the deal? That you'll die if she doesn't get her act straight?"

"I've considered that, but I know her. She's never had any real responsibility in her life. She's been incredibly sheltered and spoiled, and I know it's going to take something huge to make her accept that she has to grow up."

"Isn't the threat of her own sister dying huge enough?"

"Maybe, but maybe not. I have to accept my vision for what it is. It's not really my job to question it."

"That's bullshit," he said, slamming his hand against the phone book. "I'm leaving, and I don't want you to ever come near me again. Do you understand?"

Lauren shook her head. "You know, if you go back to your old life, the men who were chasing me might find you."

"I guess I'll have to take that risk. I'm not going to give them any information about you, I promise."

"They have awful ways of getting information, and they'll simply kill you if you don't cooperate."

"Then I'll die. I'd much rather do that than stand by on some goddamn beach and watch you die."

"Please, Carson, don't do this."

"Those guys are after you, not me. I don't think you have anything to worry about."

"If you leave, you'll be putting my life in as much danger as you would if you stayed here."

"Your knife-wielding cousin up there isn't going to go for me sticking around here."

She said nothing, because he was right. Most likely, the witch hunters had gotten tired of trying to track down any leads for her in San Francisco. She was being overly paranoid. Probably enough time had passed now that he would be safe to return to the city.

"You can take Macy's car back to her," she said, and her heart sank as she accepted the inevitable.

12

Carson had been able to cancel his credit cards after his wallet was stolen, but now he had only five hundred dollars he'd borrowed from Lauren.

About halfway to San Francisco, he started feeling the symptoms of withdrawal in a big way. His hands shook, his vision went blurry, and he had a craving so deep and intense it was all he could do to keep from turning the car around and driving straight back to L.A., straight back to Lauren.

She hadn't been kidding about the addiction thing.

After their time in Vegas, he hadn't felt this shitty. Yes, he'd experienced some physical side effects of being apart from her—sleepless nights, intense craving, uncontrolled fantasies—but he'd channeled some of that reaction into his obsession over finding her again.

Now, however, he knew it was over. He'd do everything in his power to stay away from her. So not only were his physical reactions more intense because he'd spent more time with her, but also his emotions were suffering from what he suspected, if he examined it closely, was a broken heart.

He was a little surprised he could still drive the car without wrecking it, given his out-of-control body and mind. Sex had most definitely dumbed him down, as Lauren's study had proven it would.

He thought of his lost wallet, of the risk he'd taken in going out on the street, of how sluggish and stupid he felt right now. He really was acting dumber than usual, and it had to be a side effect of all the sex they'd been having.

He couldn't say he hadn't been warned. He only hoped he hadn't lost so much IQ that he was making mistakes he wasn't even aware of.

He drove north on I-5 and tried to remember why he was leaving. He had to stay away from Lauren to save her life. That alone was worth any amount of pain, and he could endure this physical distress if he knew he was preventing her vision from coming to fruition.

The premonition couldn't come true if he wasn't with her. He just had to remember that.

When these awful feelings intensified, and he was tempted to go running back into her arms, he had to remember that he was saving Lauren's life every day he didn't see her again. It seemed a cruel twist of fate, but maybe it was all for the best after all.

Maybe his parents had been right all those years ago in claiming people of different races were set up to face too many problems as a couple. He and Lauren had certainly proven their point.

But that thought only made him furious. No, his parents were asses.

And someday, somehow, he'd find a way to help Lauren aside from staying away from her. As his hands shook, and he struggled to keep his eyes focused on the road ahead, he promised himself he would find a way to protect her if it was the last thing he did.

CARSON POWERED UP the computer on his desk and tried to work up some kind of enthusiastic feeling for being back at work. A look at his e-mail told him he had 1568 new messages waiting for him, and a glance at his intray told him he had enough work backed up now to keep him busy for, oh, say, the next year. So much for Joey Brennan filling in as Creative Director during the past week.

He downed a long drink of his espresso—his second—and set the cup down as he observed his own shaking hands. He was still experiencing the withdrawal symptoms and he was sleeping like shit. His craving for Lauren was so intense he couldn't even imagine how he'd managed to drive away from her.

But he was feeling better than the day before.

He held on to that.

There should have been some kind of satisfaction in being back in his normal life, but Carson felt only blah. He now saw the pointlessness that he'd suspected while in L.A.—his empty apartment, his voice mail full of messages from people he didn't really care about hearing from, his goddamn job.

Carson realized, upon setting foot back in the Bronson and Wade offices, that he absolutely, without-a-doubt, hated his job.

Through his twenties he'd kidded himself with the notion that he was on the fast track, that he had a killer job in a desirable profession and that was all that mattered. He was being creatively challenged, and how many people ever got to say that about their work?

The advertising world had been a perfect setting for letting him fool himself into believing what the rest of the world said about him—that he was a party boy, a spoiled brat, a good-time guy just out for the next thrill and the next hot babe.

Carson, he was now realizing, had ironically fallen for his own spin. He was an ad man. He was supposed to know better than to fall for the slick package, the surface message, or even the subliminal one.

But he had. And now, why was he so surprised to discover the urge to run away from the whole gig, join the Peace Corps, or maybe expatriate to Bali to buy a nice little hut on the beach? He'd forgotten who he even was.

He opened a message from his boss about a major client who wasn't happy with the direction of their campaign, and his eyes glazed over. He didn't give a damn.

Instead of replying, he closed the message, picked up the phone, and dialed Griffin.

A few rings later, Griffin answered with a, "Hey, man, you're alive. It's about time you called me."

"Sorry, it's been a crazy week, to say the least. I'll explain it all later, or at least I'll try," he lied, not sure what he could really even say about Lauren, L.A. or witches without betraying Lauren's trust. At the very least he knew he would never reveal her true identity. He'd have to make up a good tall tale to explain his absence and Lauren's weird behavior the night they'd gone to her apartment—and why the apartment was ransacked for that matter.

"So you hooked up with Lauren, eh?"

"Don't want to kiss and tell, you know," Carson said, embarrassed at the stiffness in his own voice.

It didn't sound like something he'd say. Until recently, he'd been the king of kissing and telling Griffin the *Reader's Digest* version of his sexual exploits.

"Dude, I get it. You're falling hard for her. We pretty much already knew that."

"I didn't call to talk chicks, honestly. I was actually hoping to talk shop."

"What's up at good old Bronson and Wade, anyway?"

"Can't say we're doing all that great without you and Macy. You can rest assured you were valuable members of the company."

"Give me a break. There were probably five hundred equally talented people lined up to take my job."

Carson sighed. "No kidding. I had to interview them all."

"I know, I know. Sorry to have made your job more difficult, man."

"Hey, I should be glad you're gone, right? It means I'm getting the fat paycheck now instead of you." He was trying to sound cheery, but instead, his voice came out flat.

"What's really going on?" Griffin said.

Carson toyed with a pen on his desk, spinning it with his fingers, attempting to ignore the sick feeling in his gut. But finally, he knew he couldn't keep his worry inside any longer. He'd have to spill it and risk sounding like an idiot.

"Do you ever feel like…um…we're selling our souls in this business?"

He braced himself for a verbal assault, but instead Griffin laughed. "We work in advertising. Of course we're selling our souls. Isn't that a given?"

"How do you live with it? Doesn't it ever start to feel shitty?"

"I don't know, man. I guess it's easier for you to feel unsatisfied when you've got your trust fund to fall back on."

"Sorry, dude. It wasn't a fair question."

"I guess I look at it as a way to earn a paycheck. And I'm always up for a creative challenge."

"And you don't mind bending over and taking it in the ass from clients every day," Carson said, then immediately regretted insulting his best friend yet again.

But again, Griffin surprised him by laughing. "Guess not. I mean, sure, it gets to me sometimes. But I don't take the job too seriously. It's not my whole life or anything."

Of course it wasn't, because Griffin had started his own company, putting himself in a situation where he got to make all the decisions and pick and choose clients. And he had Macy, too, who was probably a hell of a lot more fulfilling than any job.

Carson had only begun to get a taste of what it was like to have something besides work define his existence. And he wanted a bigger taste. He wanted to pull up to the table and have a five-course meal that didn't include the advertising world.

"I'm just getting this feeling that I'm living the wrong life or something."

"Give it some time, man. It takes a few days to get back in the workaday groove."

"No, it's bigger than that. I can't be an advertising whore and ever really be happy with my life."

"So what, you're going to become a trust fund hippie? Turn on, tune in and drop out of your day job?"

"I don't know, man. I don't know."

"This is going to sound gay, but remember that time we went on that adventure tour of Costa Rica? We were hiking through the jungle and river rafting and diving off cliffs and shit, and right in the middle of it, I looked at you and said I could hardly recognize you?"

"Yeah, I remember." It had been one of the happiest times in his life, living nearly free of the civilized world, away from all the trappings and the success and the expectations. Away from everything that weighed him down in life.

"That's what this conversation is reminding me of. I haven't seen that side of you in a long time."

"I guess I left it in Costa Rica."

"You seemed more like…yourself then. More like a guy at rest in his own skin, not trying to put on an act for anyone."

"I seem like I'm putting on an act?" Carson said, glancing out the door of his office and hoping no one was lurking nearby eavesdropping on this ridiculously heartfelt conversation. Carson didn't do heartfelt on the job, or anywhere outside of bed.

"Not exactly. I think it's only something I notice because I've seen that other side of you. I've seen the wild, untamed Carson."

"Jungle Boogie Carson?"

"Yeah, man. I think maybe you belong in the jungle, and not the urban one, if you know what I mean."

"Maybe I *am* putting on an act. Or I have been, all these years. That's what scares me most. I started believing my own act."

"It's a good act. I think everyone believes you're the slick, easygoing, good-time guy you make yourself out to be."

"I'm thinking about quitting my job," Carson blurted out, surprised to hear the words spoken aloud himself.

"Yeah, well, I can't say I'd blame you for a second, since I did it myself."

"I just don't know what the hell I want to do."

"At the risk of sounding like a motivational speaker, sometimes you have to make the leap, and then the answer presents itself."

Carson felt a wisecrack on the tip of his tongue, but he held it back. Maybe Griffin was right. Maybe he just needed to leap, without knowing what was at the bottom of the cliff. He thought of Lauren and her quest to live by her own rules, and he realized she'd inspired him. She'd made him want to create some rules of his own.

"You went away for a week and came back sounding like a different person," Griffin said. "What the hell happened to you on that trip, anyway?"

Carson stopped spinning the pen and noticed the Web site advertised on the side of it. Yet another stinking advertisement. His whole life had become messages designed to sell things, designed to make someone, somewhere, more money, and he was goddamn sick of it. He wasn't sure he could take another day of corporate hell.

He flicked the pen off his desk, and it went sailing across the room, hit the wall and fell to the floor.

"Someday I'll tell you everything," Carson said. "But for now I've gotta go. Thanks for listening to me whine," he said distractedly and hung up the phone.

He continued to stare at the pen, and he knew. Whatever his future held, it wasn't here. It wasn't in this slick, shiny office at Bronson and Wade. And it wasn't in the slick, shiny world of advertising, either. His wild side was calling to him, and he had to follow that voice, wherever it led.

He turned back to his computer, opened up a blank e-mail message, and began typing his resignation letter.

13

LARS DID NOT ENJOY torturing mortals. Rarely did his work call for him to harm one of his own race, and when it did, he hated every moment of it. He was not a cruel man by nature. His work was to protect humanity, not to harm it, and he would have avoided doing so if he could.

But there were occasions such as this, when the mortal world and the supernatural world mixed in an unnatural way, forcing him to lie in wait as he did now. Next to him, Noam was breathing noisily.

"Could you shut the hell up for five minutes? I'm getting damn sick of listening to your nose whistle."

"Screw you," he said in his native Czech. "I've got allergies."

"He should be here any minute now."

"Bastard deserves to die for making it with the witch I want to do."

"We're not going to kill him yet. We're going to get the information we need, and then kill him."

"So what's the plan? You grab him and I inject him with the drug?"

"Yeah. You'd better get the needle ready," Lars said, handing Noam the medical bag they kept behind the driver's seat.

"I've never killed a mortal. Have you?"

Lars nodded. "Once. It's an unfortunate part of the job. You'll come to accept it in time," he said to the younger man, who'd only been his apprentice for six months now.

"What if we capture this guy and he won't talk no matter what? We kill him anyway?"

"Sadly, we'll have no choice."

"Maybe we can use him as bait to lure the witch into our hands."

Lars nodded. "It's possible. That's a last resort, though. Too many uncontrollable variables."

Outside, it had grown completely dark now, which worked to their advantage. They would have to work quickly, and they would have to be ready for any unforeseen circumstance. San Francisco was not the teeming den of witches that L.A. was, but the city had its share.

With any luck, in a matter of days, it would have one less for good.

Noam was glaring out the front window of the van. At nineteen, he was already becoming a decent witch hunter, but he had a lot to learn. Lars could remember himself at that age, twenty years ago, and he remembered his unquenchable idealism, his thirst to free the world of the unnatural balance the witches created.

"My father was killed by a witch," Noam said, and Lars was surprised to hear it. The kid rarely talked about himself. "Killed in the line of duty."

"I'm sorry to hear it. We all have someone we love who was lost to them."

"I swore I'd avenge his life. But if I'm killing another human, that's not exactly vengeance, is it?"

"You have to look at the big picture. This Carson McCullen is one step along the path to eradicating the witches. Don't get bogged down in the details."

"Yeah," the kid said. "I guess you're right."

A movement from the sidewalk up ahead caught Lars's eye. "Hey, that's him," he said, nodding at the man coming toward them. "That's the one we saw on the camera from the witch's apartment."

Noam readied the needle, and the two men exited the van silently. They headed toward the witch's consort, the cool night air enveloping them. Fog was pouring in from the ocean to the west, providing the street and sidewalk with a misty diffusion that aided their plans.

In a matter of seconds, they were upon the man, and he eyed them warily as they parted as if to let him pass between them. But in a lightning-fast movement, Noam had inserted the drug into the man's arm, and Lars caught him as he crumpled to the ground. The two men supported Carson's weight as they walked with his limp body back to the van, and then they dropped his body in the back. The two men climbed in behind him and closed the doors.

A few minutes later, they had him bound with rope in case he gained consciousness before the ride to The Order's Northern California operation center was complete. They were one step closer to capturing Lauren Parish.

A witch foolish enough to go on CNN for her own career glory would be foolish enough to tell them everything they needed to know to take down the entire clan. Lars was sure of it. He'd known, ever since seeing her on the news, that she alone was the key to The Order's success. She was too bold, too proud, not careful like the cowardly elders.

Lauren Parish would be the beginning of the end of the Beauville Clan. But his cock got hard in his pants when he thought of the witch. She was beautiful, even more so than the other female witches he'd seen. She aroused him in a way that he hated. It was impure, unnatural. It was out of balance with nature to desire a witch the way he desired her.

He was not proud of his urge. But as he watched the San Francisco streets pass by while Noam drove, he could think only of taking the witch. He would succumb to his desire if he had half a chance. No harm would come of it, if he was going to kill her anyway.

Surely, one good screw would cure him. And she would hate it, so it would be a form of torture, as well. He could use rape to gain the information he needed.

His erection didn't settle down. Instead, he could

feel his cock leaking seminal fluid in his underpants as he thought of taking the witch. He detested that she could have such an effect on him. He would punish her dearly for that.

"WHAT DO YOU KNOW about Lauren Parish," the man demanded.

Carson blinked at the harsh light, and he felt something warm on his forehead, oozing into his eye. He tried to move his hand to wipe at his eye, but he found that both hands were tied behind his back. He tugged harder, and the rope that bound his wrists cut into his skin.

"Who?" he asked, trying to buy himself a little time.

"Don't play games with me."

Carson could not see the man clearly with the bright light so close to his face. He could only see the dark form of the man on the other side of the light, his face covered by a black ski mask. The man lifted his arm, and then Carson felt the impact of something hard against the side of his head.

He reeled to the side, then was snapped back into place by the ropes that held him in the chair.

"What do you know?"

Carson said nothing. His mind raced to recall his most recent memory before awakening in this chair, in this room, with this man.

He remembered walking along the sidewalk toward his apartment after having gotten off the

Muni after work, his head buzzing with the fact that he'd just resigned from his job. He remembered it being dark, and cold. And then, nothing.

They must have been lying in wait for him. And judging by the throbbing in the back of his arm, like a bee sting, they must have injected him with some kind of drug.

He heard movement from the direction of the man behind the light, and then he felt a stinging slap in the face. Then another. And another.

Carson inhaled sharply at the pain, and he tried to think of whatever tips he'd read in the survival handbook he'd gotten from his brother for Christmas a few years ago. What had the damn thing said about how to survive being tied up and bitch-slapped for information?

Or worse.

The slapping stopped, and Carson had to admit to himself that it was probably the easy part. Something worse had to be coming soon for his enjoyment, or else they wouldn't have needed to tie him up so tightly.

"Let me tell you how this will work," the man said, and Carson noticed for the first time his accent, which sounded Slavic, or maybe German, but he hadn't spent enough time in Europe to know for sure.

"How what will work?"

"You give us the information we need, and we will not kill you."

"And if I don't have the information you need?"

"We kill you."

"You've got the wrong guy," Carson said, pissed at himself for not having read that damn survival guide more closely—for not having memorized it from cover to cover.

"I'm not stupid, Carson McCullen. I know who you are, and I know your relationship to Lauren Parish."

Carson went silent, admitting nothing. He wasn't sure if it would do him any more good to lie and continue denying he even knew Lauren. Or if it was better to play dumb and act as though he didn't know she was a witch.

"Is she worth losing your life over?" the man asked.

Carson concentrated on memorizing everything he could about his captor. The man's gray eye color, the pale skin tone visible through the openings in the ski mask, his wiry build, his black clothes.

"No," he said finally. "She isn't. I barely know her."

And then he remembered something he'd heard about what soldiers were trained to do when captured by enemy troops and questioned. They were told to give only their name, rank and serial number.

Did this occasion count as a capture by enemy troops? Did the rules of war apply here? Were the goals of a U.S. soldier held hostage even remotely similar to his goal in this situation, whatever this situation was?

He didn't want to die, and he didn't want to give away any information about Lauren.

"Do you always screw women you barely

know?" the man said as he sat down at the table across from Carson.

"Occasionally."

Carson thought then of his profession, what he got paid to do for a living in the advertising world. He had to sell a bill of goods to this guy. In short, lie to him. He might not have been a soldier, but he'd been well trained as an ad man.

Which, oddly, probably made him more ruthless than any soldier.

"I should tell you, we know how to kill you and dispose of your body without getting caught," the man said.

"Great. Thanks for letting me know," Carson said wryly, realizing too late that this probably wasn't the time for sarcasm.

And sure enough, the comment earned him another sharp slap. He winced at the stinging that lingered in the side of his face, complemented now by an aching eye.

"These little slaps will start to feel like a welcome respite from what will come after them. Shall I tell you what else will happen?"

"Sure, why not."

"I have a dog," the man said. "He is crazy for the taste of blood. I cut you anywhere, and he will come and attack."

Sounded like loads of fun, though Carson thought it wise to keep the sarcastic comment to himself this time.

"I will ensure the blood is coming from your groin, so he will attack there. If you are unlucky, he will tear your testicles right off. Would you like that?"

Did this guy ever get a yes to that question?

"No thanks. I'd like to pass on that one."

"So then you will cooperate."

Carson nodded, trying his best to look obedient, or however it was a cowed captor was supposed to look.

This was his chance, finally, to prove to himself he really could rise to any challenge. He'd always longed for one of these defining moments, where he could rise above privilege and luck and prove that he was a man to be reckoned with. He wanted to prove he had courage, that he could think on his feet and be counted upon in a crisis.

This was his one chance that would never come to him while working his life away in an advertising firm or whiling away his personal life jumping from one easy relationship to another.

Right here and now, he could not only save Lauren, but he could save his own soul.

"Yes," he lied. "I'll cooperate."

14

LAUREN AWOKE SWEATING, a scream trapped in her throat, her mouth open wide as if she really were crying out for dear life. She inhaled sharply and exhaled, struggling to catch her breath.

The images were too real to have been a dream.

She'd seen Carson tied to a chair, being beaten by a man in a ski mask. She'd felt a grave sense of doom about the situation. And now that she was awake, she understood that it had been a vision.

Not a dream.

Somewhere, Carson had been captured by the witch hunters.

As soon as her mind was free of that vision, another struck her. First the blinding white light, and then an image of Carson stumbling along a road, a cut on his forehead. Over his shoulder, a sign read Hwy 1, Carmel 30 miles.

She rarely had two visions in a row, and she closed her eyes, willing something else to come to her, some other clue to let her know what had happened to Carson, or how she could help.

But nothing else came, of course. She'd been given more than she could have hoped for, except absolute proof he was still alive.

She hadn't protected him, and now he might die. There was a chance they all would, if he talked.

She sat up in bed and blinked at the alarm clock, whose red numbers said it was nearly four-thirty in the morning. Her heart was thudding frantically in her chest. She wiped the sweat from her forehead with her palm.

She had to do something.

God, only five days had passed since Carson had left L.A. How had this happened? How had she let him wander into the hands of the witch hunters? How had she gotten so careless in so many ways? She would not forgive herself, if he was hurt. She wasn't sure how she could go on living with such an awful weight on her conscience.

Lauren got out of bed and dressed, pulled her hair into a ponytail, then went in search of Sebastian. She found him in his office staring at a computer screen, on which there was some spreadsheet that must relate to the nightclub business.

"I need your help," she said before he'd even realized she was there.

He startled, then regarded her calmly. "What is it?"

"The Order has Carson—or had him. We have to find him and help him."

He answered her with a cold, unfeeling stare.

"Sebastian, Carson has a lot of information about us. If they make him talk—"

"We're screwed."

"Exactly."

"Do you see now why I didn't approve of your bringing him here? Humans don't understand the gravity of our situation."

"Spare me the lecture, okay? The damage is done, and we have to try to undo it."

"How do you know what happened?"

"I saw it."

"When?"

"Just now, while I was sleeping."

"You're sure it was a vision and not a dream?"

Lauren nodded.

"You think they caught him in San Francisco?"

"That would be my guess. I saw two visions, one of him being tortured, and another of him stumbling along what looked to be Highway 1, thirty miles from Carmel."

The raven tattoo on Sebastian's arm vanished, and Lauren knew where it had gone—in search of Carson.

"Do I have to tell you what's going to happen if we find the mortal alive?" Sebastian asked.

Of course he didn't. Lauren's stomach lurched, and she cast her eyes down as if she was acknowledging some inevitable sad fact. Though in reality, she'd never let her cousin harm Carson. Not in a million years.

"I'm finished with being patient about him. It's time he pays his dues for entering our world."

"He didn't ask to enter it." Lauren couldn't help pointing the fact out. "It was my fault he came here."

Her cousin nodded. "Have you learned your lesson?"

"Of course."

"And you understand why he has to die?"

Her anger flared, and she didn't dare make herself consider why she was so desperate to keep Carson safe, aside from her sense of personal responsibility to him. "Why not kill me instead? I'm the one who's at fault."

"His death will have a dual purpose—to remind you not to be so reckless, and to keep him from ever endangering us again."

"But if we have the uprising soon, we won't need to worry about him endangering us. The whole world will know who we are."

Sebastian looked at her without expression. "We don't really know when or if the uprising will happen, do we?"

"Corinne seems to think it will happen soon."

"Corinne is young. She has no sense of time."

"She knows more than we do."

"You're not talking me out of taking Carson's life. It's necessary, Lauren. There's no getting around it. I was a fool for letting him be away from us alive for this long."

Lauren's stomach knotted itself tightly. "How can you take someone else's life into your hands so casually? You never used to be that way, cousin."

"I used to be a naive fool," he said flatly.

"You've changed," she said.

"So have you."

Lauren knew the way to Sebastian's heart wasn't this route. She decided to drop the subject for now. "Has the raven found anything yet?"

Sebastian closed his eyes and went completely still for a few moments. When he opened his eyes again, he shook his head. "Not yet."

"I'm going to pack. I think we need to leave for San Francisco as soon as possible. I can go without you if you'd prefer."

"No, I'm going, too. But I have some business to take care of here before we leave. And we should give the raven some time to seek out Carson first."

Lauren nodded, stood and left the office. Her heart was pounding again, and the sickening fear that they might be too late to help Carson clenched her insides. She would try to have another vision, but for now all she had was a sense of doom. Even if they caught up with him and were able to help him escape, she'd still have to save him from Sebastian.

She needed to talk to her little sister because she wasn't positive she could hold off Sebastian on her own. They rarely used cell phones to talk, so she went outside in the early-morning darkness to the pay phone down the block and dialed Corinne's number with a calling card.

After a few rings, her sister answered, sounding as

though she'd been awakened from a dead sleep. "Lauren?" she said in a groggy voice. "Are you okay?"

Without caller ID, she was relying on her intuition to know who was calling.

"Yes, I'm fine. But my friend Carson isn't, and I need your help finding him."

"Carson who?" her sister said, then yawned.

Lauren explained her relationship to the mortal, and then she steeled herself against the humiliation of a lecture from her own little sister. But none came.

Instead, Corinne yawned again and said, "And you're waking me up at *what* time because of this?"

"I'm sorry. I would call another time if I could, but this is an emergency. I need your help now."

"I don't know what you think I can do."

"For one thing, I need you to tell me if you have a sense of what's about to happen. Do you think The Order is close to us?"

Corinne was silent for a few moments, during which time Lauren imagined her sister lying in bed, her long red hair splayed on the pillow and her eyes closed as she tried to summon a sense of the situation.

"I think we still have some time before there is a major clash with The Order, but I don't know how much. Maybe a few years, maybe a year, maybe six months."

"Is that all you're getting?"

"No." And then, a long pause. When she finally spoke again, her voice sounded distant and strange.

"Your vision of you with the man on the beach—it's immediate. It will happen soon."

Lauren blinked, knowing her sister was right.

"If it happens before I see you again," she said, "please remember that I love you."

"I love you, too, Lauren." It wasn't like Corinne to sound vulnerable, but for once, she did.

Lauren couldn't take it. She didn't want to break down and cry. "I have to go," she said and hung up the phone.

Her time had come, whether she was ready or not. She tried not to feel sorry for herself, but she did anyway.

She didn't want to die. She was nowhere near ready to leave this earth. She had way too much living left to do.

SOMETHING WASN'T RIGHT.

Lars had heard the shuffling sound in the rear of the van, but he'd assumed it was simply Carson McCullen stirring in his sleep. The last time he'd checked on McCullen, the man had been knocked out cold, with his hands and feet bound.

But when Lars heard the rear doors of the van open, and caught a fleeting glimpse of McCullen's back as he jumped from the van, he got his first sense that he'd been had.

The bastard was escaping.

But how?

"Stop the van!" he said, lapsing into Czech to

Noam, who was already cursing and pulling over to the side of the road.

Lars scrambled out of the van as it came to a stop, catching the movement of Carson's body as he rolled through the brush and down the hillside. The fool would be lucky if he survived the jump from the van. If he wanted to commit suicide, that was fine by Lars. It would save him having to kill the uncooperative idiot.

As he hurried down the hillside after McCullen, his mind scrambled to understand how he'd escaped in the first place. Perhaps if McCullen hadn't really been unconscious, as he'd seemed to be, and if he'd spent the past three hours in the van working his way loose from his binding, rather than sleeping as Lars had assumed he'd been…

He should have known better than to trust McCullen. He had claimed Lauren Parish was staying at a safe house off of Highway 1, somewhere near Big Sur. He hadn't been very specific with the details, claiming he'd seen the house only once in the dark and couldn't remember much about it, but he would know the place when he saw it.

Lars had knocked him out with a sharp blow to the head, to be safe, tied him up, and they'd set off toward Big Sur, planning to wake McCullen once they were close to their destination.

But now… Now Lars knew he'd been had. He'd never met a human before who'd been willing to die for a witch, so this man had caught him off guard with his stubbornness. Fool had probably gotten so addicted to his witch lover that he could no longer think straight.

Lars tripped on a rock and went tumbling, falling head over heels down the steep hillside, banging himself against brush and rock until he finally came to rest on the beach, his head still spinning. He blinked up at the sky and took inventory of himself. No real damage.

Nearby, he could hear footsteps, probably Noam's, but all other sound was drowned out by the ocean crashing against the beach. Lars sat up and looked around. McCullen was nowhere in sight, but Noam was making his way down the beach, looking left and right.

"Do you see him?" Lars called out as he stood and brushed himself off.

Noam held out his hands and shook his head.

Damn it.

The two men searched until sunset, first the beach, then the woods nearby, and finally they went back to the van and started driving slowly, hoping they'd see something from the road.

In the dark, their task was considerably harder.

Lars stared out at the ocean, at the moon rising over it, and his gut told him they were getting closer to Lauren Parish. Or was that just a foolish, desperate hope, based on how little had gone right today?

"Don't be so pissed off. We'll find him, and we'll find the witch," Noam said, breaking a long brooding silence that had settled between the two men, each probably blaming the other for their escaped prisoner.

"You didn't tie the ropes tightly enough," Lars spat.

"You didn't knock him out like you thought you did," Noam answered, his voice taking on a surly tone.

"You didn't refill the supply of tranquilizers like you should have. If you had, I wouldn't have needed to knock him out."

Lars glared ahead, truly angrier at himself than at the kid, who was young enough to be allowed a few mistakes. Lars knew the source of his mistake. He'd gotten sloppy out of desire. He'd allowed himself to become consumed with thoughts of having the witch, burying his cock inside her, and he had let his usual diligence slide.

He would not forgive himself for that.

Such was the danger of addiction. And he had to remember that he first served The Order. That was his purpose in life, and nothing could stand in the way of it. He believed in his work. He could not let desire interfere.

Never again.

He felt the weight of the gun in its holster against his rib cage, hidden beneath his jacket, and he made himself a promise.

When he found Lauren Parish, he would not let desire overcome him again. He would shoot to kill.

LAUREN SET SEBASTIAN'S BMW on cruise control and glanced at the clock on the dash. It would be dark soon, they had another few hours before they'd reach San Francisco, and she couldn't stop brooding about her own doom.

A witch foretelling his or her own death was not unusual. But Lauren had always hated knowing the circumstances of her own demise. Even knowing that it would probably be the galvanizing action for the uprising didn't help. She didn't want to be a martyr, she wanted to be alive. And now her time was almost up.

She felt twinges of regret about not taking her life more seriously. She would have done a few things differently. She would have loved the people she wanted to love instead of worrying about the rules. She would have let herself live more fully, more honestly…more everything.

Beside her in the passenger seat, Sebastian was sleeping. A sleeping lion, he seemed, likely to awaken and do damage at any moment. The danger he posed to Carson had not escaped her, but she had to trust that, in the end, he wouldn't do anything against her wishes.

The raven was still missing from his arm, still looking for Carson. When it left Sebastian for this long, it exhausted him, put him to sleep. She desperately wanted to know what the bird was seeing now, but it wouldn't do any good to wake her cousin. The raven would return when it had seen what they were looking for.

Outside, the coast stretched on forever north. But

Lauren barely registered the scenery. Her entire being was caught up in the feeling of doom she'd had ever since waking up with the vision of Carson. She couldn't figure out which she felt worse about—that she would soon die, or that Carson might soon be dead himself.

She hated that she'd ever involved him in her life, and she equally hated that once she'd done so, she didn't have the courage to throw out all the rules and let things happen naturally between them.

Maybe they could have proven the elders wrong and had a happy relationship. Maybe Carson could have eventually gotten his fill of her and moved on without any more pain than occurred when a normal romance ended.

Maybe, maybe, maybe. She didn't want to live with such regrets.

If by some miracle she could save herself and Carson, she wanted to give their relationship a real chance.

A movement in the corner of her eye caught her attention, and she glanced down to see the raven tattoo had returned to Sebastian's arm. After a few minutes, he stirred, yawning and stretching. When he opened his eyes, Lauren glanced over at him.

"What did you see?" she asked.

He squinted at the road ahead. "I saw his apartment is empty, so we know he's not there."

"That's not very helpful."

"I wasn't finished. I saw him there on the

highway, just as you predicted. We're only a few miles from his location now."

Lauren's mouth went dry, and she accelerated. When they rounded a bend several minutes later, she could see a man on the side of the road in the distance.

"There he is!" Lauren's heart thudded wildly when, closer, she could see that it was indeed Carson stumbling along the side of the road, the way he had been in her vision.

She pulled the car over behind him.

"This could be a trap, you know," Sebastian said. "I don't think The Order would let him escape without a reason."

"You're right, but we can't leave him here bleeding." She was scrambling out of the car even as she said it.

"Carson!" she called out, and he turned to her.

There was a gash on his forehead, along with dried blood. He looked at her as if she was an apparition.

She hurried to his side. "Are you okay?"

"Lauren, wow. How did you find me?"

"I had a vision of you here with a Highway 1 sign in the background."

"You drove all the way up Highway 1 looking for me?"

"There isn't any time to talk now. I'll explain it all later. Just get in the car with me and let's go."

He spotted Sebastian now in the driver's seat. "I'm not going anywhere with him."

"Don't be stupid, Carson. He's not going to hurt you, but those bastards who did that to you," she said, nodding to his head injury, "will kill us all if they catch up to us."

"What are you talking about?" he said, lifting his hand to his forehead.

He winced when he touched the wound. "What the hell?"

"Do you remember what happened to you?"

He shook his head, frowning as he seemed to try to recall anything. "I remember a room…and a bright light…and being tied to a chair…."

"Nothing else?"

"I don't even remember getting hit on the head."

"It was probably a hard enough impact to make you lose your short-term memory."

"I have no idea how I got here, either."

But Lauren didn't voice her other fear, that whatever had happened to him had been horrific enough to make him block it out.

"We have to go, please," she said again. "Come on."

"You think someone's chasing us?"

"The Order kidnapped you, and I have no idea if they're watching us right now."

He shook his head. "I'm not getting in a car with that guy."

Before she could argue with him any further, the

sound of a twig snapping in the nearby woods caught her attention, and she turned to it. But she saw no one.

"Listen, we have to go *now.* We could all die if we don't hurry."

He seemed to take her seriously then, but a white van screeched around the bend and came careening toward them. Lauren grasped Carson's hand and pulled him in the only direction they could go—toward the beach.

The moon had just risen over the Pacific, providing a little light, but not enough to make it an easy trek down the hillside. She heard a crash, the crunch of metal against metal, and she thought of Sebastian. The sound of screeching tires, and a car engine revving reached her, but she was too far away to guess what was happening.

Soon there was only the sounds of their feet crunching against the dry coastal ground cover, and their ragged breath as they raced toward the beach.

Toward the scene she had been hoping all her life to avoid.

Tears prickled at Lauren's eyes again. This was it. The event she'd been dreading, the place her entire life had been moving toward.

They finally hit the beach, and they made their way across the dry loose sand—too difficult to run fast on—toward the ocean and the wet, hard-packed sand nearest it. Behind them, Lauren could hear someone else scrambling down the hillside.

She said a silent prayer for Sebastian, but she

suspected he would be okay. He, more than anyone else she'd ever met, was invincible, regardless of the changes in him.

Carson was looking to her as they ran, trying to say something. "Where are we going?"

"I don't know, but we need to get off the beach as soon as we can. There's nowhere to hide here."

She regretted now that they hadn't taken the more difficult route into the woods. After all, she'd never had a vision of herself dying in the woods. She needed to get the hell away from this place, this beach with the moon watching over her death.

But when she looked over at Carson again, the moment felt eerily familiar, and she knew it had finally arrived.

15

THE DEAFENING BURST of gunfire at first seemed like a dream to Carson, as if he hadn't really heard it. Maybe his mind was playing tricks on him. Maybe it had been the crashing surf. That had to be it.

He glanced over at Lauren in the instant after he imagined the sound. To his horror he saw her falling forward onto the sand. A dark stain was spreading across her light-colored top, and in his confusion he imagined she must have tripped over a rock, that he just needed to reach down and grab her hand and pull her to her feet again.

His heart was pounding so wildly he could hardly inhale as he bent down, but she wasn't trying to get back up. She was lying facedown on the sand.

Another gunshot. And another.

He dropped to the sand and flattened himself on top of Lauren, stupidly hoping to shield her from the bullets.

When he looked in the direction of the gunshots, he saw two men who'd been pursuing them, both aiming guns in his direction.

But in the blink of an eye, one man fell to the ground, and then the other, watching the first man fall, was struck by some sharp flash of metal and fell, as well.

Carson's mind could not process the events at once. He could think only of Lauren beneath him, of how to keep her safe. He watched the men for a moment longer, but they lay on the ground, not moving. Then he eased himself off Lauren and saw what he did not want to see.

Her back was covered in blood. He could feel the dampness now on his own shirt, and he reached out and touched her back as if to confirm that his eyes weren't fooling him.

He felt as if he were moving in both slow motion and fast forward at the same time, as if the universe was somehow slowing down as it sped up.

This couldn't be happening.

"Lauren," he said, but she didn't stir. "Lauren, please, can you hear me?" he said as he turned her over and found the front of her as bloody as the back.

She'd been shot. Just as she'd said. He would witness her death. He *had* witnessed her death.

But no. He had to save her. Keep her alive.

This couldn't be happening.

He felt her neck for a pulse, but his hands shook wildly, and he couldn't be sure if he was feeling the right spot. He tried to remember what he'd learned of CPR from being a lifeguard in high school, or what he'd learned about first aid before going on his first backpacking trip, but his brain wasn't working.

Finally a coherent thought emerged. He had to stop the bleeding.

He held his hand over the wound, but then thought of how she was bleeding from the back, too, and he started to take off his shirt, when he heard footsteps coming across the sand.

He looked up to see Sebastian running toward them. There was a flutter of black from his arm, and the raven flew to Lauren, hovered over her, and then vanished into her chest.

Carson stared, dumbfounded, unable to process what his eyes had just seen.

Sebastian, breathing heavily, dropped to his knees beside his cousin. His expression was stricken with grief, and tears dampened his cheeks.

"I don't know if that will save her," he said.

"What did you do?"

"I've stopped the wound from bleeding any more, I think. I have to get her to a witch doctor right away."

"We should call 911. We have to get her to a hospital."

"No. I'll take her to a doctor near here. I can't risk anyone asking questions about how she was shot."

"I'll help you carry her to the car," Carson said, knowing by now it did no good to argue with the man. He cared about Lauren almost as much as Carson did, so he had to trust that Sebastian would do right by her.

What other choice did he have?

"First," Sebastian said, looking at him coldly. "Help me dump those bodies into the ocean." He nodded at the men lying on the ground nearby.

Carson looked down at Lauren's face, deathly pale in the moonlight. The rotting scent of sealife in the ocean air made him want to vomit.

This could not be happening.

But it was.

The two men went to the dead bodies, and Sebastian bent and pulled a knife from each of their chests, wiped the blades on his jeans, and inserted them back into leather holsters inside his boots. Carson winced at the sight of the wounds, but said nothing.

He helped Sebastian lift each of the bodies and carry them to the surf, where they heaved them as hard as they could into the cold dark ocean.

"Help me with her now," Sebastian said, and Carson followed along, a zombie helping to carry the limp body of his lover up the hillside.

They lay her in the backseat of Sebastian's car, and the man closed the door and turned to Carson.

"I should kill you now," he said. "I was going to, but you tried to protect her. I can see that."

Carson nodded, saying nothing, his throat constricted at the realization that he had failed miserably. He glanced one more time at her face, too still and too pale and his throat seized up again.

"I loved her," Carson said, much to his own surprise. But once the words had exited his mouth, he understood that they were true.

She wasn't an addiction. It was a feeling of having found the one woman who made him feel whole like no other. She was his cure for a life of numbness. She was his everything.

And now she lay in the back of a car dying. Or, perhaps, already dead.

"Never speak of these events again," Sebastian said. "Do you understand?"

Carson nodded.

"Lauren was right that there are some elements of fate we can't change. Just remember that," he said, and he got in the car and sped away.

Carson watched the car's taillights quickly grow smaller, and then the car rounded a bend in the road and was gone. And here he was alone, at night, somewhere on Highway 1, with a bloodstained shirt, a head wound, and no idea how he'd gotten here.

He looked up at the full moon, at its lonely glow, and knew that this was real. He was here, Lauren was probably dead, and two men's bodies floated in the ocean down below. The gash on his head began to throb as the adrenaline drained from his body, and he reached up and touched it gingerly, trying to guess the extent of the damage.

Hard to tell. He was still up and walking around. But he had no recollection of the hours or days or however long it had been between the time he'd walked toward his apartment after work, and when Lauren had found him limping along the side of the road here.

Other aches and pains began to register, and he was starting to get the picture that whatever had happened to him hadn't been good. It had been, most likely, painful enough that he'd blocked out the memory of it.

Standing at the edge of the road, he looked left, then right. San Francisco was to the north, judging by a sign up ahead that said Carmel was in thirty more miles. So he began walking in that direction.

SEBASTIAN WAS NOT SURE he had made the right decision in letting the mortal live. Hell, the guy looked bashed up enough that he might very well not have made it back to civilization before collapsing dead himself.

But when the moment had come that he should have pressed the blade of his knife into Carson McCullen's neck, he could not make himself do it. He had thought of Maia, of loving someone he couldn't have, and his heart had rebelled at the thought of doing the same thing to Lauren, if by divine grace she somehow survived.

So he left the matter of their fates to chance, and abandoned Carson on the side of the road. Only time would tell if he had done the right thing.

He was a romantic fool.

As he turned into the driveway of the witch doctor's Carmel estate, he blinked back tears. He had never been so scared in his life as he had when he saw Lauren fall to the ground from the gunshot wound. Not even in Bretagne as a little boy, hiding in the woods from the witch hunters.

She had told him over and over that it was her fate to die there on the beach, but he had only realized as he saw it happen how much he had refused to believe it was true.

He still refused to believe it was true.

He had failed his cousin by not saving her, and if by some miracle the part of him wedged inside her chest, attempting to keep her alive, did save her, he would not have to look into her eyes and tell her that he had killed Carson.

So, a fool he was. But he owed her that.

He slammed on his brakes when he reached the end of the driveway, killed the engine, and honked the car horn several times. Then he hurried to the backseat and lifted Lauren into his arms.

He'd already called ahead to their distant cousin Dmitri, to let him know they were on their way and to be ready to tend to Lauren's wound, and as he reached the top of the stone staircase at the entry to the house, the large door opened, and Dmitri stood there already dressed for surgery.

"Bring her downstairs," he said. "Does she have a pulse?"

"I don't think so," Sebastian said, his stomach revolting at the words. "I can't feel one."

At the bottom of the stairs, they reached a room that was brightly lit. Inside, there was an operating table, and a woman Sebastian didn't recognize was preparing instruments for surgery.

He lay Lauren on the table, and Dmitri cut open her top and looked at the wound, his expression grave. "The bullet may have penetrated her heart," he said.

Sebastian felt as if the air had grown thinner, and he needed to sit down.

"Do you think she'll be okay?"

"You should wait outside," Dmitri said. "You don't look well."

"I shape-shifted to stop the bleeding," Sebastian explained. "I'm getting tired from doing so, I guess."

"I will take care of her from here. You return to your full form and go rest for a while."

Sebastian closed his eyes and willed the raven back to his arm. He could feel the strange sensation of slipping from the inside of Lauren's chest, and he could see the dark red of her blood and tissue, and then it was all gone. The tattoo was in its place again.

He glanced at his cousin's pale deathly face as he left the room, and he could not let go of the thought that he had failed her.

Hours later, when Sebastian awoke, drenched in sweat and his heart racing, in a warm room lit by sunlight, he could not say how much time had passed. He did not recognize his surroundings, but the luxury of the linens and the bedroom reminded him that he was at Dmitri's estate, and then the memories of the night before flooded his head.

He had slept fitfully, dreaming awful nightmares

and reliving the events at the beach. He did not know how the surgery had gone, he realized now, and he shot out of bed to find out.

The house was quiet except for a few servants moving about performing their daily chores. Sebastian stopped a maid and asked if she knew where Dmitri was, but she didn't.

He went downstairs to the room where he'd taken Lauren the night before, but the door was locked, and no sound came from within. Muttering a curse, he went back upstairs and wandered around until he found Dmitri in his office.

"What happened?" he said, even though the older man was on the phone.

"I'll call you back," Dmitri said to whomever he was speaking, then hung up the phone and regarded Sebastian. "Good morning. It doesn't look as if you slept well."

Sebastian looked down at himself and saw that he was still in his clothes from the day before. He probably looked like hell.

"What happened?" he asked again. "Is she okay?"

"The bullet passed through her chest cavity and exited from the front. There was damage to her heart. I repaired the tissue as best I could, but please keep in mind I'm not a heart surgeon."

"Is she alive?"

"Her heart stopped beating for a while—I'm not sure how long. We were able to get it beating again, but she's not awake yet. If her brain was deprived of oxygen for very long, she could suffer severe damage."

Sebastian closed his eyes and tried to form a coherent thought. How would he live with himself if he let Lauren die? Damn her stupid vision and her freaking claims that her death was for a good cause. She was too young and vibrant to die.

"When will we know anything?"

"Her body has suffered a major trauma. With some luck, she'll awaken soon and we can tell if she has suffered any permanent damage to her brain."

"And without luck?"

"She may remain in a coma, or she may never be the same again. Or, she may die from the trauma. We should prepare ourselves for any of these eventualities as we hope for the best."

Sebastian took a deep breath. He would have to call her family and tell them the news. But not yet. "I want to see her," he said, and Dmitri nodded.

His cousin led him back downstairs to the room that had been locked. He inserted a key and led Sebastian into the darkened room, where a monitor registered Lauren's vital signs. A slow steady heartbeat blipped across the screen.

The man flicked on a light, and Sebastian saw that a nurse sat at Lauren's bedside, making notes on a clipboard. "Can you give him a few moments alone?" Dmitri said to the woman.

She nodded and left the room.

"Why was the door locked?" Sebastian asked.

"Just as a safeguard. I have to protect myself from the possibility of a police search. If I'm ever caught performing surgeries here, I will be put in jail where I won't be able to help the clan at all."

Sebastian nodded.

"Let Anna know when you're finished visiting, and she'll come back and wait at Lauren's bedside again."

"Is it necessary to have someone with her all the time?"

"With witches who've undergone surgery, it is a wise idea. Our supernatural powers can go haywire when we've suffered a major trauma. It's rare, but I've seen witches accidentally harm themselves while in a coma or while recovering. I'm just covering all the bases."

"Thank you," Sebastian said, and his cousin left the room and closed the door.

He turned to Lauren's body lying on the bed in the middle of the room, and he forced himself to look at her face. She still looked as if she was dead. The color was gone from her features, and her pale skin was a stark contrast to her dark hair.

Sebastian pulled the chair close to her bed, sat and took her long delicate hand in his. It was cool and lifeless.

"Lauren, I hope you can hear me. It's me, Sebastian."

He watched her face for some sign that she'd heard, but there was nothing.

"I did everything I could to save you," he said. "And I'm more sorry than you'll ever know that you got hurt. I know you've got that damn theory about how your death will be the thing that makes Corinne straighten up and learn to control her powers well enough to lead the uprising, but I think you're wrong. I think we need you here, too, if we're ever going to be successful."

He stopped and stared at her hand in his. She'd been his closest friend when they were kids, and he'd always imagined that someday, they'd each have kids who would grow up playing together, being best friends. Tears flooded his eyes at that thought.

He never would have admitted to a soul what a sentimental fool he was, but if anyone knew his true nature, it was probably Lauren. Which made the fact that she was lying here nearly dead hurt even more. If she died, a part of him would die, too.

"Listen Lauren. If there's any way you can pull yourself out of this enough to hear me, you have to do it."

He paused again and squeezed her hand, desperate for something—anything—to get through to her.

"Carson is alive. I let him live for you, you know, so don't ever say I didn't do you a favor. I know you care for him, and you have to get better so you can make sure he doesn't screw everything up for us."

He stopped and watched her face. Still no reaction.

"You see, I'm relying on you to get better so you can keep up with him. You know we can't have some mortal walking around knowing as much about the clan as he knows. If you don't get better, I might have to hunt him down and kill him after all," he said, then immediately regretted it.

Maybe she couldn't take hearing anything stressful right now. But if he knew Lauren at all, he knew she'd get pissed off and fight before she'd give in.

"So get better, so you can watch over that damn mortal. He'd be devastated if you died."

Sebastian kissed her limp hand, then stood and kissed her forehead, too. "Get better, cousin," he said. "Please get better."

LAUREN WAS IN THE MIDDLE of a black place. She felt as if she was suffocating from the blackness. There was nothing to see, nothing to touch, nothing to breathe. A sense of panic rose up in her, and then she realized she could breathe after all.

Her lungs still worked in the blackness. In, out, in, out. She simply had to will them to work, and they did.

But she could see nothing and feel nothing, except for a piercing pain in her chest. It would not go away, instead grew more and more intense.

And then, nothing.

Blackness.

Later, Sebastian's voice. Some part of her watched him talking to her, only half hearing the words. Some part of her sat above them both and felt a heavy sadness that would not go away. She wanted to comfort him, to tell him that all his fighting on her behalf was for nothing and that he should let her go. But she could not.

Later still, more blackness.

And then a fading to brown, to red, to pink, to white. She felt lighter than air, and the pain was gone, or else she simply had entered a place where she could not feel.

She saw herself lying on the bed, and Sebastian was beside her again. He was talking to her, but she heard no words. Her sadness was gone, and she felt only light. She felt as if she had become white light, and she was floating, filling up the space with lightness. There was no longer any part of her connected to that old body, that dying self.

She regarded herself curiously and wondered if she was dead.

Later still came the nightmares, the horrific images of the moments before the bullet had grazed her heart. She saw Carson, with the gash on his head and, she sensed, other injuries not so easily apparent. She saw Sebastian killing the two men who'd been chasing them, and she saw the bodies tossed into the surf. She saw herself, bleeding on the sand, her body lifeless.

She felt as if she was trapped in a nightmare she could not wake from, and she wanted to scream, to pull herself away from the pain and the fear and the sadness. She imagined that she was crying out and thrashing on the bed, and then she could hear her own voice, a dreadful moan. But she didn't know whether she was asking for life or death.

16

THE PROBLEM with giving up his fast-track career, Carson discovered, was that he then had to figure out what the hell to do with himself.

"Catch!" Macy called out, and Carson held up his hand and caught the set of keys careening toward him.

"What're these for?" he asked.

"Can you lock up the office when you're done?"

"Sure, where you going?" he asked as he saved the file he was working on.

"Griffin should be back in a minute, and we've got an off-site meeting with a potential new client."

Macy and Griffin's receptionist had quit a week ago, leaving them screwed until they hired someone new. Carson, suddenly free of a job himself, offered to help them out in the interim.

He hadn't mentioned the fact that he didn't feel like being alone and useless right now, not when he had no idea what had happened to Lauren, and no one to even ask if she was okay.

He'd thought of driving back to L.A. to find Sebastian and demand to know the truth, but part of him was too afraid to make the trek right now. What if the news wasn't what he wanted to hear? What if she hadn't survived? Part of him had to know the truth, and part of him was too much of a goddamn coward to face it right now.

He'd only started feeling halfway himself again a few days ago. After hitchhiking back to San Francisco thanks to the mercy of a truck driver who hadn't been too put off by his scruffy appearance, a trip to the hospital had confirmed he had a concussion, was in need of sixty stitches, and had suffered various other minor injuries.

He'd been bruised from head to toe, had a fractured rib, and two of his fingernails were missing. The hospital staff had eyed him warily when he swore he couldn't remember what had happened, and they'd forced him to file a police report, but he'd avoided revealing any details about Lauren or her family, or the men who'd been after them.

"What's wrong?" Macy asked.

"Hmm?" he said, jarred out of his thoughts.

"You spaced out there for a minute. You've been doing that a lot lately."

Carson shrugged. "It's nothing."

Macy came back from the doorway and sat on the edge of the desk. "Griffin and I are worried about you. That's the real reason we're letting you work here, because, frankly, you suck as a receptionist."

She smiled at him, but he could barely muster the energy to smile back.

"Are you sure that head injury didn't do any permanent damage?"

Griffin came into the office. "Hey, gang's all here. What's going on?"

"I was just telling Carson that we think he's turning into a nutcase," Macy said.

Griffin smiled. "I thought we weren't supposed to use the word *nutcase* around the n-u-t-c-a-s-e."

"Funny, asshole. I'm fine. I'm just suffering a…you know…broken heart or whatever. Cue the violins now please."

He turned back to the computer monitor and opened a Web browser, intent on looking busy so they'd leave him alone.

"Is that really all it is?" Macy asked. "You weren't probed by aliens or anything while you were gone?"

"That would have been preferable to being dumped, but no, no extraterrestrial probings occurred."

"Damn," Griffin said.

"Don't you two have to be somewhere?" Carson asked, glancing meaningfully at his watch.

"Nah," Griffin said. "I forgot to tell Macy, the meeting's postponed an hour."

"It's about time you fill us in on what really happened with Lauren," Macy said. "She's my best friend, after all. I think I deserve to know what's going on with her."

Carson sighed. He'd been bracing himself for the inquisition, and he knew he couldn't make any more excuses. It was time to make up a really good lie.

"Far as I know," Carson said. "Lauren's fine. She swore me to secrecy about her whereabouts and the reason she had to disappear so quickly from the city, but I can assure you when I left her, she was her usual self."

"I don't get it. Why'd you show up back here looking like you'd had the hell beaten out of you?" Griffin asked.

"I told you, my rental car broke down on the way to Carmel for a little soul-searching getaway. A couple of guys robbed me and kicked my ass when I was trying to hitchhike to the next town."

"Did these guys have, you know, green skin, weird bulbous heads, long probing fingers?"

"Shut the hell up," Carson said, but he couldn't help laughing. It felt good to laugh at something, even if for a moment.

"Did Lauren give you any idea when we'd hear from her again?"

"No, I think she's gotta lie low for a while. But she told me to assure you she really is fine, and she'll be in touch as soon as she can."

Macy was twisting her long blond hair around her finger, and her mouth formed a thin line, but she seemed to accept his answer this time. "If you say so, but if I don't hear from her soon, I'm going to hire a P.I. and start tracking her down myself."

Carson shook his head. "I don't think you want to mess with Lauren. She seemed adamant that we leave her alone for now."

At least he'd gotten through the worst of the withdrawal symptoms since being apart from Lauren. His hands had stopped shaking, he hadn't needed a cigarette in days, and he was down to three cups of coffee in the morning. He even slept on occasion, though not for long, and not without nightmares.

Memories of his time in captivity had started coming back to him. Snapshots of unpleasant and painful moments, torture, his pretending to cooperate with his captors to save himself, only to be tortured even more, and then find that he still had managed to lead Lauren right into their hands.

He would never forgive himself for that.

"There you go again, spacing out," Macy said.

He looked up at her and saw the worried expression on her face.

"Why don't you skip the receptionist gig and come with us to this meeting?" Griffin asked. "We could use your creative expertise."

Carson shook his head. "I'd love to help you out, but my advertising days are done."

Griffin shrugged. "Okay, but the offer stands—you can come work with us any time you change your mind."

"I think I'll stick with playing computer games," Carson said, and navigated to an online game site.

Coloring flashing blocks and mindless Ping-Pong computer games were about the most challenging things he cared to manage at the moment.

"Okay, I guess we'll head on out and beat the traffic," Griffin said, and he and Macy left the building.

Alone, Carson stared at the computer screen without really seeing it. This was the part where he was supposed to be putting his life back together and moving on. This was the part where he was supposed to be relieved to have survived.

But all he felt was miserable. All he felt was that he should have been the one to die.

"COUSIN?"

It was Sebastian's voice. Lauren had been hearing it for what seemed like forever, but now she could hear it more clearly. She opened her mouth and croaked a reply.

"Sebastian," she said. Her voice sounded as though her throat had been stuffed with dry leaves.

She opened her eyes and saw a soft overhead light. Next to her, she could hear the beep of some kind of medical machine, and she could hear Sebastian's voice again.

"Lauren, you're going to be fine. I'll get you some water," he said.

She watched him leave the room and come back not with a glass, but with a syringe of water. He put it to her lips and told her to swallow as he gently pressed a little at a time into her mouth.

"The doctor said your throat would be dry, and you'd be hungry, but that you should not take in too much food or drink at once."

Lauren swallowed the water. It felt good against her parched throat.

"What happened?" she said. "Where am I?"

He sat on the edge of the bed and smiled at her. It was rare for Sebastian to smile, and it surprised her, even in her current groggy state.

"We're at cousin Dmitri's house. I'll explain it all soon enough. For now, you should rest."

"Carson," she said. "Where is he? Is he okay?"

Sebastian's smile disappeared, but she sensed none of the hostility she'd come to expect. "He's fine. Don't worry about him."

"Thank you for not hurting him," she said. "He's someone I care very much about."

"I know," he said quietly.

But she didn't think he really knew. Not the full extent of it. She herself hadn't known, until they were on the beach together, and she sensed her life was about to end.

At that moment, all the pretense had fallen away, all the surface crap that didn't matter vanished, and she'd been filled with one solid, unmistakable emotion.

"You were shot in the heart, but it looks like that vision of yours wasn't quite true."

She smiled weakly. "I think I did die," she said. "But I guess I couldn't have known I'd come back to life."

"Thank God you did."

"How long was I dead?"

"Dmitri doesn't know for sure. Apparently it

wasn't long, or else you'd have suffered serious brain damage, according to him."

"Wow," she whispered. "Close call."

"Can you remember anything?"

She nodded, not really ready to talk about it.

He smiled. "Do you feel brain damaged?"

"Not any more than usual."

"I'm supposed to ask the nurse to come in and check you out. I guess she'll ask you some questions and stuff to make sure you're still playing with a full deck."

"Thank you," Lauren said. "I know you saved me, and I know you were with me here the whole time."

He said nothing for a while, and then, "I could not have lived with myself if I'd let you die. I hope you can forgive me for screwing up your vision."

She smiled, but tears filled her eyes. "I forgive you, of course. I didn't want to die."

But she hadn't realized how much she'd wanted to stay alive until she'd felt Carson's body, alive against her, shielding her dying body from the gunfire.

"Your sister's going to be overjoyed to hear from you. We'll call her in a little while, once you're feeling able."

Corinne. She missed her baby sister so much right now. She wanted to see her. "Can she come here?"

"I don't think it would be safe, but we'll get you two together as soon as we can. She was devastated when she heard you'd been shot. I think you were right about that part at least—she might have finally gotten the reality check she needed to understand it's time to stand up to The Order."

"I'm glad I didn't have to die for her to get the message."

"Me, too," Sebastian said, grasping her hand in his. "We all are. How did you know I was with you all this time?"

"I could see you—I could see us both at times. I was sort of watching the whole thing from up above."

"Wow," he whispered. "Maybe you can tell me more later."

"How long was I unconscious?"

"For almost a week."

She wanted to demand he find Carson for her, bring him to her immediately, but she knew that wasn't going to happen. If she cared at all about the mortal, she would stay away from him for good.

"I'd better go get the nurse," Sebastian said, and he left the room.

Lauren tried taking a deep breath, wincing only a little at the pain in her chest. She looked down at her injured body, covered in a crisp white sheet, and she said a silent prayer of thanks that she was alive.

Maybe a near-death experience was what it took to make her understand what mattered in her life. And if so, she was grateful for the bullet that had pierced her chest. Growing within her, she knew, was a will to overcome her injuries, overcome her fears, and overcome anything else that stood in the way of witches never living in fear again.

Lauren would be there to see the uprising. She would be there to help lead it. She would never again live in fear.

17

LAUREN SPENT NEARLY two weeks at Dmitri's house recovering. There was nowhere else for her to go for the time being anyway. But finally, thanks to the witch trait of accelerated powers of healing, she was strong again, and she was restless, and she made preparations to leave. Sebastian wasn't thrilled with the idea, but he'd already mother-henned her half to death.

She wasn't sure yet where she would go, but she knew she had to leave. Standing on the front steps of Dmitri's house, she felt a hand on her arm, and she turned to see Sebastian.

"If you continue, cousin, you're signing up for your own death for real this time," he said.

"What are you talking about?"

"You're not free to wander around anymore. You have to be more careful than ever."

"I'm not going to keep living in fear of The Order."

"It isn't just them. Aunt Leda told me the elders have put a death order on you if you're found consorting with a human again."

Lauren blinked at the news. Her body took a moment to register it, and then she felt the weight of her burden settling in her stomach. Her family was supposed to love her and protect her, not order her death. Or, at least, that's what normal families did. Not for the first time in her life, she wished like hell she hadn't been born a witch.

She jerked her arm out of Sebastian's grasp. "And what? I survived getting shot just so you can carry out my murder like a good little soldier?"

Sebastian leveled his cold gaze at her. "I would never harm you, Lauren. You should know that by now. But you're putting me in a difficult position. My job is to protect witches, and you're making it hard for me to do that when I'm having to expend all my energy on this goddamn mortal boyfriend of yours."

"I'm sorry. I'll get away from you. I can go on from here without your help."

"Lauren, think about this. Is your life worth sacrificing for some mortal?"

"It's not about that anymore. It's about me being able to control my own destiny."

Sebastian sighed. "I'm a supporter of the uprising as much as you are, but there are some rules we have to agree to live by if we want to survive."

"I hate to tell you this, but you're starting to sound like my mother."

"Sorry, but head games aren't going to work with me. Like your mother, I'm worried about you."

"There are some rules I don't agree with, and I'm not going to spend any more of my life trying to avoid breaking the elders' archaic rules."

"There's nothing archaic about not mixing with humans. You're going to dilute the power of the witch clan if you mate with a mortal and produce children."

"Do you know that for a fact?"

"It *is* a fact."

"Which one of us here is the scientist?"

Sebastian glared at her. "What's your point?"

"Genetics don't work that way. One of the greatest threats to the witch clan is inbreeding. The elders' rules are exactly what will do us in as a race, and trying to keep us from mixing with mortals smacks of racism to me."

"We're not exactly a race, you know. It's more than that."

"No, it isn't. Just like with any other ethnic group, our abilities are all in our genetic coding."

"How can our powers not get diluted if we mate with mortals?"

"For one thing, we'll introduce much-needed diversity into our gene pool. Gene pools become increasingly unpredictable as diversity decreases. That's how we manage to have a witch as powerful as Corinne, but it's also how we have fools as useless as our cousin Teal."

"So you think you can reduce the explanation of our supernatural powers to something as simple as genetic coding just like what makes my hair brown or my eyes green?"

"That's exactly what it is."

"That doesn't make any goddamn sense."

"We have no way of knowing for sure since we've had to hide from the lens of modern science."

"So have you been secretly researching this stuff or something?"

In her dreams. Lauren had originally gone into medical research hoping that someday she'd be able to help the world understand witches without persecuting them. But so far, she'd been sidetracked by other projects, like the sexual dumbing-down effect study.

"I've played around a little on my own, studying my own DNA, but I have never done any real research. It's too risky under the current circumstances, and I don't have the support of the elders or the funding that would go along with that support."

"I don't suppose the elders are going to be able to keep us hidden from science forever."

"After the uprising, I think I might dedicate my career to helping mortals understand witches through science."

"It's a noble goal, but you may not even be around for the uprising if you continue with Carson."

Lauren stared out at the cypress trees lining the lawn, and a feeling of intense sadness overcame her. She couldn't see the way forward from here. She'd somehow survived sure death on the beach, and now, her family would kill her unless she stayed away from Carson.

Sebastian wasn't saying it, but they'd likely kill Carson, too.

She couldn't be the cause of his life being threatened again. If she really cared about him, she had to get the hell away from him for good.

A car went by, and she understood what she was facing now. Saying goodbye to everything she loved—San Francisco, her friends, her job, her family…and Carson. She would have to leave it all behind and start a new life somewhere else.

"Promise me something, okay?" she said to Sebastian. "I'm only going to ask you for this one thing, and if you love me, you'll do it."

Sebastian regarded her seriously. "I can't say yes until you tell me what it is."

"Protect Carson after I'm gone. Witch blood does flow through his veins, you know."

Her cousin was silent for a while, and then he nodded. "I'll do what I can."

18

THREE WEEKS HAD PASSED since Carson had watched Lauren get shot on the beach, and he tried to tell himself he was moving on. He was lying.

He'd tried researching new careers on the Internet. He'd gotten a Peace Corps application and filled it out, but he'd never submitted it. And he'd contemplated spending a year at a yoga ashram in India. Nothing quite sounded like the right thing to do.

And then one day he'd been walking along the docks in Sausalito, and he'd spotted a little yacht for sale. He decided on the spot to buy it. He'd had some vague idea he could live in the thing and sail around the world, but mostly he sat on the deck watching the fog roll in, and he brooded.

But today there was no fog. It was one of those perfect crystal blue San Francisco days when the water sparkled like diamonds and sailboats of every color crowded the bay. Carson sat in his usual spot on the deck, feeling as though he should have been doing something. The sunshine did have a vague energizing effect, and the Elmore Leonard novel he'd been reading wasn't quite cutting it for a satisfying activity.

Maybe he'd sail out to the Farallon Islands and watch for whales, or head down the coast, or…

"Hey," a female voice said.

Carson looked up, and his heart nearly stopped at the sight of Lauren standing on the dock.

She smiled. "Can I come aboard?"

He dropped his book on the deck and was off the boat in a split second. "You're okay," he said dumbly as he took her into his arms and pulled her to him.

"I am," she said. "I am."

And then they were kissing. Desperate, hungry kisses that weren't quite satisfying enough, because he needed all of her at once, not just her mouth, not just her tongue. He lifted her up as they kissed, and then he thought of her chest wound.

"Oh shit," he muttered, setting her back down. "Am I hurting you?"

She laughed. "I'm okay—witches heal faster than humans. You can manhandle me as much as you want."

He held her at arm's length and let his gaze linger on her then, taking in every detail. She looked more beautiful than ever, if a bit paler than usual. She wore a black sundress that hugged her torso and exposed her angular shoulders, and tiny black thong sandals that exposed only a small scar on her foot where before a bandage had been.

"I never thought I'd get to see you again. Thank you for coming here, but…is it safe?"

She shook her head. "I can only stay for a little while. I wanted to see you before I left," she said, and something about her voice changed.

Her smile disappeared, and so did his.

"Where are you going?"

"I can't tell you," she said. "But I thought you deserved to know I'm okay, and I owe you a face-to-face apology for all the danger I put you in. I'm so sorry, Carson."

"No, you don't need to apologize."

She said nothing, then eyed the yacht. "Is this yours?"

He nodded. "I was thinking about sailing around the world or something, but I guess I haven't quite mustered the energy yet."

"Macy told me. She sounded worried about you, which is part of the reason I wanted to see you myself."

"Don't worry about me," he said. "I'm fine. Just trying to figure out what to do with myself since I quit my job."

She frowned. "Why did you?"

"I'm done being an advertising whore."

"Good for you. I'm sure you'll find your calling eventually. Just give yourself some time to figure it out."

"Yeah, I guess."

"Want to show me around the boat?"

"Sure, come on board," he said, hopping onto the

deck himself, then extending a hand to help Lauren aboard.

"Down here's the bed," he said, smiling as he motioned to the stairway.

"Oh?" She smiled. "We'd better not go there then."

"Not even once more for old times' sake?"

She shook her head. "I couldn't do that to you again."

"Hey, to be honest, the withdrawal symptoms weren't that bad," he lied.

"I'm glad, but I also have strict orders from my doctor—no sexual intercourse for another few weeks."

"Wow, that's brutal."

She shrugged. "It hasn't been an issue since we've been apart."

"Could I maybe, just, you know, go down on you? One last time?"

Lauren laughed. "You're relentless."

He closed the distance between them and took her into his arms again. Then he kissed her with all the desperate, pent-up passion he felt. When they finally broke the kiss, he asked, "What am I supposed to do with that?"

"I'm sorry," she whispered, but he took her hand and led her below deck and into his bedroom.

She tried to protest as he eased her back onto the bed, but he said, "Please, just this once."

Then he stretched out beside her, careful not to let the weight of his body rest on her torso, and kissed her again, this time more slowly.

He wanted to memorize every inch of her, commit the taste and feel of her to his memory so permanently he would never forget a single detail. Because if she was going to be an addiction that he could never have, then the memory of her would have to be his cure. She smelled like a tropical flower, and her skin was so soft and warm, it reminded him of Caribbean water.

He tugged her dress down and tasted her breasts, then paused to kiss the jagged red scar on her chest. He traced it gently with his fingers and memorized it too. She buried her fingers in his hair and squirmed against him, and he knew when he dipped his fingers into her panties, he'd find her soaking wet.

Then he lowered himself, pulled off her panties, and spread her legs wide, memorizing again her delicious pink folds. When he kissed her there, and inhaled her perfect scent, he almost cried. This was as good as it would ever be, as good as it was going to get.

LAUREN SHOULD HAVE protested, but the truth was that she was as addicted to Carson as he would ever be to her. As he licked her and touched her, bringing her closer and closer to orgasm, she felt her eyes grow damp. She didn't want to say goodbye to him. She wanted to stay here in his bed forever.

He knew how to work her body, and as he touched her in all the right places, she was able, for a little while, to forget. And she gave in to the pleasure one last time. She came hard against his mouth, crying out, gasping, grinding herself against him as the waves of pleasure washed over her.

Then she was still. Catching her breath. He was kissing her belly. Reality intruded again.

"Thank you," she whispered. "I hope you're going to let me return the favor."

"Are you sure your doctor would okay it?"

She smiled at him. "I'm pretty sure he didn't say anything about oral sex."

But he sensed that her mood had changed, and when she tried to sit up, he slid up next to her again and held her in place. "We don't have to say goodbye, you know."

She closed her eyes against their stinging. "Carson, please don't. You know the deal."

"No, I don't. Why don't you fill me in?"

"I mean, you know I'm bad for you, and that people in my world would never accept our relationship. It's just easier if we say goodbye now."

"Where are you going?"

"I've decided it's best if I leave the country and stay hidden for a while. I'm too easy a target—for The Order and other witches. I'll be needed when it's time for the uprising to begin."

"Let me go with you," he said.

"I just told you why that won't work," she said. "Please don't make it harder than it already is."

But some little voice inside her wanted to rebel and told her to hear him out.

"I can leave the country with you. There's nothing keeping me here. I'll help you with the uprising. I don't give a damn what your relatives think, and you shouldn't, either."

"Carson, not only is my life in danger because of The Order, but also the witch clan has a death order on me if I'm caught with a mortal again. They'll kill you, too, if we're found out."

His expression went grim, and he was silent for a while. Lauren felt unwelcome tears building in her eyes. She blinked them away.

Finally, he said, "I have been sitting on this damn boat wondering what the point of my life is, and then you appeared. You, the woman who made me feel what it's like to really be alive."

"I can't put you in any more danger," she said.

"Let me choose that. Please. I think it's my purpose in life now to protect you, to be the human voice for your cause. When your family sees that I can help, they won't want to kill me."

She shook her head, but his words reminded her of the growing feeling she had. The more she thought about the uprising, the more she knew that they would need the help of the mortal world. They just couldn't do it alone.

"We'll go away together until it's time for the uprising to begin. Let me be with you. I don't even have a life here anymore. I might as well be dead if you're not in it."

Suddenly, she was finding it hard to breathe.

"Why would you want to help?"

He looked at her seriously. "Because I love you. Because, when I thought you might be dead, I couldn't find any reason to go on living. I can't think of anything I'd rather be doing than giving us a chance to be together."

Lauren tried to come up with an argument against his words. She was supposed to be protecting him now, not getting him into even more trouble. But…he loved her.

"I love you, too," she said, because she couldn't stop herself.

And she did. Enough to defy the elders' order. Enough to not stand in the way of what he felt was his destiny. Her intuition was screaming that it was the right thing to do.

Then she remembered the vow she'd made to herself when she'd awoken from the coma, that she'd never live in fear again.

He leaned in and kissed her gently again, then said, "Let me go with you. Let me help."

"Okay," she whispered, letting go of the last vestige of fear. "Come with me."

* * * * *

My Secret Life *by Lori Wilde*

Society diva Katie Winfield first encounters sexy bachelor Liam James, with his broad chest and winning smile, at a masquerade ball. Now Liam wants to uncover the delectable Katie – from head to toe…

Turn the page for a sneak preview…

Available from Mills & Boon® Blaze® in October 2008

My Secret Life

by

Lori Wilde

Resentment pummeled Liam's stomach like a heavyweight boxer finishing off his wobbly-kneed opponent. Reflexively, he curled his fist around the birth certificate autographed by his biological father. The desire to punch something was so strong he could taste it.

Raw, bitter, black.

For the last twelve years he'd worked toward this moment, worked and waited, and Delancy had pulled the rug right out from under him. What should he do now?

You'll go at him again. You picked the wrong time, the wrong place, that's all.

His mother had never wanted him to do this. She was happy now, married to a great guy and living on a farm in upstate New York. She thought he should just forget about Finn Delancy and be proud of everything he'd accomplished without his old man's help.

But it wasn't that simple for Liam. He couldn't let it go. Anger twisted him up inside. The place was filled with privileged blue bloods, no doubt many of whom thought they could treat people any way they wanted and get away with it.

Liam blazed a hard gaze around the room. Frivolous, pampered rich people throwing silly costume parties. If they really wanted to give to charity, just write a check and don't waste money on lavish celebrations.

You're richer than most of them.

Yes, but he'd gotten his money the hard way. He'd earned every penny of it, not had it handed to him on a platinum platter.

Adrenaline, anger and frustration coursed through him. He needed to dissipate these feelings. Needed to get a firm grip on his emotions. Exercise. He needed exercise. A run in the park never failed to give him back his sense of control.

He had to get the hell out of here.

But then something caught his eye that made Liam forget everything except the fact he hadn't had sex in almost a year.

There, on the other side of the ballroom, stood a gorgeous vixen in a French maid costume and she was staring straight at him, as if he were the man of her most forbidden midnight fantasies.

Coyly, she tossed her auburn wig.

Liam drove his hand through his own wig.

She licked her lips.

Drawing in a ragged breath, he hooked his thumbs through his belt loop.

Her eyes widened, and he saw a telltale red flush spread from her generous cleavage up her long slender throat.

His body hardened and he shifted, widening his stance, pointing his boots in her direction.

She lowered her eyelashes, dropped her hands. His gaze fell to the creamy inside of her wrist, and then tracked up her smooth, delicate skin to her shoulders. She peeked at him again and then slyly winked. Even with the barrier of her black mask cloaking most of her face, he was absolutely certain she was winking at him.

Boldly, Liam winked back.

Why the hell not? Sex was better than jogging for blowing off steam and after what had happened before with Delancy, he could certainly do with the distraction.

And she was one fine distraction with those shapely legs encased in lust-arousing black fishnet stockings. He could easily imagine himself tugging that silky material over the curve of her calf.

She angled him a long, lingering look.

He caught it, held it.

Quickly, she looked away again, but there was no mistaking her invitation.

Come play with me.

His blood revved hot.

She turned and walked away.

The thundering in his veins intensified. Curiosity grabbed him by the short hairs and hung on tight. Who was this mysterious woman? Did he know her? Something about her seemed vaguely familiar, but he couldn't put his finger on what it was.

She made her way through the crowd, hips rolling seductively, as aloof as the blue-blooded princess she undoubtedly was. When she got to the doorway, she paused. Her long fingers stroked the door casing as she tossed him a glance over her shoulder. She looked damned provocative, even in a room chock-full of people dressed in suggestive garb.

Follow me, her eyes whispered.

Normally, Liam wasn't the type of guy who allowed his libido to overrule his common sense. But he was horny and desperately needing something to salve his battered ego, and she was hot and willing.

Why not go for it?

You shouldn't let your anger at Delancy drive you to casual sex with a frisky member of the Ladies League simply to prove you can bed the social elite.

Maybe not, but his gaze was ensnared on her full, rich mouth that was clearly made for kissing. She pursed her lips, slowly blew him a kiss and then crooked her index finger.

This way.

Liam felt the impact of the gesture slam low in his groin. Simultaneously, hormones and endorphins lit up both his body and his brain. He gulped against the sheer force of the sensation. This French maid wanted to have some fun. Why shouldn't he be the one to accommodate her?

He shook his head. What kind of spell had she cast over him? His tongue was cemented to the roof of his mouth.

His eyes were transfixed by her lithe form. His nose twitched, suddenly sensitized to the scent of seduction in the air. His ears filled with a blinding white roaring noise.

She strutted off a second time.

Mesmerized, he watched her hips sway.

Liam went all Neanderthal then and lumbered after her. *Must have woman.*

By the time he reached where she'd been standing, she was already in the archway of another room. The place could have been completely empty. That's how unaware he was of the crowd jostling around them.

The French maid paused again, but this time she did not look back. Apparently, she'd assumed he would follow.

She was correct.

Sending her auburn curls bouncing over her shoulders with a toss of her head, she turned to the right and started down a long corridor.

Liam made a beeline after her.

People were all around him, talking, laughing, joking, drinking, but he could have been stranded on a deserted island or trapped in a timeless vortex. He was that focused on Miss French Maid's fanny as she slipped through the costumed throng.

She winnowed around a man the size of a boxcar dressed like Paul Bunyan and Liam couldn't see her anymore. He quickened his pace, but at the next doorway, Paul Bunyan turned, blocking his path.

"Excuse me." Liam stepped to his right.

Paul Bunyan moved in the same direction at the exact same moment.

Liam corrected, angling to the left.

So did Bunyan.

Was this on purpose? What was happening here? Liam frowned.

"Shall we dance?" Paul Bunyan chuckled, and Liam realized he'd been unnecessarily suspicious. By the time he got around the guy, he found himself faced with a long hallway filled with doors. His French maid had vanished.

"Dammit," he muttered.

It's all for the best. He was feeling much too vulnerable to be indulging in anonymous sex. That kind of solace, while great in the moment, wouldn't fix anything. It wouldn't make up for the aching for a real father that had dogged his bones since he was a kid.

He stood there in the corridor, staring at the doors, wondering if she was behind one, not wanting to leave in case she reappeared. A minute ticked past. And then another.

Face it. She's gone.

He turned to retrace his steps when suddenly the door behind him opened and a hand reached out to grab him by the scruff of his collar.

Long, manicured fingernails tickled the back of his neck and the next thing Liam knew, he was being hauled into a pitch black closet.

The French maid wrapped her arms around him and covered his face in kisses. At least he hoped it was the French maid.

She murmured something in French. He didn't understand the language, but he did get the gist of her suggestive message. He tried to take a step back to clear his head, but her fingers were frantically working the buttons of his puffy white pirate shirt.

"Slow down," he said, or rather tried to say. His throat was twisted so tight with need the sounds came out as scarcely more than an excited groan.

Her mind-boggling aroma, which smelled like a cross between apricots and stargazer lilies, filled his nose and shot up his desire. He could see absolutely nothing in the darkness, but the rest of his senses were fully attuned and ready to be indulged.

"What…how…who…" He wrenched out the words, unable to form a coherent thought.

"Shh." She placed an index finger over his lips. Her skin tasted forbidden.

He thought of truffles and Russian caviar and saffron, the most expensive spice in the world. His nerve endings blazed. In the back of his mind, far off in the distance, sounding as if it had been locked up in a dry, dusty trunk for centuries, his muffled conscience tried to get his attention.

Hey, sport, this seems awfully odd. Sexy babe coming on to you, no strings attached. You know there's always strings attached. Something's wrong. Pull your head out of the hormone soup. Think this through. Last thing you want is to be like your old man. Hey, hey…

His scruples got no further because his brain short-circuited, closing off everything except the exquisite glory of her hot little mouth on his.